PRAISE FOR
FIRST-DEGREE FUDGE

"An action-filled story with a likable heroine and a fun setting. And, oh, that fudge! I'm swooning. I hope Ava Oosterling and her family and friends take me back to Door County, Wisconsin, for another nibble soon."

—JoAnna Carl, national bestselling author of the Chocoholic Mysteries

"Christine DeSmet has whipped up a melt-in-your-mouth gem of a tale. One is definitely not going to be enough!"

—Hannah Reed, national bestselling author of *Beewitched*

"The first in a new series set in the 'Cape Cod of the Midwest,' *First-Degree Fudge* is a lighthearted confection that cozy mystery readers will devour."

—Lucy Burdette, author of *Murder with Ganache*

"As palatable as a fresh pan of Belgian fudge, this debut will delight candy aficionados and mystery lovers with its fast pace, quirky cast, and twist after twist. A must read!"

—Liz Mugavero, author of *A Biscuit, a Casket*

continued . . .

"Interesting characters enhance this mystery . . . plenty of romantic tension. The mystery evolves nicely with a few good twists and turns that lead to a surprising villain."

—*RT Book Reviews* (4 stars)

"Will have readers drooling with its descriptions of heroine Ava Oosterling's confections. Set in a small Wisconsin town on Lake Michigan, readers will enjoy the down-home atmosphere and quirky characters." —Debbie's Book Bag

"Ava Oosterling and her cast of characters are going to charm the socks off the cozy-mystery world. . . . If you like your cozy mysteries with a lot of small-town charm, along with a dollop of fudge, you'll love the new Fudge Shop Mystery series!" —Feathered Quill Book Reviews

"First-Degree Fudge will tingle your sweet tooth at the first mention of Cinderella Pink Fudge." —*The Washington Post*

ALSO BY CHRISTINE DESMET

The Fudge Shop Mysteries
First-Degree Fudge

Hot Fudge Frame-Up

A Fudge Shop Mystery

Christine DeSmet

OBSIDIAN
Published by the Penguin Group
Penguin Group (USA) LLC, 375 Hudson Street,
New York, New York 10014

USA | Canada | UK | Ireland | Australia | New Zealand | India | South Africa | China
penguin.com
A Penguin Random House Company

First published by Obsidian, an imprint of New American Library,
a division of Penguin Group (USA) LLC

First Printing, June 2014

ISBN 978-0-451-41648-3

Printed in the United States of America
10 9 8 7 6 5 4 3 2 1

To supporters of Door County's Eagle Bluff Lighthouse—
named "Featured Lighthouse of 2014" by the
Great Lakes Lighthouse Festival—
and lighthouse lovers everywhere

Chapter 1

Everything and everyone has a purpose in life, and a place, my grandmother Sophie always said. "And everyone and everything can be good and then go bad. Lloyd Mueller is like beer fudge. Enjoy it now because it only has a shelf life of about three days."

I shivered at what she'd just insinuated. But nobody contradicted my Belgian grandmother, especially when she was upset. And yet I plunged in like a ninny. "Grandma, Lloyd is a good landlord. Or was. At least he's giving me a refund for making me move out of this rental cabin early. He's bringing the check to the meeting at the fudge shop. And please don't talk about him having a shelf life." My skin rippled again, this time with big goose bumps. "You make it sound like somebody will do him in for having me move."

"Bah and booyah! Maybe he should watch out! You're moving out of this lovely cabin and then moving into the storage room of your fudge shop? Whoever heard of living in a fudge shop! This is going to be trouble for you and worse for Lloyd!" Exclamation points spat out of her mouth as my grandmother splashed suds about the fudge utensils in my cabin's kitchen sink.

My cabin was one of several rentals along the three-block length of Duck Marsh Street in Fishers' Harbor, a tourist town on peninsular Door County, Wisconsin, which juts into Lake Michigan. Our county was known as the Cape Cod of the Midwest. In the summer our village's population of two hundred swelled to a couple of thousand when the condos and summer homes filled with vacationers from Chicago and beyond.

"I don't like it," Grandma said, persisting. We Belgians are like that, the old "dog on a bone," never giving up. "He's up to no good."

I had to admit I felt the same way. Everybody knew everybody's business here. Lloyd was the richest man in town by far. All we knew was that he intended to buy the Blue Heron Inn, but he wasn't telling anybody his intentions except to say it wouldn't be an inn anymore. People all over town were nervous about the secrecy. Even Lloyd's ex-wife, Libby—who got along with him fine—had told my grandma she was worried about the mysterious surprise he had cooking for Fishers' Harbor. Libby said he wouldn't even tell her. What did that mean? That he was up to no good, as Grandma said?

It was hard for me to worry too much about this big secret at the moment. I was in the living room packing books in a hurry in sticky July humidity. It was Friday morning after the Fourth, and I'd told Lloyd I'd be out by Sunday. I could fuss and ask for thirty days' notice, but Lloyd—for all his faults—was also my grandfather's old high school buddy. Besides, I liked the thought of living in a fudge shop. The early-morning fog was being steamed by the sun, steeping me like a tea bag. My long brown hair in a twist atop my head was coming undone on my damp neck, and my trademark pink blouse was beginning to stick to my back.

I'd been up since five, the water had been cut off in my fudge shop today, and the birdcall clock over the sink had just cardinal-chirped eight o'clock, which panicked me. In a half hour I had to meet up with the fudge contest judges and confectioner chef contestants at my shop. Fortunately, Oosterlings' Live Bait, Bobbers & Belgian Fudge & Beer was only about thirty feet away across my backyard. It sat on the docks of our Lake Michigan harbor.

Grandma said amid pans rattling in the sink, "I don't see why you can't live in our sunporch for now."

Grandma and Grandpa Oosterling lived across the way, in one of only two cabins on this street not owned by Lloyd Mueller. Moving in with my Grandma Sophie and Grandpa Gil would be convenient, but I was thirty-two, and I'd heard too many jokes about thirtysomethings moving back in with family to be comfortable with the invitation.

"Grandma, I'll be fine. I need to worry about settling on a new fudge flavor for next week's contest." I tossed more cookbooks and scriptwriting books into the next empty box sitting near me on the floor by the couch.

"You like Brussels sprouts."

"Sprout fudge?" I swallowed down my gag reflex, then heard her squelch a giggle. My grandma was like that, always keeping me on my toes. "What fairy tale is that based on?" From the start of my business I had decided that all my fudge flavors for females had to be named for a fairy tale.

Grandma said, "The story of the Three Bears. Porridge fudge."

Smiling at that flavor, I countered, "Maybe a Goldilocks flavor, something in gold? I'm not sure what flavor that could be, but it needs to be as nice as my cherry-vanilla Cinderella Pink Fudge." The Cinderella fudge had become an instant hit with the tourists. "I want something gal pals will savor with a fine Door County wine or that their little girls would find cute and fun for their tea parties. I'm starting to panic."

"Ah, the sweet success of your first fudge flavor is pressuring you." Grandma Sophie wrestled a big stainless steel mixer bowl into the sink. "Come over for dinner tonight and we'll brainstorm. And move your stuff into our cabin. Whoever heard of living in a storage room amid milk, cream, and mice!"

"There are no mice in my fudge shop, Grandma. There's only Titus here in the cabin, in the bottom cupboard."

"I can't believe you named a mouse. Bah."

"Well, he wouldn't climb into my traps for cheese or even peanut butter, so I figured I'd give him a name and then just call him out of hiding."

"Booyah to you." The word "booyah" refers to a traditional Belgian celebration stew made with chicken and vegetables, but now the word is used all the time as a cheer word. Grandma continued as she swished suds around the bowl. "That mouse will have more living space than you. And moving now is the worst possible time to do it in your life. Lloyd should be ashamed of himself for telling the new owner you'd be gone by Sunday sometime. Who do you suppose he sold these cabins to?"

"Maybe Libby's learned more. I'll ask her. I have to stop over at the lighthouse later with her batch of fudge anyway." I sneezed from the books as I packed another box on the floor. I hadn't dusted anything since I arrived in town in late April. Opening and operating the fudge shop had kept me too busy. "Grandma, maybe we should just be happy that Lloyd isn't letting the inn sit empty and become a home for Titus's relatives."

"I suppose you're right. Not many people want to move into a place where a murder happened."

I shivered all over again for the umpteenth time just thinking about my involvement. Back in May my fudge had been stuck down the throat of an actress who was choked to death. The killer had tried to pin it all on the newbie back in town—me. I wondered now if some relative of the murdered woman had bought my cabin in order to be close to her spirit. Was my landlord afraid I'd be freaked out? Try to stop the sale?

But I had more important worries. The First Annual Fishers' Harbor Fudge Festival was being held a week from tomorrow—Saturday. Back in May I'd been conned into sponsoring a fudge contest by my girlfriend's new boyfriend. John Schultz was a tourism and tour promoter out of Milwaukee who looked for any angle to bring himself up to Door County to visit Pauline Mertens. John had convinced me that a fudge contest would help me look like a good business member of the community while making amends for drawing bad karma to Fishers' Harbor with the murder involving my fudge. The taste-off next Saturday afternoon would be followed by an adult prom dance in the evening outside the fudge shop on the docks. The prom was also hatched by John, with Pauline's blessing. I couldn't say no to Pauline. She felt sorry for me. I'd never been to a prom because as a teenager I was a too-tall, athletic, nerd-farm-girl that the boys passed in the hallway as if I were invisible.

Unfortunately, things were going wrong. While anybody could enter the fudge contest, John had created a celebrity panel consisting of me and two chefs to draw publicity to the fudge festival. His guest celebrity chef contestants, who had arrived this past Monday for a two-week stay, had taken over the six copper kettles in my shop—as in *not sharing* them with me at all. And I couldn't seem to come up with a new fudge flavor that would knock everybody's socks off. What's more, I had to find or make a prom dress—something that wouldn't reveal how much fudge I'd eaten in the past couple of months. My excited and desperate friends Pauline and Laura Rousseau were coming over later this morning with yet another set of fabric swatches and dress patterns. Laura was two weeks away from delivering twins and desperate to fill her time after the doctor told her to quit her job.

Rapid-fire knocking on my front door was followed by my young, red-haired shop assistant, Cody Fjelstad, yelling through the screen, "Miss Oosterling! Come quick!"

My mother was with him. She hollered from behind Cody, "Ava honey, your shop's being destroyed!"

"What?" The nonsensical news kept me rooted for just a second on the floor.

Cody opened the screen door, then waved frantically. "Get a move on, Miss Oosterling. Your chefs are chasing each other around the shop with fudge cutters. They keep saying they're going to kill each other."

My fudge shop and all my freshly made fudge were being held hostage by two chefs with circular knives.

When I rushed in through the back door of my shop, Kelsey King, a petite blonde from Portland, Oregon, and Piers Molinsky, a portly giant from Chicago, were wielding fudge cutters from their stances on both ends of my white, marble-slab table. My freshly made Cinderella Pink Fudge lay hostage in its pans between them. Kelsey and Piers had fudge cutters poised over the pans.

Fudge cutters look like pizza cutters—round, sharp disks. Kelsey held up a cutter with one disk while Piers had one with multiple disks that could cause a lot of quick damage if tossed at Kelsey.

I stood in shock behind my old-fashioned cash register, thinking I might need it as protection.

My mom muttered behind my back, "I forgot to tell you about the smell, too."

The grab bag of aromas in the place made me pause. What had the chefs been up to in only a few minutes' time this morning? I'd left the place just an hour ago and nobody had been here but my grandpa Gil and a few fishermen. It had smelled of the strong fresh coffee we always had on hand and my new batch of cherry-vanilla pink perfection fudge. Now the bait-and-fudge shop smelled of bacon, of all things, and a heady, earthy mix of spices such as nutmeg, cinnamon, ginger, and maybe some anise and orange peel tossed in.

I called out from behind my small fortress, "What's wrong with you two? Stop!"

Piers, his chubby face red, his furry brown eyebrows pinched together, kept his gaze lasered on his enemy across the marble table as he picked up a pan of my fudge.

My heart rate accelerated. "Put the fudge down, Piers."

Piers ignored me, growling at Kelsey, "You do not belong

in this contest. This is what fudge looks like." He waved my pan of Cinderella Pink Fudge in the air.

Behind me, my mother whined in panic or disgust or both.

Kelsey snatched up the other pan of my fudge, waving her fudge cutter over it as she glared at Piers. "You see this fudge? This is your face!"

She slashed at my pretty pink fudge.

My mother screamed, nearly turning me deaf. I gasped, stunned for a moment, waiting for my hearing to come back.

Cody, whose dream was to be a law officer or park ranger, grabbed one of my four-foot spatulas from a nearby copper kettle. "I'll stop 'em, Miss Oosterling."

"No, Ranger, don't. Stand back." Cody liked being called "Ranger," especially after he had helped me solve the murder in May and our county sheriff had awarded him a good-citizenship star. Cody was eighteen and had a mild form of Asperger's. He was making remarkable progress toward independent living with the help of a social worker friend of mine.

I could've used the sheriff's help at the moment. Ordinarily, my popular pink fudge sat in front of the big bay window to cure and to entice tourists. Now there was nobody waiting, just the view of Lake Michigan lapping up against the boats rocking at their moorings. Any customers there to buy fudge or bait had scattered to save their lives. Even if I called Sheriff Tollefson or a deputy, the sheriff's office was a half hour's drive away in Sturgeon Bay.

I glanced to the bait-shop side of the place. "Gilpa?" The word came out strangled in my tight throat. Since a little girl I'd called Grandpa Gil the shortcut name of "Gilpa."

Ranger said, "He took a fisherman out just as I got here."

I appealed again to the chefs. "This is silly. It's going to be a beautiful day. Why start it out with a fight?"

Neither looked at me. Instead, they started a volley of words while shaking the fudge cutters and my fudge all about in the air. The glass in the bay window within inches of them was vibrating from the intensity.

I hesitated going over to the two on my own. Kelsey's blond cuteness and petite frame rendered her deceivingly harmless-looking. But she was a fitness guru who ran a health spa. She knew karate and ate the bark off trees. I was probably smelling bark cooking in the aromas floating about us. Piers, whose bulk reflected his love of the muffin tops he'd made famous in Chicago, growled like a bear at Kelsey.

Piers used his fudge cutter to gouge out and flick a good-sized portion of my precious pink confection onto the floor. He smashed it with the heel of one boot. "This is your face."

We all cried out in pain—me, Cody, my mom, and two customers who popped up from behind a shelving unit filled with handmade Cinderella Pink dolls, purses, and teacups. I recognized the ladies from my grandmother's church group. They rushed out, screaming something about "saints and sinners." The cowbell on the door clanged. A teacup fell to the floor in their wake and broke.

Those ladies would spread the gossip fast, so I had to take action. I used the weapon that always worked. "There could be *TV cameras* on you right now for all you know. I think that's John coming down the docks right now."

My mother whimpered, "Oh no."

John Schultz had been videotaping us every spare moment of his time. To keep things manageable for his videotaping, John wanted just three celebrity contestants—me and these two trying to kill one another. He'd scoured his universe of contacts in the travel industry and come up with Piers and Kelsey. I'm sad to say I approved them. Shows my talent for judging people. John had insisted that he tape the fudge contest activities this week and the next, with the hopes of ending up on a cable channel. He'd get a show of his own, he said, and I'd get fudge fame. But John wasn't coming down the docks right now; I'd lied.

Fortunately, my lie worked like a hose on two fighting

cats. Kelsey broke into tears, dropping her fudge cutter on the marble slab. She looked around for the camera on her. It was pitiful. I almost wished John were here. Piers whipped off his white apron, then used it to swab my ruined pink fudge off the floor. He, too, looked about for the camera, smiling, which galled me.

"Were you two faking? Practicing?" I asked. "You gave my mother a heart attack."

"I'm so sorry," Piers said, turning into a teddy bear. "Please forgive me, Ava. You were so kind to invite me, and yet I did this to you. Sorry."

His words were stilted, obviously an act for the nonexistent camera. At least he was being polite again to me and my fudge.

Kelsey, though, slapped a hand on the marble table. "Sorry? That's all you've got to say for cheating? He was hogging the copper kettles again for his hog that he's cooking." Her shoulders hunched up to her earlobes in a shudder. "He's putting hog bits into the fudge."

"Hog bits?" I asked.

"Bacon," Piers said, pulling his shoulders back in pride. "I'm experimenting with bacon fudge."

Kelsey sniped, "He took over four of the kettles. Then he put bacon in one of my kettles of boiling ingredients so I'd have to throw it out. After I did, I looked away for just a moment, and he'd tossed more bacon—meat—into my kettle. Yewww."

My mother touched my arm. "Honey, I have to finish making deliveries. Maybe you should come with me and let them cool down."

Kelsey said with a big fake smile, "That cow truck you drive is just the cutest thing, Florine."

Mom—Florine, never Flo—drove a black-and-white-cow-motif minivan around the county, delivering our farm's organic cream, cheeses, milk, and butter to various restaurants and to my fudge shop each day. When I'd contacted Kelsey King weeks ago in Portland, where she had a fledgling TV show featuring organics, she'd been thrilled to hear about our farm's organic nature. She agreed instantly to the adventure of being a contestant in a fudge contest in Door County. I tried to use that modicum of respect to quell the fight now.

"Kelsey, my mother can replace all of your ingredients with fresh ones right now. And maybe the bacon falling into your fudge mix was a mistake."

"No, it wasn't." Her fake smile stiffened.

I turned to look up at Piers. "Why do you need four kettles? You were each assigned two to use. Two for each of you, with two left for me."

That's when the smells in the place became a warning along with the odd sounds of audible gulps, lapping, and growls. I looked at the north wall area behind our short counter and glass shelving where the six kettles sat over their open-flame heating units. "Oh my gosh!"

Two copper kettles had bubbled over, oozing sugar and mystery ingredients—and bite-sized bacon pieces—onto the floor. A troublemaking furry brown dog belonging to my ex-husband—the infamous bigamist—leaped about in the middle of canine nirvana, slurping up bacon bits as fast as his long pink tongue could operate. We were lucky the dog hadn't knocked over the open flames and caused a fire. Ironically, my ex had named the dog "Lucky" after his gambling prowess—my ex's prowess and not the dog's. Since my ex had come back to town for utility construction business in May, the dog seemed to get loose and show up just about every other day in my shop. I glanced toward the door now with my heartbeat racing a bit in nervous trepidation. The dog's rogue appearances usually brought my ex, Dillon Rivers, through the door soon after.

Cody the "Ranger" dashed over to turn off the burners. He grabbed the gangly water spaniel, who was now rolling in the bacon goop on the floor. "Harbor, no! Come with me." Cody had dubbed the dog Harbor the first day the dog sneaked into our shop because the gregarious animal loved to fling himself into the harbor water outside our front door.

The dog with two names was always a mess unless he was secured with a leash. Lucky Harbor also loved to steal fudge if I didn't watch him. Chocolate isn't good for dogs; it can be fatal. I dashed over to Gilpa's side of the shop for a piece of twine. Lucky Harbor began barking so loudly in protest over leaving his puddle of bacon that everybody in the shop had their hands clamped over their ears.

"Please take him into the back somewhere for now, Ranger. Tie him to a doorknob or something."

Piers said, "At least the dog shows good taste."

Piers found a spoon, then began ladling up the mess on the floor. "You weren't using your kettles, Ava, so I took them over, thinking I was doing you a favor. You weren't here when I arrived. You didn't see Kelsey sabotaging the ingredients."

Kelsey yelped, "You liar." She grabbed the fudge cutter again to wave at him. "You're the one sabotaging me, you sausage hick from Chicago!"

At that moment, two of the four fudge judges arrived through the front door: my landlord, Lloyd Mueller; and a local cookbook author, Professor Alex Faust. One of the people ducking and running earlier had looked like my third judge—Dotty Klubertanz, the unofficial head of the church ladies in Door County. Dotty knew her sweets. The fourth judge was Erik Gustafson, our new village president.

My grandmother—who desperately wanted to be a fudge judge so she could vote for me—came in through the back door, finally catching up with us. "What's that smell?"

"Bacon," I said.

"No, the other smell. Like dirt cooking."

Kelsey seethed at Piers. "That's the smell of my ruined fudge."

Piers snapped, "It's real dirt. She's putting black dirt in chocolate fudge! Says they cook with dirt in Japan."

Kelsey flew at Piers with a karate kick, which he caught

in his beefy hands, but he slipped on the oozing syrup and bacon fat on the floor. They slid out from behind my glass counter loaded with various fudges, landing on their backs in the goo. I rushed to help, but Kelsey got up fast to push me away so she could go at Piers again. I grabbed her in an armlock to break it up—

Just as Dillon Rivers charged through the door. The cowbell clanged against the wall. "Whoa, are we puttin' bets down on who wins this wrestling match? I've got five bucks on the fudge lady."

I let go of Kelsey.

My tall, killer-handsome ex swept off his hard hat, combing his chestnut-colored hair with his fingers. His muscular chest was bare and glistening already from morning exertion. Both my heart and my stomach did a flippity-flop.

My mother groaned. She did not like Dillon. She said to me, "I'll call the sheriff." She was thumb-dialing her phone as she said it.

Grandma said, "I'll buzz Gil." She dug in her jeans for her phone.

Professor Faust, a genial, sixtysomething, gray-haired guy in a blue shirt and tan pants, stood wide-eyed. He was carrying a stack of his latest cookbook. "Perhaps this isn't a good time for a meeting of the judges? Where can I leave my books? They're all signed."

Everybody ignored Professor Faust because that's what happened when Dillon was in a room, especially with his shirt off.

"Hey there," Dillon said, with a look that said he knew exactly what he was doing to me. He slipped on a neon yellow T-shirt with his construction company logo on it that he'd had shoved in a back pocket. "Anybody see my dog? And what's this I hear about the fudge shop closing and the contest being canceled?"

Ugh, Grandma's gossipy church-lady friends must have met him on the docks.

I said to Dillon, "We're in the middle of something. Your

dog's in the back. You'll need to take him for a swim before you let him in your truck."

Dillon chuckled as he looked me up and down. "Maybe you'd like to go for a swim, too." He sniffed at me. "You smell like bacon. I'd better ask you to the prom before other guys get a whiff of you."

"Very funny," I said.

My mother rushed between us, clicking off her phone. "Honey, come with me to the lighthouse. Now."

At first, her urgency was lost on me. Kelsey and Piers were arguing again while cleaning up the slippery floor, and the dog was barking from the back. Cody had come back into the main shop to boss Kelsey and Piers; Cody obsessed about germs and cleanliness in the fudge shop.

Lloyd had just arrived. With his salt-and-pepper mustache wiggling, he rubbed his bald head in confusion. His gaze fixed on Kelsey for a long moment. He looked as if he were about to admonish the petite thing for bad behavior, but then he blinked and let it pass. He held up an envelope in the other hand. It had to be my rent reimbursement. "Should I hang on to this check and come back another time? This doesn't look like a good time for a meeting."

Grandma was on him like flies on fish left too long in the sun. Shaking a finger under his nose, almost touching his mustache, she said, "This is your fault, Lloyd. You're ruining my granddaughter's life. Why?"

Dillon said, "Hold on there, Sophie. The man's an upstanding citizen."

My grandmother muttered Belgian words under her breath as she advanced on Dillon.

My mother and I hustled Grandma Sophie out the door before another fight started. I felt bad that my ex was such an object of scorn, because he was a decent enough guy. But Florine and Sophie blamed Dillon for whisking me away to Las Vegas eight years ago to marry him in one of those youthful, stupid indiscretions that not even I can believe I did after looking back on it.

I put thoughts of Dillon aside as Mom was erratically driving ten miles an hour over the speed limit through the back streets of Fishers' Harbor and then even faster on Highway 42 barely outside the village. We were heading northerly, with glimpses of Lake Michigan going by like flipped pages in a book.

"Mom, slow down. There are tourists all over the place." Tourists often stopped their vehicles at the oddest times to gawk at our spectacular scenery of the lake or to find the quaint art shops tucked away in the woodlands.

Grandma gasped when Mom hit the horn and swerved around a slowing car ahead of us on the two-lane highway. "Florine, what the hell—?"

Mom veered into the entrance to Peninsula State Park. We went through the park gates, then headed down Shore Road, which went to the Eagle Bluff Lighthouse.

I told Mom, "I forgot Libby's fudge."

Mom barely missed a hen turkey and her poults that were strutting across the blacktop. Before I could complain again, I noticed the sheriff's car with its red-and-blue lights swirling in front of the lighthouse.

The lighthouse was made of Cream City brick with a red roof on top of its main house and atop the cupola tower. In the morning sun, the four-story tower had a yellow glow but with red-and-blue striations.

"What's going on, Mom?"

Her knuckles were white on the steering wheel. "The sheriff said Libby found something that he wants you to look at."

"Me? Why didn't you tell me?" I knew why. My mother did not handle stress or my adventurous life very well.

We parked next to the cruiser. Before we got out, my mother had a shaky hand on my arm. "Honey, are you in some kind of trouble again?"

"No," I said, though I always seemed to be in trouble and not know it. I searched my brain for something that would require a sheriff but came up with nothing. The fighting confectioner chefs were the only issue that came close to needing law enforcement interference of late. "Is Libby all right?"

She paled. "I forgot to ask. When I called the sheriff he just said something had happened out here, and he needed you."

By then Sheriff Jordy Tollefson came out to greet us. He was about six feet four inches tall; he had six inches on me. Jordy was in his early forties, lean, a runner, with the demeanor of a marine—perfection and precision. He escorted us inside, into the small room that served as the gift shop. A window had been busted.

Libby was sitting on a stool by the register counter, sniffling into a tissue. When she saw us, she rushed over to hug Grandma.

"Oh, Sophie, I'm so glad you're here. And I'm so sorry it has to involve your granddaughter."

A tiny bomb went off inside my stomach. I looked up at Jordy's stern face and steady brown eyes and said, "What happened?"

Jordy picked up a Baggie off the counter. It held a rock. "Somebody sent this through the window."

Then he picked up another Baggie with a piece of paper in it. It was ruled paper, the kind that kids use to learn to print letters. In perfect orange crayon, the note said *Somebody will die if you don't convince Lloyd to throw the contest. Miss Oosterling must not win.*

Blood drained from my head. I looked at Libby wrapped in my grandmother's arms and said, "Who would do such a thing? It's a silly fudge contest. I'm so sorry, Libby. Somebody's threatening you and Lloyd?"

My mother said to me, "Honey, you don't seem to get it. Somebody's threatening *you*."

Chapter 2

I wasn't allowed to touch the orange-crayon note that said I must not win. My mother assumed the "somebody will die" part of the note meant me. Sheriff Tollefson let me read the printed letters on ruled paper through the plastic bag that sat on Libby's register counter. The walls of the small gift shop closed in on me. The space used to be the winter kitchen for the lighthouse keeper and his family back in 1898 when it was built. I'm sure they made lovely meals here back then, but right now I felt like I was chewing on tacks.

"This has to be a kid's prank," I said. "Did you question the campers in the park, Jordy?"

"Yes, and the parents still around this morning verified their kids were in their tents and campers all night. But I have to catch up with one family that a witness said left around six this morning."

"There ya go. They left early because their child is the guilty party."

My mother's long exhalation of breath wasn't a sigh of relief. That was her signal that I was misreading the cues again. Jordy's stern demeanor confirmed it.

He picked up the plastic bag. "I doubt some kid would even care about a fudge contest."

"I beg to differ," I said, fluffing my ponytail to accentuate my indignation, but fear pricked down my spine a vertebra at a time. My fudge contest could be ruined with my shop suffering great embarrassment—again. The May murder involving my fudge stuck with me like gum under my flip-flops. Clearly somebody wanted to distract me again. Already I imagined Pauline's boyfriend, John Schultz, interviewing me about death threats and then showing the video of the "fatal fudge confectioner" to TV food or travel channel executives.

As Jordy poked around the gift store's postcards, photos, and books, I was thunderstruck with a realization. I had crayons in my shop that kids used when they visited. I often grabbed them to make window signs, as did Gilpa . . . and my guest confectioners. Could the confectioners have tossed this rock? I wasn't about to offer them up to Jordy without proof, though I was tempted. But my contest would be ruined and that darn Kelsey would sue me for defamation of her character, such as it was.

Grandma saved me from Jordy's piercing gaze. "Jordy, I have my suspicions about who might have done this."

"Who?"

"Lloyd Mueller."

Libby coughed. "My ex? Oh no, Sophie, we get along fine. Just yesterday I made homemade lingonberry pancakes for him and dropped those off at his house. He sent me home with wonderful chocolate-cherry coffee beans he'd found at the Chocolate Chicken."

The Chocolate Chicken was a coffee shop about six miles south of Fishers' Harbor in Egg Harbor. It also carried my Cinderella Pink Fudge. Eat cherry-vanilla fudge with a dark-roasted coffee laced with a hint of chocolate and Door County cherries, and well, now you know how to find Heaven.

Jordy asked my grandmother, "Why would you think Lloyd Mueller would do this?"

"He's tossing my granddaughter out on her butt. He's gone senile. And all this secrecy about buying the Blue Heron Inn and selling his properties—"

Jordy flipped his gaze to Libby. "Does Lloyd have any reason to threaten you? Anything about the real estate?"

"Why, no. I'm not involved. We've been divorced a decade. He doesn't tell me anything about his financial affairs, which is fine with me."

The sheriff picked up his clipboard, perched on a nearby bookshelf, then gave me his full attention. "Who would want you to lose the contest?"

My mother's withering sigh nudged me. With trepidation, I confessed, "My rivals. My mom just called your department about them fighting at the fudge shop this morning."

Jordy consulted his smartphone. "Am I reading this right? Fudge cutters as weapons? What the heck—?"

"You know how chefs can be. Very competitive."

"But how is that connected to throwing a rock through the lighthouse window out here in the park?"

"One of my guest confectioners, Kelsey King, comes out to the park regularly looking for edible plants. And she hates me."

Libby perked up. "Oh my stars, I remember something from last night. As I was closing, a skinny woman and a big man were near the wall out back with some chubby guy with a camera. The cameraman was telling them to throw stuff at each other, and they started tossing twigs, and then chased each other over the wall. I heard some mighty bad words. They must have tumbled down that steep hill to the water's edge."

Jordy's pen picked up speed. "So this cameraman likes to stir up trouble?"

Ugh. Pauline would hate me if her boyfriend got questioned about the broken window and threat.

"Jordy, the guy is taping the chefs for a possible TV series. On TV all the chefs act mad and yell. It's a put-on. Television likes conflict," I said.

Jordy jotted that down. "So, Ava, Kelsey King tossed this rock through the window for the TV show?"

"She or the other chef, Piers Molinsky." Another theory came to mind that could keep Jordy from blaming John. "Piers doesn't like Kelsey. He may have done it on his own because he knows she's out here a lot, too, and she'd get blamed. He said this morning she was cooking with dirt, and some of the best dirt in Door County is right here in Peninsula State Park."

His pen hung in the air. "Cooking with dirt?"

My mom said, "With hog bits. That's what she called Piers's bacon that spilled into her copper kettle."

Grandma Sophie said, "Those two are fake chefs, if you ask me. I'd do a background check on them, Jordy."

"And," I said, "I have orange crayons at my shop. Have you seen the new tea table that Verona Klubertanz's dad made, Jordy? It's made from Wisconsin black cherry trees and is quite lovely, and there could be a connection to the perpetrator with the rock."

I grabbed a notepad and pen from Libby's counter to sketch a couple of hexagons connected by a line. "That's the chemical formula for wood. Paper is a step away from that." I added another sketch. "Wood is essentially cellulose, which is a carbohydrate, but of course we can't eat this form of carbs. Cows and termites have microorganisms in their intestines that can convert the cellulose of wood to glucose. Do you see the connection to fudge now? And this crime?"

Jordy blinked several times. I'd learned in May that he hated chemical formulas and thus I could distract him and probably sell him swampland if I wished. However, this time he sighed heavily and smiled. "Enough of your tricks. We'll be looking at the paper thoroughly. I'll want to take a look at the paper in your shop to see if it matches somehow."

My mom's head was bobbing rapidly. "Good idea."

I told Jordy he was welcome to look around my shop.

He asked, "Where's this guy with the TV camera? I'd like to question him."

Oh, fudge. Jordy wasn't buying my theory that the rock

might have been thrown by Piers or Kelsey. But as much as I thought John Schultz was an oaf and didn't deserve Pauline, I'd never betray my BFF—Best Friend Forever—since kindergarten. "John likely showed up at the shop just as we were leaving. Maybe your deputy is talking with him now and has cleared him?"

Jordy pulled out his phone again. His thumb scrolled through screens. "Yeah, your camera guy's there with a crowd on the docks. My new deputy is handling this one, so I'd better go help her out. She's from the city. I'm sure she's seen her share of crazies, but not people trying to kill each other with fudge cutters and crayons."

After the sheriff left, Mom, Grandma, and I helped Libby clean up. I taped cellophane over the broken window so birds and chipmunks wouldn't be inclined to visit. Libby seemed relieved to know the whole incident might have been part of an argument between my miserable guest chefs. I promised her it wouldn't happen again. Libby thanked us all for the help because she had a tour coming at ten and a book-signing event with an author after that.

"Professor Faust?" I asked.

"Indeed. His book about Wisconsin's food heritage is so wonderful. You've read it?"

"I haven't had time. He dropped off copies at my shop, though, so I'll take a look soon." As part of the warm-up to the fudge festival next weekend, all Door County shopkeepers were sharing their sales space with fellow businesspeople and artists to help publicize one another. Fudge was the draw, but I was hoping the entire county would benefit from the festival.

Libby said, "Take a look at the book, dear, because he mentions the bait shop in it."

Grandma perked up. "Gil never mentioned that."

"Grandma, Gilpa's too cheap to buy a new book. Even if I wrote it, he'd wait for it to be remaindered in a sale bin."

"You're right, Ava honey. He's a darn old cheap Belgian.

I'll come back later, Libby, for the signing, and buy several copies."

As we went out the door, Libby yelled after us, "Better make his favorite dinner first before you show him all those expensive books and your empty wallet."

We laughed.

Our smiles evaporated when we arrived at the crowded harbor. My mother had intended to drop us off and drive onward to Sister Bay to make a cheese delivery to Al Johnson's Swedish Restaurant, but she changed her mind when she saw the sheriff's cruiser with the red-and-blues on. Another smaller department car sat next to it.

"What do you suppose is going on now?" my mom asked as she got out.

Grandma said, "Florine, why don't you go on and make your deliveries before that cheese in this van gets moldy from neglect? You know how you get when you're worried."

Mom's sighing usually turned into babbling when she became stressed. Babbling often descended into cleaning everything in sight, which was handy when I was a teenager because while she was yelling at me to clean my room she'd actually be cleaning my room. Since the fudge shop now needed a thorough scrubbing, I was inclined to let Mom foment more stress.

Mom said to Grandma, "You should be worried, too, because that's my father-in-law—also known as your husband—in the middle of the fuss."

Sure enough, Grandpa Gil—with his distinctive silver hair—was waving his hands between the sheriff and his female deputy on one side of him, with my two chef combatants on the other side. They were near the door of our bait-and-fudge shop, a little way from the wooden pier where Gilpa had docked his fishing trawler, *Sophie's Journey*.

I helped Grandma Sophie out of the van. Wind gusts off Lake Michigan caught her long, thick wavy white hair that hung past her shoulders, whipping it into the look of a swirling cloud. The breeze tugged at my ponytail and buffeted my pink blouse.

The pungent smells of bacon and overheated chocolate mingled with the sweet aroma of cherry-vanilla fudge. Seagulls screeched and sparrows chattered as they landed amid the crowd's feet and on the dock's picnic tables, looking for scraps.

As I headed into the fray, I spotted Dillon Rivers coming out of our shop. My heart skipped a beat. I tucked a strand of loose hair behind an ear. If Mom saw him she'd turn into a babbling bulldog trying to protect me from him. I whipped back toward the cow minivan. "Grandma, you stay here with Mom. I can handle this."

After I pushed through the throng of tourists and a few locals, I found my chefs with their hands handcuffed in front of them. The woman deputy was holding her ground against my grandfather, who was demanding the cuffs come off.

I gave my grandpa a hug and asked, "What's going on?" He smelled of the clean spray that spat from Lake Michigan's freshwater waves.

He broke into a big smile. "Look at this ruckus. We're going to sell out of all my live bait, bobbers and beer, and your Belgian fudge. All because of this dandy new lady county cop."

The deputy looked maybe twenty-five. She was Hispanic with large mesmerizingly beautiful cocoa-colored eyes that matched her regulation shirt. Her black hair was in a thick braid twisted into a knot at the nape of her neck. She wore tan pants and a tan department ball cap. She had each of her hands on an arm of both chefs.

Jordy wore a pissed look. "I've already spent way too much time on this. Get in the cars. One in each."

Kelsey rattled her handcuffs. "I'm innocent. But you can take this fry cook."

Piers growled, "I'm not a cook. I'm a bakery chef."

"You're half-baked." Kelsey flipped her long blond

tresses around as if she were an indignant filly. "I'll sue all of you, and you're first, Half-Baked."

So the fight was still raging. Cameras and cell phones clicked. I saw Lloyd Mueller shaking his head in disgust. The fudge contest was melting away faster than fancy Belgian chocolate left on a dashboard under the July sun.

Dillon barged into the fray. Women adjusted their hair and licked their lips. Even the young deputy gave Dillon the once-over.

He was looking at me with concern on his chiseled face. "Al and I are almost done fixing a leak in the pipes out under Main Street. You should have your water back within a half hour. I'll send Al back to check on the water pressure later. You want to join us for coffee now or lunch later?"

Al Kvalheim had been the street and water guy in town since before I was born, my grandpa had told me. Al loved getting dirty and greasy, just like Grandpa. He was portly, short, bald, and heavily wrinkled. He was one of the few people around who still smoked. Al was the opposite of Dillon, so I couldn't imagine how they got along so well. Dillon's invitation to join them for coffee was a lifeline being thrown my way, but I had to pass.

I edged closer and whispered, "My mother's over there. It'd be best if you left now before she blows up at you in front of the crowd."

He whispered back, "You're sure you're okay?"

I nodded. Dillon left, but in his stead my landlord stepped forward, rubbing his bald head in a thoughtful gesture. Lloyd indicated Kelsey and Piers with a nod. "It might do these two good to sit in our fine county jail. We can always replace them with local cooks or bakers. The fudge contest could be a pie contest."

"Lloyd!" I screeched. "You can't suggest such a thing. I already have a new fudge flavor in development." *Liar.*

"Another pink flavor? I'm a businessman. I'm starting to feel foolish about pink fudge for a festival."

Lloyd had obviously been around my friend Pauline

lately. Every time she taught summer enrichment courses, the alliteration was as catching as a cold bug. I looked back at my shop window, and sure enough, she was hiding inside, waiting. She waved what looked like swatches of fabric.

Kelsey stomped her petite purple canvas shoes, barely missing Jordy's uniform black shoes as she tossed her mane in Lloyd's direction. "I happen to like pink. Who are you again?"

I couldn't tell if she meant that rhetorically or she hadn't paid attention at all this week. As a fudge judge, Lloyd had stopped by a few times.

Piers scoffed. "Mr. Mueller is a fudge judge because he's the richest man in town and Ava's landlord and some old friend of her grandfather's. Ava invited him so she could figure out what he's up to with his offer to buy the Blue Heron Inn."

The crowd gasped, and so did I, because it was true, though I'd never said any of that aloud. Lloyd narrowed his eyes at me.

"Crap," Kelsey said, her gaze shooting to the sky, "do we have to put up with some little real estate intrigue in this town, too? Everybody bulldozes old stuff for new condos. End of story. Boring."

Lloyd muttered, "You're not even close. Maybe we should let Half-Baked finish you off."

Jordy held up a hand. "That's it. The two in handcuffs, get in the cars. We're going over to the state park for a visit."

Piers and Kelsey looked stunned, guilty maybe.

Kelsey began to cry—certainly a ploy. "Is this about the dirt? I'm sorry. I didn't mean to take anything from the park. They really do eat dirt in meals in Japan. And India. Africa, too. Some believe it builds your immunities naturally. In some cultures, pregnant women eat dirt. And I only took a few red clover flowers and chickweed. Chickweed is just a neglected weed, but it's superrich in vitamins and omega-6 fatty acid derivatives. I'm just trying to infuse fudge with healthful richness to cancel out the calories from the sugar."

Oh my gosh, Piers hadn't been kidding earlier. Kelsey really was cooking with dirt. And she was "infusing" vitamins into fudge? Infusion is a technical term in cooking circles. This woman was more of a competitor than I originally thought.

Jordy and his new deputy led Piers and Kelsey through the assemblage to the squad cars. I trotted behind, trying to think of some way to sound supportive of my chefs. But then my gaze caught John rounding a corner from Main Street with Dotty and Lois on his heels. A camera paired with the best gossips in Door County felt threatening to me.

I slipped inside my shop, which was crowded with fishermen and several little girls who were in Pauline Mertens's summer enrichment class. They were in the Cinderella Pink Fudge aisle, fingering the homemade dolls with pink lace dresses and the hand-painted pink tea sets and pink sparkly purses.

Cody was positioning a tall stack of Professor Faust's *Wisconsin's Edible Heritage* on the corner of the cash register counter.

Cody's social worker, Sam Peterson, burst in from the back of the shop just as my grandmother cut through from the front door to head home. My mom must have left to finally finish her delivery route.

Grandma gave Sam a hug. "You lunk, how are you? When you comin' for supper?"

"Whenever Gil says it's okay for me to court his wife," Sam said with a chuckle, looking impeccable as usual, from the perfect side part in his short blond hair to the crisp white shirt and tie.

"I'm past the courting stage, but my granddaughter's available."

Although I could see that coming, I still grew hot in the face.

Ever since I moved back to Fishers' Harbor in late April, Grandma had wanted me to rekindle my romance with Sam Peterson. We'd been engaged once upon a time. But the circumstances of our breakup eight years ago still weighed heavily on me. Even having a friendship with Sam remained awkward. I had jilted him at the altar on the evening of our wedding rehearsal—the evening I ran away with Dillon Rivers to Las Vegas.

The two men were opposites, which probably meant I had a split personality. Dillon swaggered through life like a confident cowboy, while Sam calculated his actions, which I suppose appealed to the scientific bent in me.

Sam turned to his business with Cody after my grandmother continued through the back of the fudge shop.

My friends Pauline Mertens—who was weighed down with two big bags—and a very pregnant Laura Rousseau edged through the crowded shop. Pauline was fanning herself with a hand.

She said, "This is like high school before the prom, the guys checking you out."

"Stop it. Guys never checked me out. I was too tall."

Laura laughed. "Can we sit down before I pee my pants? The babies are kicking."

"Sure." We went to the marble-topped table by the window, where I kept a stool. Laura settled onto it while I said to Pauline, "I'm afraid I can't demonstrate my fudge making for your class at the moment. It's a mess over there." I pointed toward the sticky explosion we'd had earlier around the copper kettles. The table in front of us was a mess, too, with pink fudge confetti scattered across the white marble.

Pauline sniffed the air. "Smells like you had a bacon-and-eggs breakfast in here. Starting up a diner?"

"Something like that."

"Don't worry about the girls not getting a fudge show today. Two of the moms agreed to come here to take over their field trip. They're going to the Eagle Bluff Lighthouse."

The images of the orange crayon lettering on the ruled paper came to me. Had Kelsey and Piers really thrown that rock? Did they want me to lose the contest that badly? Or did the orange crayon come from that camping family that left the park early? I excused myself to look for the ruled paper by the kids' table in the shop and found none. I also looked under the cash register counter but didn't see any ruled paper.

When I returned to the marble-topped table, Pauline had dropped her two big bags on the floor. One bag was her big purse that carried her summer enrichment classroom supplies, including everything from stickers to Sharpies, to dozens of little sticky notes and scissors. The other bag appeared stuffed with Butterick patterns and fabric swatches for the prom dress she and Laura insisted on making me.

Pauline looked down her nose at me, like a teacher does with her students. "It'd be great to get your invitation to the dance on video."

It was her way of telling me John had come in and had sneaked up behind me. I turned around to find the appendage on his face—the video camera—recording me while his other hand held a professional-looking light. John wore his usual hideous Hawaiian shirt, baggy shorts with multiple pockets, and sandals. My gaze was always drawn to his hairy feet.

"Cinderella!" he boomed. "The fudge shop owner torn between Fishers' Harbor's two most eligible bachelors. Besides me."

John tipped his head up and Pauline bent down to kiss him on the lips. The two had met in May during the unusual circumstances of the murder at the Blue Heron Inn. John was my height—two inches shorter than Pauline—and he was definitely a generation older, in his fifties somewhere by the looks of the gray sideburns and gray strands dappled throughout his head of brown hair. He was always loud and boastful, bordering on boorish, in my opinion. These facts failed to matter to Pauline, who had regressed to high school romance mode.

Another fisherman came in and headed over to my grandpa's bait shop area. Grandpa was still outside, so I called over, "I'll be right there."

I gave John a scowl to send him away. He followed the fisherman.

Pauline muttered, "Be nice."

"There's something you need to know about John."

A smile burst on her face. She grabbed my shoulders. "Sam's coming this way."

Sam's crisp white shirt, dark tie, and clean tan pants were a stark contrast to my limp pink blouse, dirty denim shorts, and bare legs covered with dust and bits of Cinderella Pink Fudge.

Pauline and Laura excused themselves from the corner behind me, saying something about using the restroom. But they stood secretly behind Sam with rapt anticipation on their faces. My gal pals were so transparent.

"Hi, Sam." My throat closed. Panic had struck. Did I want Sam to invite me to the fudge festival dance? To make our debut as a couple? Confusion swirled inside me worse than a waterspout on Lake Michigan. "Uh, didn't you want to take some fudge back to the office?"

"I came for more than fudge."

The shop silenced. The minnow tank bubbled. The air conditioner pinged from the wall on Grandpa's side of the shop.

My grandmother's friends popped in then just in time, the cowbell clanking on the door, busting apart the awkward moment.

Sam's shoulders relaxed, as if he'd been saved. "I meant to say, I came for more fudge. Yes, to take back to the office. And I'm here to take Cody with me to his group meeting."

"Oh, sorry. I forgot," I said, greatly relieved. Cody met every Friday with young adults like himself who had Asperger's or other challenges that were helped by Sam's coaching them on life skills.

I hurried behind the counter. "Ranger, I'll take over the registers while you wrap things for Mr. Peterson and your group today." I lowered my voice. "The cameras are rolling. Make everything look extra special. Real Hollywood."

"You got it, Miss Oosterling."

Cody loved wrapping the fudge. He pulled out crinkly, stiff party cellophane and shiny satin ribbons to wrap individual pieces of Cinderella Pink Fudge. I believed that our customers should feel like fairy-tale royalty when they received Belgian fudge from Oosterlings', as if the customers were the king and queen of Belgium. My fudge was therefore made with the finest cream and milk from my parents' farm, delivered fresh daily. Their two hundred Door County cows fed on beautiful green grass pastures on rolling hills overlooking Lake Michigan. Biting into a piece of my Belgian fudge transported a royal fudge highness into that bucolic scenery.

John's camera captured Cody wrapping the pleasantly pungent, pink cherry-vanilla fudge with marzipan fairy wings atop each piece.

Then John surprised Sam by swinging the camera on him and asking, "Why is Ava Oosterling such a special lady?"

"Her fudge tastes good for breakfast," Sam said in his matter-of-fact baritone voice.

With a tiny smile to myself at Sam's funny response, I left the counter to rejoin my friends by the window, but was stopped by Grandma's friends.

Dotty Klubertanz—one of the fudge judges—and Lois Forbes thrust dollar bills at me.

I asked, "What kind of fudge can I get for you ladies?"

"Oh, it's not for fudge," Dotty said. A plump lady in her sixties with short white hair, she had on pink denim clamdigger pants and a pink T-shirt with sequined butterflies. "We came to pay you for the cup we broke during that frightening episode earlier."

Lois, nodding her red-dyed head of hair excessively, said, "Your cooking buddies said they wanted to kill each other. Do you think they would really commit murder? Are you starting to feel paranoid about bad things following you?"

"Ladies, lightning does not strike twice," I said, though my inner warning system recalled the note at the lighthouse said somebody would die.

"What's wrong, dear?" Dotty asked. "You're shivering."

I handed back Dotty's money. "It's the air-conditioning. I'm used to hotter weather. You owe me nothing. Accidents happen. It's part of doing business. Besides, I owe you two a lot for helping me get this business under way." Since May, the two had been guardian angels, bragging about me on their social media networks. Dotty, being a judge, felt slightly biased in my favor; however, her being the head church lady meant she'd be the toughest judge. She'd be honest about which fudge flavor was truly the best at Saturday's final tasting.

I asked, "Have you ladies heard anything about what Lloyd's up to with the properties on Duck Marsh Street? Or the inn up on the hill?"

Lois's eyes widened again. "Scuttlebutt is they're going to tear it down—"

"I thought it had historical significance."

Dotty shrugged. "That doesn't matter when you have that million-dollar view of Lake Michigan on top of that little bluff. Word is Lloyd wants to build a big condo building for the Chicago people coming up here for vacations."

"I was sure Lloyd Mueller muttered something this morning that seemed to say that wasn't going to happen." Now I was racking my brain to remember what he'd said.

Dotty said, "He lives in that old house that was built before 1900. Maybe he's tired of old things and wants to live in something new for once in his life."

Lois added, "Enjoy a new beginning on his way to the gated community in the sky."

"The Pearly Gates," said Dotty.

Lois took my hands in hers. "Ava, that's not all. We've heard that right behind your shop, where the rental cabins are now, he plans to install a helipad so the rich Chicago people can hop from here out to their vacation homes on Chambers Island and up to Washington Island without waiting for the ferries."

This sounded like gossip. "I doubt they'd take down all

those cabins on my street just so helicopters can come and go."

Dotty shook her head. "The helipad is only part of it. We heard that whoever is buying the cabins will be working with the village to expand the harbor, too."

Lois fingered her red hairdo. "We heard the buyer wants to dredge right here where we're standing. Your fudge shop would be torn down."

Chapter 3

While I was reeling from the gossip about the demise of my fudge shop, Cody and Sam waved on their way out.

Cody said, "See you after lunch, Miss Oosterling. We're stopping in Ephraim for ice cream and burgers at Wilson's after group meeting."

Ephraim was a quaint, tiny village on Lake Michigan between Fishers' Harbor and Sister Bay. It was Wisconsin's only dry town, and it enforced a code that every house and building had to be painted predominantly in shades of white or gray. Wilson's Restaurant and Ice Cream Parlor—with its daring red-and-white-striped awnings—was where everybody stopped for the best milk shakes and sundaes in Door County.

John tailed after them but not before catching a loud, smacking kiss from Pauline. Somehow I knew Pauline was headed for heartache with this bloke.

Lois looked at her watch. "We have to scoot. I have to wash six stained glass windows before lunchtime."

"Wait," I said, reaching out to touch her papery arm. "This thing about them bulldozing this building is just gossip, right? You haven't heard anything official?" I couldn't imagine that my family would be the last to know about this.

Lois patted my hand on her arm. "We'll ask around. It's

our turn to clean St. Bernie's for the weekend services. Then we've got to head to St. Ann's near Egg Harbor. They've got that Sunday dinner and raffle this weekend."

The women accepted fudge from me for the raffle. They swooned over the wrapping paper that matched Dotty's pink outfit, then left.

Feeling numb from their news, I took care of the fishermen who had been patiently waiting. Where had Grandpa disappeared to? He had been getting distracted a lot lately, taking long breaks. With a small net, I fished out live minnows from the gurgling tank to put in the customers' minnow buckets. The men grabbed beers and cartons of worms from the stand-up cooler in the corner. They also bought my beer fudge that came packaged in a six-pack beer carton. I used discarded cartons from my friends Ronny and Nancy Jenks, who ran the Troubled Trout Bar on the north edge of town.

After the fishermen left, a racket erupted from the back.

To my dismay, Dillon's dog was in my small galley kitchen. He must have come in the back door when Sam or Grandma left. Sometimes the door didn't quite latch. The refrigerator door was hanging open. The chocolate-colored hunting spaniel was lapping up a stick of butter amid spilled milk from a carton he'd retrieved. The dog had a rope leash on, but it'd come undone. Cody must have tied him to the refrigerator door handle, thinking the dog would be out of the way and safe until Dillon came again to pick him up.

"Come on, Harbor, or Lucky, or whoever you are. Maybe Mr. Troublemaker?"

The rope tying him to the refrigerator had been chewed through. Lucky Harbor chewed through twine most every day, but it was cheap stuff and Grandpa had it around in big rolls for fishermen and boaters to buy for tying all sorts of odds and ends like their sails and tarps. I refused to buy a real leash or accept the many Dillon offered to me; somehow that would be admitting that the dog and Dillon were permanent in my life.

I led the bouncing, chocolate brown American water spaniel out with me into the shop area, then tied him to one of the legs of the heavy marble table. I told him to lie down. He did.

Laura and Pauline had spread out several fabric swatches. I cringed at the shiny pastels staring back at me on the smooth white marble surface.

Pauline swept her black hair over a shoulder, smiling down at me in her sly way. "Ava, guess which color your dress is going to be."

"You know I hate this game, Pauline. Listen, I have other more important things to talk to you both about."

"Come on, Ava, this is your time to shine. Pick a color for your dress. Your grandpa wants A.M. and P.M. to enjoy this. Do it for him."

My grandpa had named her P.M. for Pauline Mertens and me A.M. for Ava Mathilde (my middle name) when we were youngsters. He'd say things like "Be good all a.m. and p.m. for your grandma Sophie, A.M. and P.M."

"Surprise me, Pauline. You know I hate dresses. I look dowdy in them."

Laura was leaning against a corner of the tall table, rubbing her big belly. "That's because you buy everything at the big-box store down in Sturgeon Bay. This is going to be something I custom-sew for you. And please, I need something to do this weekend besides feel these babies kicking me."

Laura was talented at everything. She was a short, cute woman with luminous blue eyes and a blond bob that framed her face perfectly. Until a month ago, she'd run her own bakery shop and school, the Luscious Ladle, in Sister Bay. Her doctor had advised her to get off her feet now and not lift anything heavier than ten pounds since she had a risky pregnancy. On top of that, her husband was deployed with the U.S. Army on the other side of the world, so she had no help at home. But she had A.M. and P.M. to take care of her a.m. and p.m.

I had relented about the sewing, for Laura's sake. She had to be bored, sitting at home all the time. "Okay, you two. What should I wear?"

Pauline held up two swatches—a shimmering, rich brown satin the color of Belgian chocolate fudge when it glistened in a copper kettle over a flame, and the other a royal blue silk so iridescent it could have been made of silvery blue butterfly wings.

Laura giggled behind her hands.

I thrummed the cool marble with the fingers of one hand. "What are you two up to?"

"Oh, nothing." Pauline dangled the swatches in front of me again. "Take your pick. Which color do you like the best?"

"They're both nice. I can't decide."

Pauline sighed. "Pick something. I have to get to the school for the Butterflies' fudge parade meeting."

Pauline had decided that the fudge festival needed a kids' parade down Main Street next Saturday in order to qualify as a real festival. She called her summer school group of six little girls—now in my store fingering the dolls—the Butterflies. She'd already plastered every window in town with posters to make sure all the tourists knew about the "Fudge Fluttering Parade at the Fudge Festival."

"Okay, blue looks good," I said, not caring and still reeling with the thought of this building being demolished. But had I heard Dotty and Lois correctly? I was slipping today. Lloyd had said something significant I'd missed, too. And I still had to tell Pauline my suspicions about John and the stupid rock thrown through the window at the lighthouse. "Definitely the blue."

Pauline high-fived Laura, then said, "That's who you should marry, not to mention go with to the prom dance next week."

"Marry who?"

"Sam. He has blue eyes. This material matches his eyes."

Laura said, "The brown satin matches Dillon's."

I snatched the material out of their hands, then tossed the swatches on the white marble. "I can't believe you two would have me pick a husband using fabric swatches."

They enjoyed giggles at my expense as I strutted back across the shop floor to finish cleaning up the morning's disaster. The copper kettles needed washing, but I had no water yet. Dillon had said it'd be on in a half hour. That was any minute.

Pauline came after me. "I'm sorry. We were just having some fun."

"I'm okay. It's just that this whole day has been weird. Lloyd even dissed my fudge. He thought pink fudge was silly. And if we lose the celebrity contestants, he's ready to change it to a pie contest. And he's Grandpa's best friend. I don't think Lloyd is feeling well because of the pressure from the big secret sale of his property."

The dog barked. Pauline and I jerked our heads to look. Laura had slipped off the stool and was leaning with her forehead on the cool marble table. We dashed over.

"Laura? What's wrong?" I asked. "I can grab some water from Grandpa's cooler."

Laura lifted up her head. "I'm okay." Her skin nearly matched the white marble.

Pauline said, "No, you're not. We're taking you to the clinic."

"I'll get my truck. Pauline, can you handle her alone for the moment?" It was a redundant question because Pauline was six feet tall and strong from all our basketball playing we still did for fun and her wrestling kids every day. Laura was all of five feet four inches, maybe, and except for her belly, as skinny-limbed as a willow tree.

I raced through the back and across the lawn to Duck Marsh Street, where my yellow Chevy pickup truck was parked. I drove it up over the curb and right across the lawn to the fudge shop's back door, where we loaded Laura into the front passenger seat. Pauline folded herself into the narrow backseat with her two bags.

Laura's lips looked bluish.

"Are you having the babies?" I asked, my heart beating like a bass drum in my head.

"No, I don't think so," she whispered. "I'm just nauseated. Maybe from the humidity today."

I had just hit the gas hard, spurting up grass and dirt from under my tires, when I stopped with much more care for my pregnant passenger, then backed up.

Pauline screeched from behind me, "What's wrong?"

"The dog. Cody's not around and Gilpa won't pay any attention. The dog'll get loose and eat all my fudge, and chocolate is toxic to dogs."

It took me less than thirty seconds to retrieve the spaniel. As soon as he leaped into the backseat behind me with Pauline, he licked her face profusely.

"*Ick*. Make him stop."

"Lucky Harbor, do you want some fudge?"

That worked to draw his attention. While I didn't give him fudge ever, he'd somehow learned the word meant he got a substitute treat. I fished in a pocket where I'd begun keeping Goldfish crackers for him and tossed one behind my shoulder. His teeth clacked with the snatch.

I wove through backstreets to avoid the tourist traffic, then hit Highway 42. We decided to head for Sturgeon Bay's hospital. There was a clinic before then, but no mere clinic that fixed cuts and gave shots could help a woman with blood pressure problems and carrying twins.

Traffic was heavier, though, on the two-lane highway. Tourists were out in full force, stopping at quaint shops or restaurants tucked behind borders of white daisies and pink rudbeckias. I had to brake several times, then use the gravel shoulders to pass cars.

Laura was scary-quiet next to me. The only noises in the pickup were Lucky Harbor panting behind my ear and the air-conditioning fan struggling. I tried small talk.

"Have either of you heard the rumor that whoever the

buyer is for the cabins might offer my grandfather money to tear down my shop?"

"No," said Pauline. "That's silly. Where'd you hear that?"

"Dotty and Lois just a bit ago."

"*Hmm.* They're usually half-right."

Laura stirred, lifting her head. "Your grandfather owns it. And he owns his house. You'd have heard about an offer by now."

"You're right. So it's just gossip."

Pauline said, "Where would you move your fudge business? I don't recall much that's empty around here."

"Except the Blue Heron Inn, which is closed and owned by somebody out east."

"There's that creepy empty mansion over at the other end of Fishers' Harbor where . . ."

Pauline purposely didn't finish that sentence. My shoulders hunched up in a huge shudder. I'd almost been murdered in May in that big old yellow house by the woman who had run the Blue Heron Inn. She'd murdered a visiting actress at the inn, trying to pin it on me with my fudge stuffed down the actress's throat. Then, after I suspected her treachery, I went in search of Gilpa and Cody, who had both gone missing. They'd been left for dead in an old cistern in the basement of the empty mansion. Isabelle Boone had planned to shove me in that cistern, too, and brick us all into our tomb. By distracting her with a precious Steuben statue of hers that I'd threatened to break, I'd subdued her. The whole episode made me vow never to go back to that empty, three-story mausoleum. Ironically, I'd always thought I wanted to live in a big house, particularly after living in efficiencies in Los Angeles, but I was changing my mind. Big houses brought me bad luck.

Pauline said, "John wants to go to the fish boil tonight at the Troubled Trout. Are you guys game?"

That was nicer small talk. "I'm game," I said, with great cheer in my voice for Laura. "They serve the whitefish with a nice garlic butter and that cherry salsa. I heard they have watermelon tonight, too, with sweet pickle ice cream."

Laura rolled down her window, then threw up into the wind.

Lucky Harbor barked sharply behind me as Pauline thumped the back of my head with a finger in admonishment for making Laura sick.

Pauline said, "Sometimes, A.M., you forget to engage your brain before you speak."

She was right.

From there on out, I didn't say a word all the way to Sturgeon Bay.

About an hour later, the nurses had moved Laura from the emergency room into a private room. She wasn't having the babies yet. The doctor wanted Laura to go her full term. The babies needed all the time inside Mom they could get. Laura's blood pressure wasn't normal, so the doc was keeping her overnight to get that regulated.

Laura was too young for this kind of trouble. She was in her midtwenties, but right now in the bed she looked about fifteen. I'd met her in May when I'd needed some white chocolate to make Cinderella Pink Fudge in a pinch. She had made the best hot cheesy bread and shared it with us that day at her shop, the Luscious Ladle. She'd needed our help carrying the heavy loaves to the nearby Al Johnson's Swedish Restaurant. Now, almost two months later, she needed Pauline and me; I felt like we were sisters.

Minutes later, as Pauline and I walked down a staircase that led to a side door, I said, "I wish her husband could come home."

Laura had said he was on a special mission, and messages could be sent through to him, but she'd refused to pursue it. She didn't want to alarm her husband for just a blood pressure correction and an overnight stay. I ached for her, though, because of how lonely she must be. I was surrounded by family and too many men, and she had none. Her relatives were in other states, too, and she didn't want them rushing to her side needlessly.

The echoing slap of our shoes in the quiet stairwell and the antiseptic smell somehow contributed to my sadness for Laura.

We left the hospital by the side door, then circled around to the E.R. parking area.

When we got back to my pickup, the dog was gone. "Crap." I'd left the windows down because of the hot day. "Dillon's going to kill me."

"Stop using that word. *Kill*. I don't allow it in my classroom."

"Have you forgotten I was almost killed in May, and now there are silly notes that insinuate I might be killed? If I had a perfume named after me, it'd be the 'Scent of Killing.'"

"Don't snap at me, Ava. What silly notes?" Pauline put an arm around my shoulders.

"Sorry. It's been a rough morning." I explained the lighthouse episode and the note.

Pauline said, "And here I thought those two chefs were merely being arrested for fighting. They could be murderers. Is your fudge contest falling apart?"

She was likely worried for John and his big dream for a culinary travel show. "I'm sure by now Jordy's had the two chefs take a look at the window and nothing came of it, so John is safe. The rock was likely thrown by some kid from the campground. Let's find Dillon's dog. Is there a grocery store or candy shop nearby? That dog loves to eat and he has a sixth sense for sniffing out sugar."

We were climbing into the front seats when Pauline pointed through the windshield toward the emergency room doors. "Look."

Lucky Harbor was curled up in the deep shade by a big brown flowerpot, sleeping. We hadn't seen him at first because he matched the color of the pot.

Pauline said, "He was waiting for you to come back through that way because that's the way you went inside, not the other exit. He's smarter than you."

"That's easy enough," I said. I got back out of the truck and called, "Want some fudge?"

The furry brown head popped up; then he bounded to me with his tail wagging. After a Goldfish, I gave him a head scratch. "Let's go back to the fudge shop."

He raced to the truck, going to the back, expecting me to lower the tailgate. Obviously Dillon let him ride often in the open truck bed, but that was around Fishers' Harbor at twenty miles an hour.

"No, Lucky Harbor. You get the whole backseat to yourself. Come."

After I got in, he slurped the back of my neck as I pulled out of the hospital's parking area.

The sun was beginning to move overhead by the time we got near Fishers' Harbor. It was nearly noon. I trusted Gilpa would be handling the shop just fine, so instead of driving into Fishers' Harbor, I took a right turn off Highway 42 just before town and went inland.

"Where we going?" Pauline asked. "I'm supposed to be meeting with my Butterflies' parents to start making their parade costumes."

"Wasn't Bethany volunteering to help? She can handle it." Bethany Bjorklund was Cody's girlfriend—in his eyes, anyway. Whatever the relationship, she was kind, and she signed on to help with the fudge festival and the fudge shop parade floats.

Pauline fished her phone from her humongous purse, sending paper scraps and notepads and pens flying. "I'll call her. So, where are we going?"

"To Lloyd Mueller's. All this secrecy about the property that affects my grandparents is odd. And him dissing my pink fudge is double-fudge odd. Lloyd acts like he's scared of something."

"You're reading too much into this."

"Pauline, that note said Lloyd should throw the contest, so I don't win."

"It was a prank. You know how your life works. As soon as you have a few good days, you end up with something bad. Right now we're in the good."

"How do you know that?"

"You're not dead, for one thing."

"That's not funny."

"Please, can't we just leave well enough alone?" She was stuffing papers and pens back into her purse. "I don't think anything good can come of poking a stick at a bear in his cave."

"Lloyd is not a bear. He's my grandfather's best friend."

"You're walking right into something really bad, Ava."

"Pauline, you're not helping."

"Sorry."

Lloyd lived in a large, late-1800s, two-story white house with black shutters on a wooded hill on the outskirts of Fishers' Harbor. The land rose just high enough so you could glimpse the boating traffic on Lake Michigan to the north over the tops of the maple trees and village buildings. A Swedish fishing fleet captain had built the house the year before he lost his life on the lake in a wintry squall.

I'd visited Lloyd's home a few times as a little girl with my grandpa and grandma and remembered it feeling huge and very dark inside. We pulled to a stop a few feet from a cherry red door in the circular brick driveway. Several robins were fighting over the water spraying and cascading from a sizable, but plain, three-tiered concrete fountain that rose above my height in the center of the circle.

"Lucky birds," I mumbled to Pauline. "They have water this morning."

Pauline and I were barely out of the pickup when the home's front door popped open. Lloyd came forward with a limp that seemed endemic to being in one's seventies. Gilpa and Grandma had similar limps, especially in the evenings after a long day. Lloyd was dressed in a teal golf polo shirt bearing a designer shark logo and matching plaid shorts that grazed the wrinkles above his knees. His legs were skinny as cornstalks. He wore sporty white golfing shoes. One hand massaged his salt-and-pepper mustache. Sunlight highlighted the age spots atop his bald head. His eyes penetrated me in a way that chilled.

Maybe Pauline had been right; we'd made a mistake coming here unannounced.

"Hello, Lloyd. Listen, I can come back later, but could we set up a time to talk about the fudge contest?"

"Ava," he said, his countenance softening as he reached out his hands to clasp mine with priestlike solemnity, "we must talk about your fudge, indeed. Fishers' Harbor is in trouble. You and I were threatened. Somebody's gonna die, I heard. And I know who it is."

Chapter 4

Lloyd glanced about the outdoor environs as if he feared somebody were spying on us. He ushered Pauline and me inside. I left Lucky Harbor outside to enjoy the shade trees. Or to run home to Dillon. Dillon's backhoe was grinding away only three-quarters of a mile away in our downtown.

Inside the house, the air-conditioning refreshed us with dehumidified air. We followed Lloyd through a breathtaking, open layout filled with Wisconsin wildlife prints on the walls and tasteful sandstone-colored leather furniture as well as a dining room area with a resplendent cherry-wood-and-glass table and matching cherry chairs. A collection of cups and saucers—in vintage floral patterns—filled three wide shelves of a glass-fronted cupboard. The second story had been opened up in the center of the living area to create a rotunda with a stained glass dome skylight. It dripped hues of gold, red, emerald green, and blue onto the dark oak floors.

Lloyd led us into a library in the back with floor-to-ceiling windows overlooking a massive rose garden sporting blooms of every color imaginable, from sunny yellow to pale peach, to even a smoky blue. Bees worked the flowers in a choreographed fashion.

I said, "Did you know flowers give off electricity? The

bees detect it. There's a true attraction between flowers and bees that goes beyond the color or even the perfume."

"You've always been a science whiz. Your grandpa is so proud of you. And grateful that you've come back to stay in Door County."

I beamed like a little kid who'd just received an A on her botany project.

He motioned for me to take a seat in an antique wicker chair filled with floral cushions. He then pointed out one for Pauline, saying, "And you're keeping up Wisconsin's proud heritage as the country's birthplace of kindergarten. We Germans had a hand in that."

Our state was founded in 1848 with a constitution guaranteeing an education for every child, starting at the age of four. Wisconsin's first kindergarten began in 1856. A German invented the "kindergarten" concept and coined the term. I could imagine Pauline's little Butterflies frolicking amid the aisles of Lloyd's rosebushes.

Lloyd took bottles of water from a compact refrigerator under a table behind us that served as a desk. He gave a bottle to me, then Pauline. Lloyd opened a bottle, too, but didn't sit down with us. He paced with his limp, as if agitated with the malady or something else—like his mention of somebody dying. Pauline blabbered on about her Butterflies decorating little red wagons with Cinderella Pink Fudge fairy-tale designs for the parade a week from tomorrow. I could tell her antennae for trouble were up, too.

I was eager to get to our serious subject. "Lloyd, I take it you talked with Libby about the rock thrown through her window?"

"She called me this morning just after she'd unlocked the door at the lighthouse. I advised her to call the sheriff right away."

"We think it's just a kid from the campground."

Lloyd flashed me a look that said I was wrong. "There are people around Door County who disagree with how I run my business affairs. I hope that doesn't include you."

Goose bumps popped up on my arms. "I must admit I've been wondering why I'd have to be out of my cabin by Sunday. It was sudden."

"Has your grandfather questioned it?"

"No."

"Because he understands how these deals work." Lloyd eased his scarecrow body into a chair to my left. He put his water bottle on the side table between us, then paused, as if to draw sustenance from the floral view. "To make sure this deal went through, I had to guarantee all the cabins I rent would be emptied posthaste. I even paid extra to speed up your boyfriend's construction company work on the Main Street water mains."

"Dillon's not my boyfriend."

Pauline choked.

I ignored her. "Are you turning Duck Marsh Street into condos and a helipad?"

He rubbed his head. "Of course not. And I can't say anything about the project until the deal goes through."

"When is that?"

"We sign the papers tomorrow night over dinner."

"Who's 'we'?"

He shook a finger at me but with a smile behind it. "I'm sworn to secrecy. Business deals are like that. But let's talk about that threatening note. I don't think you should go through with your fudge contest."

"But a lot of people have already entered. And a pie contest is too ordinary."

Pauline said, "Belgians are known for pies. And the word 'Belgian' is part of your shop's name."

"It's Oosterlings' Live Bait, Bobbers and Belgian *Fudge*, Pauline, not Belgian *Pies*."

"Don't forget you swapped out the apostrophe on that sign to the plural form, then tacked up 'Beer' again on the end of the sign. Just tack up the word 'Pie' after that and you're good to go."

Belgian stubbornness fits with the feisty personality of

everybody who founded Fishers' Harbor, including those hearty Icelanders, Swedes, Finns, Norwegians, and Germans. In fact, while other towns dropped the apostrophe at the end of their town name long ago—Baileys Harbor, Rowleys Bay, Gills Rock—Fishers' Harbor had proudly claimed fame over the years for their little apostrophe that set them apart.

I turned back to Lloyd. "This note and rock event is just a kid's prank. It'd be silly to stop the fudge contest now. I'm willing to defy whoever's threatening us."

Pauline choked. She did that a lot around me.

Lloyd's cheeks pinked with excitement. "Give the contest lots of publicity. See who gets upset about it. When they threaten us again, we nab them."

Pauline said, "Both of you are nuts. You're talking about possibly teasing somebody out to kill one of you."

"Pauline, you used the 'K' word."

"I know, but this is scary and my kindergarteners aren't around."

"John will love the fudge contest if it gets bigger and flashier. You should love this idea, Pauline."

Lloyd got up again to limp about. "That note has to be taken seriously. This is not a fictional adventure like your little television show you worked on in L.A."

Everybody called the situation comedy I worked at in Los Angeles for about seven years a "little" show. That bugged me, and yet I was glad to be away from the miserable, manic bunch of guys who wrote the *Topsy-Turvy Girls*. They didn't let me get more than an occasional idea written into the scripts after they bought my first script, which landed me a job. I ended up in charge of things like the cast's chow, and that's how I began making fudge. I had needed a creative outlet and more money to live on.

Lloyd limped over to his bookshelves. They covered three walls, floor to ceiling. A wooden ladder on wheels was mounted on each section for easy access to the top shelves. He bent down and from a lower shelf chose several slender paperback volumes from one spot. With reverence in his motions, he placed the stack in my lap, then sat down.

"Those are yours to keep. Come back anytime to that section of the shelves and take more."

The books were community cookbooks, the kind that churches and clubs put together with their members to sell as a fund-raiser. My parents and grandparents had several tucked away in cupboards and drawers. The covers on some of these were deteriorating. Lignin in wood that's left unbleached when used in papers like newsprint will turn yellow and brown when exposed to air. I eased a cover open. The copyright was 1906!

"Oh, Lloyd. These are antiques filled with heirloom recipes."

"Those particular ones belonged to my grandmother and mother. A couple are from the Old Country." He meant Germany. "They're yours to keep."

"Lloyd, I can't accept these. They belong to your family."

"I don't have much for family, nobody here in the States, anyway. Shirttail relatives back in Germany certainly. And Libby doesn't want the books. After you asked me to be a fudge judge, it prompted me to look up old recipes for fudge. I knew nothing about the candy confection. Those books might give you ideas for better flavors and colors than that modern pink stuff. Fudge has been around for years and with roots in Europe. I have a chocolate cup in my collection, which you viewed in passing minutes ago. When I was a boy, it was common to enjoy hot chocolate with a confection on a rainy afternoon."

I understood now what he was all about. He hadn't been dissing my fudge; he was dissing my whole approach to the contest. "You think the contest should educate people about our heritage in Door County? I should make the contest bigger than just little old me trying out new flavors? I should create a fervor for fudge?"

Pauline rolled her eyes at my Fs.

"Smart woman," he said. "But you have to act fast. After

I sell off my properties, the new owner may eventually build those ugly condos and that chopper pad unless you get the people around here excited about your fudge in a deep way. You have to help people believe the fudge shop is fine where it is, and so are the cabins on Duck Marsh Street."

"Somebody wants me to fail, though, if that note is to be believed. Some person with an orange crayon wants you to convince the fudge judges to make me lose." It struck me that perhaps a kid wouldn't care enough about a fudge contest to write such a note. A shiver zipped up my back and neck and into my hair.

Lloyd got up again, slower this time. "The bigger you get, the harder it is to fail. Fishers' Harbor has never had a fudge festival. Mostly, people around here sell clay pots and covered ceramic pie plates with cherries on top. And the woodworkers? *Ach du lieber*. They trot out painted birdhouses and garden gnomes."

"But that's what tourists like to buy. And Door County is actually filled with loads of lovely artists of fine art, including artists renting out your buildings in our downtown. The great art here probably graces many a home in Chicago."

"Ah yes, we are Chicago's playground. Now you're thinking big. Being a fudge judge got me thinking, too. You Belgians have what you call your kermis festivals."

"Harvest festivals." In the Belgian areas of Door County below Sturgeon Bay, every hamlet held a harvest festival August through early October. But there was nothing in July. And nothing like a kermis in the top half of Door County, though the Swedes, Finns, and Norwegians had their share of wonderful festivals. A kermis was bawdy fun, with plenty of music and Belgian beer flowing, booyah and other hearty foods, the unique Belgian pies, and games like bocce ball as well as card games. But putting on a kermis was a daunting thought. "You want me to start a kermis for Fishers' Harbor?"

"Your doubting tone troubles me. Like your pink fudge."

He took a few rocking, bowlegged steps again, as if walking off a kink.

I peered again at the gifts in my lap. A sudden, horrid thought came to me. "You're not suffering from something terminal, are you?"

"I'm fine. But I want you to do something about this threat that Libby found this morning. I must warn you that I believe our young village president and the past president would like nothing more than seeing you and your fudge put on a ship and floated out of here, preferably in a storm."

That made me sit up straight. "Erik Gustafson and Mercy Fogg want me ruined, or worse?"

Pauline said to me, "I thought you and Mercy had patched up your differences."

"Not since she reported the dog in my shop and got me that demerit on my last health inspection. Then she crowed about it online, which Lois saw and told my grandmother."

Mercy Fogg was fifty-nine—in my parents' age group—and a know-it-all. She was bitter about losing the spring election to nineteen-year-old Erik after she'd served as president of the village for twenty years. She now felt it her business to root out any shopkeeper who mistakenly forgot some regulation or got behind on taxes. She'd dinged some of Lloyd's renters, including the quaint Klubertanz Market on Main Street, the coffee shop, and even The Wise Owl—our little bookstore where tourists browsed for old maps and used and new books to read on a deck overlooking Lake Michigan.

"Erik's always been nice to me, so he's not our culprit."

Looking down on me in my chair, Lloyd said, "Erik told me the other day Piers Molinsky slipped him some cash. A bribe to throw the contest, I assumed."

"When was this?"

"This past Tuesday."

It sounded like the "Confectioner's Conflict" had started earlier than I knew. If bribes were cooking by Tuesday, the chefs had likely been cooking up trouble since the time they arrived on Sunday. I had met them the first time on Monday. Erik might consider a bribe, because he was practically a kid and as poor as the rest of us. Now I imagined that Erik had thrown the rock, thinking the silly trick would be blamed on a little kid, which it almost had been.

"Did Erik keep the cash?"

"Erik clammed up. I don't believe he wanted me to know about the cash, but it slipped out when we were discussing the tax bills on my properties and how hard it is to make a living here. We essentially feed off tourist money June through the end of October, and then the county shuts down for winter and we go batty from boredom. It's a wonder I haven't killed myself before now."

Pauline and I exchanged a look of concern. I reminded Lloyd that winters here now included a lot of activities like snowshoeing and snowmobiling as well as ice-skating and ice-fishing. And nothing could beat Christmas in Door County with all the old-fashioned downtowns festooned with lights.

But Lloyd's agitation and pacing again signaled something deeper worrying him.

I suggested, "Perhaps you should tell these things to Sheriff Tollefson."

"I'd rather you talk with him." Lloyd slumped into his chair again.

"Jordy gets miffed at me for trying to do his job."

Pauline said, "The real reason Jordy gets miffed is that he's here to protect the citizens and you almost got yourself killed on his watch. You should have waited for him before going into that creepy mansion basement back in May."

Lloyd laughed out loud. He turned to view his roses. Bees scored the air outside.

I said to Lloyd, "But if Piers is bribing Erik, this means I need to tell Piers to leave town and get a new contestant."

Lloyd said, "You might consider Miss King needs a ticket out of here, too."

My stomach tightened. "Is there something I should know about her?"

"Let's just say she likes to be friendly to get what she wants. How well did you vet these chefs? Is either of them real?"

"Actually, John Schultz found them. And what do you mean she's 'friendly'?"

He waved me off. "Do you trust this Schultz guy?"

Pauline stood up, flipping her hair off her shoulders. "There's nothing wrong with John. He runs a tour business. I'm sure he checked into their backgrounds."

But doubt lingered in the air as Lloyd's potent insinuation hung there. I also recalled now how he had practically glared at the two chefs, particularly Kelsey, when Lloyd walked in on all the trouble. I had the ugly thought that maybe Piers was part of some Chicago mobster element. And Kelsey cooked with dirt because of some trendy thing going on, so who knew what she was willing to do? "Friendly" had a sexual connotation. I shivered again.

Lloyd said, "Be careful who you trust, Ava, as you embark on your new venture for your fudge shop and for our community. You can have access to my entire library for your research on Door County's history, food, and fudge. I'll give you a key to the house."

"That's nice of you, but these cookbooks will be enough. Thanks, Lloyd."

"No, it's not enough. You and I received a threatening note. We must find the culprit. And you deserve more than my forcing you to move into your fudge shop."

"That was my choice."

"That's kind of you to say, but I feel awful now. Would you consider moving into the Blue Heron Inn after I secure its purchase tomorrow night?"

Unease swept through me like a gale off the lake. The inn was the location of the murderous debut of my Cinderella Pink Fairy Tale Fudge. "I'm not sure that's a good idea, Lloyd."

Pauline waved her hand around like one of her kindergarten kids. "She'd love to make fudge in that big, new kitchen in the inn. She accepts."

Lloyd's chuckle turned into a cough. He backed away from us to withdraw a handkerchief from a pocket. My instincts said he'd been lying about his health being fine.

I said, "It'd have to be temporary, Lloyd. It's just too big a place for me to think about keeping up alone."

"Let me clarify," he said. "I'll kick you out of the inn within a few weeks. I haven't told anybody, but I plan to turn it into elderly housing for people like me, single and ready to live simply with others of my own age who aren't boring."

"That's a great idea," I said. "Fishers' Harbor has nothing like it."

"So you'll move into the inn on Sunday and stay for a few weeks? And fight this fudge terrorism we're up against?"

"If our village president and Piers Molinsky are up to no good trying to make me back out of my own contest, I can't take that lying down. So, yes, Lloyd," I said, attempting to keep the tremulousness out of my voice, "I'll move into the Blue Heron Inn on Sunday."

Pauline was clapping. "So, who are you going to tell first? Dillon or Sam? This is the finest fudge contest and festival for old flames and confectionary flavor aficionados far and wide."

"It's F week, isn't it?"

She nodded.

Chapter 5

When we left Lloyd to get in my truck, we found the fudge-colored dog lying in the water in the fountain's bottom tier. He was lapping at cascading droplets.

"Harbor, get out of there!" He was decidedly not "Lucky" at the moment.

He leaped out with a splash, then shook, spraying me. Water went up my nose. He trotted to my truck door.

"Oh no, you don't." I went to the back to open the tailgate. He leaped in, his tail wagging, his pink tongue flicking droplets into the air. I pulled at my soaked pink blouse, plastered to my skin and bra. "Darn dog."

Pauline said, "You can't fault the dog for that. He's a water spaniel, after all. Blame Dillon."

"You think Dillon planned for me to get soaked?"

"He may not have planned this, but Dillon is about fun and I suspect he doesn't mind thinking about his dog with you. Sure gives him an excuse to come by all the time."

"That's just plain silly."

"No, it's good. You need more fun in your life. And the guy isn't all bad, not if he owns a dog that loves the smell of your fudge."

I kept the speedometer under twenty miles an hour so I didn't bounce Lucky Harbor out onto the streets. I didn't see Dillon as we passed orange cones around the construction at the intersection of Main Street and the side street that took us down to the harbor. But Dillon was waiting for me in the shop. So was Sam.

The centrifugal pull of the two handsome men overwhelmed me as I paused inside the front door, hugging Lloyd's moldering cookbooks. Dillon's tan was getting deeper by the day from his construction work, his biceps and shoulders becoming more sculpted under his neon yellow T-shirt. Sam was no slouch, either. He was a runner and enjoyed fishing, activities that gave him a burnished, rough edge in summer. A sun-bleached lock of his blond hair rested unnoticed and rakish on his forehead. I pivoted toward some customers to regulate my breathing.

Pauline's Butterflies were there, too, with Bethany. They'd gone to the lighthouse for their tour.

The littlest Butterfly, five-year-old Verona Klubertanz, who was Dotty's granddaughter, danced to me with her shoulder-length dark curls bouncing. "Hello, Miss Oosterling. We came to make fudge! Look. I made fairy wings!"

She held out a hand filled with squishy pink fudge that had to be the leftovers from this morning's fight. I bent down, but had to compete with Lucky Harbor's nose poking at the girl's fudge.

Dillon rescued us, reaching for the dog's collar. "Lucky, let's put you outside."

"Miss Oosterling," Cody called from the cash register counter. "I let the Butterflies use the messy pieces you wouldn't be able to sell anyway." Ordinarily, when the Butterflies came to the shop for an artful experience, I mixed up chocolate modeling paste. The girls loved making edible objects and creatures.

I told Verona, "Those are perfect wings. You're going to be a first-rate confectioner someday."

"I want to be a fairy. They can fly. Look!" In her other sticky hand, she held up one of the dolls we had for sale and floated it through the air.

Bethany rushed over to take the doll. "Not today, honey.

Let's put that back on the shelf, please. Sorry, Ava." As Bethany shooed the girl away, she said, "While you were gone, Verona's dad stopped by with a box of fresh jams for you and Gil. He brought raspberry, denim, and hedgerow." Travis's denim flavor was the color of denim and came from blueberries and rhubarb combined. Hedgerow was a blend from bushes supposedly found along hedgerows, such as blackberry, raspberry, and blueberry. "I put the jars on the kitchen counter until you could price them, and gave Travis fudge to sell at the market."

"Thanks, Bethany." The strawberries and rhubarb seasons were pretty much past now, but the raspberries were just coming on in the county. In a week or so, we'd also be picking the county's famous and bountiful cherries. Travis made a cherry-apple butter that used to be served at the Blue Heron Inn. I made a mental note of what I would serve at the inn—then caught myself. I reminded myself I would be moving in temporarily only and alone and not as a bed-and-breakfast operator, and only because of the industrial kitchen.

Pauline hurried after Bethany and the little girls gathering in the doll aisle like real butterflies puddling around a water puddle.

I headed behind the cash register counter to stash the cookbooks for later reading when the shop wasn't busy.

The cash register *ka-chinged* as Cody rang up purchases of fudge he'd neatly wrapped. We'd just sold out of the Cinderella Pink Fudge and Cody said we also needed more luster dust. Cody loved how luster dust made fudge sparkle. I'd need to get busy with my kettles and make fudge fast in order to fulfill my obligations for sharing my fudge with businesses this weekend. A quick sweep with my eyes told me Piers and Kelsey weren't around. I relaxed, but only a little. Dillon and Sam were there for a reason—probably me.

Dillon was now outside the bay window, tossing something into the water. His dog flew into the harbor in a belly-flop splash. The sight made me smile because of the pure joy I saw in both man and dog. Pauline was right; I hungered for such play myself.

Sam, on the other hand, was standing at the glass-enclosed fudge case with a list. He'd told me that family counseling went better when everybody was fed fudge first. He said that fudge got them reminiscing about old times. I also found that a surprising number of people remembered making fudge with their grandmothers or mothers on a Saturday night or at holidays. They'd watch television or a rental movie while eating a fresh batch of the savory, sugary chocolate treat. The thought made me feel good about Lloyd's suggestion that I should become more knowledgeable about my shop's heritage. I'd have to sit down soon with a copy of Alex Faust's cookbook to see what he'd said about the bait shop's history.

Sam said, "I finished moving your boxes from the cabin into the back storage room for you. Your grandmother asked me to help you out."

I realized the healthy glow I'd seen earlier on him was actually sweat. His white shirt had wilted. I didn't have the heart to tell Sam I didn't need to move into the shop.

"Thanks. Can you excuse me, Sam? I've got more of the maple fudge back in the kitchen for you."

Sam followed me to the kitchen to the right, uncharacteristic of him. I was nervous, thinking something intimate was about to happen. Was I hoping for it?

"Is there something you need to talk to me about, Sam?"

"No, but I wondered if you needed those boxes moved around in that room."

So that was all he wanted—to lug boxes. "No, but thanks. My grandfather sort of chucked stuff in there over the years, and we'll have to sort through it all. But you can help me haul fudge ingredients out to the copper kettles if you're in a mood to move things."

I had Sam reach up high for the kilo bars of white chocolate where the dog couldn't reach them while I checked the refrigerator for cream. Mom had been back sometime during my absence and had left plenty.

Sam said, "Let me get the cream for you."

"Thanks, Sam." His closeness created an agitation in my veins, but he seemed oblivious as his arms grew fuller. "Don't you have other appointments today?"

"It's lunch hour."

I'd forgotten. That's why Dillon was here, too. He'd promised to check on me. Maybe I was like a sister to Sam and Dillon, and that's all we had. As I reached up for some more chocolate bars, Sam came behind me to reach over my head. His breaths puffed into my hair in a ragged rhythm. My imagination saw his lips edging forward to kiss my ear. I held my breath, but Sam just went ahead and got the chocolate down.

Sam had forgiven me for jilting him, but his social worker training made him live by plans. He preferred an orderly life. I'd been a messy character in his past, and I was messy now. He likely wanted to fix me, or at least analyze what he'd done wrong to make me leave him. The thing that scared me was that Sam probably did indeed have all the answers to retool my life. If I wanted to let him, he'd make me his "project." He'd had college classes about love. He was trained to run personality tests on people. Sam would know who might be a perfect match for me. Or not. I wondered what he'd say about a fabric swatch test.

I took frozen Door County cherries out of the freezer and put them in the microwave to thaw. Some batches of Cinderella Pink Fudge I made with dried cherries and other batches with whole berries. I was still wishing a new fairy-tale flavor would pop into my head that would have a winning edge. Goldilocks still didn't seem right to me. Gold-colored things were butter, dandelions, and maybe yellow tomatoes. None of those would work for a fudge flavor.

"Can you put the kilo bars in the melter and turn it on, Sam?"

"Sure, Ava."

Out of the corner of my eye I saw him lick his lips, as if he were nervous. My insides began to flutter. I stared through the microwave window at my thawing cherries.

Then Sam's hands touched my shoulders from behind and turned me around. His blue eyes looked confused. I put my hands on his chest, intending to push him away, but his heartbeat tickled my right palm. My heartbeat quickened a little, but I had to admit Sam was taking way too long to sweep me into his arms for a kiss. I was beginning to wonder about my attractiveness.

His blue gaze swept me up and down. "Would it be okay if we met sometime to discuss things?"

"What things?"

"Well, I thought we might need to meet to discuss possibly dating."

Any sexy feelings I'd had a moment ago evaporated. "Have a meeting to discuss dating?"

Oh dear. I'd obviously become unapproachable, not worth romancing at all. I was merely an item on a meeting agenda. But I'd been a sucker for his politeness since high school. He'd been a senior football player and I'd been a sophomore starter in basketball when we noticed each other. He always dry-cleaned his letter jacket before he'd give it to me to wear. I had ached when he graduated before me and left Door County for college. And then we'd reconnected and fallen in love all over again, becoming engaged. After all that history he wanted a *meeting*? About the possibility of *dating*? Would I need to do research or fill out questionnaires and report back at future meetings? I was being treated like a client, not a sexy woman worth romancing. What had happened to us? To me? Why hadn't he grabbed me and tried to have his way with me right here on the floor?

Dillon poked his head in, saving me. Sam and I turned to unwrapping the chocolate bars to put in the industrial melter. Dillon said, "Hey, Ava, you going to the fish boil tonight? I heard they have a good band."

"Yeah, I'll be there," I said.

"Great. I have something to talk to you about. I'll save ya a spot on the beach."

Dillon left.

Sam started to say something but then excused himself, too.

I collapsed against my counter until my phone buzzed in the pocket of my denim shorts. It was Libby. She reminded me she needed more fudge for the weekend. "You can deliver it anytime later tonight, Ava. I'm going to the fish boil, but I plan to come back out to the lighthouse to catch up on cleaning. I keep finding broken glass in the oddest places."

"I'll stop by, Libby." I was glad to have an excuse to leave the fish boil early, in case I needed to escape Dillon. Or Sam.

I also didn't want to meet up with Piers and Kelsey tonight, or Erik Gustafson. I'd be tempted to ask him why he'd accepted a bribe from Piers and then written a silly note to toss through a window with a rock. I imagined Kelsey karate-kicking both of them and Piers trying to toss Kelsey into the steel drum used to boil the fish.

For the remainder of the afternoon I made fudge in my copper kettles, showing the process to tourists. They loved trying their hand at raising the long wooden paddles to whip the mixture. The whipping was essential to get the crystals just right so that the fudge came out smooth and not too grainy. Everything had to be timed right and at the right temperature or you could end up with something hard as glass or rubbery as taffy.

To my surprise, Piers and Kelsey took over the kettles around two o'clock while I loafed my fresh pink fudge on the marble slab at the front window. The chefs were quiet, as if they'd vowed over lunchtime to change their personalities. I swallowed my trepidations and asked them to join me at the fish boil; after all, it was even more important now to get the judges and contestants together for a chat about how the judging would be presented to the public a week from Saturday. And watching Lloyd and Piers interact could get interesting, since Lloyd knew about the bribe.

When I got to the fish boil that evening behind the Troubled Trout, a good country-swing band provided the music and Piers and Kelsey were engaged in separate conversations on opposite sides of the crowd on the beach. It almost didn't register with me that the man Kelsey was talking with was Lloyd, of all people. At first I assumed it was merely a judge-contestant conversation, but then they walked together behind a potted evergreen near the path to the parking lot. They were still in my view, though hidden from most of the crowd, including my grandparents and Libby. My grandparents and Libby sat near the big fire and its boiling pot, where the big fillets of fish were lowered in for cooking. Professor Faust was walking up to them.

Back behind the evergreen, Kelsey had one hand on Lloyd's forearm, with a drink in her other hand. Then her free hand traveled up to touch his cheek. I gulped at her brazenness. She wore a smile that was so big it gave "friendly" a new definition. My heart was racing. Was she coming on to him right here in public? It grew more curious when Lloyd headed back to the outdoor bar, where he seemed to be lecturing Erik, maybe to cut off Kelsey's drinks. Erik scowled at Lloyd, said something, then gave him the brush-off, walking away while Lloyd's mouth still moved, presumably spewing more advice to Erik. Lloyd limped from the bar and made his way toward Libby and my grandparents. Kelsey, still by herself at the edge of the crowd, was watching Lloyd's retreat and laughing.

It dawned on me to look for Piers to see what he was up to. He'd wended his way through the crowd a little from the other direction, but he'd planted himself behind a couple of people, as if he were hiding. He was staring hard and cold at the group that now included the professor, Lloyd, Libby, and my grandparents.

A chill swept over me. What was going on? Common sense kicked in then. Piers was in a direct line to Kelsey. His hard look had to be for her. I didn't blame him for trying to admonish her trampy behavior.

Pauline had found John in the crowd, so I was alone. And out of sorts, reeling from witnessing the obvious flirting between Kelsey and Lloyd, while I was still thinking about Sam's wanting a meeting before we could even date.

Feeling dull, I wended my way alone toward the outdoor bar near the building for a glass of wine. Before I could get there, Dillon grabbed me for a barefoot dance in the sand. He had a way of sensing my moods. He knew when I needed laughter. Or a dog. By now, the town was used to seeing the "runaway couple" and didn't pay us much heed. When we finished dancing, Dillon escorted me closer to the water's edge where it was more private. A skein of pink across the water advertised the impending sunset.

"I can't stay long," he said. "I'm training Lucky on scent-trailing this evening over at the park."

"How's he doing?"

"He flushed a possum and a pheasant the other day like a pro." Dillon dipped a bare foot into the lake, splashing my feet with the cool, clear water. The shadows creeping in with the sunset gave Dillon's face a seriousness that was uncharacteristic of him. "I was wondering if you'd like to join me and my mother for dinner some night when she's here. She's coming for a visit."

I hadn't seen Cathy Rivers in years, and I'd always liked her. But joining them for dinner might give her the wrong impression. I said so.

Dillon laughed. "She always liked you better than me. She still reminds me about how stupid I was to let you go."

"We were young. We moved on."

"You inspired me when you dumped me."

"Inspired you? How?"

"A year after we parted, I saw your name in the credits on your TV show. You were making something of yourself, while I wasn't. So I went back to college and finished up my engineering degree. This humor guy got serious." He kicked water at me again. "I gotta get Lucky and head to the park before it gets too dark on us."

While watching him disappear into the crowd, I hugged my arms, feeling raw and unstable. Dillon had always been a nice guy—until the bigamy charge. But I reminded myself that was long ago. This May, when he showed up at my fudge shop after I hadn't seen him for eight years, it'd been the night of Cody's senior prom, held on the harbor dock by the shop. Cody had finally got the guts to ask Bethany to the prom. It was a magical night of lights and dancing, a Cinderella fairy-tale atmosphere. Days before the prom, Cody and I had found a stray dog. I'd called the shelter about him. To my shock, Dillon came to my door the night of the big dance to collect his dog.

I had reeled with emotions at the sight of Dillon. I'd loved him, then hated him. There had been no in-between. But there he stood, filling the doorway, his chestnut hair flying wild in the breezes off the harbor, the glint in his chocolate-colored eyes shining down on me like the moon that night. Magical.

After we married in Las Vegas, there'd been that same magic for a while. We honeymooned at the Grand Canyon, then drove Route 66 all the way through Santa Monica to the ocean. But then a month later, Chloe from Nantucket and Sharee Ann from Biloxi and their lawyers contacted me, telling me they were also married to Dillon. I got my annulment and headed to Los Angeles and the ocean. I couldn't go home, but I needed to be near water. I'd grown up in Door County amid the wonderful hug of Lake Michigan that surrounded the land, and I needed to be hugged in a big way after being betrayed by Dillon and making a fool of myself with my family and with Sam. To purge myself of my mistake of marrying so fast, I leaped into writing about my experiences, teaching myself to write TV scripts while waitressing at Jerry's Famous Deli in Burbank.

When I finally returned home, Pauline had said she

heard that Dillon had been put away for five years. That wasn't true. She'd just lied to make me feel good.

Dillon told me in May, "The initial sentence could have been for five years, because it was a Class D felony for bigamy and another couple of years for financial fraud. But none of it but being stupid was my fault."

While he had indeed married Chloe in some youthful exuberance a couple of years after one of our college breakups, Dillon had quickly divorced her. He'd thought their paperwork had been filed correctly. He apologized to me for the Chloe thing.

Sharee Ann was another mistake and another matter. She was a groupie who followed Dillon on his comedy club route. But the groupie who didn't also want to be a devoted wife spent her time forging Dillon's signature on a lot of credit card purchases and using aliases.

At one point, the lawyers thought it appeared Dillon had been married to three women at once, including me in the mix, because of all the delayed filing of various paperwork, including divorce papers. But the dates were sorted out and Sharee Ann finally got her own trial. The rest of us were free.

Dillon had spent a couple of months in jail before the bigamy charge was finally cleared. I found out the only reason he spent time in jail instead of getting out on bail was that he refused to let his rich parents fork over the money. So underneath it all, he had his principles intact.

On that night of his return in May, I kept him standing at first in the doorway and didn't let him in. I still wasn't sure what to do with him or how to act. My foot itched to kick him in the you-know-whats. I let him do the talking, letting him squirm, grovel, apologize, and beg my forgiveness.

He finished with "I've quit the comedy circuit. I don't party much. I finished college and went to work for my dad's construction company. I'm a bona fide civil engineer. I build streets, roads, and bridges, and I'm civil while doing my engineering."

He had smiled at his little play on words. I relented and smiled back. It was hard to stay mad at Dillon.

The trouble now? I ached to get in a fast car with the guy and zip down the road with the tunes on loud. Dillon had loved freedom and a fast life. It made me wonder if having his construction job and a dog were enough for him. When would he get tired of the ordinary life and have to do something wild to stoke his inner fire?

On that starry Cinderella night in May, with the music and laughter outside, Dillon had taken me in his arms and waltzed me one-two-three around the fudge shop. His dog followed us, making me giggle. Dillon laughed, too, his deep voice filling the aisles as we danced amid the perfumes of fudge flavors and bygone memories. I'm sure some of the high school couples must have seen us, but nobody had ever said a word to me about that night. It was as if that dance in the fudge shop was my and Dillon's little sacred secret.

Pauline joined me now at the shoreline. "That's a wistful smile if I ever saw one. Dillon?"

"No," I lied a little bit. "I was thinking about how much I like it here in Door County, and how much I want to do right by the people here, especially my family. I want to prove myself."

Everybody was dancing and singing along to old cover tunes from the eighties and nineties. The sunset was strafing the harbor with a fiery collection of colors. Sailboats were coming in for the day. As the sun lowered into the horizon in an orange glow behind the buildings and high bluff where the empty Blue Heron Inn sat, I thought about the orange crayon and the threat to me, and Lloyd's stern talk when we'd met at his house. Just as the day was turning to night and growing chillier, I, too, felt a dark force descending on Fishers' Harbor. The day had been filled with fights, threats, and secrets. Lloyd seemed to think the safety of Fishers' Harbor had been splintered.

In the distance we finally saw the Chambers Island Lighthouse beacon, a speck glowing in the dark seven miles away in Lake Michigan. Strings of lights came on behind the Troubled Trout. Pauline and I stayed late, drinking wine and talking about boyfriends and how wonderful basketball had been for us, starting with our grade school years near Brussels, Wisconsin, in lower Door County.

Satiated with nostalgia, I went home and crawled into bed in my cabin. But melancholy seeped in like a wisp of wind through the screens. What would it be like to roll over and see . . . who? Dillon? Sam? Or was there someone else lurking out there that I hadn't noticed? Someone writing notes about me with an orange crayon? I got up amid a shiver to close and lock my windows, something I never imagined doing in Fishers' Harbor.

By Saturday morning, I'd decided that making fudge was better than worrying about men or orange crayon messages likely made by bored kids. Lloyd had to be off his rocker. There was no way Erik Gustafson—a star football player only a year ago for our little consolidated school—would ever accept a bribe or participate in shenanigans with Piers.

Gilpa's fishing trawler, *Sophie's Journey*, was easing into the harbor, so I hurried to make a fresh pot of his strong black coffee. Cody had discovered the secret to Gilpa's coffee back in May—extra scoops of fresh grounds with pinches of cocoa and sugar out of my kitchen to jazz it up. Our coffee was almost as good as what you could get at the Chocolate Chicken or with the hearty pancake breakfast that came with eggs, meatballs, and lingonberries at Al Johnson's Swedish Restaurant.

Libby called me around eight thirty. I was mortified. I'd forgotten to run the fudge out to her last night. I couldn't have driven anyway, not after enjoying that second glass of Door County cherry-moscato blend wine with Pauline.

When I got to the Eagle Bluff Lighthouse at nine, before the place would open for tourists, I encountered Lucky Harbor racing about in the clearing that was flanked by lilac bushes and an old cream brick outhouse to the east, and yards away to the west, a fuel storage building with a red-brown metal hip roof. The woodland lay beyond to the east and west. The dog circled the brush-flanked outbuildings, making rustling noises, as if looking for something. When the dog spotted me, he raced for me. I ducked into the shop and closed the door, handing off my fudge to Libby.

"Dillon's dog is out there," I said. "He's a little nuts and he loves fudge. Keep your door closed."

"He's a pretty dog, though. Dillon brings him around a lot. The kids love him. I saw them last night out here but didn't expect them back on a Saturday morning."

"The dog probably ran away on his own. He does that a lot. I'll collect him and take him back. Bye, Libby. And again, I apologize for not coming out last night."

"Pshaw, you deserved a night of fun after yesterday. No harm done at all."

When I left, I closed the screen door quickly behind me, making sure it was latched solidly so Lucky Harbor couldn't slip in. Sure enough, the dog was at my feet, his tongue dripping from his exertion.

"Lucky Harbor, slow down."

He raced away behind the lighthouse this time, circling it and coming back to me again. He did that a second and third time. I still didn't see Dillon. Maybe, I thought, the dog knew Dillon was behind the tower, resting from his hike and taking in the view of Lake Michigan.

As I headed for the corner of the lighthouse, Lucky Harbor startled me when he reversed course to come back to me. He jumped up on me, barking. When he raced away again, I scooted faster. The gravel around the tower's base crunched underfoot.

Just past the squared-off corner of the four-story tower, hidden from view of the parking lot, a figure was sprawled across the gravel and grass. My stomach dropped to my feet. "Dillon!"

I rushed over amid the dog's shrill barks.

Chapter 6

It wasn't Dillon. The pants and shoes I'd spotted first had only looked like Dillon's from a distance. At the base of the cream brick tower lay Lloyd Mueller, dead.

My screams brought Libby charging around the brick building. She fainted at the sight, crumpling onto the green lawn. I called nine-one-one while trying to stop Lucky Harbor from licking Libby's face. The dog meant well; he was whining.

Libby came to by the time I talked with a dispatcher. I helped Libby up. Her short, lithe body was shaking. She was around ten years younger than Lloyd, and had always seemed to defy aging—until now. With her tears flowing, she ran her hands into her dyed black bob—scrunching her hair as if to pull it out—then fell to her knees in the gravel by Lloyd's body. "Lloyd! Lloyd!"

Lucky Harbor plunked his muddy, dirty front paws on my white blouse as he implored me to do something. I pushed him gently back to the ground, then squatted next to Libby and put an arm around her slender quaking shoulders. "I'm so sorry, Libby."

A siren erupted in the near distance. The volunteer emergency medical technicians were on their way. We were only a few minutes from the firehouse on the outskirts of Fishers' Harbor.

Lloyd lay on his back, his bald head at a cockeyed angle, his eyes open, his mouth slightly agape under his mustache. He looked stunned by his own demise. An arm was crumpled awkwardly under him, the elbow poking out toward us. His shirt and pants looked impeccable, as usual. There were no bushes to break his fall or tear his clothing. He'd landed squarely on gravel, just missing a small concrete pad on the ground as well as iron pipe railings on a staircase leading to the back door of the lighthouse. I didn't see any blood, but I suspected there might be plenty underneath his head, seeping into the gravel. I wasn't about to move him or look.

Amid her sobs, Libby touched Lloyd's face a couple of times, her hand shrinking back each time.

Tears welled up in my eyes. My throat clogged again.

Soon, our EMTs—Ronny and Nancy Jenks—hustled up behind us. I helped Libby back away.

Jordy's deputy, Maria Vasquez, showed up. Maria had been on her way to check in with me at the fudge shop about yesterday's transgressions when she heard this call come in from the lighthouse. Maria and I took Libby to a nearby picnic table while the EMTs assessed Lloyd.

We sat down, with me across from Libby and the deputy. They had their backs to the goings-on with Lloyd's body, but I had a clear view if I wanted it. I focused on Maria and Libby instead. Lucky Harbor settled on the grass next to me, panting and looking about, on alert. I wondered where Dillon was.

Maria looked at me with dark eyes hooded with concern. "Did you . . . ?"

She wanted to know if one of us had seen him fall. "No," I said. "The dog was carrying on and I followed him around to the lake side of the lighthouse and that's how I found Lloyd."

"Lloyd had been working on the tower?" Deputy Vasquez handed a tissue to Libby next to her.

Libby said, "No. Or at least I don't think so. I hadn't seen him since last night right after the fish boil. He dropped me off at my house." She pointed off in the direction of the road into the park. "I just live across Highway 42."

"You stay here for now, please." The deputy patted Libby's shoulder, then left. She returned with a camera and proceeded to take photos. She also used a measuring tape, making notes or diagrams as she went.

Nancy and Ronny stood to the side, looking glum. While the deputy couldn't presume anything, the thought of suicide rose inside me, and I believed in the EMTs as well.

The surroundings were incongruous to the awful event. Lake Michigan rippled and sparkled just yards from us. The breezes were balmier today, the humidity not so oppressive as yesterday. My short-sleeved white blouse didn't stick to me. The temperature was around eighty degrees. Kids' laughter came from far off in the park's campgrounds somewhere.

As the gusty winds off the lake buffeted us, yesterday's conversation with Lloyd bounced in my head. He'd been seriously concerned about his land deal and my fudge contest. He also said he knew who had written the threatening note, insinuating it had been Erik and Piers. He'd mentioned Kelsey being "friendly," which I'd witnessed later. On top of that, he wanted me to move into the Blue Heron Inn. This mishmash of things made me uneasy now. It felt like Lloyd had some hidden agenda or secret, and that he had been pushing me toward helping him with something. But what? And why? Was he afraid of somebody? Or just under too much pressure? In addition, I couldn't ignore his health problem; he had been uncomfortable yesterday. He'd also started giving away his things—his cookbook collection. Had that been a plea for help, too? Had he seen in me something of a daughter he could trust? Because he trusted my grandfather?

With my heart heavy as stone, I called my grandmother to tell her the news. She went silent for a long moment. Grandpa would take this news about his best friend's death even harder.

After I got off the phone, Libby muttered, "I don't understand. Why would he do this?"

She obviously thought he'd committed suicide, too.

I said, "It had to be an accident. Maybe he was up there taking a look from the tower to envision the changes his real estate sale would bring to Fishers' Harbor. I heard he was signing the contract tonight, Libby."

"Tonight?"

I was a little surprised she didn't know, but I let it pass. They were a divorced couple, and sharing lingonberry pancakes now and then didn't mean they shared everything. "Maybe he was having second thoughts and came here to think. Or to talk with you about tonight. It was probably dewy and slippery up there on the iron walkway. And it's so narrow up there." I imagined him stretching out a kink in his hip or legs as I'd seen him do yesterday at his house, then tipping off-kilter. "My grandmother will be here any minute, Libby."

She nodded. The whites around her big, dark brown eyes were red from crying. I got up and came around the picnic bench to give her another hug.

The memory of the note startled me again. *Somebody will die if you don't convince Lloyd to throw the contest. Miss Oosterling must not win.*

I had the good sense not to say anything that might exacerbate Libby's pain.

When Sheriff Tollefson arrived a half hour later, he shot across the grass straight for me where I stood holding on to the dog. My grandma was with Libby. The sheriff repeated questions I'd already been asked by Deputy Vasquez. Then he got to the note. "Did you talk with Lloyd about throwing the contest? Did Lloyd feel threatened by anybody?"

Fear swept through me at the realization the sheriff thought this might have been a murder. I told Jordy about visiting Lloyd yesterday around the lunch hour with Pauline. "He seemed mixed up emotionally, Jordy." I told Jordy about the cookbooks, the key to the house, Lloyd's wish for my career, and the proposed move into the Blue Heron Inn. "You should check with his doctor. Maybe he knew he was dying and was trying to get everything in order before he passed away."

Jordy made a note. "Do you think he was capable of suicide?"

The lump in my throat enlarged. I recalled all the pressures Lloyd must have been under from the townspeople. "Maybe."

"Somebody wrote Lloyd's name in that note, but not the other judges of your contest. Those would be . . . ?"

"Our village president, Erik Gustafson, Professor Alex Faust from the University of Wisconsin in Green Bay, and Dotty Klubertanz."

"What about your testy contestants? They seem capable of harming people they don't like."

"With fudge cutters? You don't think Piers or Kelsey murdered him, do you?"

"Could they have driven him . . . over the edge, literally? Any pressure on Lloyd from them?"

I had to tell Jordy about Kelsey's unwanted "friendliness" toward Lloyd, and that Lloyd said Piers had bribed Erik last Tuesday. "But I have no proof of that bribe, Jordy. Piers may have offered money to Erik, but maybe Erik didn't accept it or he returned the money. Lloyd didn't elaborate and I didn't ask."

"If there was a bribe, maybe Erik was embarrassed or fearful after saying something to Lloyd."

"You're speculating, Jordy."

"True, but I'm trying to jog your memory. Piers is a beefy, big guy. And Erik was a football player. You can bet I'll ask them some questions later, too."

The insinuation was clear: Piers or Erik could have muscled Lloyd up the circular staircase and thrown him off the tower.

"Jordy, Lloyd said he was signing a contract tonight over dinner with somebody. He didn't mention who or where, but maybe that's a lead to track down. And he gave me old cookbooks, with a speech about doing grand things for the town. It all seems odd now that I look back on it. Maybe there was something else going on."

The EMTs passed us with Lloyd's body bagged on a stretcher.

Deputy Vasquez walked up to us with her camera and tape measure. "I haven't found anything in the perimeter. We haven't had rain in a while, so no obvious footprints. I'll secure the lighthouse and take a look inside and at the top. The EMTs said it looks like he broke his neck in the fall. There's rigor mortis in the body and lividity."

"Thanks, Maria," Jordy said.

Maria followed the EMTs.

I said, "She seems really good."

"Fresh out of Madison College."

That was a tech school in Madison, the state's capital. "Why'd she take a job up here?"

"Her parents work in the orchards and dairy farms right here in Door County. The County Board of Supervisors approved her position because they want us to write more speeding tickets to feed the county's coffers. The only real law enforcement work we get is pretty much with you."

Jordy had on his usual stone face, but I considered it a backhanded compliment. Then Jordy said, "The note said Lloyd should throw the contest and make sure you lost. Who wants to harm *you*? And why, Ava?"

My brain sputtered like a boat motor trying to back up. "I make fudge; what's not to love about me?" But a seed of concern had sprouted in me. "What does 'lividity' mean?"

"When his heart stopped the blood began to settle and pool. Gravity pulls it down. The skin looks bruised. Lividity will help us pinpoint the time of death."

"When will you know that?"

He scowled at me. "Let me handle this, especially since it may involve serious threats to you. I don't want to find you fighting with a murderer in a basement again."

"You sound like you care." I let a grin slide across my lips. "Maybe I should ask you to the dance next weekend, just for my own protection."

He scoffed. "You'll most likely get plenty of close protection from Sam and Dillon."

He walked away before I could respond. I found it interesting that Jordy had a sense of humor. And concern for my safety.

Lucky Harbor sat in the front shotgun seat, his nose out the window, sniffing the breeze, as I drove into town. When the brown spaniel spotted Dillon on Main Street, the dog's tail began slapping the seat. He barked. It was only a little after ten, and few tourists were about, so I easily found a parking spot.

I left the dog inside because I didn't have a leash. I crossed the street where Dillon stood in his neon yellow hard hat and T-shirt beside a pile of gravel and a pit along a curb in front of The Wise Owl. Workmen were lowering a pipe into the pit. When I told Dillon the news, he gathered me in his arms in front of everybody. He felt solid, warm, and just what I needed. Tears filled my eyes, which ordinarily I hated. But the image of my grandpa's best friend's crooked form lying on the gravel overwhelmed me.

Dillon murmured into my ear, "I'm so sorry, for everybody. Your poor grandparents. Poor Libby. And you. Do you want to step over to the coffee shop? I'll buy."

"No, but thanks. I'd better get to the fudge shop. Grandma said Gilpa was just coming in from a fishing tour when I called her earlier."

"I could come with you."

"No, you have to work." While I felt in need of his support, I was wary of rekindling a deeper dependence on him.

He said, "Take the dog if you want. Lucky is a pretty good listener."

I pointed out my shirt. "He's good about getting me dirty. Why was he over in the park by himself?"

"Because last night he treed a possum before we left the park, and so he ran away on me earlier this morning to find that possum again. I figured either he'd come back on his own or I'd go fetch him during my break this morning."

Dillon and I crossed the street to get to my truck and his dog.

He ruffled the dog's neck and ears, then took a leash from a pocket. "Hey, boy. What did you see over there at the lighthouse?" Dillon handed me the leash. "Take him. A dog is a good buddy in times of stress. A car crash taught me the value of a dog."

"When was this?"

"Remember my Porsche?"

Red, loud, and fast. Like a magic carpet, the roadster ferried us to Las Vegas and then to Route 66 to the ocean. A thread of the thrilling memory dangled inside me like a rope teasing me to climb it. "What happened?"

"Crashed it the year after you left me. Going too fast and missed a corner. I ended up in the hospital with a broken leg and wrist and depression over my sorry state. A hospital volunteer brought in a dog for me to commune with."

"Let me guess. An American water spaniel?"

He grinned. "No, a golden retriever. But then I got interested in dogs and found out Wisconsin had its very own official breed of dog, the American water spaniel. I held off on getting one until I finished my degrees and got situated in Dad's construction company, but thinking about what a dog had meant to me kept me going and pushing forward. Sound silly?"

My heart was melting, damn him. "No, not silly at all."

"You'll take him for a little while today, then? Your grandpa might need him, too."

He had me with the mention of Gilpa. "Okay." The fudge-colored dog panted up at me and wagged his tail as if he knew human language. "Come on, Lucky Harbor."

Dillon gave me a thumbs-up. "I'll pick him up by lunch-time. Want me to bring a sandwich over for you?"

I almost objected, then thought better of it. I might need an excuse to get out of the fudge shop after news of Lloyd's death hit the gossip mills. Everybody would be dropping by to ask me to recount finding the body.

"Sure, Dillon. Thanks. See ya later."

When I got back into the truck, the dog's big brown eyes seemed to want to tell me something.

Another one of those odd chills prickled my back. This dog had been frantic at the lighthouse. Dillon's question came to mind. What did the dog see? A suicide? Or something more sinister? I recalled how he'd been snuffling about the grounds at the lighthouse with a determined ferocity. Had Lucky Harbor been only upset about finding a dead person? Or had he detected some other scent in the grass that was distinctive? I started the truck's engine, letting the roar erase the horrible speculation creeping into my brain.

Chapter 7

The shop buzzed with fishermen and tourists buying gear and fudge when I walked in around ten thirty with Lucky Harbor.

Professor Alex Faust was there with more copies of *Wisconsin's Edible Heritage* stacked on the counter while he talked with Cody at the register. It had slipped my mind that he was signing copies today outside at one of the round bistro tables. He fumbled in his briefcase filled with papers, tourist brochures and our *Peninsula Pulse* magazine, and a tablet computer. Upon seeing me, he snapped shut the briefcase and handed me bookmarks with a smile.

"You'll be outside this morning, Alex," I said.

"What a glorious day," he said with great exuberance. He hadn't heard about Lloyd's death obviously. He went outside with his armful of books and briefcase. Customers snaked in a line behind him. He had a certain amount of fame, which is why I'd suggested to John he'd be a good fudge judge.

I helped the professor push together both of the two small tables with chairs that I'd added to our outdoor landscape for summer tourists. Gilpa's rough-hewn wooden benches along the walls were still there, too, perfect for fishermen pulling on waders. I'd also put up planters with red geraniums under both of the big bay windows. We Belgians didn't eat dirt like Kelsey's famous restaurant find in Japan, but we knew how to turn dirt into beautiful floribunda art.

I didn't see my grandpa, so I went back inside and rang up a fisherman's purchase of bobbers for his son. I went back over to my register with the dog in tow to tell Cody the horrible news.

Cody's gaze fell to the floor. He was just out of high school, with short red hair cut in a cute, spiky cap of fuzz that made him look younger than eighteen, even cherub-like. Because he had Asperger's, I knew from talking to Sam that Cody might be in a quandary as to how to react.

"It's okay, Ranger, if you don't say anything. None of us knows what to say. But we can still smile at customers."

"Thanks." He showed me a printout. "I did inventory when I got here. There's a pink purse and a Cinderella doll missing."

"You're sure?" It was ridiculous to ask, because Cody was meticulous. He liked things clean, shiny, and in their place. I remembered little Verona Klubertanz and her friends in the shop yesterday. Verona had clutched a doll with her sticky fudge fingers and Bethany had to ask her to put it down. I'd have to ask Pauline if Verona or other girls showed up at summer school today with the doll.

Professor Faust came back in to collect the rest of his books. His gray hair stood out every which way in tufts after being mussed from the harbor breezes. I gave him the news about Lloyd.

Alex set his books back down. "How horrible. And unfortunate timing. I talked with your village president only yesterday about the Duck Marsh Street properties."

"Why?"

"The cabins have historical significance. I told Erik that he should ask for a delay of the sale of the properties until the village can join forces with the historic preservation society. The village needs to take a closer look and be involved with preserving rather than destroying."

"When did you talk with Erik?"

"It was a brief conversation in the morning. It was after the ruckus here. I had turned my car onto Main Street and seen Erik coming out of the coffee shop, so I pulled over. I told him saving the cabins instead of allowing Lloyd to demolish them could create a tourist attraction. It should be possible to trace the ownership back to the original Swedes, Finns, and Belgians who built them in the 1800s. I suggested to Erik that perhaps Lloyd had already done those title searches and somebody should ask him to provide that information to the public."

"You don't think the preservation society would sue Lloyd, do you?"

"Perhaps. I have to be honest—that would be my advice. History is important to me."

This type of pressure might have pushed Lloyd to take his own life. With trepidation, I asked, "What was Lloyd's reaction to this?"

"I didn't talk with him about this specifically. I suspected Lloyd was intent on selling the properties, so it'd do me no good to get in some argument. We had to get along as judges, after all, for your fudge contest. But Erik agreed with me and felt honoring the stories behind the cabins could be a historically significant project for Fishers' Harbor. He said he'd speak with Lloyd. I was going to speak with Lloyd today. God rest his soul."

"But this notion of preserving the cottages can't be new."

"You're correct. Many months back when I was researching my cookbook's chapter on Door County, I discovered Lloyd owned a lot of real estate and knew a lot of history about the area. I heard about Lloyd's offer to buy the Blue Heron Inn if he could scrape together the money. It's an unfortunate irony that as he's about to buy the inn where a death occurred, his own death occurs. It's like the Blue Heron Inn is jinxed."

A prickly unease crawled over me because Lloyd had been so joyous about me moving into the empty inn.

I excused myself to find my grandfather, taking Lucky Harbor with me.

Once outside, the brown dog skittered fast down the wooden planks of our pier, heading straight for *Sophie's Journey*. He leaped over the boat's railing, then disappeared inside. As I got closer, I could see him inside the open cabin, licking my grandfather's face. The dog then launched into the water to paddle for the shallower, reedy marsh area where he loved to catch frogs.

My grandfather was covered in black oil, which was, as always, in his thick silver hair. His mood was as dark as his looks. With a mug of coffee in his gnarled hands, Gilpa sat at the small table bolted to the floor in the middle of the cabin. I sat down across from him. The trawler rocked on a wave that washed in from a passing speedboat.

"Sorry about Lloyd, Gilpa."

He nodded, watching the dog plop about for frogs. Gilpa's eyes were rheumy, the lids red. "His passing isn't good at all."

"He was a good man."

"Did I ever tell you he got a hole in one at the golf course but never bragged about it?"

"Yes, Gilpa. You were both in your twenties, I believe."

"Lloyd spent his entire life trying to get another hole in one."

"I saw him yesterday on his way to golf. He remembered I liked science. And he gave me cookbooks."

"He was kind to our family. He let us buy the house instead of renting. Same for the bait shop."

I'd heard the story before. Lloyd had bought the cabins and bait shop not long after college. He'd inherited money, but he'd always worked hard at odd jobs, saving every penny. After I was born and my grandparents moved off the farm, Lloyd sold them the house and shop. That's how they came to transplant themselves from the Belgian community around Brussels and move here amid the Swedes and others of Fishers' Harbor. I suspected the deal's terms had been generous; my grandparents had been poor, and still weren't all that well off.

"Gilpa, do you want me to put up a sign inside that there are no more fishing excursions today or this weekend?"

"No, Ava honey. Just like that dog, I need to be in the water. Lloyd would want me to get that 'hole in one' today. He used to always catch bigger fish than me, too. He was good at everything."

"So are you, Gilpa."

He gestured toward the back of the boat. "Not with these damn engines. Hunks of metal are defeating me today."

"Maybe Lloyd left you a pile of money and you can buy yourself a new boat finally, one with big, shiny new engines."

"Oh, I doubt that. Libby's getting it all, I'm sure, or a big share of it. He loved her still, you know."

"I think she still loved him, too. Which confuses me when I think of him committing suicide right where Libby worked. He wouldn't do that to her if he loved her." But doubt nagged me. "Would he?"

Grandpa sipped his coffee. "Your grandma says he treated Libby with a raw deal, but divorce and bachelorhood suited Lloyd. He just liked doing things without consulting others. He always was a private man."

"He told P.M. and me that he was signing a contract with somebody tonight. Do you know who that was?"

"You mean the buyer for Duck Marsh Street and your cabin? He wouldn't even tell me. But I respected that. His business was his business; my business is mine. We Belgians don't go sticking our noses into other people's affairs. We don't need trouble. The Old Country taught us that in World War Two. Gotta stay neutral."

"But Belgium was overrun by everybody, Grandpa. It wasn't that they were just neutral. It was that the Belgians chose not to get in a fight."

"Which makes me wonder about you."

"In what way?"

"Those goofy fudge makers of yours fighting like that yesterday in your shop was a shameful thing."

His scolding was given with love. I said, "I won't let it happen again."

"Good. I understand that P.M.'s boyfriend stirred up this batch of fun called the fudge contest, but don't let the doofus turn it into a circus, honey. You let guys run your life before on that little TV series and don't get me started on you-know-who." He meant Dillon Rivers. "A.M. and P.M. are my favorite superheroine duo. You have special powers and must rule your own life. Remember that." He winked at me.

I winked back. "Thanks, Grandpa. I love you."

"Love you."

When I got up to go, he said, "Mercy Fogg was here earlier looking for you."

I sagged. "What did she want?"

"Something about how two of the judges had to disqualify themselves from the judging because they were doing underhanded stuff. Whatever that means."

Oh, crap. The bribe came to mind. Rumors must have spread around town already. I told my grandpa about Piers allegedly handing Erik some money, and Lloyd learning about it. "Lloyd also told Pauline and me that Mercy's not to be trusted." A fact I now realized I'd forgotten to mention to Jordy and that I hadn't pursued with Lloyd. "Do you know of anything going on between Mercy and Lloyd?"

My grandpa spilled his coffee on his hands. "Dammit. Sorry for my French, but I just remembered something."

He made his way off the boat posthaste while muttering, "Mercy is more than a busybody. Come with me. I want to show you something. At least I hope it's still there."

Lucky Harbor leaped up onto the pier, then shook lake water all over us.

The three of us went around to the back of the shop. The dog had to stay outside. Grandpa led me into the storage room that was opposite the kitchen.

The room was sixteen by twelve and filled to the brim with boxes of supplies for our respective shops. My boxes of books and other things that Sam had moved for me were stacked near the doorway. Shelves lined all the walls except for a small window facing south and the end of the harbor's parking lot. I had planned to get Cody to help me turn the space into some semblance of a sitting room with a sofa hide-a-bed this weekend. With Lloyd's death, though, I assumed I'd be able to stay in my cabin longer.

My grandpa shoved aside boxes until he got to the back corner.

"What are we looking for, Grandpa?"

"A box Lloyd gave me to hang on to maybe five years ago."

"What's in it?"

"You'll have to look at it to believe it."

Gilpa knelt on the floor in the back corner. He whipped out his pocketknife and used the little corkscrew to poke into a wooden plank. He pulled up a trapdoor.

"Has that secret door always been here?"

"Since the day I bought the place. This room was filled with old fishing nets then." He stretched an arm down into hole. "When I cleared out the nets, one of them snagged on a sliver of wood and when I pulled hard, up came the door. It was probably put in by a fisherman long ago when he needed a place to hide his wages while he returned to his trawler on the lake. They could be out there for days and weeks sometimes."

"No banks around here in those days."

From the maw below the floorboards, he pulled up a roughly hewn wooden chest about the size of my grandmother's jewelry box, about a foot wide by eight inches front to back and six inches deep. Gilpa set it on the dusty floor. Rusted iron hinges held the lid in place. There was no lock, just an iron pin through the front latch. Grandpa wiggled the pin, but it wouldn't budge. He got up, then put the box against the wall before giving it a kick to loosen the rust. The pin rattled loose.

The box was filled with letters and small jewelry boxes, and autographed golf balls.

Grandpa said, "This is Lloyd's honesty box."

"What the heck is that?" I knelt beside him.

He opened a ring box. "It's still here. Safe and sound."

While he sighed with relief I marveled at the lovely emerald sparkler in a rectangular cut. After my unfortunate adventure in May in which diamonds had been hidden in my kitchen and my fudge, I hesitated touching the ring. "Why is this here, Gilpa?"

"Lloyd gave me these things for safekeeping. This was Libby's engagement ring. He didn't want Libby to get her hands on it."

"Why?"

"Honey, the reason for their divorce was Libby's gambling."

"Oh my. Does Grandma know about this?"

"She's always known that Libby and Mercy Fogg have enjoyed gambling over at the casino." The Oneida Casino was near the airport on the west edge of Green Bay, maybe an hour and fifteen minutes from Fishers' Harbor when traffic is light. "But your grandma doesn't know about this box. Lloyd didn't want anybody to know. I'll have to hand this over to the executor of his estate."

"So Lloyd saved things of Libby's he didn't want her to pawn?"

"That's right. Lloyd was sentimental. He knew that one day Libby would have quit gambling and then regretted getting rid of her ring. He felt that someday she'd be honest with herself about herself."

"Thus the name 'honesty' box. That's interesting because for all his sentimentality, Lloyd was about to turn Duck Marsh Street into a condo development. Professor Faust just told me that months ago he'd suggested somebody try to convince Lloyd to preserve my cabin and the others. The professor was about to talk to Lloyd about it just before he died."

"I don't know about their discussions. But Faust is right. There was plenty of brouhaha about the cabins months ago. It's died down lately. Lloyd was a shrewd businessman, far shrewder than I ever cared about being myself, and condos would certainly help my business and yours. We'd have many more people with money living right outside our back door."

No wonder I hadn't heard much about the property since coming home. My grandpa was all for razing the cabins for the sake of our business.

He handed me the emerald engagement ring. The gem glowed in the sunbeam coming through the small window. "Why didn't he put this in a bank deposit box?"

"Because Libby and Mercy could find out about the ring at a bank if anybody talked. He didn't want to be bugged about it. He planned to quietly give this stuff back to her someday."

"He was a kind man, and yet he kept these things from Libby, which was sort of mean. I don't know what to think of him now."

"He meant well."

"Grandma was also mighty mad at him for tossing me out of the cabin and tossing Libby out of the marriage and the big house he lived in."

Grandpa patted my shoulder. "Don't you worry about your grandma. I'll tell her about this box as soon as I can today. She'll understand about my promise to Lloyd."

I handed the ring back. "But we came here because I'd mentioned Mercy Fogg."

He put the ring back in its box, then began fishing about in the other small boxes and letters in the chest. The oil residue on his hands was smudging the envelopes. He came up with a fistful of letters tied together. "These must be it."

"What?"

"Love letters. Or threatening letters. Probably both. From Mercy."

This time I didn't hesitate. I snatched a couple of smudged envelopes to look inside. "Mercy is a horrible poet."

"But very good at rhyming threatening notes. Look at this one."

I read aloud the note he handed me. "*Lloyd, Lloyd, handsome as any star on celluloid/Date me, love me, share with me a life/Or I'll tell everyone I know that you stole from your wife.* Oh, Grandpa, this is nasty. And how did she know Lloyd kept things from his wife?"

"I'm sure Libby speculated about precious things she couldn't find, and then Mercy took up the cause and confronted Lloyd. He likely told her to mind her own business, but it was too late. Mercy had guessed what he was doing."

"Mercy is always trying to run things her way. Trying to run my life at times, and Libby's life, it appears."

"Nothing came of it, but I'm sure this chest is filled with all kinds of evidence of her threats. If the poor woman ever sued him, Lloyd would've come here to fetch this to stop her silly stuff and clear his name."

Cold reality crackled through me. "Grandpa, we need to show this collection to Sheriff Tollefson." I reminded him of the rock and note thrown through the lighthouse window. "Maybe Mercy did that to cause trouble for Lloyd? Maybe she wanted to rekindle something with him?"

Grandpa shook his head. "I don't know about that, Ava honey. It's been about five years since Lloyd gave me anything to put in this box. I was sure her mooning over him was over."

My phone buzzed in my pocket. It was Pauline texting that Laura Rousseau had been released from the hospital.

"Grandpa, Pauline and I are going down to Sturgeon Bay to pick up Laura. I could take the box with me and give it to the sheriff for safekeeping until we know who the executor is for Lloyd."

He ran an oily hand over his already-smudged face, which now had a tear streaking down it. "I'm gonna miss Lloyd."

I fell into his arms. "I'm so sorry, Gilpa."

* * *

I left Lucky Harbor with Gilpa. A half hour later Pauline and I were in my yellow pickup truck with the chest in the backseat and going down Highway 42 when a car failed to yield at the stop sign to my left on a country road intersection. I swerved, but then we were sailing in the air.

Chapter 8

I came to hanging sideways in my seat belt. The truck had come to rest on its side.

Pauline was lying against her door and the ground below me where her window was open to the grass.

"Pauline?"

She grunted. "I think we rolled all the way over."

"I wasn't going fast enough to do more."

"For once."

By the time we unbuckled—carefully with arms bracing at all angles—several people had stopped on Highway 42 to render aid. We climbed out through the window of my door by using the steering wheel as a step. A woman handed me tissues. "You're bleeding."

Blood was trickling down the left side of my face from somewhere on my head. Pauline was working kinks out of an elbow and had grass sticking out of an ear.

It took about twenty minutes for Deputy Maria Vasquez to show up, lights flashing. She joined us in the grassy field. "Everybody okay?"

The sun made me squint. "Yeah. Just a cut."

She wore an official brimmed hat today with her brown-and-tan uniform. Her glossy black hair was in a neat braid that draped over a shoulder. She took our report as the tourists went on their way. None of them had seen what had happened except one person thought he'd seen a dark car heading off down the crossroad. My yellow truck was a dented mess, but our seat belts had saved us.

Dillon showed up in his white construction company truck. He trotted down the embankment. "You okay?"

"Yeah, we're fine," I said, accepting a fresh tissue from him. "Somebody ran a stop sign and I swerved to get out of the way."

Dillon's fingers probed gently at the top of my head. "You might need a stitch or two."

Pauline came to look. "Yeah, your brains are oozing out."

I had to smile. I said to Dillon, "We were headed to the hospital anyway to pick up Laura."

Deputy Vasquez said, "I can take you."

"No," Dillon said, "I can take them."

Before this got ridiculous, I said, "Dillon, we'll go with the deputy. I'm sure making a report will take a while and you've got to get back to Al and your crew."

His dark eyes intensified with concern. "You're sure you're okay?"

"Just shaken up."

"I'll get your things from the truck. A couple of purses?"

"And a wooden box. It was in the backseat."

He hoisted himself up and onto the tipped truck's driver's door, then lowered himself inside. He popped up with Pauline's giant purse, but not my cross-body bag with my wallet and cell phone.

He hopped down. "No other purse. There wasn't a box."

"It couldn't have just disappeared like that."

Deputy Vasquez said, "Your windows were open. People don't realize the centrifugal force that happens in a rollover. People get flung out right through the windows if they don't wear seat belts. Your purse and box are here someplace."

We walked the truck's perimeter. My purse turned up under a tuft of clover in bloom, but the small chest—which wasn't light enough to be flung too far—was nowhere to be found.

The deputy and Dillon inspected the truck.

Pauline said, "Do you suppose somebody took it while we were stunned in the truck for a couple of minutes?"

Dillon asked, "What was in the box?"

"Any valuables?" Maria asked with renewed interest.

Nausea was filling me suddenly. "Yes. The box belonged to Lloyd Mueller."

"The dead guy?"

I nodded.

Maria said, "Is there a chance anybody would want to harm you to get this box?"

"Yes."

Maria asked that we finish making our report at the sheriff's office. We sat in Jordy Tollefson's interrogation room at a six-foot plain brown table and on blue plastic chairs. I'd been here before—too many times.

Jordy Tollefson wasn't happy to see me. "Maria says somebody may be out to harm you because of a wooden box."

Mercy Fogg came to mind. Had she found out I had the box with her incriminating notes and come after me? Or had Piers Molinsky found out I knew about him bribing Erik? Was he afraid I'd ruin his career?

"All I know for sure is that somebody aimed their car at me."

"You're saying the car was a weapon?" Jordy asked. "This wasn't just an accident?"

"Your deputy brought up the possibility."

Jordy laid out blank forms in front of him from a file folder and began writing. He knew my address by heart, not a great testimony to me. "I thought I told you to stay out of trouble."

"That was yesterday."

"Maria tells me you said the box had jewels in it. You're not involved in another jewel heist, are you?" He was referring to the diamonds that had been stolen in New York before ending up in my fudge in May.

"No. There was just the one ring, and miscellaneous costume jewelry. The ring looked valuable. It's a green emerald engagement ring about the size of my fingernail." I showed him a pinkie finger, complete with broken nail.

"That's a whopper of an emerald."

"It was a whopper of an accident. There's a thief loose in Door County, Jordy. Maybe worse."

Pauline groaned. "You don't know that. Could we come back later? She's not coherent because she needs stitches in her head."

"My brains aren't falling out, Pauline. I know what I feel and what I've seen. There was bad karma swirling around Lloyd right before he died. Several people could have been upset with him, even mad at him, maybe scared he'd tell their secrets."

"Like what? Explain your evidence to me." Jordy sat back, looking me straight in the eye.

What did I have for solid evidence? I swallowed hard. I looked from Pauline to Jordy and said, "Well, one secret that both Pauline and I witnessed was Lloyd confessing that he was bothered by Kelsey King being too 'friendly,' as he called it. Then I saw them having a disagreement at the fish boil."

Shaking his head, Jordy continued filling out the form. "You realize that's not hard evidence of a damn thing, don't you?"

Pauline said, "Let me take her to the hospital."

Jordy kept his eyes trained to the form. "She's not bleeding on my papers, so let's finish this up. Ava, describe the box and contents, please."

"I didn't see much of the contents beyond Mercy's crappy poems professing love and threatening Lloyd. Mercy was saying she'd tell Lloyd's wife about him hoarding her ring or other things. Those aren't the exact words, but it was clear Mercy suspected him of hiding valuables from Libby. At least that's what my grandfather and I concluded."

"So you've involved Gil?" Jordy shook his head again as he wrote.

"Actually, he involved me. I knew nothing about the box until Grandpa said Mercy was looking for me earlier today. Then he remembered the box."

"Why was Mercy looking for you?"

"I don't know. Something about the fudge judges. I haven't asked her."

"Well, don't ask her."

"Why not?"

"I want to talk with her first." Jordy sat back. "But I don't have much here unless she confesses. Maria said there were no skid marks. It looked like you and the other vehicle cleanly missed each other. Did you hear a horn?"

"No horns. I was in the ditch fast. I guess I was trying to outrun the car."

"You don't remember being bumped by the other vehicle?"

"No."

"What'd it look like?"

"A blur. Darkish."

"Dark what?"

"Like a big mouse maybe."

"A big mouse?" Jordy looked at me queasylike.

Pauline offered, "She has a mouse in her kitchen. He's grayish brown."

Shaking his head, he muttered while writing, "A dark blur, mouse colored." He handed me the form. "If it looks like we got all the details correct, please sign."

While I read, I noticed the neat, printed lettering. "You know, Jordy, this looks just like the orange crayon lettering on that note we found in the lighthouse."

Jordy paled, as if I'd caught him missing a crucial clue. "What's your point?"

"I'm not accusing you of throwing the rock. I was just noting how neat your printing is when you're here in your office. You're relaxed, right?"

"Yeah. I still don't get your point."

"If the person writing the threatening note was relaxed,

it probably rules out an excited kid doing mischief. What do you think, Pauline?"

She rubbed her aching elbow. "True. Kids in a hurry usually slant their letters every which way or run them together."

I asked Jordy, "Could we look at the note again from the lighthouse?"

He gave me a puckered expression I'd never seen before. But he gathered up the files and my signed statement, then left. He came back with the plastic bag. We peered at the note through the plastic.

Pauline said, "Very careful lettering, neat. Moderate orange color, medium hand pressure."

I said, "The person was comfortable with the crime he, or she, was about to commit."

Jordy sat back, blowing air across his lips. "Since when did you become a handwriting expert?"

"Just now. I get these flashes of inspiration."

"You were hit in the head inside your truck. The truck inspired you."

"Whatever the cause, doesn't it seem plausible that the note's threat is connected to Lloyd's death and my accident? The note says somebody will die. Lloyd died. And somebody is after me. Somebody followed me. And for some reason they picked up that box."

"But Lloyd Mueller's death looks like an accident. Maria confirmed that it was very dewy and slippery up there on the tower."

"You don't believe it was a suicide any more than I do. You're a pro. You have to think murder until you rule it out. That note targeted me."

"It said *somebody* will die if you don't lose the fudge contest. So stop making fudge if you believe that note is serious and don't want others to die." Jordy speared me with a serious stare.

"I can't stop. I have to make a living. And besides, my fudge is my art. A reporter in May called me a fudge sculptor."

Pauline grabbed my arm. "We need to get you checked out at the hospital." She turned to Jordy. "I was in the truck, too. That car came right at us. Then the wooden box disappeared while we were hanging in the truck. Somebody is trying to frame Ava or harm her."

"Frame her? For what?" Jordy leaned forward.

"Ava was your suspect in a murder back in May. What if somebody's trying to blame Lloyd's death on her and her family? To throw you off?"

I added, "It's a hot fudge frame-up, Jordy. Start questioning perps."

He leaned forward over the note to peer at us pointedly. His shoulders appeared broader, more menacing. "Door County has a population of about twenty-eight thousand people. Add to that the several thousands vacationing here right now. Which adults do you two propose I start questioning?"

"Just Mercy Fogg," I said, incredulous as to how dense Jordy was today while I'd been hit on my noggin and was feeling brilliantly clear. Maybe he was hungry. I was feeling a little hungry and dizzy myself. The clock on the wall behind him was striking noon. "Mercy will still have the wooden chest hidden in her trunk if you get to her fast enough."

"What kind of car does she drive?"

He had me. I said, "I only see her driving school buses or county road graders. Look her up in the vehicle license database." He winced as I went on. "Pauline and I have to get to the hospital. And I sorely need to get back to make fudge. Jordy, did you know science has proven that chocolate fudge makes people amorous?"

His face turned red. "What's your point?"

"If you take some of my Cinderella Pink Fudge with you to question Mercy, she might want to spill her guts about what she did. Sam uses my fudge at his client meetings. I bet feeding fudge to prisoners would work better than lie detector tests and torture. Can we go?"

"Not fast enough," he said.

But I sat there, captured by my revelations, bubbling in my head like Belgian chocolate. My gut said Lloyd's death was murder. I couldn't prove it, but murder suspects popped up: Mercy and Piers, Erik and Kelsey, and some mysterious wannabe buyer of a good portion of Fishers' Harbor. I *needed* to make fudge now because that could reveal the killer. I rattled off the suspects to Jordy.

Jordy rose off his chair with the Baggie in hand. "I can't question Mercy or anybody just because you suggest it, Ava."

"This is sounding more and more like working in television. My executive producer nixed most everything I came up with."

"Maybe you had bad ideas." He leaned over the table at me. "Don't stir up trouble that can hurt Libby. If rumors explode, Libby's going to be devastated. If there's been a murder, let me handle the nightmare that will create for Libby. Getting lawyers involved will turn Fishers' Harbor upside down, and we just got over a big legal mess with you in the middle of it."

"It sounds like you're warning me to keep quiet."

"Ava Oosterling." He spat out my name like it was a swearword. "You don't get it." He tapped a finger on the table like a repeater rifle. "I'm trying to tell you to stay safe. Rumors can get out of hand and become dangerous. One little peep out of you that Mercy Fogg may have harmed Lloyd and you could ruin her job driving the school bus and working for the county. Then she'll sue your tiny little ass off and win."

After he left the room, Pauline said, "I think he likes you. That ass comment was sort of sweet."

Jordy called a wrecker service to haul my truck to a salvage yard, but I intervened to have it delivered to an auto body shop on the outskirts of Fishers' Harbor; I couldn't bear to give up on my yellow truck.

The sheriff dropped us off at the hospital. I called Mom to have her pick us up and take us home. Three stitches pulled my scalp back together. Pauline and I got pamphlets about concussions. No X-rays were taken because we seemed in good shape, but we were advised to have somebody check on us regularly for the next twenty-four hours. If we got headaches, we were to head to the emergency room.

Escaping death had given me an adrenaline rush. Pauline was less enthused about that method for boosting one's energy. But I was eager to make fudge with a new flavor. Fairy tales popped into my head: Goldilocks and the Three Bears, Hansel and Gretel, Rapunzel, Red Riding Hood, the Princess and the Pea, Snow White, and Thumbelina. There were other tales, too, that could warrant magical fudge flavors, such as Shakespeare's Romeo and Juliet, or Robin Hood and Maid Marian. There were beautiful Native American tales, too, and tragic ones like the maiden who'd allegedly been separated from her lover, and after he died she wanted to join him, so she leaped from a high, rocky bluff overlooking the Mississippi River. The town of Maiden Rock, Wisconsin, got its name allegedly from that tale.

I doubted Lloyd had jumped off the Eagle Bluff Lighthouse for a lover. Had he slipped? I didn't believe his death was an accident any more than I believed my getting run off the road was an accident.

We picked up Laura and wheeled her out of the hospital into the fresh air. She kept shaking her head over everything that had transpired since we dropped her off here yesterday morning. I handed her a bottle of water.

She took a swig. "At least you're alive. I don't know how to react to Lloyd's death."

Joining us, Pauline said, "Ava's reacting by making fudge."

Laura said, "I need to take your measurements for the dress I have in mind."

"What color?" Pauline asked me, flipping her long, dark

hair off a shoulder in her authoritative way. She had a bluish green bruise forming along her right cheek.

"Oh no," I said, "we're not going into a discussion again about Dillon and Sam."

Pauline said, "I was thinking tan, to match Jordy's uniform."

Pauline told Laura about the "tiny ass" comment. They broke into laughter.

Laura pleaded, "Stop, or I'll pee my pants. Again."

Then I laughed, too. Everybody should have friends like these.

My mother arrived in her sports utility vehicle this time instead of the cow minivan. She babbled admonishments at us as she hugged us.

"You could have killed yourself," she scolded me. "I should kill you for trying to kill yourself."

"Mom, stop with the 'kill' word. It's not allowed in front of Pauline."

She pointed us into our seats like we were children. "You're staying with your grandparents tonight."

"No, Mom, my cabin is fine."

"Who's going to check on you at midnight and two and four in the morning? Never mind. I'll call you. If you don't answer, I'll call an ambulance."

Laura said, "I'll stay with her."

"I don't have an extra bed," I protested. "Just the lumpy sofa."

As we drove away from the hospital, we decided Pauline would sleep at Laura's in Sister Bay because Laura had a two-bedroom ranch house with a real bed in the second bedroom. I relented and told Mom I'd sleep in Grandma Sophie's sunroom on the foldout sofa.

Mom asked, "Who's helping you at the shop? You shouldn't be doing anything at the shop. You need to rest."

"Mom, really, the seat belt held me in. The crash was like riding a roller coaster."

"Be sure to call your dad. He'll want to hear your voice."

"Will do, Mom."

"Maybe I should stay with you at the fudge shop."

Ugh! "No, Mom, it's not necessary. Other people will be around. Like customers." The only trick that worked to calm Mom's worry gene was talking about her work on the farm. "How many new calves are you feeding lately?"

"Oh gosh, ten. They're the cutest things, too. One has markings on it that look like a cat's head, and there's an outline of the United States on another calf."

She once found the profile of Elvis and named that calf Graceland. We heard about a lot more famous people's silhouettes on calf hide, which would bore you like it bored us. But Mom was sweet in her own way. I loved her for it.

When Mom dropped us off at the shop, the harbor was crowded as usual after lunch. I was starving, but tourists were milling about waiting for my show. After Memorial Day, I'd begun a practice of making fresh Cinderella Pink Fudge around one o'clock every Saturday for sure and most days of the week to entice the tourists and fishers after lunch. What I'd said to Jordy about the science of fudge was true—chocolate smells have been proven in experiments to increase sales. With the addition of fudge making in copper kettles over open flames, Grandpa noticed sales of his bobbers and bait had risen because people lingered longer, thus making more impulse buys.

To my surprise, Piers was stirring away peacefully at a copper kettle on one end of my north wall area, with Kelsey stirring at the other end of the row of kettles. They'd separated themselves with four kettles in between.

John Schultz was interviewing customers on camera. A little boy was saying his favorite vacation pastimes were gutting fish and eating fudge.

As soon as Pauline caught John's eye, she melted into tears and told him about the accident. This side of Pauline was new for me. What was it about goofball John in his Hawaiian shirts that made her go weak? I didn't "get" him at all. But then, my choices in men hadn't worked out, so I wasn't an expert on attraction.

I tossed on a white bib apron to cover my messy clothes. I'd washed up pretty well at the hospital, so my arms and legs were clean. I twisted my hair into a bun at the back of my head, sticking a pen off the counter through it to hold it in place. The stitches pulled on the top of my head, but I gritted my teeth against the annoyance.

Cody helped me gather ingredients from the kitchen. I didn't tell him about the accident; he sometimes had trouble processing my painful adventures and would get as upset as Mom.

In minutes the crowd was watching me and the guest confectioners create spirals of luscious, liquid dark and white chocolate high in the air with our long wooden ladles. The air became thick with the ambrosial perfume that teased the tongue and made mouths water.

I told the crowd, "The cherries are high in antioxidants and their enzymes help ease muscle inflammation and pain of arthritis and strenuous exercise. The melatonin in tart cherries also helps keep your sleep cycle on track."

One woman in the crowd fanned herself and said, "Your fudge will help me sleep through the night? I'm buying out the shop right now."

The crowd chuckled.

As I was creating cherry-vanilla pink perfection fudge next to Piers, he made the big mistake of opening his mouth.

"Well, some people don't sleep much at all. Ask Miss Dirt Eater murder suspect where she was this morning early."

Since nobody had said anything publicly about "murder," his word choice was curious.

To my left, still a couple of kettles away, Kelsey stopped stirring what looked like butterscotch fudge with balls hidden in it. "The only murder around here is going to be you. I was collecting dandelions, which are edible and legal."

So that's what was in her pot—whole dandelion blossoms.

The crowd had quieted.

Piers looked into John's camera. "Fudge is something that builds character and brings friends together. Even in death. Guess who was out in the park before Lloyd Mueller died."

Even I gasped with the crowd at that bold statement on camera.

Kelsey lifted her four-foot wooden paddle and whacked Piers on the back. Butterscotch fudge and flower blossoms splattered everywhere, a blossom smacking me in the neck before it blobbed onto my formerly pristine apron.

Customers herded their children out the front door.

I pleaded with John, "Please stop recording."

Pauline coaxed the camera off his face while I turned to Kelsey. "Take a break." I ripped the fudge-paddle weapon out of her hands.

"I have a contract with Mr. Schultz. I'm not leaving."

"I'll find you another kitchen to cook in. Come back in two hours for your orders." I had no idea what I was saying, but I'd had enough of these two. "Piers, you, too. Take a break."

"Why me?"

"Because every time you two cook here, Cody and I have to spend two hours cleaning up. You also can come back in two hours for further instructions."

Kelsey and Piers hurried out, muttering curse words. John trotted after them. I imagined this playing out as the cliff-hanger right before a commercial break on TV.

The small crowd that was left erupted into applause. White-haired Dotty and her redheaded friend, Lois, popped up from around the end cap of a shelving unit where they'd ducked for cover.

Dotty, sparkling in a pink sequined T-shirt said, "You tell 'em, honey."

Lois nodded. "Those two are weird. But she's a cute little blonde."

"Don't get too close to her, Lois," I said. "She's lethal with her feet."

The cowbell clanked. John returned. "I need more shots

of you alone making fudge. Can we do maybe a half hour more of taping?"

Dotty said, "With the way she looks? Nothing doing."

I took slight offense. "What's wrong with the way I look?" The white apron had butterscotch on it, but that was all.

Dotty said, "This disheveled outfit won't do, not if you want to be successful with your show."

"It's John's show."

"Pshaw. It's our show, too. Door County could become famous on TV. We have to think about how we're portrayed on the boob tube." Dotty preened in her pink sparkles, hinting for John to record her. Dotty was taking her fudge judgeship seriously, it appeared.

John said, "Love that color. That's what this place needs—more color!"

Lois said to me, "I have just *the thing* to cure your dull, drab appearance, Ava. I'll drop by after Mass tomorrow with a surprise." She paused for effect while John recorded. "Stay tuned. Oh, I love saying that."

Dotty said, "And you said it well."

I was doomed. Some faraway, fuzzy part of my brain reminded me of the disaster the church ladies had created in May when they'd turned my shop into a rummage sale of homemade things like beer hats. Those were made from beer cans cut up and knitted together, usually in the ever-popular green and gold for the Green Bay Packers.

Pauline and Laura helped clean up the shop while I made Cinderella Pink Fudge for the tourists. Laura also took my measurements for a dress while I was held captive stirring my ingredients. That spurred talk about the upcoming dance as well as memories about everybody's prom and what they wore.

Pauline and Laura left within the hour, about the time I was loafing the pink fudge on the white marble slab. With a wooden tool, I worked the hot, runny fudge until it cooled and stiffened enough that I could knead it with my hands around its edges. It ended up looking like a pretty pink meat loaf made of chocolate. Then I let it sit on the slab to harden in front of the window with its afternoon shade.

Exhaustion struck me as I finished, but my mind—filled with the delectable aromas—had revved up with questions. What had Kelsey seen at the park, if anything? Why was Piers eager to accuse her of murder? Who had stolen the box?

I needed to lie down to let the answers filter out like bubbles being released from fudge in the whipping process. First, though, I made phone calls to solve the "Confectioners' Conflict." After writing down separate instructions for Kelsey and Piers, I left them each an envelope next to the cash register. They now had secret missions in Door County. I felt like I was the host of some survivor reality TV show.

By the time the tourists went off to other activities in the midafternoon, I was ready to leave, too, and crawl into a bed. Then Mercy Fogg showed up.

Mercy burst in, blowing right past me at the window. She was almost my height, but much stockier with substantial arm muscles. A woman with a wide face and an abundance of bouncy blond curls, she sometimes looked clownish. Today she had on yellow clam-digger pants and a black sleeveless top with a red felt flower pinned to it.

I ducked below my marble table. Cody was at Grandpa's register helping some fishers. My grandfather had gone home to be with my grandmother, both of them grieving Lloyd.

"Where's Ava Oosterling?"

"She was in an accident, Miss Fogg." He'd heard about my rollover from some of the tourists.

"When you see her, tell her I need to talk with her about Dillon Rivers. He's up to no good again."

She left without detecting me. I had just come out of my hiding place when Sam came in. He followed me to the counter.

"Your mother and father both called me. I'm supposed to watch you."

My parents were matchmakers. I rolled my eyes, but a yawn slipped out. "I need a nap is all."

"I'll watch you nap. Your mother said you have a concussion."

"Sam, really, I'm fine. No concussion."

Cody called over, "Miss Oosterling, I can take care of the shop."

"We're pretty busy. I should stay."

"Don't you trust me?"

Cody knew the "trust" issue could get me. I hadn't trusted him in May when I first hired him through Sam. I was still ashamed with the way I considered Cody's Asperger's condition to be some hindrance when it wasn't at all. He just went at things differently. Sam had told me that Cody had a good chance of becoming a fairly average adult like the rest of us.

Sam challenged me, too, with a hike of an eyebrow.

Properly chastised, I said, "All right. I'll take the rest of the day off. Ranger, you're in charge."

Sam escorted me through the back door and into the sunshine dappling my backyard lawn. Sam asked, "What did Mercy want? I almost got barreled over by her."

"Something about Dillon. Another one of her many rumors, I'm sure."

"Maybe you should listen to this one. I heard it today, too, at the Troubled Trout during lunch. Customers were putting bets down about it."

I stopped in the middle of my yard. "Bets about what?"

"Dillon might buy the cabins on your street as well as the Blue Heron Inn. He might be your new landlord. Or is he more than that to you, Ava?"

A growl escaped me.

Chapter 9

Sam grabbed me before I could run off to find Dillon and pummel him. "Hold on," Sam said. "Let me finish. It's not true. She made it up. I'm just relaying the gossip."

"Why is Mercy saying that Dillon is buying Lloyd's property? And then what? Does she have him and me getting remarried?"

"Who knows? Mercy can't stand it that John didn't invite her to be a fudge judge, or that you didn't suggest her name, so now she has a grudge. She has to find a way to make herself important."

The rumors got me thinking about new angles concerning the murder. "Dillon is a civil engineer whose company is working for our village. If he or his family was investing in property here, he'd have to reveal his conflict of interest to our village president. But I'm not sure I can trust Erik Gustafson anymore."

"What's going on with Erik?" Sam's eyes sparkled despite us standing in the shade of the giant maples along Duck Marsh Street.

"I learned today from Grandpa that Mercy and Libby are old gambling buddies. Mercy might know more about Lloyd's dealings than we all think. Maybe Lloyd and Dillon's family know one another. They'd be in the same circles if money counted, certainly." I sagged, knowing I needed to ask Dillon some pointed questions.

Sam put an arm around me. His steadiness kept me from collapsing. The day was catching up with me. And I still had to tell Grandpa I'd lost the precious box. My grandparents had certainly heard about my rollover accident from Mom, but I hadn't told Mom about the missing box. So Grandpa didn't know I'd messed up—yet again. I gave Sam a spontaneous hug. He hugged me back.

"What's wrong?" he asked.

"My grandfather's going to be so disappointed in me."

I told him about what had transpired yesterday at Lloyd's house and about the contents of the box. Sam didn't say anything or judge me; he just draped an arm around me to escort me the few yards across the street to my grandparents' cabin.

My grandparents were in their backyard garden. When bad things happen, we Belgians garden or go into our fields. Or make fudge, in my case. Belgians came to Door County in the 1850s because farmland was a buck and a quarter an acre. Professor Faust had told me that our country advertised in Belgium and neighboring countries for workers. The Belgians tamed the land and forests in Door County, becoming famous for shingle-making, too. By 1860, four million handmade shingles were shipped out of Brussels, Wisconsin. My grandparents' talented hands had turned most of their sunny yard into rows of beans, peas, squash, tomatoes, Brussels sprouts, cabbages, potato hills, and more. A section was dedicated to gladiolas as well as candy-striped zinnias. A breeze buffeted a silvery blue and a yellow little sulfur atop the blossoms.

Grandpa was bent over a row of winter onions. He loved to eat onions with cottage cheese.

My grandma came over with a tin pail overflowing with pea pods. "You're here for supper, Sam?"

"Just making sure your granddaughter got home okay."

Grandma went into the house, but Sam relieved Grandpa Gil of his armful of onions and took those over to the coiled hose next to the house for washing.

I confessed about the missing chest, telling Grandpa my suspicions that maybe it had been stolen by the person who caused the accident, who might also be the person threatening me. "Possibly the same person who took Lloyd's life, Grandpa."

He soured at that. "Lloyd's death was an awful accident, honey. And the box could've been taken by anybody stopping by and you just never noticed."

Sam went into the house.

Grandpa got the hose and walked the end of it to the garden, where he set up a sprinkler. "Lloyd's death and the missing box are scaring me, Ava. You and I went through a horrid experience back in May. Let's stay out of this."

He sat down in a nearby yellow Adirondack chair. "I called Libby to express my condolences. Lloyd has no close relatives here, so she's making the arrangements. The funeral is Tuesday at St. Ann's."

Lloyd was Lutheran, and St. Ann's was a Catholic church, but St. Ann's could hold a lot more people than our local Lutheran church. St. Ann's basement was also where Lloyd, Grandpa, and other guys participated in community card game fund-raisers.

Grandpa's remark about Lloyd's lack of relatives reminded me of the old cookbooks Lloyd had given me. I made a mental note to go through them early tomorrow morning when it was quiet at the shop.

"Gilpa, did you say anything to Libby about the letters and her engagement ring in that box?"

"No, A.M. I figured that would be coming from the sheriff when he returned the things."

"We're going to have to tell Libby soon before Mercy hears about it and makes our lives miserable." Mercy's visit to the shop earlier was troubling me. I told Grandpa the rumor Sam had heard. "I don't want to believe in Mercy's rumors, but Dillon also told me that his mother was coming for a visit."

"You think his mother might be the secret partner?"

"Gilpa, the last time I saw her she was working on developing property in South Padre Island, Texas. Cathy Rivers specializes in that sort of real estate project."

Grandpa scooted forward in the Adirondack chair. "If the Rivers family is buying up Lloyd's property . . . Ava Mathilde, forgive me, but I have nothing good to say about your ex."

A burning desire to call Dillon had to be saved for later. Grandma Sophie had made one of Grandpa's favorite Belgian meals. She insisted Sam stay for supper. I could barely keep my eyes open, but we stuffed ourselves with hot dandelion potato salad made with bacon, meat loaf topped with winter onions and browned until crisp under the broiler, shredded red cabbage tossed in vinegar with a touch of honey, slices of mild cheddar cheese from our own farm, and sweet gherkin pickles Grandma had canned last fall.

We had a choice of three pies: raspberry-rhubarb, cherry, or Belgian rice. The ingredients for the thick, custardlike rice pie included rice, butter, cream, brown sugar, several eggs with their whites whipped and folded in, and vanilla. Pies are a calling card of Belgians. And they're not small. The pie tin we Belgians use from the Old Country is twelve and a half inches in diameter, while the normal pie dish in this country is eight or nine inches across. When you came to a Door County kermis, you might find thirty different flavors of pies. I suspected Grandma would be taking the remainder of these pies to Libby Mueller tomorrow so that Libby had something to offer the people dropping by to express condolences. Grandma would also be making more pies to take to Tuesday's funeral lunch. Funerals and weddings were often potluck affairs around here because it was customary to invite the whole community.

Sam ate a small slice from all three pies. It was as if he'd reverted to his football-playing days.

Grandpa said to me, "Your grandmother used to make a dozen pies for the Belgian Days celebration down in Brussels. But like everything else in life, that custom got put aside because lives got busier."

I recalled that Lloyd had suggested I start a kermis in Fishers' Harbor. "On what days were Belgian Days, Gilpa?"

"Second week of July."

"The same weekend as our current fudge festival?"

"Seems so."

"We have to do something about it, Gilpa. We have to resurrect Belgian Days. What do you think, Sam?"

He finished a mouthful of cherry pie. "If it means you're serving this pie, this Swede will become Belgian for a day."

All of us laughed.

"We'll make it a Founders' Day instead to celebrate all of Fishers' Harbor's early immigrants. And, Grandpa, you just gave me an idea for next Saturday. I have to match a fairy tale with a fudge flavor and a pie flavor—a trifecta. We'll raffle off the pies, too, to raise money for next year's Founders' Day."

Sam asked, "Which pie and fudge flavors? Rice fudge? What fairy tale is that?"

I enjoyed the levity after my weird day. "I'm not sure yet. We agreed to each have two flavors in the contest. But I'm going to use old traditional flavors and tales." I thought about Lloyd's historical cookbooks in his house, and him suggesting I create something big for our community as a way to protect myself from Erik and Mercy, who allegedly were in a conspiracy to see me fail.

At the end of our supper, Gilpa excused himself to get a good night's sleep.

I escorted Sam outside onto my grandparents' front porch. The sun was dropping behind the bluff and behind their cabin. The street and lawns were scored with shadows that looked like graphite outlines of the tree limbs above. I could hear muffled voices in other rental cabins. Across from us, my cabin was decrepit-looking, its foundation sagging low into the earth.

Sam asked, "Do you ever wonder who lived in that cabin when it was first built?"

"No, Sam. But now it seems really important to know everything about its history."

"Before it's torn down?"

"Yeah."

Sam seemed to want to linger. "I'd hate to move from my house."

Panic caught fire inside me. "I'm tired, Sam. I hope you don't mind . . ."

"Oh, sure. Sorry. Good night."

Sam stepped off the porch quickly. Too quickly. I felt bad about shooing him away. He loped up the street for a long walk home—to a house across town he'd picked out long ago for us to live in together.

I went back inside my grandparents' cabin to call Dillon, to ask about his mother's intentions, but the last thing I remembered was collapsing in the hide-a-bed in the sunroom.

The smell of bacon frying, whole-wheat pancakes, and warm cherry syrup roused me at five a.m. My grandfather had already left to open up for the fishers. Grandma Sophie told me I'd slept like a rock since collapsing around seven o'clock last night. I'd slept ten hours! She'd checked on me throughout.

"You must be exhausted, Grandma. I'm sorry."

"The need for sleep evaporates when I'm protecting my little duckling."

She fed me a delectable pancake painted with a smiley face in tasty red cherry syrup. Grandma's kitchen atmosphere filled me, too. The room hadn't changed much in the twenty-some years they'd lived here, except for a new stainless steel refrigerator and stove. The black-and-white floor tiles were original, and even the electric clock above the sink in the shape of a copper pot still kept time perfectly. It matched the antique copper gelatin molds on one wall. The entire place sparkled because it was cleaned with love. It made me think about Grandpa saying that Lloyd still loved Libby. It saddened me that maybe Libby didn't realize how Lloyd had looked out for her over the years.

"Grandma, what did Libby think about Lloyd's secrecy over his real estate deal?"

Her arms paused in a sudsy sink. "I thought he was a rat, but Libby was never one to blame him for anything. She's devastated by his death. I'm sure she's eager to find out what's going on, just like the rest of us."

Grandma went back to washing dishes.

I wasn't sure if Grandpa had told her about Lloyd's secret box, so I was limited in what I dared ask. "There was another cabin owner yet on this street not too long ago. Did they sell out?"

"Oh yes. Lloyd bought that cabin a few months ago."

"So your cabin is the only one that Lloyd didn't own on all three blocks?"

Grandma Sophie grabbed a dish towel. "What are you getting at?"

"It's odd the entire street would be bought for a condo development—or as Lois and Dotty say, 'a helipad for the rich'—but the buyer would build around your cabin."

Grandma slid into the chair across from me, the dish towel balled in her hands. "Build around it? Oh my. They do that in big cities. Build high-rises around some dumpy house or church."

"Did Lloyd mention moving this house?"

"They'll have to move this cabin over my dead body!" She tossed the towel toward the counter.

"Grandma, it's odd you weren't asked to sell. Unless Lloyd left it up to the new owner to pressure you."

"Lloyd would never have done that to us."

But I'd already learned that Lloyd was secretive. It would be awful if the new owner *were* Cathy Rivers, Dillon's mother. That would devastate my grandmother. "Are you sure Lloyd never even hinted to you and Grandpa about this new owner?"

"Not that I'm aware of, Ava, and your grandpa and I don't keep secrets."

Hmm. That wasn't true. I excused myself to go to my fudge shop.

It was six a.m., late by my grandpa's standards, by the time I got to Oosterlings' Live Bait, Bobbers & Belgian Fudge & Beer. I had showered, put my hair into a knot on top of my head, and then changed into my Sunday best—a fresh sleeveless white blouse and denim knee-length shorts and sturdy athletic shoes.

Because it was Sunday, I refrained from calling Dillon this early. As Pauline said, I had a habit of poking bears awake in their caves; nothing good came of doing that. Instead, I planned to look through Lloyd's old cookbooks. There had to be some special reason he'd plunked those in my lap.

The usual cadre of fishermen was milling about, buying minnows and six-packs of fudge and beer to take out on their excursions. One guy was filling his Thermos from Grandpa's coffeepot. Gilpa was wheeling and dealing a price for his fishing guide services with a man and his son, so I knew he'd be taking *Sophie's Journey* out onto Lake Michigan, leaving me alone to tend both registers.

I expected a good crowd later. On Sundays the tourists did last-minute shopping before clearing out of their cabins and condos. The sunrise and a breeze were busting up the gray blanket of fog in our harbor; humidity was predicted to stick around and the sixty-degree temperature would climb to around eighty later.

After Gilpa's customers left, I blocked the front door open to take advantage of the cool air and sweet smell of the freshwater lake. I wiped dew off the front tables outside, then watered the geraniums.

When I went to retrieve the cookbooks from under the counter, they were missing. Thinking that perhaps Cody had put them somewhere for safekeeping, I searched every drawer, shelf, and even in our safe, which was hidden under a shelf next to the floor in my galley kitchen. They hadn't been set aside in the storage room, either.

When I returned to the front, Professor Faust stood at the counter, holding the cookbooks. "Your employee Cody allowed me to peruse these. I promised to return them this morning. I hope that was okay? I asked him to be sure to let you know I had them." He set the small stack on the counter.

"Perfect timing. I was just looking for them, coincidentally. What did you think?"

He ran a hand through his windblown gray hair. His hazel eyes grew as twinkly as the luster dust I put on my fudge. "The church ones in particular carry a treasure trove of names and personal notes referencing people who came over directly from the old countries in the mid-1800s. This is like a genealogical tree for the Fishers' Harbor area."

His excitement made the professor look younger than his sixty years. He had dressed more youthful today, too, in tan chinos and deck shoes, and a plain polo shirt in a green color that matched his eyes.

He pulled a slim cookbook from the stack. "This one from the Lutheran church I found particularly interesting." With great care, his fingers parted the pages. He let the double-page spread splay before me.

To my amazement, there was a recipe for fudge from a Ruth Mueller. I asked, "A relative of Lloyd's, I believe?"

"His grandmother."

"How can you be sure?"

"I called Libby. She confirmed it."

The professor showed me pages with recipes by Ruth Mueller in all the cookbooks Lloyd had given me. There were several for cakes, including one for German chocolate cake with its gooey, caramel-coconut frosting. But the fudge recipe drew my attention. It was simple, with no temperature mentioned. Usually you had to boil and stir fudge until it reached 238 degrees on a candy thermometer. This recipe said to "stir the bubbly mixture while your children dance with their father around the woodstove until they're tired."

The words made me smile. "Lloyd's grandmother had a sweet sense of humor. That's a novel way of telling time for fudge." I closed the books. "Would you like some coffee?"

"Thank you, but I'm on my way to set up an outdoor booth at the lighthouse."

"The Eagle Bluff Lighthouse?"

"Yes. The campground affords me a new audience every day for my book sales. I've never sold so many books."

"Why outdoors?"

"Officer Vasquez said not to cross the police tape."

This alarmed me. "But I thought they'd finished looking around yesterday after we found Lloyd."

"Oh no. I was over there to do a book signing later yesterday and found I couldn't get in. A woman officer was there for another look."

So Jordy perhaps had taken my suspicions to heart yesterday. Or he was just doing his job. I asked the professor, "Do you think it was murder? Or did Lloyd somehow fall off?"

He shrugged. "I only knew Lloyd through your contest. He was a genial man who loved his golf. I doubt he had enemies, and I don't see a happy man like that leaping to his death."

"So you think it was an accident?"

"I've been to the top of a few of Door County's ten lighthouses, including that one while doing my research, and all of them have good railings and good footing. I suppose, though, if one leaned too far out and a foot came up, throwing you off balance . . ."

I could see it on his face, though, that he didn't believe Lloyd had slipped. I said, "Lloyd golfed a lot, which requires good balance."

We grew somber. Lloyd had been murdered.

My mother's words on Friday echoed back. She'd pointed out the threat in the note had been to me. Both Lloyd and I had been mentioned. Lloyd was dead. Was I next? My insides thrashed about like our lake in the throes of a storm.

The professor touched my arm. "Ava? What's wrong?"

I was shaking. "We have a . . . murderer among us. Don't we?"

"Oh, I doubt that. Wouldn't such a person have left Door County already?"

"Of course you're right." But I needed to change the subject. "Could you sign one of your books for me? I'm sorry I've been so busy that I haven't had a chance to ask you before now."

After signing my copy of *Wisconsin's Edible Heritage*, the professor said, "Take a look in my index and you'll find Oosterlings."

While he went to look at fudge in the glass case, I flipped to the page. A couple of paragraphs noted how fish were brought off Lake Michigan and stored in ice in shacks. During bad weather the fishermen would even sleep in the same shack until the weather cleared. The "shack" was our bait shop. An old photo showed a sign at the front door: Mueller's Fishing Company. That didn't surprise me because Gilpa had bought the shop from Lloyd Mueller.

"Then it's true what my grandfather and I thought," I said, musing out loud while thinking about the secret cavity under the floorboards in the storage room.

"What is?"

I told him about our theory that fishermen probably used the floor as a hiding place for their wages or other things.

The professor's eyes popped. He withdrew a notepad and pen from a pocket. "The cabins on your street were built to house fishermen and lumbermen who could be gone for weeks. Perhaps Lloyd Mueller found treasures, and that's why he kept buying the cabins on Duck Marsh Street—they were filled with treasures. Have you looked under the floor of your grandparents' cabin? And yours? Have you given this little fudge shop a thorough search? You could be rich, Ava, and you just don't know it."

Chapter 10

The idea of riches hidden under the floor of our cabins—or under the fudge shop—kept me in good spirits as tourists filtered in on Sunday morning. If I found booty I'd buy Gilpa a new boat. I'd just received a call from the Coast Guard that he and the fishermen he'd taken out were stranded on Lake Michigan out past Chambers Island, about seven miles out. They were fine, but they'd need a tow. My grandpa's problems with his old fishing trawler happened as often as mosquito bites in the woods. When I arrived in May, on the very day of my Cinderella Pink Fudge debut at the Blue Heron Inn, Gilpa had been stranded on the lake with guests from the bed-and-breakfast.

By ten o'clock the shop was bustling and my stitches were itching again. I freed the ponytail knot atop my head, then got busy selling all ten of my current fudge flavors, including local favorites of walnut, maple, coffee, and butterscotch, as well as Cinderella Pink Fudge and Worms-in-Dirt Fudge. John and Pauline arrived as I finished wrapping pink paper around an order of Cinderella Fudge.

Pauline and John looked way too satiated, as if they'd had more than just breakfast in bed this morning. Pauline was striking with her long brown-black hair feathering over a lightweight red hoodie sweatshirt that matched red shorts that showed off her athletic legs. She'd put on makeup to hide the big bruise lining her face.

John, on the other hand, wore his usual Hawaiian shirt—this one with red wineglasses dotting it—which looked like a muumuu on his portly frame. He wore his usual baggy shorts and sandals. John laid his video camera and light on Gilpa's cash register counter, then helped himself to coffee.

Pauline rushed to my register. She whispered, "Lloyd was murdered. Just like we surmised. It's on the front page of the online *Door County Advocate* this morning."

Pauline moved aside while I rang up a purchase of two pink purses for a mom and her daughter. Cody had Sundays off, but I was wishing I had an assistant today so I could escape to go over to the lighthouse to look around. After the customers left, I said as much to Pauline.

"No," she said, "this time let's not get involved. I have better things to worry about."

"I can see that." I tilted my head toward John, who was scuffling about the bait shop. He picked up a foam cooler, then began measuring off a lot of the rope from the round bale I usually stole from to cut a length to tie up Lucky Harbor. "What's he doing?"

Pauline's tall body slumped. "He said he wants to face his fear. Help me stop him."

"I've wanted to stop John since you met him."

"Don't start."

"Okay, okay. Sorry. What's his fear?"

"Water. He's going out in a boat today."

"But he gets seasick." I recalled that in May John had gotten sick that Sunday morning on my grandfather's boat and had to be brought back in before the tour even got under way. The delay had caused Gilpa and his remaining passengers to end up in a storm on Lake Michigan, with the boat breaking down. I'd even thought for a time that it was a ploy and John had perhaps murdered the famous actress during my fudge's debut.

I set Pauline at ease. "John won't have to go out with Gilpa. I just got a call that he's stranded again."

"Not your grandfather's boat. John's not going fishing. He signed up for a shipwreck diving tour with lessons." She shuddered. "He signed up only a half hour ago over the phone. He wants to take underwater pictures of treasure for his TV show."

Going diving to view shipwrecks was big business for Door County. We had one of the world's best collections of freshwater shipwreck sites in the world. Schooners hauling everything from lumber to Christmas trees to ore and gold had sunk within several yards of the shore at some points.

Pauline was whispering between clenched teeth now. "John said you and the professor were talking about sunken treasure. The minute John got off the phone with Professor Faust this morning, he changed his plans. We were going to visit wineries today with the professor, but now John's determined to learn to scuba dive." She placed a hand over her heart. "Look at John, Ava. He's a bowling ball. He'll sink and never come up."

I almost said that'd be a good thing, but I held my tongue. "Listen, P.M., John knows what he's doing."

The place was getting more crowded. Several men had come in and were talking with John as they shopped for bobbers, bait, and beer. John was joking with them, discussing the best way to signal from underwater if he were in trouble. Pauline peered at me with pure misery all over her face. I was saved when I saw Cody coming down the dock toward the open door with Sam and Dillon, along with his dog. Dillon and Sam weren't enemies, but they had certainly given each other polite distance. Until now.

Pauline abandoned me to head over to John.

"Good morning," I said to the trio as they walked across the wooden floor, all of them wearing boating shoes. "What's up? Cody, it's your day off, remember?"

Dillon said, "We're going fishing together. And scuba diving. It was Cody's idea."

Cody said, "Yeah, I asked Sam and Dillon to go. Did you know Dillon already knows how to scuba dive?"

I stared in disbelief at the three men. Other women had paused, too. Dillon was a tall, dark, muscular specimen wearing a black T-shirt under a denim jacket and low-slung jeans. Sam was a blond good ol' boy who looked yummy in a light blue polo shirt that stretched across his broad shoulders. He wore khaki shorts that made him look fun instead of his usual stuffy self. Cody, with his red hair full of cowlicks and face full of freckles, was a charmer, too.

I said, "This Sunday must be something special for guys because John is going scuba diving for shipwrecks."

Dillon grabbed a fudge sample from the plate I kept atop the glass case. "We're going out on the same boat. Moose Lindstrom's *Super Catch I.*"

Moose—or Carl—was Gilpa's chief competitor. My grandpa refused to admit it, but he was jealous of that brand-new big, superliner style of boat with its air-conditioned cabin, kitchenette, and lounge, not to mention its massive engines, which purred and didn't grunt and puff smoke like a broken-down antique farm tractor.

I came around the register counter to whisper, "John's never been scuba diving. Don't let him go. He gets seasick. He's just doing this to prove something to Pauline."

Cody whispered, "Because he wants to marry her?"

"Where'd you hear that?"

"I didn't. I just looked at him. Sam says that it's important to read a person's face. John's face says he's going to ask her to marry him soon."

I flashed Sam an admonishment. "Sam, read my face. You can't be serious. John is not right for Pauline. She knows nothing about him."

Cody said, "They've known each other for two and a half months. Since the other murder. Now they have two murders here in Door County in common. They're developing what's called a history together. Right, Sam?"

Sam shrugged.

I tried again. "Cody, John's not even as mature as you."

"He's in his fifties. I asked him. And Sam is two years older than you, and Dillon is six years older. You like them both, don't you? Despite them being older?"

Now Dillon and Sam were hiding smiles behind their hands. Even Dillon's dog was standing there, wagging his tail at me.

All this bonding among men was going too far, particularly if it was going to end up with my friend getting hurt by John Schultz. "Have all of you forgotten that John found Piers and Kelsey for this fudge contest and they could be murder suspects?"

Cody said, "But John doesn't fight. He won't murder Pauline."

I swallowed my shock yet again.

Dillon came to my rescue. "Where are the conflicting confectioners, by the way?"

"Sleeping in, I'm sure. I don't care. It's peaceful here." I turned back to Sam. "What are you up to with this expedition?"

"Living what I preach. We have to get along with people. And Cody invited me."

Cody said, "Dillon and Sam don't want to fight over you like the chefs do. I asked them both their intentions."

Dillon's dark eyes crackled with humor. Sam kept nodding like some bobblehead doll. This was so unlike Sam to put up with Dillon. But Sam would do anything for Cody and I could see now that Cody was playing matchmaker.

Dotty and Lois saved me. They came in with their arms loaded down with mounds of shiny, frilly, lacy fabric. The three men and Lucky Harbor drifted over to join John and desperate Pauline.

Dotty had a pink rosebud tucked in her short white hair behind an ear. "We're here with your surprise."

Lois also had a rose in her red hair. She foisted her armload of fluffy lace and satin fabric into my arms. "These are for you!"

Lace tickled my nose. I sneezed. "What are these things?"

"Aprons," Dotty said.

She placed her pile on my counter with great reverence. I tossed my pile on top. Dotty held up a gauzy pinafore apron with wide pink satin ruffle ribbons for ties at the waist. The shoulder straps were made from the same satin ruffles, with an added white lace overlay. The same lace and satin trimmed the entire skirt. It looked like something from a 1950s or 1960s television show. *The Dick Van Dyke Show* came to mind; my grandmother loved watching it in reruns.

Oohs and *aahs* went up from the women and girls next to the glass fudge cabinet.

Dotty said, "Try it on."

"Yes," said Lois, "it's perfect for you."

"I have aprons already," I said, grabbing the plain cotton chef's apron on a hook behind me.

Lois hustled behind the cash register and swiped it out of my hands. "Oh, sweetheart, we're here to cheer you up."

"I don't need cheering."

Pauline stepped up to the register. "Yes, you do. Try the darn thing on. It's cute."

I could tell she was eager to get a little revenge on me for my comments about John.

"Since when do I have to be cute?" I was about to disparage the pink fluffy bit of cloth when I saw the disheartened looks on the faces of Dotty and Lois. I plastered on a fake smile. "You two made all these, didn't you?"

They nodded.

Lois said, "Along with the other church ladies in our group. We want you and Door County to look good on camera for Mr. Schultz's TV show. I stayed up until midnight sewing. I almost fell asleep in church this morning. But with your lovely complexion, pink is you. With the summer sun's highlights, your hair is almost auburn." Lois held the pink apron up to my body and turned to Dotty. "Don't you think she looks like Audrey Hepburn in *Breakfast at Tiffany's*?"

Dotty nodded. "My mother and I watched that movie together when I was young. We rent it every Mother's Day now." Dotty teared up.

Lois said to me, "You're our Holly Golightly. That was the character's name in the movie, you know."

Gulp. These women were in their early sixties—and with quick calculations I realized they'd been maybe ten when they saw that 1961 classic romantic comedy movie. Somehow they were picturing me as Audrey Hepburn through the innocence of their formerly young eyes. Maybe this was good for me. Research on nostalgia has proven it has great powers for health and healing. Amused, I figured my stitched head would heal faster if I played along.

I put the apron over my plain white blouse and denim shorts. Pauline tied it in back.

A chorus of *oohs* and *aahs* preceded the women's applause. My face was flaming again. Flustered, I picked up an apron and thrust it at Pauline. It was a frilly pile of white lace with red roses on it, which matched her red sweatshirt and shorts.

Lois patted her red hair. "I'm partial to that one, too. Ava, it's made with Belgian lace I got long ago from your grandmother. We'd made aprons for all the servers for some Valentine's Day family dinner at St. Bernie's."

Pauline twirled in place. Then she shoved me around in a circle to model mine until I was dizzy. Giggles rippled through the shop.

Bethany emerged from the crowd to tie on a powder blue lace apron, and then a few other women joined us. We were soon modeling them for one another, laughing, and . . .

The men over in the bait shop—Sam, Dillon, Cody, John, and the other male customers—stood like statues with open mouths.

Then John licked his lips—lasciviously.

Sam blinked a lot, a crooked smile making him look drunk.

Cody kept nodding like a bobble head at Bethany.

Dillon hiked an eyebrow in a way that was akin to a bull pawing the earth.

An unwanted sizzle zipped up and down my body.

Before I could untie the sash of my apron, chatter broke loose. The women and girls and men were all buying things with gusto. There was a lineup of men at the fudge counter, something I'd never seen before.

The aprons had changed the axis of the earth. I heard stories about aprons of grandmothers with pockets filled with candy, about traditional appliquéd aprons used at Christmas dinners, and more tales about serviceable flour sack aprons used during threshing season; still more aprons were used to shell peas on a porch on a summer evening.

This evolved into sharing fudge recipes their grandmothers made. I made notes.

I hauled out Lloyd's cookbooks to let people take a look. The women saw Ruth Mueller's name. Some promised to ask at home to see what their relatives remembered about the Muellers. One man thought he recalled his grandfather saying something about the bait shop being used during Prohibition to hide booze. But other men and women argued no way would a Mueller be caught up in that.

As if on cue, Mercy Fogg showed up. She marched right up to me. "I want to talk with you about Lloyd's murderer. Who happens to be in your employ."

Chapter 11

Mercy looked evil, dressed in a uniform black jacket over a gray blouse and gray pants.

"Want to try on an apron, Mercy? How about some coffee?" The last cup had been in the pot so long I hoped she'd taste its bitterness and flee. Mean of me, but I still couldn't forgive Mercy for reporting Lucky Harbor's presence in my shop to the state health inspectors.

Mercy had a small digital camera around her neck. A button on her jacket said BIRD PEOPLE ARE THE REAL TWEETERS.

"You're here to buy fudge for your birding group today?"

Mercy huffed. "No. I was up at seven busing them around Door County, but that crap is over with. Dumped them off for a picnic lunch they're having at Peninsula State Park. That's why I'm here, honey bunny."

"My name is Ava."

"Ava Mathilde Oosterling. Yeah, yeah. I'm Mercy Annabelle Fogg. Now that we've got the niceties over with, I want to tell you that Lloyd's murderer—your stupid girlie guest chef you hired—was on the lighthouse tower this a.m. at daybreak. It was almost like she was a bird singing about her guilt."

Ah, it was Kelsey, and not Cody, she was calling a murderer. "Singing? On the lighthouse?"

"You heard me. What's-her-face was up there. Let me show you."

Mercy turned on her digital camera, then advanced the photos until she found one that showed the pink glow of sunrise on the vertical, squared edge of the Eagle Bluff Lighthouse tower. At the top, behind the railing, stood a slim person with blond hair. I saw no yellow crime scene tape around the perimeter at the bottom and asked Mercy about it.

"Kelsey King probably took it down herself."

I stared at the photo, incredulous. "Maybe that's not her. It's hard to tell one blonde from the next."

Mercy's blue eyes burned into me. "I've got blond hair. You're saying you can't tell me from Miss Skinny Bones?"

"Point taken, Mercy." The photo scared me, to be frank. This was a bold move to do at a crime scene. "Did you talk to her?"

"No. We were in the woods and we were headed the other way on Tramper's Delight Trail. I was last on the trail and heard singing behind me. I looked back and there she was."

"She was really singing?"

"Man, you don't listen, do you? Talking to you is hard work."

I pretty much deserved that remark. "Why did you rush to tell me this? Why not the sheriff? Or did you call Jordy already?"

"No, I didn't. I . . . I forgot my wallet this morning with my driver's license."

A tickle came to my insides. I'd caught "Miss Perfect" Mercy Fogg in an indiscretion? I should have been jubilant. But darn, I went soft and felt sorry for her. Hadn't we all forgotten our driver's license at least once and driven illegally? Besides, maybe if I gave her this one she'd go easy on me the next time she caught me in one of my many mistakes or spotted Dillon's dog licking the glass case or putting a paw on the edge of the marble table.

The photo didn't convince me this was Kelsey King,

though. "She was supposed to be working late at a new vegetarian restaurant I hooked her up with called Legumes and 'Toes in Egg Harbor. She'd be sleeping in." The 'Toes stood for Potatoes.

"Oh, she was at Legs and Toes. But not cooking. I was there with Libby last night. They had a woman folksinger, but after she started, Kelsey came out of the kitchen, grabbed the guitar right from the woman, and began strumming and singing."

"Yikes. That assignment was supposed to keep her out of trouble."

"Afraid not. The other singer stalked off."

"Was Kelsey any good?"

"Nobody barfed up their dinner."

I squinted at the photo on the camera again. My body went cold. "We have to call the sheriff, in case she's still out there." I pulled up the ruffled apron skirt and retrieved my phone out of my shorts pocket. "I need to get out there. To talk to her."

"You think she . . . ?" Mercy used a hand to mimic Kelsey diving to her death.

"Mercy, please don't kid around. It's slippery up there. Accidents happen. I'll never live with myself if something happens to her."

I tried Kelsey's phone number. It flipped me to voice mail. I left a message for her to call me. "She's obviously not dealing well with me or this fudge contest."

"What did you do to her?"

I called nine-one-one. When I got off the phone, I realized my dilemma. I had no vehicle. I raced to Pauline and asked her to drive me out to the lighthouse.

"Sorry. John and I walked over here from his motel."

Ugh again. She'd stayed with Mr. Hairy Toes at his motel last night. "Can you take over the registers?"

"What're you up to?"

"Kelsey's in trouble. Doing stupid things. Maybe because of me. She's out at the lighthouse."

"Doing what?"

"Playing detective maybe."

"But you were suspicious of her."

"I still am. She's crazy and unpredictable. Pauline, this is serious. We have to hurry."

Mercy said, "I'm going back to the park to pick up the bird-watchers."

She was insinuating I could ride with her. Never.

"No, I can borrow my grandmother's SUV." But when I phoned, Grandma was gone and there was no answer. Obviously, she was still in church or somewhere with her phone turned off, maybe over at Libby Mueller's house.

I knew that Dotty and Lois weren't far away after leaving the fudge shop, so I phoned Dotty. They were happy to take over the cash registers. I felt a disaster coming on, but I had to trust them anyway.

Within the next minute Pauline and I were seated behind Mercy as she drove the yellow school bus a bit too fast out of the harbor's parking lot. Squirrels dove under nearby cars.

Mercy turned onto Main Street in Fishers' Harbor, slowing into the twenty-five-mile-an-hour speed limit and coming to a dead stop in summer tourist traffic.

"Can't you push it a little, Mercy?"

She couldn't. But it gave me a moment to consider other suspects in Lloyd's murder—the people who rented his properties on Main Street. They included a collection of artists in a couple of buildings, plus Travis Klubertanz and his wife, who ran the market, and Milton Hendrickson—the elderly gentleman who ran The Wise Owl Bookstore. Pauline knew the artists because they often taught art over at the school; she said they seemed solid and happy with their rent arrangement with Lloyd. I knew Travis; a busy young father working a small farm plus a grocery and with little kids didn't have time for murder. I also couldn't imagine elderly Milton tossing anything heavier than a book off the lighthouse tower. Milton was also part of the group of guys that played cards with my grandfather and Lloyd.

We weaved around Dillon's construction equipment.

Pauline asked, "When will the construction ever end?"

Mercy and I said simultaneously, "We have two seasons in Wisconsin. Winter and construction." It was a common saying.

As Mercy navigated the bus northward to the edge of town, I worried about Kelsey King out at the park. Or whoever it was. It didn't make sense that if she was up late cooking or singing at Legumes and 'Toes, she'd be up this morning early to go to the tower.

I must have mumbled that out loud because Pauline said, "Unless she was snooping around and making sure they didn't find her lined paper and crayons."

"Maria and Jordy surely would have found those things by now."

Mercy said, "Libby told me all about the note."

"You two are good friends," I said, hoping for more information. "Even though there's a good difference in your ages. She's much older than you." I said that to butter up Mercy. Libby was in her early sixties, only slightly older than Mercy. "How'd you and Libby meet?"

"On a gambling bus heading for the Oneida Casino."

"You still go?" I recalled how sad the gambling had made Lloyd.

"Not so much. We go over to the Troubled Trout now and then. You been there lately?"

"No."

Mercy eased the bus around a car being parallel-parked. "You should go. You'd be surprised what you can put money on these days."

Pauline said, "The last time Ava gambled, she ended up with a bigamist, a divorce, and then an annulment and no money."

"But I learned to write TV scripts and make fudge," I countered. "And I can navigate the L.A. freeways." I turned to Mercy, or more correctly, the back of her blond head. "You'd enjoy the challenge of driving a bus out in L.A., Mercy."

"No, thanks."

I agreed with her. Five blocks and only a couple of lanes of traffic in our little town was a picnic compared to clogged six-lane freeways.

We beat the local officers to the park.

The yellow tape was gone from around the lighthouse, just as Mercy's photo had showed. The tape was balled up under a bush near the split-rail fence.

I headed to the solid green front door of the gift shop, where I almost fell on my butt after trying the doorknob. The place was locked. "She must be here yet." I slapped on the door and yelled, "Kelsey?"

Pauline asked, "You're assuming she had a key and just waltzed in?"

"She got up to the top of that tower somehow. Let's go around back."

Mercy said, "I'm not going. Libby told me all about how Lloyd had looked."

The vision of Lloyd splayed on his back with his arm crooked and under him came back to me. I shook off goose pimples forming. "Pauline, come on."

Pauline looked down at me. "Maybe we should wait for Jordy."

"Oh, for heaven's sake. Kelsey might still be up on the tower and need talking down." I ran around back.

Pauline and Mercy trotted behind me, our footfalls crunching in the gravel.

There was no one on the ground, to our relief.

We looked up. We didn't see anyone, but that didn't mean Kelsey wasn't crouched on the outdoor deck on the other side and trying to avoid us.

"Kelsey!" I called again.

There was no response, but then Mercy said, "There!" She pointed toward the nearby woods and Tramper's Delight Trail.

A figure was disappearing into the brush. I took up the chase.

* * *

A siren wailed in the distance as Pauline and I raced down the park's woodland trail. Mercy stayed behind.

After a small bend in the trail, I glimpsed Kelsey or whoever it was duck into the understory.

Pauline said, puffing beside me, "We're going to lose her."

"No, we're not."

But we did. Thick ferns and brush and prickly downed fir trees pushed back at us. We came to a halt amid mosquitoes and black flies attacking us for their lunch.

A rustling from afar put me in motion again. "Come on." As I pushed at an opening in the brush, I called out, "Kelsey? Stop! Kelsey, we can work this out!"

We scrambled through thorny berry bushes snagging our clothes and loose hair.

"Let's go back," Pauline said. "Let her go."

"No, Pauline. We're closing in." I could still hear branches slapping in the near distance ahead of us.

We came to a deer trail where the footing was easier. We were huffing pretty hard by now, but I forced myself to run faster. We had to pause to step over downed limbs and even a small birch tree trunk, rotted just enough to be shedding its white bark in sheets that made footing slippery. Something was grunting and flailing about in the woods not too far from us.

"Kelsey?"

In a small clearing we came upon Lucky Harbor playing with an old rope maybe five feet in length. He whipped it about as if it were a snake he was trying to kill. As soon as he saw us, he barreled at me, leaping up on me with his front paws on my blouse, leaving green grass stains. He was wet and covered in cockleburs.

"What are you doing here?" I asked him. "You're supposed to be on a boat fishing and finding shipwrecks in Lake Michigan."

Pauline cried out, "Something's happened to John. They had to come back because John's sick, or worse. I need to get back. Crap, I left my purse on the bus."

"Pauline, get a grip. I'll call Dillon."

My phone was always in my pocket. When I called Dillon, I found out that Lucky Harbor had jumped ship right in the harbor as usual to chase frogs. Dillon had been just about to call me to watch for him. The men were okay and the *Super Catch I* was closing in on a shallow shipwreck site in Lake Michigan. John had had his first diving lesson and had done well.

Pauline held a hand over her heart while breathing hard from our exertion. "John isn't careful, you know. He doesn't think things through."

I was picking burrs out of Lucky Harbor's curly fur and tossing them far into the underbrush. "That's an understatement. What is it exactly that you see in him? You two are such opposites."

"Maybe that's it."

"Is this a serious relationship?" I let the dog go for a romp.

"What are you getting at?"

I couldn't bear to broach the "marriage" word. "I was going to say something about messy, sloppy John not deserving you, but you're more a mess right now than he usually is."

"You, too."

Our shorts had threads torn from them, our legs and arms were striped with bloody scratches, and her red hoodie had been plastered with some sort of sticky weed seeds.

The dog brought the rope to me. By now it was pretty slobbery. I told him, "No. Drop it."

He did.

Pauline said, "Dillon's done a good job with him. You, too. You make a nice threesome." She had one of her devil looks.

"Stop it, Pauline."

"If Laura and I can't get you to pick a date via picking fabric swatches, then maybe we can use this dog. Dogs are good judges of people."

"If that's true, I must remind you that the dog keeps running *away* from Dillon, not *to* Dillon. Shouldn't that tell you something?"

"You're going to have to choose somebody for that prom next Saturday night."

"If there is one. Kelsey is nuts and maybe she murdered Lloyd Mueller because she was upset about this fudge contest and Lloyd spurning her overtures to hook up."

"Nobody murders somebody for refusing to have sex with them."

"But what if they did have sex and she was afraid Lloyd was going to tell somebody about it and disqualify her from the fudge contest? He almost told both of us about them having sex."

"He said she was 'friendly' and then changed the subject. For a guy his age that word doesn't mean sex necessarily."

As usual, schoolteacher Pauline was right. I began heading back the way we came. Lucky Harbor bounced ahead of us, his head barely popping above the tall ferns.

Pauline said, "Being on the tower this morning was awful risky because it was so public. Why would she do that?"

"Maybe she's trying to make it look like she's nuts so she'll get off in court."

"It's all far-fetched. That couldn't have been her on that tower. Mercy is a known liar and manipulator."

I agreed with Pauline. Then I got mad. "That darn woman got us out here for nothing. That was probably some dumb kid from the campground we just chased."

It wasn't long before we were back on the comfortable hiking trail. Lucky Harbor ran hard ahead of us, halting here and there to sniff something.

Pauline said, "What kind of nose does that dog have?"

I smiled at her. "My thoughts exactly after I found Lloyd. The dog was everywhere smelling the bushes, the grounds, everything. I'm betting he saw Lloyd fall."

"So if Lloyd's death is a murder, that dog might have seen the murderer, too?"

"Maybe. Or maybe not if it was early morning and pretty dark yet."

"Could he sniff around for the box for us?"

We were walking faster now. The dog was ahead of us, loping toward the trailhead.

"Nifty idea," I said, "but we don't have anything from the box to let the dog smell."

"But you have the hole in your fudge shop's storage room floor. He could smell around in that."

"That's brilliant, Pauline."

"Thanks, Sherlock. Just call me Watson."

"Not Sherlock. I'm Poirot. He was a Belgian detective."

"Did Poirot have a buddy? Who am I?" Pauline asked.

"Hastings. Poirot's buddy was Captain Arthur Hastings of the police force. Hastings had a penchant for women with auburn hair."

"You make me sound like a lesbian for liking you."

"Liking women might be better than liking John."

"There you go again. You know little about him. You're not being a very supportive best friend lately."

"All right. Sorry." But as her best friend I was wondering about John's background. I'd trusted him to set up the fudge contest and here we were, chasing after one of John's choices in chefs who was running away from us in the woods and who could be a murderer.

As we headed out of the woods, I saw that the bus was gone. "Damn. She left us."

"That woman is nasty. And she has my purse in that bus. How could she dump us like that?"

"Because Jordy's here."

A few yards from where the bus had been parked, Jordy's tall frame leaned against his squad car, his regulation-brimmed brown hat leveling his dark gaze at me.

Chapter 12

For having a runner's trim body, Jordy could look mighty muscular and imposing when he wanted to, like now when his gaze pinioned me. "What the hell is going on out here? My dispatcher calls me about a possible suicide in progress and I end up getting run off Shore Road in the park by a yellow school bus going like a bat outta hell."

"That was Mercy Fogg. You didn't ticket her?"

"No, because I was in a hurry to get here to stop a suicide. I don't suppose you're going to take a dive off the lighthouse and make my future bright."

Pauline smirked, but I didn't find my own demise all that funny. The sun was high in the sky now, deepening the shade under Jordy's hat brim as he stepped toward me. My stomach acid crashed about like waves on the lake hitting the shoreline not far from us.

"Jordy—"

"Sheriff Tollefson. Now tell me what's going on out here."

"Mercy Fogg told us she saw Kelsey King on top of the tower early this morning when they were bird-watching."

"What was she doing?"

"Mercy was escorting a birding group."

"Not her. Miss King."

"Kelsey was singing."

Jordy swiped at his face, as if he wanted to wipe away the

vision of me. "I'll assume this is leading to something. How early was this?"

"Probably eight or nine o'clock. Earlier maybe. I didn't ask Mercy for an exact time, but it wasn't too long ago. It was near the end of their birding."

"It's almost noon now. So you think Kelsey King stayed up on the tower for hours waiting for you to come out here now to watch her commit suicide?"

We were interrupted by Lucky Harbor running helter-skelter between us and around us. This time, his antics clicked with me.

"He wants us to follow him, Sheriff."

I trotted fast after Lucky Harbor, who had already rushed in a brown blur behind the lighthouse. The dog was performing nose-to-ground figure eights all the way to the rock wall that protected people from falling down the steep bluff.

We raced to the waist-high wall. I expected to see another body. But there wasn't any. Red-winged blackbirds rocketed off cattails far below us. A sailboat passed by; four people on it waved. We waved back.

Jordy said, "I need to get going. I have an appointment to see Libby Mueller at noon, and Professor Faust called me about something the two of them found earlier today at the construction site in Fishers' Harbor."

He started walking away, but Lucky Harbor charged to a lilac bush toward the west of the lighthouse and growled. All of us headed to the bush.

Pauline said, "There's a wad of paper in there."

Jordy said, "Stand back. Don't touch or disturb anything. Hang on to the dog."

The dog had slipped his collar, so I grabbed a handful of the fluffy brown fur on the back of his neck and hoped he didn't mind.

Jordy peered at the bush from several angles. "Not sure how Maria could've missed this. We scoured this place until eight o'clock last night."

With a tweezers and a small plastic bag he withdrew from a pocket, Jordy extracted the note, took a look, then sealed it before we could read it.

My instincts told me he was hiding it purposely from me. "How bad is it?"

Pauline and I crowded around him, putting on the pressure.

Jordy read it aloud. *"One down, one to go."*

Pauline said, "It looks like the same printing as the other note. Nice and neat again. Calm."

"As in calm about killing me!" I shrieked.

Lucky Harbor plopped down on top of my shoes, then leaned against my scratched-up legs. He looked up at me as if saying, "I'm here for you. I'll protect you."

I said, "Kelsey has to be the one behind all this."

Jordy asked, "You say it was her out here just now, though we have no proof. Any motive for her to do this?"

"Other than she thinks this fudge contest is stupid and she hates me and she's weird?"

Pauline said, "She doesn't hate you. She hates Piers."

"Maybe she's trying to blame this on Piers?"

Jordy said, "Trying to frame Piers Molinsky for murder is a serious charge."

I told Jordy in rapid-fire fashion what I knew about Piers trying to bribe our village president, Erik Gustafson, on Tuesday, and that Lloyd had told me about that on Friday. I added, "I'm pretty sure Piers knows Kelsey was trying to bribe Lloyd by using sex." I explained what I saw on Friday evening. "There's no love lost among them all."

"Where can I find Piers today? At your shop?"

"Later, yes, but right now you can likely find him at Laura Rousseau's shop, the Luscious Ladle, in Sister Bay. I gave him the task of coming up with new recipes for his famous muffins that would go well with chunks of my Cinderella Pink Fudge in them."

"How did you convince him to do that?"

My face grew hot under Jordy's watchful eyes, but I admitted, "I lied. I said John wanted to videotape a special segment on him with the new recipe."

Pauline said, "What a brilliant, yummy idea! Your cherry-vanilla fudge chunked up in . . . oh, I'll eat any flavor, but red velvet cake muffins with your fudge in the middle is just chewy chocolates colliding in colorful collusion."

"You're prepping a lesson on the letter C, aren't you?"

She nodded.

Jordy shook his head, but he was licking his lips. "I'll visit him later. What else ya got?"

"Professor Alex Faust said Erik told him he'd speak with Lloyd about holding off on the real estate deal so that the town could save the historic buildings on Duck Marsh Street."

"Including your cabin?"

"I'm only renting, but yeah."

Pauline offered, "There's been a rumor that a helipad is going in, and even Ava's grandparents may have to move and maybe the harbor would be redone with Oosterlings' Bait, Bobbers and Belgian Fudge and Beer being bumped off."

Jordy said, "That sounds like a motive for Gil and Sophie to wish bad things on Lloyd."

Oops. I gaped briefly at Pauline for her faux pas, then said, "My grandfather was his best friend, Jordy. But there have to be people jealous of Lloyd or mad enough at him to murder him. Somebody hauled him or forced him to the top of the lighthouse. The murderer was making a statement. Which brings me to Mercy."

"You can't keep blaming her because she's a little different," Jordy said.

"But you just saw her tear out of here, Sheriff, and Lloyd told me she couldn't be trusted. You already know she wrote threatening notes to Lloyd that I saw in that missing box. Is there any news on that missing box?"

"No, but—" He glanced at his watch. "I'm fifteen minutes late meeting Libby Mueller and the professor."

"We'll go along."

"Why?"

"Because we need a ride, first of all. You'd leave us stranded out here?"

"You have a cell phone. Call somebody."

Pauline said, "This little episode of stranding us could get out and affect your reelection."

The sheriff and I stared at her. Being impolite wasn't like Pauline.

Jordy said, "You're threatening me?"

Pauline shrank a little, more like her old self, so I stepped up and said, "She's not feeling well because Mercy stole her purse. Pauline practically has a whole year's supply for her classroom in that thing. It's worth a million. We'll need to make a lengthy report if we don't get it back."

Jordy's facial expression then reminded me of a kaleidoscope inverting its fractured images a dozen times before it came into a focus. "Both of you, in the car. Your dog, too. All of you in back, behind the barrier. And no funny business. I still can't believe all this trouble over a fudge contest."

Lucky Harbor boinked his nose into Jordy's pants at knee level. I handed Jordy some Goldfish crackers and said, "He thinks 'fudge' means 'treat.' Do you think he'd make a good police tracking dog? Could you give Pauline and me some pointers on how to train him to track killers? You guys must have some handbook on that, right?"

Jordy fed the dog his crackers, then hustled us into the backseat, slamming the door shut a bit harder than I suspected was normal.

We found Pauline's purse dumped at the corner of Shore Road and Highway 42, right next to the stop sign.

Instead of stopping at Libby's, Sheriff Tollefson took us back to my fudge shop. Jordy said his visit to Libby was official and he couldn't have us along. That sparked my curiosity, but he refused to answer my questions. Was Libby under suspicion? Probably not for real, but she of all people might know of a personal enemy of Lloyd, if there were any besides Mercy.

When we arrived in the downtown, about to turn off on the side street leading to the fudge shop, the sheriff spotted Libby standing with Professor Faust on the sidewalk a block ahead of us. They were next to Dillon's white construction truck, looking into the open truck bed. Jordy turned off his blinker for our turn and then proceeded straight ahead, parking in a space reserved for the construction workers.

He said, "I'll assume you two can walk to the shop from here."

He could assume that, but that's not what we did. Lucky Harbor struck off for the lake, though, while Pauline and I pretended to be looking in a store window.

Libby said to Jordy, "We stopped in the bookstore. The professor came out while I was finishing my purchase. He found it."

"Found what?" Jordy asked.

"The rifle. It's there." She pointed toward Dillon's truck. "That's my ex-husband's rifle. Dillon Rivers stole one of Lloyd's rifles."

"How do you know it wasn't a gift?" Jordy peered into the truck bed.

"Lloyd has a collection that's priceless. He wouldn't give it away."

Jordy slipped on latex gloves. Amid *thunks* and *clanks* he nudged tools or supplies around. He lifted the rifle gingerly by the end of the barrel.

Both Pauline and I looked away toward the window in front of us, our reflection showing our shock.

Jordy bagged the rifle, then busied himself talking with the professor and Libby. Pauline and I took off. My wobbly legs could barely get me around the corner. I stopped to lean against the building. Pauline did the same.

I whispered, "What the heck is Dillon doing with one of Lloyd's rifles?"

Pauline whispered back, "I can't even guess, but he's not going to like the greeting he's going to get when he and the others return from that diving and fishing excursion."

The bait-and-fudge shop seemed oddly normal when Pauline and I arrived close to twelve thirty. Bethany was there with girlfriends, with Butterflies in tow, who screamed with glee when they saw their teacher. They hugged Pauline—or more accurately, Pauline's legs—dragging her over to the children's table in the far corner.

My grandmother was at the shop, helping Lois and Dotty, which likely accounted for the place not becoming a church bazaar. But Grandma Sophie seemed subdued, while everybody else made a fuss about my tattered clothing and scratches.

Dotty picked a burr out of my hair that Pauline had missed during our ride in the squad car. "You see?" Dotty said. "Here you are again, a mess."

Lois agreed, laughing. "Do you realize every time we see you, you've skinned your knees or worse? This is not the look you want for TV."

I washed up quickly in the restroom in back, wondering about Grandma's mood. Out in front, Lois made me don an apron again, a frilly pink one. My stitches were bothering me, so I skipped my usual ponytail and held my hair back from my face with barrettes instead. I looked ready to star in a 1960s sitcom.

Grandma was dusting a back shelf, her back to me. Her demeanor was worrying me. I asked her with forced cheer, "Know what show this reminds me of, Grandma?"

"Dick Van Dyke Show."

A smile flickered for only a second. She got busy handing out lunch from a picnic basket. Grandma had made one of my grandfather's favorite sandwiches—peanut butter made with her homemade sweet pickles—in anticipation of him coming in soon aboard his crippled boat. She was concerned about him, but there seemed to be a deeper undercurrent. Grandpa had gotten stranded many times in the past.

I took the peanut butter–pickle sandwiches over to Pauline and the Butterflies. Grandma handed out cartons of cold milk. There was nothing better than a PB&P sandwich with cold milk. Except for fudge with ice-cold milk. I sneaked a piece of Cinderella Pink Fudge, imagining it in the middle of Piers's red velvet cake muffins. My taste buds already predicted a savory sensation in my future. Unless he was arrested. It seemed like everyone in the world around me was about to be arrested, Dillon included.

I put aside telling Grandma about our adventure in Peninsula State Park. With gossipmongers Lois and Dotty there, I had to be discreet. I lied and said Pauline and I had to chase down the dog that had gotten away from Dillon. I'd even gulped and said that Mercy had been kind enough to give us a ride.

I took Lucky Harbor over to his usual place by the upright cooler that stood against the far wall of the bait shop area. I didn't even have to tie him this time. He was so used to our routine by now that he circled in place a few times and then lay down on his own.

"Has Grandpa called lately?" I asked.

"Probably."

Probably? Grandma Sophie had just finished ringing up a carton of worms for a couple of men. After they left, she ran a hand through her cloud of white hair, shifting into a broodier mood.

"What's wrong, Grandma?"

"Your grandfather is going to lose his business if he doesn't do something about a boat."

"There must be used fishing trawlers or used engines for sale that would work well enough for his needs," I said, getting busy making a fresh pot of coffee behind Grandpa's register counter.

"He says there aren't. They all cost too much. Even the

little fishing rigs. And don't even speak of an engine. He's determined to bully what he has into working."

I went back to the kitchen to fill the carafe with water, then returned. "Why can't he borrow money like everybody else? If he has a new boat, he'll make more money than he is now because people always like riding in a new boat. He can advertise it that way."

"Ava honey, I've told him that until I'm blue in the face."

"His boat is named after you. I think he feels emotional about it."

"Oh, fiddle-faddle. It's not like getting rid of the boat is getting rid of me. And he could transfer the name to the new boat because this one will be scrapped. No, he's just being stubborn. He's paid cash for things all his life, and he can't stand the idea of being in somebody's debt." Grandma grabbed a spritzer bottle of disinfectant and scoured the already clean counter.

I was worrying about Dillon and the new development with the rifle, but I kept that to myself. Fortunately, it wasn't long before a towboat brought in Grandpa and his fishermen. When the fishermen walked into the shop, they gravitated right to me to talk about being stuck in the middle of Lake Michigan for most of the morning. I wasn't sure why I warranted their attention, but they had me packaging lots of fudge in several flavors while they tasted them all.

Grandma and Grandpa hugged, but it was a brief hug. I could tell that Grandma wanted to "discuss" the matter of the boat later.

The men eating my fudge in front of me at my register kept on chatting with me about the weather and more on Lake Michigan. When I went to check the coffeepot behind Grandpa's counter, they followed me, still talking.

Tourists piled in then for the one o'clock fudge-making show. A little boy said, "Look, Mommy, she's wearing an apron costume just like the naked woman in Daddy's magazine I found under the bed."

Tittering rippled through the shop.

Pauline sidled up to me. "Now you know why those men are so enamored with you. It's the French maid syndrome. Men like women in aprons."

"Pauline, it's only a silly apron."

"Go with it. I don't know why I didn't think of this before for the adult prom. You're going to have dates lining up now."

I brushed off the silliness. I began putting fudge ingredients in a copper kettle. Piers and Kelsey hadn't shown up, so I had all six empty kettles staring up at me, sparkling under the lights. I suspected Piers might be talking with the sheriff by now. Would Dillon be next? Kelsey was likely soaking in a tub to soothe her scratches and mosquito bites, if she was indeed the person we had chased in the park.

After Bethany and her friends left with the Butterflies, I thought Pauline would help me, but she ventured outside to sit at one of the tables. She was looking across the harbor and into the lake, waiting for John obviously. I stirred my sugar, cream, vanilla and cherry juice flavorings, and white chocolate in the copper kettle. It was pitiful to watch her pine for that charlatan. But my heart teased me with a question. If Dillon or Sam had said they were going scuba diving today for the *first time* in Lake Michigan—a huge lake that had swallowed many men over the centuries—would I be worried? I would be freakin' terrified! Was Sam foolish enough to do that? Dillon had scuba dived before, but certainly his skills must be rusty? Or not? What had he been doing during the eight years we hadn't connected? Now I was staring off through the window and across the harbor, too, concerned.

I flipped the long wooden paddle around in the gooey pink fudge ingredients extra hard, which sent a big dollop up to the ceiling. The tourists hooted and clapped profusely. Embarrassed, I was sure my skin tone matched the pink in my apron.

Settling back into my routine, I realized that my outlook on love was all wrong still. Lois and Dotty were right—I wasn't grown up. But Pauline seemed to think I'd find true love by matching fabric swatches to eye colors, or wearing an apron, or by dancing with a date at the adult prom this coming Saturday. Was it that simple? Would I meet the man of my dreams by Saturday night? Pauline believed in fairy tales even more than I did. I'd tried writing fairy tales for about seven years for a television show; I wasn't all that good at it. But if I didn't begin living my own fairy tale, how could I possibly justify creating and selling my Fairy Tale Fudge line?

I was saved from these thoughts when a flash of cardinal red flew away from the window. The bird was actually Pauline launching from her chair to race up the docks and into John Schultz's arms. She was taller, but he still picked her off her feet and swung her around. Talk about a movie scene.

I craned my neck around the heads in the crowd until I could see first Dillon, then Sam coming down the docks, too. If I were free at the moment, whose arms would I race into first? I didn't know! But I was worried for Dillon. I watched for the sheriff to show up at any moment.

I cranked the fudge ingredients harder, trying to conjure answers to everything, including my love life, with the aromatic cauldron of Belgian chocolate, thick Holstein cream, and Door County cherries.

Cody was right behind the other men, holding up a big fish that he was showing off to Pauline.

Something happened to me right in that moment that I hadn't felt since my divorce—shame. And bone-aching lonesomeness. I, too, wanted to rush out and hug and be hugged. But I couldn't because I had feelings for both men and wouldn't be able to choose which one to hug first. That's the part that shamed me. How can you love two men equally? Was I now a bigamist-of-the-heart? I was no better than Dillon Rivers, and certainly undeserving of Sam Peterson.

Then the sheriff appeared outside. My heart felt as if it fell out of my chest, maybe tumbling all the way into the vat in front of me. I watched as Sheriff Tollefson took Dillon aside and they talked. Then the two men left, walking out of view as if my window were a movie and they'd walked offscreen. Panic hit me with such a force that my hands instantly sweated on the tall ladle and I slipped forward a notch. Somebody gasped. I recovered, plastered on a smile for the tourists, and kept stirring my fudge.

By Monday morning the conundrum concerning love wasn't important anymore. I'd left several messages for Dillon, with no response. And Gilpa had tromped through the shop late—unusual for him—at seven o'clock. He gave me a cursory "Hey, A.M." as he packed up his tools, grumbling. Then he headed to his dead trawler. The cowbell gave a dull *clunk* in his wake. A misty rain peppered the tables outside and Gilpa, but he seemed to take no heed.

Frustrated, I donned a dandelion yellow bibbed apron on purpose to try to bring sunshine inside the shop. Sooner or later Gilpa would have to come back in for more of his beloved coffee. I made a new pot, spiced extra dark with cocoa, just the way Grandpa liked it. But he didn't return; I had to handle soggy customers alone.

My father called me about an hour later. A phone call from Peter Oosterling was rare, especially during milking time. "What's up, Dad?"

"Honey, your grandmother just called me, crying."

"Oh my gosh, what happened? Did she break a leg again? I'm heading right over."

"Hold on. The news is worse. She said Mercy Fogg called early this morning to tell her that your grandma and grandpa don't own the bait-and-fudge shop."

I sighed, because Mercy was a liar and troublemaker. But now I knew why Grandpa was in such a foul mood. "It's all made up, Dad."

"Mercy says that she holds the title to the shop. She says Lloyd gave it to her long ago."

This was beginning to sound serious. My mouth went dry. "Mercy can't possibly own our shop."

"It has to do with some way the real estate deal was fashioned years ago with Lloyd. Mercy might also own the cabin your grandparents are living in, since Lloyd had also sold that to your grandpa. You need to get over to your grandma's house right away, sweetie. She's very upset with your grandpa. I'll be there with your mother as soon as we finish the milking. Where's your grandpa?"

Could it be that this news was true? Why else would Grandpa practically ignore me and head straight to his boat? That's where he did all his thinking. An ache constricted my chest.

It took me a moment to realize Cody Fjelstad was standing right in front of me. "Miss Oosterling? Miss Oosterling! We're missing a bunch of inventory again. Do you think Verona shoplifted more stuff?" Cody must have come in through the back door and I never noticed in my agitated state.

I said, "The Butterflies were here yesterday. But it was crowded. Maybe it wasn't Verona."

"Should I call the church ladies to have them bring more homemade dolls and dresses to replenish the supply before your one o'clock fudge-making show?"

I wasn't listening. I whipped off the fancy apron I was wearing, not feeling the cheer of yellow anymore. "Sounds like an excellent plan, Cody. You're in charge."

"Thanks, Miss Oosterling!"

I ran through the back of the shop and then raced in the rain to my grandmother's house across Duck Marsh Street. I had to make sure Mercy Fogg wasn't stealing our shop or busting up my family.

Chapter 13

Grandmother Sophie wasn't crying or swearing. It was worse. She was throwing together a Belgian rice pie, slinging rice all over the kitchen. It was crunchy underfoot and dangerous to walk. Some of the rice had made it into the pan of water to cook. I grabbed a broom to collect the rest and throw it away, though my grandmother's floor was the kind you truly can eat from because it was so clean.

"Grandma, I'm sure it's a mistake."

"A mistake? Mercy and Lloyd were in cahoots together. They conspired to somehow take over the whole town."

"Lloyd never liked Mercy. I have proof."

"What proof?"

Oh dear.

I had to tell Grandpa's secret. "Grandpa showed me some letters and things hidden in a box at the shop— "

"What box? He didn't tell me about a box."

Oh boy.

"It was just a box of old things, but it had letters from Mercy threatening Lloyd. She wanted some of Libby's things back. Grandpa hid it for Lloyd as a favor."

She shook the pan of rice and water on the stove, which did nothing for the rice or water but seemed to give Grandma Sophie time to form civil words. "Where's this box?"

"I lost it in my truck accident on Saturday. Somebody stole it right from the scene."

"Does your grandfather know about this?"

Oh, poop.

I made Grandma Sophie sit at the kitchen table, where I filled her in on everything, including Mercy playing a trick on us at the park.

When I got done, Grandma said, "She's the author of those notes."

"Maybe. If she is, we can certainly sue her or do something that will get the bait shop back and save your house. If any of that gossip is true. But she's a chronic liar, Grandma. She's lonely and needs attention."

Tears welled in Grandma's dark eyes. Her fluffy lively white hair seemed to droop. She rubbed her garden-roughened hands. "Why didn't your grandpa tell me any of this? That old buffalo really gets my goat."

I covered her hands with mine. "Grandpa always means well, Grandma."

An hour later my parents and I sat around the kitchen table with my grandparents. The rice had been cooked and sat on the stove, waiting to be combined with its eggs and cream and put into a piecrust.

Grandpa told us he'd bought the bait shop years ago on a land contract from Lloyd, but had skipped several payments over the past five years in order to cover the taxes on it and the house. The house was paid off and not in arrears on its taxes, he was "pretty sure." In other words, he wasn't sure. My parents and I exchanged stunned gazes.

Grandma walked out of the room without a word.

The old buffalo was in the proverbial doghouse.

I knew very little about land contracts, but they are common in farm country. Much land changes hands using land contracts because you don't need to have a down payment. Such a contract is like buying furniture from one of those "rent to buy" places. Sooner or later, after a bunch of payments, you own the sofa, or in our case, the land. But if you skip payments, the land—or business—can revert to the original owner. So all your years of payments can be for naught if you're derelict or negligent. Right now Grandpa looked like both.

He sat at the kitchen table, picking at the black motor oil in the cracks of his hands. His red-plaid shirt rolled up at the sleeves was still drenched from the rain. His thick silver hair was smashed to his scalp in places while some sprigs of it were springing up as they dried.

"Dad," my father said, "how could you let this happen?"

My rib cage hurt from the pounding of my heart for Gilpa.

His thick fingers tapped the table, as if tapping an SOS. He was red in the face, as if he were about to explode. That scared me. Did his silence mean Mercy was right? Had Grandpa messed up this badly?

I felt compelled to come to his rescue. I rattled off again what I knew about Mercy and her tricks. "This could be a ruse. What if she murdered Lloyd?"

"Murder?" my mother screeched. "He committed suicide."

"Mom, it's been all over the news. The sheriff suspects murder and so do I."

"You stay out of this, Ava. You're a confectioner, not a cop. Lloyd is dead and you're no longer threatened. I need to sweep."

Dad caught her arm before she launched up to tear into cleaning the whole house. I decided to skip revealing the note found in the bush by the lighthouse yesterday that said, *One down, one to go*.

I said, "This is just part of Mercy's plan to get us all upset to cover up for what she did while village president. She's pretending to try to right something that she did wrong concerning village tax collections."

My mother said, "It's more likely she was angling for our property all along and that's why she murdered Lloyd. Poor Libby. Aren't Libby and Mercy friends?"

"Yes," I said, "gambling buddies."

My father said to my grandfather, "Florine and I will take you to the bank, Dad, to dig up the land contract in the lockbox and see what it says. Even if Mercy is lying, I want to be prepared before I confront her."

I remembered what Professor Faust had told me. "The professor said something about the titles of the properties being easy to look up in county records. Maybe that's all online. I'll check."

"Sounds good," my dad said. "Now, who's going to go talk to Mom?" He meant my grandmother.

Gilpa finally spoke. "I'd better leave her alone for now." He flinched, but he was so uncharacteristically subdued that dread ran through me. Were the bait shop and this quaint cabin home no longer owned by our family? Were we left with nothing? Heck, we didn't even have a boat that worked.

"I'll talk with Grandma," I said, not having a clue what to say to a woman who felt she'd been betrayed by her husband of over fifty years. But my heart told me I had to fix this. Somehow this felt like my fault. If I hadn't agreed to the fudge contest, Lloyd and I wouldn't have been threatened. Something about bringing attention to the building that housed Oosterlings' Live Bait, Bobbers & Belgian Fudge & Beer had sparked these disasters.

After my parents and Grandpa left, I dawdled in thought, stirring the cold rice in its pan for lack of something else to do. I was so upset with Mercy that I could have run her over with her own bus if she stood outside on the street right now. Had she run me off the road? She was a professional driver. She could've committed the murder, too. She had motive enough. She could be the one threatening to kill me. She wanted my family and me out of the way so she could take over Lloyd's property and get rich. It would be just like her to want to put in a helipad and learn how to pilot a helicopter so she could ferry Chicago's rich people up here to their condos. I shivered at how bold her plan had been. And simple.

But was it too simple? Mercy had never struck me as a dumb person, so doubts niggled me. Mercy was probably right about the land contract returning the ownership of the bait shop to somebody. If that owner was Mercy, how the heck did Lloyd hand the land contract over to her? If it was so, why hadn't Mercy spoken up about this until now?

This was feeling complicated. I knew two people who could help me with my questions about real estate history in Door County: Professor Alex Faust and Dillon Rivers's mother. I wondered if Cathy Rivers had arrived yet in Fishers' Harbor for her visit. Did she know yet about the rifle being found in her son's truck? There was only one way to find out. Call Dillon—the one person my parents and grandparents loved to hate. It'd surely be ironic if he could help us get out of this pickle.

While sitting in my grandparents' front sunroom, I called the professor. He was in his car when I called, heading to a book signing over in Jacksonport on the other side of the county. Libby was with him; after his signing they were headed north to the Cana Island Lighthouse, where she was going to introduce him to her docent friends at that location. I set up a date to meet with the professor later.

When Dillon answered in person this time, I asked almost breathlessly, "You weren't arrested, were you?"

"No. But I got to visit the justice building in Sturgeon Bay for a couple of hours. What do you know?"

"Pauline and I saw the professor and Libby show the sheriff the rifle in the back of your truck yesterday. Who could've put it there, Dillon?"

"I don't know, but it's not a funny joke." His voice was rough with irritation. "I just got a call back from the sheriff. It seems the rifle was recently fired, and the sheriff knows I'm out in the woods with my dog a lot, training him to hunt. I carry my gun to get the dog used to its presence, but I've never fired it. He accused me of firing this rifle."

Irritated myself now at the sheriff, I got up to pace in front of the sofa bed. "But, Dillon, you're innocent."

"My fingerprints are on the rifle."

That landed like a bomb in my ear. I almost dropped the phone. "Really?"

"A few weeks back when I was in town setting up the construction schedule, Lloyd invited me over for a look at his gun collection. He'd heard I was out with Lucky a lot."

"Oh no." I sagged onto the sofa. "This doesn't sound good."

"It gets worse. The reason the sheriff called this morning is that not only did the rifle have my fingerprints on it, but he went back out to the lighthouse and found a bullet lodged in the wooden floor of the lighthouse. From this rifle. He didn't say so, but I'm no dumb person. He thinks this rifle was involved somehow in Lloyd's death. The sheriff was hoping I'd cough up a confession."

I could barely whisper his name. "Dillon, what can I do to help?"

"I've already contacted my mother about a lawyer. She's in town now, by the way, looking for a Door County motel to invest in." The phone went quiet. I was about to ask if he was still there when he added, "Thank you for offering to help. That means a lot, Ava."

We set up a date to meet, with his mother in tow.

My grandmother vented her anger by baking pies. She wanted to take one over to Libby's house later this morning, after Libby returned from the Cana Island Lighthouse. I told Grandma I'd go with her. I needed to ask Libby a few questions about Lloyd's investments to see if Mercy or somebody else had a good motive for killing him. I suspected Libby didn't know about the hole blown in the lighthouse floor. She'd swept up the gift shop area without mentioning it, so the sheriff must have found that hole this morning early or yesterday in some other room of the lighthouse when inspecting the place without Libby around.

I hiked back to my shop through a mist and droplets plopping off the maple trees, calling Pauline and Laura on the fly to fill them in.

Pauline was at the shop fifteen minutes later, close to half past perch on the clock, or nine thirty. Fishermen who had come in out of the rain milled about, yakking at me; they were on me like wasps after a sugary drink. I wore the disgustingly frilly yellow apron because it was still handy. I smiled a lot, pretending I was feeling sunny.

Cody was wrapping pieces of Cinderella Pink Fudge from the loaves I'd made yesterday and left out on the marble slab for cooling. I escaped the men only by restocking shelves with Fairy Tale Fudge pink doll clothes that the church ladies had dropped off during the time I'd been across Duck Marsh Street.

Pauline wore an orange short-sleeved cotton knit top and matching shorts and sandals. I'd never seen this getup before. Yesterday's nice all-red outfit had been new, too.

"You look sort of like one of Dillon's orange cones. We could stand you next to an open manhole for a summer job."

"I do not look like a traffic cone. The color is tangerine."

"You look nice." I knew she was dressing up lately for you-know-who-with-hairy-feet. "But don't you have to work with the Butterflies later on the fudge floats?"

"Bethany's helping again. She's determined to earn college credits for her summer volunteer work."

"Throw some detective work into the mix. Please ask Bethany if Verona Klubertanz showed up today with any pink Fairy Tale purses or doll clothes. I'm missing more of them. Have you noticed any?"

"No, but then I wasn't inspecting the toys the girls drag along with them in their backpacks. Now tell me more about somebody trying to frame Dillon and Mercy owning your fudge shop."

I drew her behind the glass case and whispered, "She may be trying to get away with murder. She could have kept that rifle stored in her bus, then dumped it in Dillon's truck while cruising through town. We have to outsmart her."

"We? This part of 'we' won't be going into basements of mansions. And no guns. Okay?"

"Of course not. We're just going over to Libby's with my grandmother to deliver a pie. With no gun hidden in it. But I need a lookout."

"Why?" Pauline did her look-down-her-nose routine.

"I have to get inside Lloyd's manse after I meet with Libby."

"You almost got yourself killed the last time we sneaked into a house."

She was referring to the debacle in the old mansion in May. "My wrist is fine now. Falling down those stairs was nothing. Besides, Lloyd's library and office are on the first level. As is his gun collection. So, no stairs."

Laura Rousseau came through the front door, lugging a big box atop the shelf of her pregnant belly. I rushed over to relieve her. The aroma of red velvet muffins hiding cherry-vanilla fudge chunks inside assailed me right through the seams of the closed box. I'd left Piers a text message early this morning about trying the recipe for me.

"I thought Piers would bring them, Laura. This is too heavy for you."

"Piers said he was meeting Professor Faust."

Suspicion pricked me because Lloyd had said Piers had tried to bribe Erik, a fudge judge, too. Was Piers bribing Alex Faust now, too? Would Piers rig the contest this way, and murder a disagreeable judge just to triumph on John's cable TV food or travel show? I dared not even look at Pauline.

Fortunately, the aroma of muffins and fudge was distracting. I set the box down at the cash register counter. I flipped the top open and took out a luscious-looking red velvet muffin sporting a huge muffin top the size of a small plate. Laura, Pauline, and I broke the muffin up to share. There were walnuts inside, too, a surprising riff added by

Piers. The red velvet texture surrounding the gooey fudge along with the walnut crunch gave my mouth a rush. Our ability to taste and the pleasure centers in our brain react to texture as well as flavor. We gals stood there, lapping at our fingers as if we were Lucky Harbor. Chocolate, vanilla, and cherry flavors with the hint of walnut danced on our tongues. My jaw prickled pleasantly from the sensations.

The soaked fishermen in the shop had gravitated to me again, right at my elbows. I shared the muffins, holding on to the box. The men inhaled them so fast that there was an updraft of air right in front of me.

A chunky man with a long, bushy beard said, "I didn't know Cinderella herself was gonna be here dolin' out the goodies."

Another slender guy in a plaid shirt snickered to the first guy, "You wait your turn. I got in line first to try the glass slipper on her foot."

This sudden fairy-tale talk from a bunch of wet fishermen was unnerving to say the least, but taking their money was not. I rang up the fudge-laden muffins in my frilly yellow apron while Cody offered them another cup of cocoa-laced coffee.

The frenzy over the muffins bled over into a flurry by the men buying pink fudge to take with them. The chunky man with the beard stood over me at the counter, watching my every move as I bent over to wrap his box. He said, "You sure have a way with fudge. There's some dance coming up for the fudge, isn't there?"

"Yes, an adult prom."

"I was wondering . . ."

His friend punched him on the arm and then hauled him off.

Pauline rushed up to me. "He was going to ask you to the prom!"

"No, he wasn't."

"Yes, he was."

"I don't even know that man."

"Who cares? Beggars for dates can't be choosers. Want me to drag him back?"

"No, Pauline."

"Please?"

Stubborn Belgian.

Minutes later, Pauline, Laura, and I were walking out the back door of the shop, intending to drive with Grandma in her SUV with pies to visit Libby. But Sheriff Tollefson's squad car was at Grandma's house. For the second time that morning, I took off running through the rain across my lawn and Duck Marsh Street.

"Jordy, what's going on?" I asked breathlessly when I stopped in the middle of the living room.

He stood there with a pen poised over his clipboard.

My grandmother was sitting in her favorite corner of the sofa, next to her reading table. "Ava dear, he's just asking me a few questions." But her pallid face said it was more serious than that.

"About what?"

Pauline and Laura trooped in behind me. Laura was panting.

Jordy said, "It's official business. I have to ask you to leave, please."

"You can at least tell me what's going on."

My grandmother said, "My theory about Lloyd has proven true. He's bad luck. The sheriff thinks I might have had a hand in murdering him. I'll gladly take the blame after what he's done to us."

I screamed something about injustice at Jordy that Pauline and Laura echoed. To his credit, Jordy helped Laura to a chair like a gentleman should. But he explained that *because* Grandma was a close friend of Libby's, she had to be questioned. *Because* Libby was a prime suspect. *Because* the first person you look to in a murder case is the spouse. Then Jordy kicked us out of the house for his interrogation of Grandma Sophie *because* she'd consented to it. Jordy was full of answers that I didn't like.

* * *

"My grandmother a suspect in murder? What is he thinking!" As I drove to Libby Mueller's with Pauline, Laura, and the rice and raspberry pies in Grandma's sports utility vehicle, I added, "Grandma Sophie's never like this. She's smart enough to refuse to talk to the sheriff without a lawyer present. She's talking to Jordy as a way to get back at Grandpa. She wants to be arrested. This is going to blow up in all our faces big-time."

"Your face maybe, but not mine or Laura's." Pauline sat in the front passenger seat with a rice pie wrapped inside an insulated holder on her lap. It was still warm and was infusing the air with the smell of eggs and cinnamon. I'd called Libby and she'd hitched a ride back across the county with a lighthouse volunteer, leaving the professor to do his research on his own. Pauline continued. "You're being overly dramatic again. You're going to ruin your contest and your TV show if you don't stop looking at life as if it were an e-mail and you had to say everything in capital letters with a bunch of exclamation points after them."

"First of all, the fudge contest and TV show ideas were both John's. Aren't you the least bit embarrassed at how his idea has turned out? Jordy even said it—all of this happened because of the fudge contest. And how is John today, anyway?"

Asking was a mistake. Pauline launched into telling us all about how John mastered scuba diving in one day.

"Did he find any treasure?" I asked.

"He found a cup."

Laura, who had a raspberry pie sitting next to her on the backseat, asked, "That's all?"

"John thinks it's a significant cup, a very important find," Pauline said, pride oozing through her words. "He said Professor Faust told him it could've come from one of the shipwrecks that carried important goods for the well-to-do of Door County back in the 1800s, which means the ships could have had gold coins and jewelry aboard, too. He could be rich by tonight. He's going to catch up with Professor Faust to see what else he knows."

Laura asked, "What's the cup look like?"

"It has gold lettering on it. We think it's the ship captain's own personal service. Or a rich passenger's."

"What letters?" I asked.

"AVD. In an intricate script."

"Darn," I said. "The A works for Ava, but I guess I'm out of luck. No Oosterling in those letters. And I could really use the dough right now."

"John's excited. He's arranging for another dive."

Rapture was all over my friend's face. It was good to see her that way. Somehow her happiness gave me hope for my own love life.

Within ten minutes we'd gone through our tourist-laden streets and up Highway 42 toward Ephraim to a road that ran inland, southeast and opposite of Peninsula State Park. Libby Mueller lived amid a collection of older cottages, mostly one story. Long ago this was probably a lumber camp. Libby's cottage was white with black shutters. What her plain house lacked in color, her postage-stamp yard made up for with its bounty of flowers, including perennials like daisies, and annuals like marigolds, zinnias, and bachelor buttons. Both she and Lloyd had a love for flowers, it seemed.

We parked next to Libby's small, rusting gray Honda sedan.

I got out and retrieved the raspberry pie from the backseat so that Laura could climb out unencumbered.

When we got to the door, voices filtered through the screen. I punched the doorbell.

To my surprise, Kelsey King came to the door wearing pajamas. She hissed through the screen, "Are you following me?" She lifted her cell phone up and snapped a photo of me through the screen. "I'm calling the cops."

Chapter 14

If there wasn't a screen between us, I might have heaved the raspberry pie right on top of her blond head. "Kelsey, the cops, as you call them, are already at my grandmother's house, so I win. Now put the phone down and back away. We've brought pies for Libby. We're here to express our condolences." A partial lie, but I was proud of how sincere I sounded.

She flipped her blond ponytail at me as she walked away from the door.

Pauline and Laura raised their eyebrows at me. Laura whispered, "She's wearing pajamas. Did she stay overnight here?"

Pauline whispered back, "Hard to tell. The high school girls wear pajama bottoms to school in place of jeans."

Libby came to the door, swinging it open, her face springing into a teary smile. "Well, good morning, girls! Please come in."

Her short, perfect bob of dark hair and tan pants and dusty rose blouse were a stark contrast to Kelsey's slobby appearance at a little after ten on a Monday morning.

We stepped inside.

"More of Sophie's pies? What a lovely gesture. Look at those pinched piecrusts. Let's put those down over here."

"Libby, I'm so sorry about Lloyd."

"Ava, I know it was a shock for you, too, the way we found him. . . ." She leaned into me for a hug. "Thank you for being with me. He was a good man."

She led us to the small dining room table, which was only a few steps from the front door. The open kitchen was to the right and living area to the left, all flowing together. It was a normal house except for Kelsey King's presence. She was pouring herself a glass of orange juice as if she'd lived here forever with Libby.

Laura asked for directions to the bathroom, then scooted away while Pauline and I stood there agape at Kelsey.

"You two know each other?" I said, stupidly.

Kelsey said, leaning back against the kitchen counter, "Libby came to Legs and Toes last night and had my new fudge flavor for dessert." A smile slashed across her face crookedly like a fudge cutter trying to dig into me.

Libby said, "And it was very good fudge."

"What flavor?" I asked.

Kelsey laughed. "Nice try. I have a winner, wouldn't you say, Libby?"

"It's unusual, I'll give you that." Libby held up her coffeepot to offer us coffee.

I shook my head. "We can't stay long. Do you need any help, Libby, with the arrangements for tomorrow?"

"That's nice of you, but no, the funeral director seems to have it all in hand. They even ordered a big tent in case of rain and will add a loudspeaker outside if the crowd gets that big. Lloyd knew everybody. He was well liked."

By everybody but my grandmother, I thought, who was being questioned right now as a suspect. I turned my attention to Kelsey.

"A friend said you were singing atop the lighthouse tower over at the park, Kelsey. Yesterday morning early."

Kelsey shifted her weight but otherwise looked properly perplexed. "That wasn't me."

"But the friend said it was you, a petite blonde."

"His binoculars must've been dirty." Her eyes grew hard

as she drank from her glass of orange juice. The color "orange" struck me, giving me conniptions.

Libby pulled out a chair at the table for Laura as she returned. Laura said, "Thank you, Libby."

Libby said, "Are you sure you all don't want some coffee? Maybe a piece of those pies?"

Pauline and I stayed standing. Pauline said to Kelsey, "We chased somebody through the woods who looked just like you."

"It wasn't me." Kelsey plopped her glass on the counter.

Libby gave Kelsey a quick hug. "This dear girl was so exhausted from all her work at the restaurant in Egg Harbor that I told her if she was too tired to drive all the way to her condo in Sister Bay to stay with me. This little thing isn't somebody who'd be running out in the woods."

Kelsey smiled at us, triumphant. "Nice chatting with you, but I've got to change and get to the Legs and Toes to work on my fudge recipe. Libby, you'll join me for lunch after your errand? I need a taste tester." She started to walk past me, then paused. "Say, who's the new replacement judge for Lloyd? Libby would be an appropriate choice."

Sure, I thought, because somehow you've made friends with Libby. Then I saw Libby teary-eyed at the opposite end of the dining room table. My heart spoke for me. "Libby, I'd be honored if you joined the fudge contest. We'll okay it with John, too. It'd be a tribute to Lloyd. You both meant a lot to each other. And to my family." The last part was a lie, of course, what with Grandma wishing Lloyd dead.

Libby palmed away her tears. "That's a lovely gesture. My husband always gave a lot to this community. He'd want me to do this for you. I accept."

It struck me then that I didn't know exactly how Lloyd had contributed at all. He owned a street full of cabins, some of the buildings along Main Street, and a fancy historic estate home, but did he give to the school? Parks? What? I'd have to ask my grandfather, or Libby, sometime when the kickboxing confectioner wasn't in my face.

Laura rocked up from her chair. "I'm feeling puffy. I'd better get home and put my feet up."

Kelsey went on her way toward a bedroom down the hall.

Libby rushed to help Laura with her chair. "When are those babies due?"

"Couple of weeks yet. I feel like a cow."

We assured her she was too pretty for such comparisons. As we headed to the front door, Libby said, "Is your husband coming back for the birth?"

"I'm afraid not. The army has him working on something important and top secret."

Libby hugged her at the front door. "We appreciate his service. We're all here for you. Just call and let me know what I can do and I'll do it."

"Thanks, Libby."

After we were settled in grandma's SUV, Laura said from the backseat, "Kelsey was lying about everything."

I started the vehicle. "Definitely."

"That invitation to Libby for lunch was spur-of-the-moment. It felt controlling somehow, though I don't think Libby realized it."

Pauline said, "And what's this chummy relationship with Libby all of a sudden? They just met last night? And Kelsey stops by to stay over? And after we know Kelsey made a pass or two at Lloyd? This is fishy. They're not telling us the whole story."

I kept my eyes on the blacktop road. "There was only Libby's car at her place. But Kelsey must have rented a car in Green Bay after she flew in from Portland, so where is it?"

"What does she drive?" Pauline asked. "A dark car?"

"I don't know."

Laura asked, "You've never seen her car?"

"No. She just showed up at the shop, and who would think to go out to the parking lot to see what rental car she's driving?"

Pauline said, "Kelsey could've been driving Libby's car and run us into the ditch."

"If only we can prove it," I said. "She says they only just met last night."

Laura said, "It's got to be a lie. They're too chummy."

Pauline agreed. "That's how Kelsey was on top of the tower yesterday morning early. She got a key for the lighthouse from Libby. You have to also have a special key to open the hatch at the top of that staircase; only Libby would have that key, outside of the Coast Guard."

"Kelsey likely stole the keys from Libby," I said. "I noticed Libby didn't say much about the singing on the tower. She may have been as surprised as us and just didn't know what to say."

Laura asked, "So, what is Kelsey up to with all this sneaky behavior?"

"It's obvious," Pauline said as we pulled up to the stop sign in front of Highway 42. "She plans to win the fudge contest however she can do it, plus get money out of Libby."

"But Libby has no money." Then I realized my stupidity. "Of course Lloyd probably left her money because he was nice and loved her. I doubt he left her a ton of dough to gamble away, but Kelsey is stupid enough to believe Libby will come into a fortune. What if Libby's been Kelsey's mark since the first day Kelsey arrived in Fishers' Harbor?"

Laura clapped from the backseat. "You're good. Case solved."

We were almost back to Fishers' Harbor on Highway 42 heading south when my cell phone rang. I dug it out and handed it to Pauline.

"Hello, this is Pauline, Ava's secretary."

It was my father. Pauline turned on the speaker. Dad said, "I'm here at the bank. The land contract looks solid enough, but I have some bad news. Along with Lloyd's name, and your grandfather's, the contract also has Mercy Fogg's name on it. It appears she cosigned it with Lloyd."

I almost ran off the road. I pulled into a nearby gas station lot. "Is there any other paperwork? Anything to explain why her name is on it? Any notes from Lloyd?"

"No, honey, that's what we're missing. This is just the contract in your grandpa's lockbox."

After we said our good-byes, the word "box" lingered in my head. Cars pulled around me to get to the fuel pumps. "Maybe Lloyd had some of the documentation about the contract with Grandpa in that box that was stolen from us. A long shot, but . . ."

Pauline said, "So we have to find that box. If Kelsey stole it at the crash site, maybe she's also dumb enough to try and hide it in the woods? She's been over there a lot, it seems."

Laura said, "That park is huge. That's a needle in a haystack. And she could have burned it. Or tossed it in the lake."

My hunch said otherwise. "If Mercy stole those papers, she'd burn them, but maybe not Kelsey. She's ditzy. She's befriending Libby. Kelsey would've saved the box in order to curry favors from Libby."

Pauline said, "True. Maybe it's at the lighthouse. That's why she was on the tower. She was faking the reason for being there by singing. Mercy saw her up there, so maybe the box is up there."

A new realization gave me a shiver. "Libby didn't exactly seem surprised at us questioning Kelsey about singing on the tower. I'm wondering now if Libby's in on some ruse to get more of Lloyd's money, such as proving she's still part owner of his real estate. But that makes no sense since she likely inherits something anyway."

Laura offered from the backseat, "It could be that Libby's been threatened by Kelsey. If Kelsey killed Libby's ex-husband over their secret affair gone bad or their disagreement about her winning the fudge contest in hopes of gaining fame and fortune, she might be willing to threaten other lives. Maybe Libby's in fear for her life and going along with whatever Kelsey wants."

It was all starting to make sense, as strange as it was.

Jordy's words rang through my head again. "But we need hard evidence."

Pauline dug in her fat purse, which sat on the floor. "I'm writing all this down."

Pauline was using a ruled pad of paper from school. What if Kelsey had somehow stolen the paper from Pauline's purse at the fudge shop? Pauline set that bag down and walked away from it all the time. But there was no way to prove a piece of ripped paper came from Pauline's purse.

"Do you have crayons in that purse?" I asked.

"Sure. A whole box of sixty-four."

"Still have the orange one and related colors? You called the note a 'moderate orange' when we were with Jordy at his office."

Pauline pulled out the box. She hoisted the waxy sticks. "Apricot, melon, peach, yellow-orange, red-orange, burnt orange, and . . . Wait. One's missing. Salmon."

Laura croaked from the back, "Oh my gosh. Is this what's called a lead?"

"Could be," I said. "Or not. Pauline, do your kids take your crayons out of your purse?"

"Never. First thing they learn in kindergarten is never to get into Miss Mertens's things or anybody else's backpack or pockets."

"We should run that box down to Sturgeon Bay for fingerprinting."

"There's fudge smudged all over it from the Butterflies, and Jordy would also get my fingerprints."

"Yeah. And despite your protests, Verona or her friends could have swiped a crayon."

"Or maybe I just never saw it on the floor at your shop when I cleaned up after the girls."

I thumped my fingers on the top of the steering wheel. What would the *Topsy-Turvy Girls* do next on my TV show?

While I was thinking, Pauline said, "Hey, look. It's Dillon. And that's your truck."

I hadn't realized we were at the old gas station that was connected to Fishers' Harbor Auto Body. A tall overhead door was open, though we couldn't see much from this angle, what with the pumps, cars, and people in between. Dillon was looking over my vehicle's crumpled yellow tailgate. Lucky Harbor was wandering about, sniffing. Dillon must have taken an early lunch break from the Main Street construction. It was after eleven o'clock. But what was he doing with my truck? One of his hands was sliding along the top of the tailgate, and then it was caressing the crumpled steel before cupping the one good headlight that remained. My memory relived his warm hands with strong fingers that were sensitive to a woman's needs. . . . My heartbeat quickened.

I jerked in my seat.

"What's wrong?" Pauline asked.

"Nothing."

"Don't say 'nothing.' You just got hot watching Dillon Rivers touch your truck!"

"Did not."

"Now who's the stubborn Belgian?"

Laura laughed.

I steered fast back onto the highway. Because I was driving Grandma's SUV, I hoped Dillon hadn't recognized me.

Soon afterward, I veered off again and onto a back street.

"Now where are we going?" Pauline asked.

I fished in my pocket and came up with Lloyd's key.

Pauline said, "The key was okay when Lloyd was alive, but now it feels like trespassing. I'll be fired from my teaching job."

"We're not breaking in." I waved the key again.

"We need to get Laura home. She needs a rest stop."

"Lloyd has nice bathrooms." I glanced into the rearview mirror. "You're fine with this, Laura?"

"I have nothing better to do than watch birthing videos."

"This'll be more fun," I said.

Pauline printed a note on her pad, muttering, "Forced into Lloyd's house against my will. Please call nine-one-one."

"If I didn't know better, P.M., I'd think you were the one writing the threatening notes to me."

"I do own an orange crayon, A.M."

We circled inland and drove the rural road that would take us by Lloyd's on the southwest edge of the village. Instead of turning into Lloyd's lane from the main road where people might spot us, I parked Grandma's SUV around a corner on the rural road with woodland between us and Lloyd's house. "If anybody asks, we're here picking berries in the woods," I said.

Laura was puffing as we made our way through the acre of maples and pines and tall grasses. We were inside Lloyd Mueller's house within minutes. I locked the door behind us. Laura hurried to the restroom not far from the front door.

The beauty of the atrium with the stained glass skylights and warm woods on the floors stopped me again.

Pauline dropped her purse in awe. "So he just took out the floor above? That was a bold architectural move in such an old house. I never heard about this."

"That was Lloyd. He quietly went about his business."

"Too secretive, though, if you ask me. If he asked your grandpa to hide a box, and he lets Mercy put her signature on a contract without telling anybody, I'm not sure Lloyd can be trusted at all. Maybe he and Mercy had something going on."

My conniptions returned because she was right. "Mercy and Lloyd? A pair?"

"A secret affair would explain a lot of stuff. Except why would she threaten to get rid of Lloyd? Isn't that what the first note said?"

"No, it didn't." That note was burned into my brain. I repeated it out loud. *"Somebody will die if you don't con-*

vince Lloyd to throw the contest. Miss Oosterling must not win."

"So Mercy merely wanted you to lose. She didn't care who died."

"She's always wanted my business to founder. She probably thinks I'd move back to Los Angeles. If so, she and Lloyd then wouldn't have so much opposition to selling the building and land under it for the expansion of the harbor they planned." My theory was all too plausible.

"Maybe that's why Lloyd was so eager to have you move into the Blue Heron Inn? He wanted you to feel agreeable, even if the bait shop got torn down. Boy, this plan of theirs was almost too pat."

"Except somebody got too eager and greedy and murdered Lloyd and messed things up a little for the lovers. If Mercy and Lloyd were lovers." I sighed. Now the theory didn't feel right. "Lloyd was my grandpa's best friend. And Lloyd was trying to protect Libby from Mercy."

"Are you sure? Or was it all just a cover-up for an affair? Maybe what you witnessed at the fish boil that evening was more of a lovers' spat with Kelsey."

She'd just made my stomach twist in on itself. I wasn't sure of anything.

Laura rejoined us. "Where do we begin?"

"Laura, you stay downstairs and hunt through drawers, and, Pauline, you go upstairs."

"Why do I have to go upstairs?"

She'd always wanted to be boss, from the time we played house at the age of five. "You have to go upstairs because you're the tallest. You can look in the tops of closets the easiest."

"I suppose that makes sense, but if somebody comes, I can't escape like you two. I'll be stuck upstairs and they'll find me."

Laura said, "Like I'm going to be able to run?"

"Pauline," I said, giving her a stink-eyed look, "nobody will put a pregnant woman or a schoolteacher in jail."

"Oh yes, they will. Women give birth in prisons all the time and schoolteachers end up teaching poetry to felons."

"You're wasting time. I'll take the library in back. Meet me there when you're done."

We started to head off to do our spying, but then Laura noticed the cups and saucers in their cabinet. "All in pink flowers. Pink, like your famous fudge."

I hadn't made the connection when I looked at them previously.

Laura made her way down the glass cabinet like a kid at a Christmas store window. "Wedgwood Avon Cape Cod. Just like my grandmother had. And Royal Albert bone china. The Royal Country Roses pattern. Royal Doulton's 'May' pattern. Made in the late 1800s in England."

Pauline and I came in for a closer look. That's when I noticed a couple of cups and saucers were missing. Previously I'd seen shelves that were packed. But the lower shelf—the one that might go unnoticed at first—now sported cups with spaces between them as big as a hand, as if somebody had hastily reshuffled all the cups to hide thievery. I said as much to my friends.

Laura said, "But who would come in here and take a couple of cups?"

We all looked at one another with a slow burn growing on our faces. I said, "Kelsey? Maybe Mercy? If either had something going on with Lloyd, she would've been in here."

"What about Libby?" Pauline asked.

"She's visited for years. Why would she wait until now to steal two cups? But it's a good point. Maybe the cups had sentimental value."

Pauline said, "We should give her a call about this before we report it to the sheriff."

"Indeed," I said. "But it feels like Kelsey's doings again. I just don't trust her."

"Another big lead?" Laura asked.

"I don't know," I said, remembering Jordy's need for hard evidence. "We'll call it a soft and loose connection."

Pauline said, "Whatever the connection, it's odd that he dissed your cherry pink fudge when he seemed to like pink cups."

Laura pointed out, "But maybe he dissed pink because these cups belonged to Libby and they'd fought over them."

We agreed that seemed plausible, unfortunately. But we were here to find out why Lloyd was murdered and to find anything to do with my fudge shop building, not about Lloyd's cup collection.

As I passed the bottom of the staircase, I recalled the gun cabinet was tucked into the alcove on the other side. Even from a few feet away I could see that a rifle was missing. Unlike the cup shelves, you can't rearrange rifles. They fit in slots and sleeves within a cabinet. One was missing. The tiny hairs on the back of my neck lifted. I made a mental note to call Dillon as soon as we were done here.

In the library, we paused to appreciate the rose-garden view. Many shades of pink bloomed amid the full rainbow of colors. Who had come here to steal just two cups that had pink roses on them? If Libby wanted her collection back, why not just take the entire thing?

I scanned the room for a good place to start. With three walls filled with books, this could take forever, especially if Lloyd liked hiding things in books or fake boxes that looked like books. I recalled the spot where he'd withdrawn the cookbooks. If Lloyd had been trying to tell me something in code, that was the place to start.

I leaned down and grabbed slim volumes of Lutheran cookbooks from the 1980s. I was born in that era, so I thought there might be a secret message from Lloyd. I found great recipes for "Potato-Wiener Surprise" and "Tater Tot Hot Dish" and a dessert bar called "Chewios" and recipes for "Cowboy Cookies," "Raspberry Bars," and "Rocky Road Fudge Bars." I was salivating and getting hungry. It was right before lunch. The pie section of the book had me drooling, too. I even smelled the old book to see if the pie aromas were present. I remembered that Pauline and I ate paper when we were kids.

A German section of the cookbook included Schwarz-auer, a fruit soup, and Pfeffernüsse Cookies, which required ground coriander seed. Kelsey King would like that recipe. I had to give Kelsey her chops; maybe combining plants and spices with sugar could yield a great fudge. Just leave out her silly dirt. I decided to borrow the cookbook for reading later. Nobody would miss it and I would bring it back some-how, sometime.

The next handful of books to the right of the gap where Lloyd had chosen his books yielded something more inter-esting. A slim volume held recipes for preserving fish and creating fish dishes, contributed by fishermen and even a captain of a fishing boat plying Lake Michigan in the late 1800s through the 1930s. There were sketches and photos, and one sketch of a building was a dead ringer for Ooster-lings'. It was unique that this book's recipes came entirely from men. I flipped twice through the book to make sure. Some names were familiar. A Hans Mueller was perhaps a relation of Lloyd's? His grandfather perhaps. Perhaps he had been married to Ruth Mueller, the name I'd come across previously. Hans had a recipe for cooking white fish in a beer sauce. My family liked fish sautéed on endives with beer, too. Germans and Belgians were close geograph-ically in Europe and close in what their palates enjoyed.

Then, out of the blue, as I turned a page, there was the name:

Oosterling.

I sat on the floor cross-legged for a closer look.

There was no picture or sketch. The name Bram Ooster-ling was paired with the name Clément Van Damme under a recipe that showed how to bake freshwater salmon with mustard. Belgians love mustard. My parents and grandpar-ents kept at least a dozen varieties of mustard in their cup-boards. They even trekked to Middleton, Wisconsin—a suburb of Madison—once a year to the National Mustard Museum to buy selections from the thousands of mustards for sale. My dad was partial to the strong, stone-ground brown mustards. If he was in a hurry for a quick lunch or snack, he'd make himself a mustard sandwich—just mustard on hearty, stone-ground bread. After I introduced him to Laura's great cheesy bread, Pete had insisted that if he had to choose a last meal on earth, it'd be toasted cheesy bread with brown mustard and a tall glass of cold Holstein milk.

This Bram Oosterling being in the same book as Hans Mueller made me wonder: Could the Mueller-Oosterling association years ago possibly have anything to do with Lloyd being so lax with his land contract with my grandfather? Perhaps Lloyd didn't demand payments from my grandfather the way he should have because our ancestors had been friends. Or was there some pact they'd made? Did the Muellers owe something to the Oosterlings, instead of the other way around? But why? For what? That train of thought felt dangerous, though. Somebody might think my grandfather would want Lloyd dead to avoid losing the bait shop!

That book went on top of the Lutheran church cookbook to take home to show my family.

I was about to get up from my cross-legged position when I spotted it—a safe in the wall. "Found something!"

The safe was hidden low on the wall and directly behind the books Lloyd had given me. I got on my knees to try the combination lock, but the door wouldn't open.

Pauline pounded down the staircase and came into the room. "I found something, too!"

She held sheaves of oversized papers. "These were in a dresser in what must have been Libby's room. They evidently didn't sleep together when they were married."

I got up. "I found a safe, but we'll need tools to pry it open or out of the wall."

"These are plans for a new harbor." She unfolded architectural papers and laid them out on the table. "Look here." She pointed to lines that clearly showed a row of condos. "The marsh is still there. In fact, all of Duck Marsh Street is still there, but it looks like it's marked for rehab of some sort. But look at this." She tapped the condos again. "See the tiny print?"

For some reason architects are trained to print on the head of a pin. I stuck my nose down to the paper and read *Oosterlings' Fudge Shop*. Next to it was *Oosterlings' Bait Shop.*

"The plan is for separate shops?"

"A shop all your own, in a row of quaint shops built as the first floor under the condominiums. Look. There's even a window for window service. People wouldn't even need to come inside the shop for their fudge fix."

I could see that Pauline thought I'd love it. But two things bothered me: Our historical bait-and-fudge shop building would be gone, and I wouldn't be sharing any space or cocoa-laced coffee or the aromas of Fairy Tale Fudge flavors with my grandfather. Gilpa needed me. And I needed his cheery confidence in me. My heart felt like somebody had taken an ice cream scooper and hollowed it out.

I asked, "This was in Libby's room tucked inside a drawer, right? As if somebody wanted to hide it from somebody else."

"Maybe Lloyd was hiding it from Mercy."

"Could be. She was the former board president, and she's still eager to control our town. And if Lloyd and Mercy were having an affair, I doubt he'd let her go into Libby's old room. Lloyd cared about Libby."

Pauline grew thoughtful, tugging at a strand of her long hair. "Libby came over here now and then, right? They'd enjoy breakfast together once in a while."

"Yeah. Why?"

"If Kelsey or Mercy were pressuring Libby about getting in here to steal things, maybe Libby had started hiding important items from view in order to protect Lloyd. He was a pretty casual guy. Look how he invited us in and just handed you a bunch of cookbooks on the spur of the moment. Maybe Lloyd saw an opportunity to begin giving away his valuables to friends so that Kelsey and Mercy wouldn't get their hands on them."

"You may be right." Professor Faust's words about buried treasures in old houses came to mind. We'd found one safe, but were there more?

Laura waddled fast into the room, flushed. "I heard voices outside the front door. Then somebody jiggling the lock. Now what?"

"We hide." I chucked my books and the architectural drawing into Pauline's big purse.

"Oh no, you're not going to get me in trouble."

"Shhh. Give me your scissors, P.M."

"Are you planning on stabbing somebody? All I have are kindergarten scissors with rounded ends."

"Good enough for what I have in mind. Now hurry outside. Both of you."

Chapter 15

Pauline, Laura, and I were in Lloyd Mueller's rose garden when Alex Faust and Erik Gustafson surprised us by staring at us through the windows from inside the library. They must have come straight there from the front door, which made me curious. Did they know about the safe? Why were they in the house? I had made a lunch date with the professor earlier, but it didn't look like he was tracking me down for that. He and Erik looked as surprised as we were to be meeting like this.

I waved at them, then clipped a rosebud stem with Pauline's kindergarten scissors.

Pauline whispered, "You'd better come up with something good or we're toast."

"Pauline," I whispered, "trust me."

I handed off the prickly rosebud stem to her as Professor Faust and our village president came into the backyard. The professor had his briefcase along, but Erik also carried one, which I found odd. Laura handed Pauline a folded tissue to help handle the thorny stem.

"Well, hello, Professor Faust," I said. "And, Erik, how are you?"

The gray-haired professor and the nineteen-year-old stood there, looking befuddled. Erik's face was red, as if he hadn't had as much time as I to create a lie about the reasons for being here.

The professor said, "Did you walk over here from downtown? We didn't see a car out front."

Pauline said, "We came through the woods. We're doing a favor for Libby Mueller."

Pauline flashed me a bug-eyed look, directing me to finish the lie.

"We were just at Libby's delivering pies and we told her we'd help with the funeral tomorrow, so here we are picking a big bouquet of Lloyd's favorite flowers to sit beside the casket." I flexed the kindergarten scissors in my hand while I smelled another rose I'd just clipped. "Did you know these are organic? The leaves look wretched as a result of no spraying. However, the blossoms are pure as sunshine."

Erik shrugged, looking even more confused. "That's really nice."

"So why are you two here?" I asked.

Erik's head whipped toward the professor in obvious panic.

Professor Faust said, "Erik wanted my help. He says there seems to be some trouble with the real estate dealings concerning the harbor area."

I said, "Meaning Mercy Fogg might own it, including my fudge shop."

The professor slapped a hand on Erik's shoulder. "That's exactly why we're here." He held up a key. "I got a key from Libby. She said it'd be okay to look around for Lloyd's papers."

"Yes, indeed," Erik said, "I would like to resolve this before tomorrow's funeral."

Guys Erik's age never talked so formally. Had Mercy used some lie to get Erik to come here and snoop? Was a past village president helping the current village president? Erik was a fudge judge who'd possibly been bribed by Piers, and Mercy hated me. If they were all in cahoots together, I was "fudge smudged" in this plot. But what was Professor Faust's role in this subterfuge?

I directed my question to Erik. "What about the secret buyer? Has that person talked with Mercy yet? And have you been paid to keep your silence about the buyer?"

Erik, though still muscular from his football playing days last year, appeared to shrink. "Huh?" He glanced at his phone. "Hey, I guess we'll have to do this another time, Professor. I gotta go to work. Ronny needs me for the lunch hour."

The professor said, "Sure thing, kid. I'll drop you off."

"Nah. I can hike over to the bar from here."

Erik disappeared fast around the corner of the house. He bartended regularly at the Troubled Trout. In a small village, being president isn't even a half-time job; it mostly pays in stipends to cover expenses.

I said, "Erik's finding out that being an elected official can require a lot of hours and grief."

"Indeed." The professor looked at us with suspicion, which made me nervous. I felt like a kid in school and he'd report us to the principal for cutting class. "He told me that everybody wants something from him."

"Yeah, and did he mention they sometimes give him money to get something? I heard that Piers Molinsky offered him money, probably to throw the fudge contest Piers's way."

"That's unfortunate. But the lad didn't take the bribe, I'm sure. And you're down a fudge judge. Have you canceled the contest? My feelings won't be hurt if you do. My book research is heading in a new direction anyway. Away from food for a while, thank goodness."

"Libby might pinch-hit for Lloyd."

The professor nodded his approval. "What a lovely thing."

"I thought you loved writing cookbooks."

"Historically based cookbooks were the quickest way to publish with a modicum of respect and keep up with my tenured history colleagues, who seem to cough out books at will. I'm quite intrigued now by the mealtime customs and tableware brought here by the immigrants coming to the Great Lakes. My interest has been piqued by the cup that John Schultz found."

Pauline screamed next to me, "Really? He's rich?"

I worked my jaw to get my hearing back.

Alex said, "From the picture of the cup he sent me on his phone, my guess is that it could be quite valuable, perhaps gifted to a maid or laborer by a king or queen, if not stolen of course."

Pauline's eyes gleamed. "So you and John think there's more?"

"Oh yes. I'm aboard his ship, pun intended. He texted me to see if I knew a shipwreck expert. Mr. Schultz and I might collaborate on a travel show featuring the hunt for Lake Michigan treasure."

"That would be fantastic!" Pauline readjusted her purse on her shoulder, standing even taller next to me. She looked ready to burst into song.

I hated to burst her bubble. "Pauline, you forget that John is videotaping my fudge contest. That takes priority at the moment."

"You're just jealous."

The professor chuckled. "Perhaps it'll all work out if the fudge contest is canceled anyway. I suspect Libby might change her mind about your offer of becoming a judge, what with her being a grieving widow of sorts."

"She seemed okay with it. It wasn't my idea, actually. Kelsey King was at Libby's and the idea popped out of her mouth."

"Miss King?" He drew in a big draft of the rose-scented air, as if to choose his words carefully. "She's off her rocker. I've been researching the contestants."

"What'd you find on Kelsey?"

"She was arrested once for cooking with weed and selling the cookies."

Laura laughed. "Pretty common, but did she ever get into more serious trouble?"

I asked, "Or make weed fudge?"

Pauline asked, "Do you think that's why she's been in the park? She's looking for marijuana plants?"

I said, "At least we know why she might have been singing on the tower."

We all laughed. But then I sobered. "Maybe I need to disqualify her? Maybe I *should* cancel the contest. The sheriff is right. Lloyd might still be alive if it hadn't been for my fudge contest bringing the likes of Kelsey and Piers to our town."

The professor asked, "Certainly you're not blaming them for Mr. Mueller's death?"

The way he worded that brought red-faced embarrassment to me. "No, not yet, anyway. It's just that I think they thought they'd get a lot more out of this fudge festival than merely making fudge."

"More money?"

"Yes. And it all makes me feel funny about the dance coming up. How can we even think of dancing at a prom after Lloyd's death?"

Laura said, "No, don't think that, Ava. I'm determined to make you a dress and I want that dress to be worn at the prom by the fudge fairy queen. Which will be you."

Professor Faust said, "Kelsey's arrest was expunged from her record. It was a first-time offense." Then he grinned with a hiked eyebrow. "Any chance I could be your date, Ava? You'll wear one of those aprons? I thought you were fetching online in the yellow one."

"Online?"

"At the *Door County* newspaper site under its Happenings button."

"Drat. It was that chunky guy with the beard and his phone camera."

"Chunky guy who?" Pauline asked. "A new man in your life?"

"Just a guy buying bait yesterday. He liked my apron."

Laura said, "Watch out. Men read a lot into an apron.

They see a whole lifetime unfold before them, such as holidays with you and him in the kitchen, preparing the turkey with the children. I wore an apron when my husband was home on leave and look at me now."

The professor chuckled.

I was saved by a "woof" as Lucky Harbor galloped around the corner of the house, his pink tongue lolling out the side of his mouth. He leaped up on my front, panting as he got grass stains and dirt all over me.

"Where did you come from, Mr. Harbor?" I asked, pushing him down.

The dog went to the professor next, sniffing around his shoes and his pants legs.

Dillon rounded the corner. "Sorry. Lucky took off over at the auto body shop. Ava, you must have driven by."

"I thought I was incognito in my grandmother's SUV."

"He must have smelled your perfume, Ava. And yours, Professor."

Dillon pulled his dog away from sniffing the professor. Lucky Harbor stared at me in a potent way, whining. I hadn't said "fudge," but I suspected he smelled fudge on the professor and me. I asked the professor if he'd had fudge today.

"Yup. Training my palate for Saturday."

I tossed the dog a Goldfish cracker.

Dillon was stepping about the garden. "My mother has to see this garden. Ava, can you get away for lunch with us instead of dinner tonight? Then I'll bring her over here afterward; you can come with."

Pauline flashed me a mix of surprise and admonishment. She hated it when I didn't tell her every detail of my life. But lately she'd been keeping a lot of stuff from me concerning John Schultz.

I said, "I was going to grab lunch with the professor. I had some questions for him. We set it up earlier this morning."

Professor Faust waved me off. "Oh, my dear, another

time is fine. It was a great coincidence to have met you here in the backyard of Lloyd's home."

But then I wondered about us all leaving now, with the professor being left here alone. The safe was in plain sight. "I suppose you need to look around for the papers inside for Erik?"

"Oh no, my dear. I need him with me. It's like researching in a museum. These days you need an escort. I'd hate to be accused of stealing anything from Mr. Mueller's home."

"Might we talk some more soon about local history and the buildings on the harbor?"

"Beyond what's already noted in my cookbook?"

"Yes. There has to be a reason a buyer insisted on remaining secret. Erik said nothing to you?"

"Nothing. I'll go to the library in Sister Bay. They have a nice collection of local history books. Perhaps we'll find out that treasure is buried in the harbor or under floors, as we spoke of previously."

He walked away around the side of the house, leaving me to wonder again if the box from under the fudge shop floor might have a long-forgotten note about the ownership agreement between Lloyd and Grandpa. Perhaps the box itself was valuable.

"Earth to Ava," Dillon said.

"What?"

"Can we meet with my mother for lunch? She's never been to the Troubled Trout."

Pauline and Laura stood with their heads ping-ponging between Dillon and me. Both wore sly smiles. I had to confess my drooling wasn't just for the meal I imagined at the Troubled Trout. Dillon standing like Adonis amid roses made this woman's heart experience a kerfuffle. His eyes shimmered like smooth, shiny stones on our beaches with fresh Lake Michigan water rippling over them with mystery.

Swallowing to get back my composure, I said, "I'll meet you there as soon as I take Laura and Pauline home."

"Nothing doing," Pauline said. "Give me your keys, Ava.

You go with Dillon and I'll take your grandma's SUV back. I'm parked at the harbor anyway."

She trotted away and Laura waddled off before I could protest.

Dillon grinned at me in that way that made the sun brighter.

My head said to run after my friends. My body turned to jelly when an old familiar glint in his eyes held me prisoner.

The air grew still and redolent with a powerful force.

Dillon swept me into his strong arms for a kiss that tasted like the essence of roses.

I tried to protest. Really, I did. It was totally his fault that I kissed him back.

His big hands were all over me, starting a fire between us. He was whispering my name over and over. It couldn't have been me who whispered his name in return, fanning the sparks. It must have been the bees buzzing, and the breathlike breeze drifting between us.

Dillon unloosened my ponytail. My hair tumbled down across my shoulders. He nuzzled under it to kiss my neck. The rose perfume in the yard and the hint of salty man made a cocktail that teased, bringing back memories. Would Dillon pick me up, carry me inside, rush right up the stairs and into a guest bedroom? Nobody would know. . . .

Then Lucky Harbor barked.

Dillon and I parted. We stared at each other in shock.

I said, "That was a mistake."

"It didn't feel like it." Dillon backed up a step, licking his lips as if to keep tasting me.

"No, it's the setting." I gulped at the air to recover my composure, filling myself with the redolent bouquet of roses. I could even taste their essence on the air.

"Lucky for us Lucky interrupted us." He touched his mouth with two fingers, then touched my lips. "Sorry. I got carried away. It's just, you look so cute lately, and when I saw you earlier in the apron—"

"Those darn aprons."

He laughed, but I ordered my feet to work and headed toward the sunroom. "I'll go back through the house and lock up."

"What was the professor looking for in there?"

Dillon followed me inside, but he stayed businesslike. I filled him in and then led him to the safe. He crouched down, then gave the lock a spin but couldn't open it, either.

I asked, "Is there another way to get it out of the wall?"

"Sure, Ava. Use a crowbar to rip the bookcases off the wall and bring in a big saw to manhandle this old plaster and make a mess."

"I'll help."

He chuckled. "Let me think about it over lunch. This could land us in jail."

"On our TV show we used a hairpin once to open a safe."

Dillon stood up and considered the three walls of books. "Most people keep passwords and combinations in a folder next to their computer, which isn't very smart. Maybe he used books. Was this his home office?"

"Yes. I can go through every book."

"Good idea, but later. We're due for lunch with Mom."

We walked back through the hallway. The gun cabinet made me pause again. I asked Dillon, "Anything more about the rifle found in your truck?"

"No, not yet. I take it this is the cabinet where the gun belongs?"

"Yes." Something wasn't right about it. The empty space I'd seen earlier now appeared much smaller. I took a closer look. "Dillon, I swear that earlier there was space enough in here for two rifles. But now there's only one missing." I stared at the only sleeve left open, wishing now that I'd taken a much closer look earlier to verify my suspicions.

"What're you thinking?"

"That Erik or the professor returned a rifle to this cabinet minutes ago. Do you think Erik borrowed Lloyd's rifles?" Horror struck me like sudden indigestion. "You don't think Erik . . . ?"

"Was at the lighthouse with Lloyd Mueller? Shot a hole in the floor? Killed him? Don't let your imagination go too wild. If Erik returned a gun just now, there's likely a plausible explanation. He's probably a hunter and borrowed it last season and was just returning it."

"You sound like Jordy Tollefson now. Logical."

"Then you've now got two men with common sense looking out for you. A good lunch will sort this out. Let's go eat."

When we got out front, a red Corvette sat there. Dillon tossed the keys at me. "My mother's. You drive."

Dillon knew full well that I had loved his sports car—the one we'd run away to Las Vegas in eight years ago. My head said to say no.

He opened the driver's door for me. The devil inside me said this was a short ride in his *mother's* car. It wasn't *his* car. It wasn't like I was agreeing to run away and marry him again. But the way he'd kissed me just moments ago . . . I'm a heathen. I got in.

Outside the car, Lucky Harbor wagged his tail. Dillon pointed in the direction of downtown, and the dog cut through Lloyd's wooded lot.

Dillon said, "You going to let my dog beat us?"

"Not on your life, Mr. Rivers. Hold on tight to your smile, because you're about to lose it."

Revving the engine, I ripped around the fountain in front of Lloyd's house and laid rubber on his long driveway.

Dillon cranked up the tunes.

I was blissful, not thinking about murder or why somebody wanted my fudge contest to fail and to get rid of me.

Then came a troubled lunch at the Troubled Trout.

Chapter 16

Having lunch with real estate mogul Cathy Rivers should have brought me answers to help prevent Grandpa losing our shop. Cathy was sharp.

Cathy gave me a hug before we sat in a dark booth in the crowded bar area of the Troubled Trout. The seats were already taken on the deck upstairs overlooking Lake Michigan. The privacy was probably good, though. With my plain shirt covered with grass stains and my denim shorts, I felt out of place with Cathy. She still looked like a Miss Wisconsin. In her fifties now, she was my height and maintained alabaster modellike skin and a trim figure that wore a navy-and-white Ralph Lauren top and shorts with élan. Her beautiful chestnut hair sported a striking white stripe starting in her widow's peak.

Dillon sat next to his mother, discreet about not sitting next to me. But I had to shake my head with amusement as I looked around and saw people staring at us.

Cathy asked, "What's so funny?"

"I expect the betting cards behind the bar will soon include wedding dates. Why else would Dillon's mother be here meeting with me?"

She laughed it off, then got to business. "I'm glad you called Dillon, asking to meet. I'm eager to rehabilitate properties here because Door County respects its history. It doesn't tear down things; it saves them. Usually. And I'm feeling the urge to stay home now in Wisconsin. We're very similar in that way. We've both come home in the past year. We have big things ahead of us."

That felt unsettling. I wasn't sure what she was getting at.

The waitress came to take our order. I recommended the deep-fried cheese curds, of course, and the summer cherry-flavored beer made with Door County cherries. This one came from a Belgian brewer south of Madison in Flanders, Wisconsin. My grandmother had told me some shirttail relative of hers ran the brewery.

Cathy was charmed. "I'm looking forward to your fudge contest and dance. I've brought along one of my old beauty contest gowns to wear."

I suddenly felt silly for my inability to settle on fudge flavors and a dress color.

Cathy's perfect fingernails tapped the table as if calling us to order. "I went to the title office to look up the history of your shop. I also looked at old village meeting transactions and minutes—something which most people don't think to do. I wanted to find the 'intent' of the village's actions years ago. Mercy Fogg doesn't actually own your building, but she sort of does."

"Sort of?" My hands were sweating around my beer glass.

"It appears that almost ten years ago, during her tenure as village president, Lloyd Mueller was going through hard times."

"The real estate crash and the economic recession were coming on."

"Yes. Small towns everywhere had to eliminate services, and some even thought about filing for bankruptcy. Lloyd was significant to the village because of all his holdings. If he went bankrupt, that pretty much meant Fishers' Harbor would, too."

"There's too much pride here to let that happen."

"Shuttered shops affect tourism. So Mercy Fogg worked

a deal with Lloyd. To help relieve his debt to the village and pay his taxes, he adjusted the land contract ownership of your shop to include the village."

"The village of Fishers' Harbor?" I blinked hard at Cathy and Dillon.

"Yes. Mercy signed it, but as president of the village. So if your grandfather wasn't making his payments, that means it could revert to the village. The citizens would be able to sell it someday to recoup any tax payments owed the village."

My mouth went dry. "The village might own Oosterlings'?"

"Technically, it might. But not Mercy personally, no matter what her intent was then or is now."

"But if Erik decides to quit and she volunteers to step back in as village president, she'd control our bait shop. And maybe Duck Marsh Street. So everything she says is true in a way. In order to get out from under all this, the Oosterlings have to come up with a bunch of money, plus get Erik and Mercy involved with changing the land contract and ownership. I don't know where to begin."

I sagged against the back of the booth.

Cathy tapped the table again. "We haven't seen a will, or the legal documents of his corporation. There could be a trust set up for the bait shop or your grandfather for all we know. Real estate deals are complicated at this level."

"A trust? How does that work?" I took a sip of cherry beer to help me think, but it wasn't the same as making fudge. I was at Cathy's mercy.

"If there's a trust set up, that means the partners in the trust just take over the assets without a lot of fuss in probate court. There might still be a will in addition to the trust to say where personal items should go after the death, too, but a trust is a common way for people to pass along their property without a huge tax debt and probate."

"So you think there's hope that my grandfather might have been named in the trust? Or the will?" The cherry beer began to taste refreshing again.

"Yes," Cathy said. "They were best friends, after all. Do you know who Lloyd's attorney is?"

"No, why? I haven't thought to ask." I felt stupid.

"That's the next person you need to talk with. Your village president would know who that is, surely. He has to consult with the attorney to retrieve any of Lloyd's papers."

Dillon and I exchanged one of those looks: Something had been fishy at Lloyd's house earlier. I told her about being there to pick flowers hardly an hour ago and seeing Erik and Professor Faust without a lawyer in tow.

Cathy said, "But perhaps he or she was on the way."

Our meal arrived then with all local ingredients—fried cheese curds and fresh-caught Great Lakes trout drizzled with raspberry sauce, with side dishes of garden peas and baby carrots.

Dillon explained he'd shown up at the house, looking for his dog. "Erik and Alex took off with no lawyer mentioned. In fact, Alex Faust didn't even want to hang around. He forgot he should've locked up the house."

Cathy said, "They were snooping around?"

"Yes," Dillon said. "And perhaps returning a rifle, just like the one of Lloyd's left in my construction truck that matches some hole in the floor at the lighthouse."

I added, "But Erik was called to work here, so maybe that interruption caused the professor to forget about the locks."

Cathy asked for more information about the professor, so I explained his interests.

"Shipwrecks?" she asked in an ominous way. "So he's intrigued with treasure?"

I explained about John Schultz and the cup. I also added information about finding the chest under my shop floor and how the professor wondered if more hidden treasure existed in all the cabins on Duck Marsh Street. "He's going to do a little more research for me on the buildings."

"That's good. Perhaps I should meet with the professor next."

A notion flew into my brain like a gift. Dillon had been right; food helped me think. "Lloyd Mueller has what looks like a valuable collection of cups and saucers, all bone china and old, and I'm sure a couple of those cups and saucers are now missing. It's an odd coincidence that the professor is intrigued by cups found in shipwrecks in Lake Michigan."

"But it's all coincidence, unless you can find him red-handed with those cups. I certainly don't see a professor jeopardizing his job at his university for foolishly lifting a couple of cups from a house." Cathy considered the information while tasting her first cheese curd. Her face became transformed with a broad smile. "Sinfully good!"

"We make them fresh at our farm. My parents installed their own small dairy cheese processing plant."

"You've got to give me the tour."

She'd said that on autopilot. There was no way my parents wanted Cathy Rivers or her "bigamist son," as they still called him, to stop by for a tour.

Cathy read my thoughts. "Well, maybe some other time. In the future."

We enjoyed more of our trout, and then she said, "What should I wear for my meeting with this Alex Faust?"

I almost dropped my fork.

Dillon nudged her with an elbow. "Mom, I'm going to tell Dad."

It was gentle ribbing. She elbowed him back. "A woman has to use whatever weapon is in her arsenal."

I offered, "He likes yellow and aprons, if that helps."

Dillon chuckled.

Cathy asked, "How are your grandparents doing?"

I told her about their rift. "I don't think I can bear it if my grandparents aren't dancing on the docks on Saturday night."

"We'll get to the bottom of it all within a day or two, Ava. I still have friends in high places, too, if needed," Cathy said. "The governor, a Wisconsin senator on high-ranking Washington, D.C., committees, and the president of the Harley

Corporation. I can get a ride on a hog anytime to talk about the pork barrel in politics. And about the real estate in a tiny Door County village."

We clinked our beer glasses together in a toast to Cathy's power.

When the waitress came to check on us, she asked, "Did you want to get in on the pools?" She meant the betting pools behind the bar.

Dillon said, "Betting on when the lake ice will form next winter?"

The waitress enjoyed that. "No. Let me get the cards. I thought you would have heard by now."

She went to the bar, collected the betting cards from Erik, and then came back.

Several names with dollar amounts filled the squares on the cards. "This one is betting on the fudge contestants—and I'm losing! It looks like at least two-to-one odds for Piers and Kelsey."

The waitress said, "Actually, it's ten-to-one for Kelsey and six-to-one for Piers at the moment. You're at twenty-to-one odds to lose. So the payoff for you would be really good if you ended up winning. It's a five-buck minimum if you want to put your name down in a square."

I exchanged my card with Dillon's card. His was worse! I said, "This is about who I'll take as my date to the adult prom!"

Several unknown people—probably tourists here for the week's fudge festival bargains at local businesses—had grabbed squares and listed all sorts of men around town, including Dillon, Sam, even Cody and the sheriff. There was a square that said *Hot apron babe*, and it was marked with twenty dollars.

"I know who that is. The chubby, bearded fisherman. Ach. Is he winning?" I looked up in fear at the waitress.

"Oh no. Al Kvalheim is winning. He's bought the most squares, locking in the odds for a sure win so far."

I cringed, but Dillon said, "Al probably cleans up well after his many hours underground. He's actually a nice guy. I bet if you ask, he'd even give up smoking on Saturday night."

My neck prickled in a panic attack. "Al's my grandparents' age and he's got arthritis in his knees from crawling down into manholes for over thirty years."

The waitress collected the betting cards. "I guess that's a no from you on putting down a bet."

"A definite no."

After the waitress left, Cathy said, "Let me put in a good word for my son. He's a good dancer, doesn't smoke, and since everybody's betting on you two anyway, why not put some big money down on yourselves and win the whole pot?"

Dillon draped an arm around his mother's shoulders. "That's my mom, ever the practical businesswoman looking for ways to make money."

He got up and pulled out his wallet. "And I think it's a good idea. I'll be back."

"Dillon!" I called out, but too late. He was at the bar putting down who knows what kind of cash on us dancing on Saturday night.

I got back to business with Cathy. I mentioned that nobody seemed to know who the mysterious person was who'd made an offer on the harbor area and Duck Marsh Street. "Do you think Lloyd meant all along that the mystery owner was the village? It's not a real person?"

"Could be," Cathy said. "That would explain why nobody's spilled the beans on that. I should be able to confirm these things with a few phone calls or visits at county and village offices."

We decided that she'd stay after lunch to talk with Erik, and then find the professor. I still wanted to talk with Erik and Professor Faust, too, but I'd wait to hear back from Cathy before following through. This distrust of the professor felt wrongheaded to me, but we'd seen him only an hour ago with Erik Gustafson, acting strangely. Perhaps the next person I needed to talk with was Piers Molinsky, who had tried to bribe Erik. Little Fishers' Harbor was the hub of some huge conspiracy, apparently involving my little shop.

I returned to a packed Oosterlings' shortly before one o'clock. The Butterflies were fingering everything as usual. Their little-girl squeals erupted from behind shelving aisles.

The men were as bad in the bait shop. My grandfather was answering questions about spinners and what weight of fishing line to use for coho salmon, trout, and bass out on the Great Lakes. As soon as I donned an apron—a pretty thing dotted with embroidered lilac blossoms—the men began giving me furtive glances.

Cody's fingers were flying as he tied pink ribbons around packages of Cinderella Pink Fudge. Then he stuffed wrapped pieces of fudge into apron pockets.

I asked, "What're you doing, Ranger?"

"Miss Oosterling, we're getting calls for birthday gift orders, even from out of state. I even got one from your La-La Land."

Dotty and Lois trotted in from the back hallway, each loaded with a stack of aprons, even frillier than the first batch they'd brought me. Lace abounded like snowdrifts in my shop.

Dotty, dressed in a bright pink sequined T-shirt, put her stack down on the corner of the counter. She was puffing. "We sewed these fast today."

"What's going on, Dotty?"

"Oh, Ava, word has gotten out about fudge and aprons being sexy and the aprons are selling like hotcakes."

Cody said, "Sam told me that there's a picture of your fudge and you in an apron on some sexy Web site, but I didn't look, I promise."

Sexy Web site? I groaned.

Dotty said, "Young Cody called me in panic while you were out this morning because he sold out of your aprons. So we made a deal. I hope you don't mind."

"What deal?"

Lois nodded. "We turned our prayer chain into a fudge and apron chain. Our church ladies' organization is getting a cut from the apron sales here."

Dotty giggled, leaning toward me to whisper, "You look very cute on that Web site."

"I need to know what Web site. Right now."

Lois fluttered an apron in front of me. "Here, put one of our new creations on. Lilacs aren't so much you. I like this green-checkered one with the bib. I made a toque to match."

Before I could take a second breath, the women had me tied into a green-checkered cotton apron trimmed with satin and lace, and with the toque on my head. My stitches itched, but I didn't dare take the toque off for fear of some church lady flogging me into purgatory for my sin.

John Schultz was taping. I'd missed him when I'd rushed into my shop. Pauline was there, too. I raced over to her next to the child's tea table in the corner.

"Pauline, have you seen the Web site I'm on?"

"Yes, and it's tasteful. Not what you're thinking. We have our other more important thing to talk about." Pauline dragged me outside where there was a modicum of privacy on the dock. We walked toward my grandfather's dead boat. She hefted her purse in a showy way. "What am I supposed to do with these architectural plans?"

"Come over to my place after work. We'll look them over again. I have other things to tell you about anyway. I think we're closing in on the killer."

"You only 'think'? John wanted to take me to dinner tonight at the Mission Grill." It was another fancy restaurant in Sister Bay. "They have some new pheasant dish he wanted to try. He wants to get video there, too."

"Pauline, I just said the word 'killer.' Did you not hear me? Have you forgotten about our accident and the missing box? We have to find it. And Dillon's got the sheriff after him because of that rifle, and we saw odd things over at Lloyd's house, and—"

"Gee, you sure are a killjoy."

"With that ugly bruise on your face you don't want to go to some place like the Mission Grill anyway. People won't be able to eat their dinner."

She felt the side of her face that had hit the ground in the truck accident. "Is it really that bad? I put makeup on."

"Only a mud pack would cover that up. I'll see you around eight, okay?"

"John's not going to like this."

"John can use a little dieting, so don't sweat it."

"That was mean."

"I know. I'm sorry."

"You need to get a real man of your own and then you wouldn't be so jealous of me."

I ignored her. I didn't want to talk about Sam and Dillon. I stared at my grandfather's boat. "I wonder how many aprons I have to sell with fudge in the pockets to pay for a new boat. Or to buy back our building from the likes of Mercy Fogg or the village." I had a feeling Erik Gustafson wasn't going to stay long as our board president, not if he was sneaking around returning rifles. I still wanted to know why he'd been carrying a big briefcase. Or did I know? Was he looting Lloyd's property? Was the professor, too?

When I stomped back inside the shop, huge applause followed me all the way to my copper kettles. I couldn't deny loving the adulation. I sorely needed something going well in my life. After securing my green-checkered toque in place, I began explaining the science of candy making, how glass blowers and I were essentially forging and shaping the same thing with fire and heat—crystals. Fudge may have been made by cave women, because glassmaking was about that old, too.

After a full hour of entertaining customers, I took a break and exited "backstage" to my kitchen. Sam accosted me next to my chocolate melter. As in, Sam accosted me.

He grabbed me in his arms from behind, then twirled me into his shirted chest. "Do you know what you're doing to me with this new uniform?"

"Sam? What—?"

He tossed the toque from my head. His hands were in my hair as he drew my face to his in a chocolate kiss. He evidently had purchased some fudge and eaten it while standing hidden in the back of the crowd.

I broke away. "Sam! What's gotten into you?"

He grabbed for me again, holding me in his arms. "You look frisky. A Belgian filly."

"A Belgian filly? You never talk like— Oh my God, is that what they're calling me on that Web site?"

"Yeah."

I'd never experienced the casting couch while working in Los Angeles, but now it seemed I'd found the secret to my very own version of it and my own allure: fudge served in aprons.

I pushed against his chest but was held fast by the prurient need shining in his blazing blue eyes. "Get a grip, Sam. And not on me."

"Are we a date for the prom Saturday night?"

"Humph. I found out you didn't put down enough money on me over at the Troubled Trout." I served up a coquettish smile. "Pony up more money and we'll see. A woman doesn't live on fairy-tale fudge promises alone."

He let go of me, then took out his wallet. I laughed. He was acting in a new and adorable way. He was counting his cash as he walked to the kitchen door. Before leaving, he said, "I'll trade more kisses for information on your missing box. I think I know where it is."

Chapter 17

"How did you find out about the missing box? Where is it?" I asked.

Sam was smoothing his shirt after our manic kissing interlude. "I stopped by your cabin earlier to find you, then went over to your grandmother's place. Sheriff Tollefson was there and they were talking about the box."

I rushed Sam down the short hall of my shop and out the back door for privacy. We stood next to some small burning bushes I'd planted. "You didn't tell anybody else about the box, did you?"

"No, but the sheriff seems to think it's connected to the murder at the lighthouse."

"My thought exactly."

Sam swatted at a mosquito floating past. "While I was there, the sheriff got a phone call about the autopsy. There are signs on his body that Lloyd was tied up."

"So he was hauled up to the top against his will, then shoved off to make it look like a suicide. Jordy didn't think my grandmother could do such a thing, did he?"

Sam grimaced. "I got the feeling he has some evidence that points to her."

"Evidence? Like what?"

"I don't know. He wasn't saying in front of me."

"So where's the box?"

"The lighthouse."

"Jordy said that?"

"No, I did. I'm sure it's there."

"But Jordy and Maria went over that place already, right down to the fingerprints. They would have found that box."

"Exactly. That's why I think it's there. The murderer waited until after the place was cleared by the sheriff, and went back with the box. To the scene of the crime."

I gave Sam my best Poirot-style squint. "How did you come up with this stuff? This doesn't even sound like you. You sound more like me. Guessing. You usually research the facts on everything."

"I did . . . some research." Sam's face went red as a summer tomato. "I sort of, kind of, said something to Cody."

"You just said you hadn't told anybody about the box."

He held up his hands in surrender. "I didn't tell him about 'the' box. But you know how he is. He envisions himself a park ranger someday. So while you were making fudge, I asked him where he'd hide a box that had been stolen from a truck just following a murder at the lighthouse. He said killers always go back to the scene of the crime. He also said the killer would be at tomorrow's funeral."

"That happens on TV shows because it's convenient."

"Cody says it's a true phenomenon."

Squawking robins flew past in an aerial battle for territory. It felt like a warning of what was ahead for me. "We need to sneak into the lighthouse and look around when Libby isn't there."

"Why not ask for Libby's help?"

"It's complicated, Sam, but she might think I'm trying to prove Kelsey is a murderer, and Libby might panic and prevent us from looking around."

"I'll go with you."

"You're a social worker. You follow rules; you don't break them."

"You look so good in this apron . . ." His eyes had turned

to sizzling, hungry sapphires. "We'll make it legal. We'll stop by Libby's for a key and just say you forgot your purse in the gift shop."

That lie felt responsible. "I'll have Grandma call Libby. Libby will do anything for my grandmother. We'll have to go after dark, though, so nobody interrupts us."

"I'll meet you at around nine."

"That's perch on my grandfather's clock."

Sam hiked away, rounding the corner of the fudge shop building.

The taste of his chocolate kiss lingered on my lips, infusing me with confusion. I'd been kissed by Dillon and Sam on the same day, to the same effect. I wanted more. I smiled at the mere thought of meeting Sam alone in the seclusion provided by a romantic lighthouse.

But first? I had to find that Web site and get that picture of me in an apron taken down.

I was closing up at eight p.m. that Monday when Jordy appeared, ruining my blissful, hopeful mood. Everybody had gone home, even my grandfather. Lucky Harbor was gnawing on a piece of twine, his favorite activity when I refused to toss him Goldfish crackers. Once I shut off the lights, he'd scoot for Dillon's place. It had become our routine.

The cowbell clinked. Jordy was in full uniform, even wearing his fancy-brimmed hat. A chill swirled in the air. His shoulders looked broader whenever he had his official hat on.

I said crisply, "My grandmother knows nothing about the murder of Lloyd Mueller. And neither does my grandfather. That's all I have to say to you."

I walked around Jordy to open the door, meaning for both Lucky Harbor and Jordy to leave. Neither did. I snapped off the lights. The dog left, but Jordy stood in the dim light, his irises with pinpricks of white in them from boaters' lights reflecting through the windows.

Jordy switched on the lights. "I'm here on business."

He hustled past me, down a bait shop aisle. I watched his hat bob along. He came back to me, carrying the big roll of twine that I used for the dog leashes. He'd slipped a huge clear plastic bag around the roll, saying, "Evidence."

My fingers collected into sweaty fists. "Evidence of what? That you can lift thirty pounds of twine?"

"The medical examiner found a couple of pieces of fiber that he believes are twine used to tie up Lloyd before he died."

"Sam told me he was tied up."

"Your grandmother believes Lloyd was drugged, then tied up. She thinks he was carried up those stairs by some strong man. Like Dillon."

"Dillon? You *want* it to be Dillon, Jordy. My grandmother did not say that."

Jordy set down the twine, then grabbed my shoulders but in a gentle fashion. "She said that, Ava. She said that whenever Dillon came to collect his dog, the dog always either had a twine leash on him or was playing with twine, and Dillon probably had tons of twine. What's more, Dillon and his dog are always over at the park. Perhaps with one of Lloyd's rifles in hand. Dillon could easily have bumped off Lloyd."

I busted from his grasp. "For what purpose, Jordy?"

"To get Lloyd out of the way so that Dillon and his mother can negotiate for the real estate here. Heck, I'm surprised the citizens of Fishers' Harbor haven't heard that the Rivers family has made an offer on the Blue Heron Inn."

"They have?"

"That was conjecture on my part. But you wait and see. Once I hear that's true, I've got handcuffs at the ready."

"They're not murderers." I had to think fast. What was going on? My grandmother wouldn't put the finger on innocent people. My mother and father might let Dillon go to jail and squirm, but that wasn't like Sophie or Gil Oosterling.

Pauline came through the door, dropping her big, fat purse in surprise. Jordy collected the plastic-wrapped twine and left. The cowbell's clank resounded with ominous finality.

Picking up her purse, Pauline asked, "What's going on?"

I filled her in.

She said, "Maybe we should just go over and talk with your grandparents about this right now."

"I can't. I have a date with Sam to break into the lighthouse." After she gave me a look down her nose, I told her to relax. "We're going to get a key from Libby. It'll be legit. But we have to find that box. It'll have fingerprints on it and lots of revealing papers inside. I hope, anyway. If Jordy thinks Lloyd was drugged and hauled up the stairs by Dillon, finding that box could prove Dillon's innocence."

"That's the stupidest theory I've ever heard you come up with. You realize of course that the box has your fingerprints on it, as well as your grandfather's."

"Yes, but my grandfather would say to us, 'A.M. and P.M., somebody stole that box from you at the accident scene for a good reason.'"

"Maybe Dillon took it? Maybe it wasn't a coincidence he was driving by, after all."

"You just don't want me to be happy, do you? You have John, but all my boyfriends get to go to jail?" I locked the front door from the inside.

"That's your problem. You can't decide between Dillon and Sam, and then there's Jordy, and now there's that chunky, bearded fisherman, plus old Al Kvalheim and all the town's men wanting you. Not to mention you have a dog panting after you all the time."

"It's because I smell like fudge." I made a note about the twine and put it on my grandfather's counter. "At least Lucky Harbor didn't put money down on me over at the Troubled Trout. Don't make fun of me getting attention."

"Attention? You crave it but you can't handle being popular for the first time in your life. You're doing all you can to sabotage your own success because you're afraid of success, Ava Mathilde Oosterling. Even a volcano gets over its own eruption."

I was stunned. Yet she knew me better than I knew myself. "Of course I'm afraid, Pauline. Every time something good comes my way, it turns sour. And I don't know how to get out of that cycle."

"Stop thrashing about like one of those frogs in the lake that Lucky Harbor chases after. Do something worthy in your life and you might get out of that cycle. Sure, you messed up in the past pretty badly and embarrassed yourself. You feel unworthy of being loved. But eight years has passed since the Dillon debacle. It's time to take action. I tell my students all the time that old saying—excuses are the poetry of failure. You should heed it, too."

She was right. With fire in my belly I ripped off the apron and slung it toward the stack of the others still sitting on my counter. I grabbed her big purse off her shoulder. "Let's look at those architectural plans. Did you look at them again?"

"No. I've been busy calling around Door County for more red wagons for the Butterflies fudge parade on Saturday. Little Cheyenne crashed hers into a tree."

"She okay?"

"Oh yes. Verona let her help decorate her wagon, and then Cheyenne helped Paris, Madison, and Savannah."

"So it's all the rage to name girls after cities."

"But that's so yesterday. Some reality TV star just named her kid North. Within five years my kindergarten class will be like a compass filled with North, South, East, and West."

We laid out the architectural paper on the white marble table.

Notations called for rustic wood and rock from Door County, and Milwaukee Cream City brick to match our new shops with the older buildings in our village. A walkway with lovely new benches meandered by the expanded harbor that would stretch into the area where the cove was now.

On the back of the paper, we found a tiny, penciled *RCC*.

Pauline muttered, "Rivers Construction Company."

"It can't be. Dillon would have told me if his mother and father were behind this. RCC can mean anything and anybody."

We refolded the architectural plans. We left through the back door, then walked through the darkness and the dewy grass. When I flicked on the lights in my cabin, Titus scurried across the living room floor.

Pauline said, "Want me to catch him? I'm faster than you."

"Are not. And no, leave Titus alone. I'm trying to live-trap him. I bought one of those sticky papers for him to step on."

"Then what? When he's sitting there having his tiny little heart attack looking up at you while he's stuck on the sticky paper, how are you going to feel? And what does one do next with a live mouse glued to a piece of paper?"

She had a point. I felt stupid again today. "I haven't gotten that far with my plan for Titus. I certainly don't have the heart to poison him." The mouse's fate gave me a thought. "Jordy said my grandmother thought Lloyd was drugged to slow him down. Who would do that? And why? Why not just kill him fast?"

"If he were drugged, somebody could make him do something or admit to something against his will before they killed him."

"Or make him sign something."

"Or they just wanted him to cooperate as they lugged him up the lighthouse steps to the top of the tower. It seems like we know a lot of people who could gain by his demise."

Pauline flounced down with her purse on my couch, across from the fireplace. Cardboard boxes were all around her. Cody had hauled my stuff back earlier. Knowing Sam would be here any minute, I went to my bedroom to throw on a sweatshirt. I stuffed a small flashlight in my sweatshirt pocket. My phone was charged and in my denim shorts. I put on lightweight sneakers in case I needed to run fast.

Pauline was watching me scurry about. "Maybe I should go along, Poirot."

"No, Hastings. I don't want to be responsible for you."

"But I have to do something."

"Check on Laura."

"I called her before I came to the shop. She said Piers had volunteered to strip wallpaper in that old room in the back of her shop. She can't be in any fumes, of course."

"Piers sure is trying to make us believe he's Mr. Nice Guy all of a sudden. We have to talk with Erik about that bribe he offered him last Tuesday. I have a lot of things to ask Erik about."

"Ask him tomorrow at the funeral. I'm sure Erik will be there. Maybe Piers, too."

That gave me a new notion. "Piers could've hauled Lloyd up the lighthouse tower stairs. They're a tight fit for a guy his size, but that climb is relatively short and Piers is agile. He's also good with concocting recipes."

"Like those red velvet cupcakes with your Cinderella Pink Fudge bits inside. Better than any French pastry." Pauline swooned. "Do you have any? And milk?"

"No, Pauline. Stay on topic." I sat on the arm of the couch, looking down on her—a rarity for me. "Piers could've drugged Lloyd. Lloyd was tasting things made by the contestants last week, getting to know them."

"Well, if that's the case, then maybe Piers and Erik were plotting to get Lloyd out of the way so Erik could take over the real estate holdings. Maybe Piers wants the Blue Heron Inn and Erik agreed to help him."

I nodded down at Pauline. "But we still need to prove that one of those two ran us off the road. And murdered Lloyd."

Pauline got up. "The notes with the orange crayon referenced the fudge contest. This scheme had to have come about after Piers came to town and then met Erik. You left the shop several times while your guest confectioners were there making fudge. It certainly wouldn't have taken but a few minutes for Piers to snoop around and discover the box. Maybe he had decided to steal it but saw you put it in your truck on Saturday and then he came after us, waiting for us at the intersection to run us off the road."

"It's plausible. But wouldn't Piers have just stolen the ring and left the box? The ring would give him a down payment on the Blue Heron Inn."

"Are you sure your grandfather doesn't know more about all this? He lied about the land contract and lied about owning his building, Ava. And your grandmother's under suspicion now."

"Though she tried to save herself by saying Dillon was involved in the murder."

Rapping at my door sent Titus skittering into the kitchen. Sam was here. Pauline hiked off in the dark toward her car in the harbor parking lot.

I got in Sam's sports utility vehicle.

The night was chilly, but clear, with a three-quarter moon outlining buildings and making the painted lines on our Main Street and Highway 42 shimmer with an opal glow. Our windows were cracked open. I loved the fresh air here. It was crisp and clean, unlike anything I'd experienced elsewhere. The pleasant scents of cedars and fresh-mown golf course grass greeted us as we drove into Peninsula State Park. Sam had picked up the lighthouse key earlier from Libby. He reported that he hadn't seen Kelsey there.

We stopped a quarter mile from the lighthouse, parking behind bushes at a trailhead. We got out. His SUV was a dark gray, like my grandmother's. There were a lot of gray vehicles around. I would have to check on Piers Molinsky's rental car. But then I recalled that Erik Gustafson drove a tiny burnt orange hybrid car.

"Do you think Erik might have written the orange crayon notes?" I asked, folding my sweatshirt-covered arms against the chilly night. "If he likes orange, maybe that's a clue. Pauline and I think Erik and Piers have to be in this together. We could check to see if Piers drives a dark rental car."

"Later. Let's find that box. I asked Libby about it and she suggested we look in the old privy and oil house."

"You told her about the box? I thought we were going after my forgotten purse."

He shrugged. It was hard for Sam to lie about anything.

Lighthouses and homes used to have separate oil houses back in the late 1800s and early 1900s because the kerosene oil was too dangerous to keep inside a house. Kerosene replaced the more stable lard that was burned in the earliest lamps. These days, a solar panel kept the Fresnel light shining.

Sam and I stayed close to the woods as we walked along the park road toward the lighthouse. Once close to the lawn, we crouched down amid the lilacs flanking the clearing. Mosquitoes buzzed in my ears.

The beacon light shone brightly into the inky expanse of Lake Michigan. Pronounced "fruh-nel," the French Fresnel light's crystals and prisms could allow the beam to be seen forever—until the bend of the earth itself hid it from view. Looking up at the four-story tower with the light on top was hypnotic. My very own ancestors had come here by ship through the Port of New York and then on steamers through the Great Lakes. They'd left crowded Belgium when times were lean with only hope in their pockets. Belgium was a small country, one-fifth the size of Wisconsin, but was still overcrowded with almost twice our state's population of approximately six million.

I whispered, "John Schultz thinks he's going to get rich by bringing up cups brought here by our poor ancestors."

"There are plenty of wrecks, and many valuable things down there for John to find." Sam's eyes twinkled in the moonlight. "I'll take up scuba diving and find pirate's gold for you."

"You'd wear a rubber suit and flippers for me?"

"If you don't stop talking like that, Ava, we won't make it to the lighthouse."

"Get real, Sam. It's too buggy out here." I slapped a mosquito on my cheek. "Did you bring spray?"

"It's back in my vehicle."

"Then we've got to move. I'm going to be weak from blood loss soon."

We hurried to the oil house and privy, but discovered the keys Libby had given us didn't work.

"Libby knows her own keys," I said. "This is odd."

"Maybe in all her nervous excitement over us looking for this box, she gave me the wrong ones. We'll have to go back to her house."

"We're here, so let's try the lighthouse before we go."

Sam slipped the key into the gift shop door's padlock easy as pie. He popped the latch off. We entered, closing the outer door and inner screen door quietly behind us. I couldn't see much at first, but I could smell the old wood, papers, and musty, rusty antiques.

The moonlight came through the single window and limned objects, so it didn't take us long to look through the small gift shop. We went down five wooden steps into the basement next, using our flashlights. We didn't find the wooden box amid the jumble of supplies kept on boards laid across sawhorses for tables. There were two rooms, and one was empty.

Next, we went up a set of four steps to the second floor, where the family had lived. Ambient light from outside came in through two windows of the dining room, but we had to resort to my small flashlight to poke into murky corners. Protective rubber runners crisscrossed the wooden floors, softening the sounds of our footfalls.

The building was filled with original furnishings, including the rosewood Chickering piano of the William Duclon family. William had been the lighthouse keeper from 1883 to 1918, and he was buried near our town and not far from the lighthouse. I hadn't been here for a tour since grade school, but I was still impressed by the thought of living in a place with an old wood-burning stove in almost every room. The dining room had tables and chairs, and blue-and-white china hung on the walls, but no box with rusty hinges.

We didn't find it in the master bedroom with the old rope bed.

The parlor next door had a painting of kittens on the wall and another with a child with baby chicks—innocent fare that belied what might have happened here. We found the small hole in the wooden floor made by the rifle bullet, just past the ropes to keep tourists at bay and behind the right side of the small settee. Had Lloyd sat here talking innocently to his captors before going to the top? Or had he been pleading for his life? Had the rifle been shot as a warning to Lloyd? I almost couldn't stomach being in this room. As I was edging backward, a sparkle glinted under the sweep of our flashlight.

I stepped over the rope to get to the settee. "Oh my gosh, Sam, it's fudge!" The sparkle came from the edible luster dust on top of my Cinderella fudge. A half-eaten piece nestled at the far end of the settee, as if somebody had taken a bite, then had to leave the rest behind. I'd brought small plastic bags in case we'd found something. I never imagined we'd find fudge.

"What're you doing?" Sam asked.

"Bagging this." I was using a tissue to carefully pick up the piece of fudge. "Nobody eats only a portion of my fudge. And that's not bragging. It's just a fact. Somebody was eating this and had to leave it behind in a hurry. Maybe Lloyd's killer."

"Why didn't the sheriff find it?"

"Well, it is just fudge. Both times they were here they were looking for more nefarious things like weapons, so maybe this was overlooked."

"But I still don't know why you'd want to take that to the sheriff."

"Hard evidence," I said, with some satisfaction. "My fudge is very creamy and smooth and hardens just enough to retain fingerprints. Maybe the sheriff can match those to somebody. The bite marks, too, might help. Or Jordy can get saliva off the fudge for DNA."

"You are so television—did you know that? And smart."

"Thanks, Sam."

We left the parlor. I kept my eyes peeled for any other telltale fudge. As we made our way up the black, cast-iron circular staircase to the second floor, a window overlooking the lake revealed dots of lights from ships in the distance.

The children's room held two regular small beds and a trundle bed where the family's seven boys had slept. It also had a woodstove and desk. The guest bedroom to the north had beautiful blue-and-white crockery that could hide things, but they were empty. There was no box. No fudge.

On the wall before the final steps would take us up to the platform was a framed needlepoint on the wall with a saying: *Travel East/Travel West/after all/Home's Best.*

The saying could have pertained to me. With a catch in my throat, I said, "Perhaps that's the last thing Lloyd saw before he died."

We continued up the dark metal stairs, taking our time because of the steepness. The stairs were sturdy iron in a cutout design; they didn't move a bit. Hauling a body up would have taken plenty of time and strength, though I imagined Mercy Fogg could accomplish it alone, as well as Piers or Erik.

When we got to the top, we had to use one of the keys to unlock the padlock on the Plexiglas hatch above our heads. Once that was done, we stepped outside onto the high platform but had very little maneuvering room. Not wanting to look down quite yet, I focused on the beacon sprinkling fairy-tale sparkles on the water. Waves lapped and sucked against the barely visible rocks. It was a dangerous drop-off behind the wall, though once upon a time there had been a steep, ladderlike stairway down to a dock. The remains of a concrete pier still sat in the water. Had someone in a boat committed the crime and left by water, thus not being seen by anybody leaving the park at an odd hour?

As my gaze drew back from the moonlit rock wall and then came closer still to the tower, I shivered. Lloyd had been thrown to his death from where I stood. Had he been conscious? Had he seen the view of the lake over the tops of the trees that we all loved? In my imagination now, he was looking back up at me from below, repeating what he'd told me in his library, *"You have to help people believe that the fudge shop is fine where it is, and so are the cabins on Duck Marsh Street."* And from the stitchery on the wall, his voice feathered to me: *"Home's best. Home's best."*

Lloyd's ethereal voice startled me. I grabbed at the railing.

Sam pulled me back into his arms, sucking us up against the steel panels below the Fresnel prisms. "Whoa, what's wrong?"

"Lloyd's voice was in my head plain as day as if he were still alive." My skin rippled with a shudder. Had Sam just saved me from falling over the railing?

I turned and wrapped my arms around his neck in my relief. "Thanks, Sam."

He kissed me on the forehead—at the same time something bit me on the side of one cheek as a crack echoed from below.

Sam crumpled at my feet on the platform.

"Sam!"

A dark spot bloomed on his shirt.

Another crack split the air. My body pitched across Sam's chest.

Chapter 18

A bullet had grazed the top of Sam's left shoulder after spraying a chunk of paint off the metal housing under the Fresnel light and onto my cheek.

A second bullet had ricocheted, too, Deputy Maria Vasquez surmised, off the tower's railing post behind me, and then had hit me in the back of the left leg. It had barely penetrated my flesh, fortunately. Sam, however, needed a doctor to pull a tendon and flaps of skin back together.

Maria held out two plastic bags—one with my piece of fudge with the tissue still clinging to it, and another bag with a bullet. "We'll analyze the pink fudge later." Her cocoa-colored eyes were penetrating me, though not mocking. She held the other bag higher. "Looks like a slug for a thirty-ought-six hunting rifle. Pretty common for deer hunting. Except it's not deer-hunting season."

It was ten thirty at night. We sat in the blaring lights of the E.R. in Sturgeon Bay still in shock. After being shot at, I had looked up in time to glimpse somebody dressed in dark clothing including a hoodie sweatshirt slip into the woods.

Maria wasn't pleased with my observation abilities. "Everybody committing a crime wears a dark hoodie. Which direction did the person go in?"

"Toward the east. Maybe one of the hiking trails? It

might be the trail Pauline and I chased somebody down yesterday morning. Tramper's Delight."

"Who were you chasing?"

"We think Kelsey King." I told her about the chase and our suspicions.

As Sam was easing his way off the nearby table, Maria asked me, "Does Kelsey have any reason to shoot at you?"

"Besides hating me?"

Sam cleared his throat. "She doesn't hate you. She hates the fudge contest she got rooked into by John Schultz."

Maria asked, "Is that the camera guy I talked with the other day?"

"One and the same," Sam said.

"Are you friends with him?" Maria was looking at me pointedly.

My gut went queasy. "He's the boyfriend of my best friend. Is there something we should know?"

"Libby Mueller called me." Maria closed her notebook. "She said John creeped her out. He asked to get inside Lloyd Mueller's house for videotaping, but she thinks John wanted to plunder the place."

"I don't think John would steal."

"You're sure?"

The questioning was making me worried for Pauline. "He seems pretty harmless. He's obsessed with diving for treasure at the moment."

Maria was writing furiously. "Treasure hunter?"

"He just wants to get rich. The fudge contest is his plan to get on TV and get rich."

Maria said, "I need to talk with Mr. Schultz."

Pauline was going to hate me.

Sam asked Maria, "Why would Libby even suspect John Schultz of wanting to steal things from Lloyd? You're not suggesting John's a suspect in his murder."

That was so unexpected I had to grab a nearby intravenous bag stand so I didn't fall over.

Maria didn't flinch. "She said that a Professor Faust suggested she be careful."

I offered, "Professor Alex Faust is one of my fudge judges. He's a historian. He was at Lloyd Mueller's house himself this morning when I was there. Libby had given him a key. Obviously to check things out for her."

"And why were you there?"

"Picking roses for the funeral." My face went hot, but I hoped nobody would notice in the context of the E.R.

"Did you go into the house?"

"No." My whole body was on fire with my lies. I was going to burn in Hell, for sure. "I have witnesses. Pauline Mertens, Laura Rousseau, our village president, and Dillon Rivers."

Sam said, "Dillon? You were picking roses with Dillon?"

Now the fire was in Sam's eyes, leaping at me.

My heartbeat hammered into my throat. I focused on Maria. "Libby has nothing to worry about. A lot of people are watching over Lloyd's house, including the professor. Nobody's going to break in."

Sam insisted he could drive, but I knew he was just trying to be macho because he'd found out I'd been picking roses with Dillon. I pointed out, "You're one-armed and on pain pills. Now please get in." I still had his keys from the ride here from the lighthouse, so he had no choice.

He stayed mad at me. We rode in silence for about twenty minutes out of Sturgeon Bay on a quiet Highway 42. I focused on the occasional innocent eyes of raccoons reflecting back at us from the edges of the blacktop and prayed they didn't try to cross the road. The windows were rolled up against the chill that had grown into the damp cold of nighttime. Foggy mists rolled off the lake in the distance, crossing the road in front of our headlights like ghost animals, which made me nervous. My foot kept wanting to jump to the brake. The engine droned on while the tires slapped in perfect cadence across tar-filled highway cracks.

Finally, Sam muttered, "You and Dillon were inside Lloyd's house together?"

"No, Sam. It was just me. Dillon came to get his dog in the rose garden."

"What were you doing?"

"Picking roses. Like I said."

"What'd you find in the house?"

"Nothing." A part of me wanted to share more with Sam and tell him about my suspicions concerning the cups and rifles, but I also wanted to avoid talking about Dillon with Sam.

"Is it a nice house?" he asked.

"Remarkable, Sam."

"Better than the one I bought for us?"

He'd impaled my heart. "Don't go there, Sam. You have a nice house. But it's your house." I'd never been inside it.

"Not really. I bought it for our wedding present. And planted the roses for your bridal shower gift."

"Oh, Sam, please stop this." I was suffocating. I rolled down my window halfway. "We're tired. It's not a good time to talk about us, the past or the future. I'm very sorry I got you into this. It's not even like you to get involved in illegal, stupid things. It's why we split up. I knew I would hurt you sometime. Now I have. And I'm sorry you're hurt. Please forgive me, Sam, and let it go."

After another minute of the highway thrumming beneath the car, Sam said, "Dillon's been out in the woods a lot. You said his dog was out there. He hunts. He has hunting rifles."

I chose to be curious rather than upset. "You think Dillon shot at us?"

"Not at you. Me. He still loves you, you know."

"That's the most ridiculous thing I've ever heard."

"Which part? Him shooting at me? Or him loving you?"

"Sam, stop before I push you out of this vehicle and steal your truck. I need a new one, you know."

We pulled up to my cabin about fifteen minutes later. I

let him drive home alone across the village since there was zero traffic and he'd only be going twenty-five at the most.

Once he left my street, I pushed myself inside, aching all over. I was shaking, too, wrung out. I switched on my kitchen light and kicked off my shoes. Titus stared up at me, acting as if he, too, wanted to know: Who did I love? Dillon? Sam? That chunky fisherman? A dog? Or a mouse?

My head itched, my leg stung, and my cheek felt stiff where the chip of paint or metal had hit me. I could have lost an eye, I realized now. I curled up with my laptop on the couch to check for e-mails. My fingers were still quaking. I clicked on an e-mail from Pauline.

Searched RCC on the 'net. Rivers Construction Company and Riverboat Cruise Corporation both came up the most. Both based in Milwaukee. No people listed for the riverboat one, just contact info.

I trusted Dillon, for better or for worse, so I concluded the Rivers family wasn't involved with taking over Fishers' Harbor or my fudge shop. So who owned the Riverboat Cruise Corporation? I'd call them in the morning and ask. By morning I'd know who was skulking about our village. Or worse. Could the owner of this RCC acronym have murdered Lloyd? So that they could get the property cheaper? The thought still brought me back to Mercy and Erik—two people who could surely use money and who knew their way around legal documents. Erik was young enough and perhaps naive enough to think he could borrow Lloyd's rifles and get away with murder. And Erik liked the color orange.

I couldn't sleep. There was a buzz in my body keeping me wide-awake and high, an awareness that I'd almost died. I desperately needed to make fudge so that I could think straight. I put my shoes back on, then headed out into the darkness.

On Tuesday morning, I slept in after my fudge-making night. It was nearly eight a.m. by the time I got to the shop.

Cody was already there, of course. The lusty, earthy coffee smell jolted me awake. For breakfast I downed a piece of dark Belgian chocolate fudge as I sipped the dark-roasted brew.

My grandfather was yawning loudly while puttering about his shelves. If he saw the note about the missing twine roll, he didn't seem to care. Usually he growled about our sheriff's interference.

Cody was banging about, putting a copper pot in place that he'd brought from the kitchen where I'd washed it last night after midnight. "Miss Oosterling, can I teach Bethany how to make fudge while you're at that funeral this morning?"

I was tying on one of the fancy-schmancy aprons in a peach color and lost my grip on the bow behind me.

Cody came over to help. "I like this one. It's movie star shiny. You deserve a star on the walk of fame, Miss Oosterling." He sauntered to the door to point outside. "We should start our own walk of fame right outside. I could carve stars and names into the wood on the dock and on the piers. We could have a big party every time we chose somebody to add to our walk. But you'd have to be the first. You're a star from Hollywood for real."

He was buttering me up, but I liked it. "I worked for a while on a TV show, but mostly behind the scenes. I wasn't the star."

"But the apron makes you look like a real somebody. A real peach."

"You really think so?" The young guy was really working me. I pirouetted in my peach-colored, puffy pinafore apron with its shiny satin interwoven across the bodice. The pockets on top and bottom were satin, sort of like wearing peach mirrors on my boobs and on the skirt, too.

Cody clapped.

I said, "Sure, I don't mind if you teach her how to make fudge."

"Can we make more of that new recipe you made last

night?" He nodded toward the window where I'd left the new batch made at midnight under a towel on the marble table.

"Did you peek?"

His face turned a shade of red that almost matched his short haircut. "I tasted a nibble. That could win the prize on Saturday."

"You think so?"

"You bet. That's destined for Emmy swag bags."

"Let's keep it a secret, then. But I have to come up with a fairy-tale name. Plus, I need to come up with one more flavor for the judges."

"Kelsey King is making dandelion fudge and something else from plants she finds in the woods at the park. Just so she doesn't pick poisonous stuff."

As I checked the stock on my shelves, I wondered what poisonous plants were out in our woods. Certainly mushrooms. Had Kelsey poisoned Lloyd? Had she tried to scare him into voting for her and not me? That was silly. More likely, she tried to get him to give her valuable cups and saucers, or to sign something over to her. Instead of becoming groggy, the poor man had died on her. She was in good shape; I could conceive of Kelsey using ropes to winch him up a step at a time. Had she sung that Friday night or early Saturday morning, too? As she had the morning Mercy saw her. I'd have to tell Jordy to ask the campers about that. The singing could have been a cover-up. If somebody asked her what she was doing at the lighthouse, she'd say she was practicing. A lot of people liked singing in a tower or silo.

But if she murdered Lloyd or killed him by accident, why had she cozied up to Libby Mueller, the ex-wife that Lloyd had still loved in a protective way? It couldn't be, could it, that Libby was in on the murder? She was a slight woman, so I didn't see her wrestling with Lloyd or dragging his body up those stairs.

If Libby was innocent and Kelsey was a killer, then Libby was in danger from Kelsey, as my girlfriends and I had concluded earlier. The motive was clear: Kelsey wanted to take over Libby's life and live the high life in Lloyd's mansion. Libby was fearful of John doing that, but it was Kelsey who was the real culprit perhaps.

I cringed. A fudge contest should be fun. I was determined to get it back to being fun. Lloyd had loaned me books and had encouraged me to make it big and wonderful because that would save Fishers' Harbor. Again it struck me that Lloyd might have been afraid of somebody.

"Cody, you told Sam that bad guys show up at funerals of their victims. Is that true?"

"It sure is. The FBI takes down car license plate numbers and takes pictures from off in the trees where they hide. Are you thinking of taking down numbers today? The sheriff can run them later for you."

My fudge assistant was only eighteen, with a definite flair for drama. Still, the "TV" feel of this made me look forward to watching the action at the funeral today.

Moose Lindstrom walked into the shop then. His bulky, tall frame stood in the middle of our floor. First he looked me up and down pretty good with his big ol' smile; then he winked at me before turning to the other side of the shop. "Hey, Gil, I've got a proposition."

My grandfather came around an end cap on an aisle, looking disheveled. "I'm not marrying you, Moose. Got enough trouble with the marriage I've got."

Moose scratched the whiskers on his chin. "I saw ya sleepin' on that boat of yours this morning and it got me to thinkin'."

I rushed forward, my hands wringing my shiny peach apron. "Gilpa, what were you doing sleeping outside? You and Grandma have to patch things up. This is silly."

He headed to the minnow tank.

Moose gave me a silent plea for help. All I could do was shrug. Grandpa was an immovable Belgian buffalo.

Moose went at it again. "Gil, I got more business than I can shake a stick at lately, what with this good weather. But

I can't be in my boat all day long. Tires me out. I was thinking you could use the *Super Catch I* and just toss me whatever cash off the top you think is fair."

Gilpa sprinkled fish food across the top of the minnow tank, giving Moose the silent treatment.

I rushed over and snatched the box of food. "Come on, Gilpa, that's a really nice offer. And you like his boat. You piloted it that time in May, remember? It was fun. Remember how easily it cruised across the top of the waves? Your boat doesn't do that."

"I like my boat."

"Gilpa, your boat's not working and probably won't anymore. Both engines are shot. And your boat's a mess. It's all oily. Nobody wants to ride in that thing. And it doesn't have air-conditioning."

My grandfather gave me a look that shamed me for being so forward.

I swallowed hard, trying to think of something to help him get over his silly pride. "What would Lloyd want you to do? He liked new things as much as old things."

"Lloyd? New things?" My grandfather's face wrinkled in pain. "You think giving me a damn fancy boat to ride around in will get Lloyd back? Or our shop? Or your grandmother? I'm losing everything. Everything. I'm moving back to the farm."

He stomped off through the back of the shop.

I sank against the minnow tank, dropping the box of food on the floor.

Moose stuffed his hands in his pockets.

Cody had turned white. "He's mad. Maybe you should call him on his phone. Sam always says when I get mad and can't handle things because of my autism, I should call him. Maybe Gil should call Sam."

Cody's concern touched me. "It's okay, Cody. He's going to go talk with Grandma now. They'll be all right."

"I don't think so, Miss Oosterling. He's going to pack his bags and leave for good. Remember when I ran away? He has that look in his eyes, like nobody understands him. That's how I feel when people gang up on me."

My heart fell into my stomach. In May, because of my lack of patience with Cody, he'd stolen a boat and motored out to live on an island. Pauline and I had to rescue him and convince him to come home. "I ganged up on him, didn't I?"

Moose put a hand on my shoulder. "You did nothing of the kind. I pushed him. Sorry. I thought I could help."

"Did he really sleep on his boat last night?"

Moose nodded.

"Oh dear." I bit my lip in thought. I had to find a way to get Grandpa back into proper fighting mode, and back together with Grandma. I was nothing without my grandparents by my side. My grandparents were the ones who'd helped me get my start in the fudge business. My grandfather had even taken down the word "Beer" on the old sign to make room for "Belgian Fudge." I had added "Beer" back to the building later in May to show my love and respect for all he'd done for me.

I had to put my life in order once and for all. "Moose, have you ever heard of the Riverboat Cruise Corporation? They're the ones who drew up the plans for the harbor. They proposed moving the bait shop back off the dock and under some new condos."

"Oh, sure. RCC is big. They run some river cruises down in Chicago and all over the Great Lakes region."

"So who's the president of that corporation? The name isn't listed on the Internet."

"Damned if I know. You talked with Lloyd's lawyer? He'd know. He'll surely be at the funeral today." Moose bent down near my face, then whispered, "Whoever Lloyd named in his trust is going to get mighty rich. Rumor around town is that Mercy Fogg knocked him off so she and Libby could live the high life together in that mansion."

A nasty image of Mercy—and Kelsey, two nutty women—sharing that magnificent house with Libby plagued me as I readied to go to the funeral that Tuesday morning. Lloyd wouldn't want any of that to happen to his estate. Lloyd had entrusted me with a key for the place and I somehow felt protective of the house now.

I called the Riverboat Cruise Corporation and asked for the owner's name. The phone got forwarded to five different people and some calliope music before I concluded I'd just gotten the royal brush-off.

I went home to dress for the funeral.

Funerals call for a dress. I hated dresses, but I still had a royal blue sheath with pockets that I used to wear to writer gatherings in L.A. It hid the ten pounds I'd gained since opening my fudge shop. I left my hair loose about my shoulders. I slipped on tan high heels. The nick in my leg from the bullet was covered by a small flesh-colored bandage, but there was no pain, just a stiffness. The heels registered loud clicking noises as I walked across my cabin's floorboards. Titus didn't recognize me. The poor mouse darted helter-skelter from the kitchen into the living area, then cowered under the couch and stuck his nose out to look at me again. I put one of the Oosterling cheese curds on the floor for him to munch on while I was gone.

I called Pauline to pick me up because I didn't want to come between my grandparents by asking for a ride with them. I crossed my fingers, hoping those two would drive together to the funeral and patch things up. That reminded me that I'd have to call the auto body shop about the assessment for my yellow truck and then touch base with my insurance company.

Pauline was wearing a cherry red sheath with matching tan shoes. We almost looked like twins. That tended to happen with us, starting in kindergarten.

We were on the highway heading southwest out of Fishers' Harbor when I asked her to turn around.

"What's wrong?"

"We forgot the roses. We told everybody we were picking roses for the funeral."

Pauline circled back down the highway, soon pulling up in front of Lloyd's house by the fountain. I got out my key.

Pauline said, "We shouldn't go inside."

"We need to put the roses in something, unless you're offering your purse as a vase to sit next to the casket."

"No. Every time you ask me to stuff anything in my purse, bad things happen to us."

"Nothing bad happened when you put the architectural plans in your purse."

"So far. We stole those plans from this house, though."

When we got inside Lloyd's historic home, we quickly saw that it'd been ransacked.

Chapter 19

Drawers in the dining area's side table were left open but not dumped, just pawed through and left messy. Furniture had been moved around. Cushions were tossed. The cups were still intact in their cupboard, save for the couple I still thought had been stolen.

"The guns and the safe," I said.

We hurried down the cool air-conditioned hallway. A hunting rifle was missing, which didn't surprise me. We headed to the library.

"Oh my," we said in unison.

Many sections of Lloyd's shelves had been emptied. But oddly enough, they hadn't been tossed about. His precious cookbooks were in small stacks on the floor, as if somebody had been going through them methodically. To look for the safe's combination.

I rushed to the lower shelf in the middle of the back wall. The safe was still closed and locked. Chinks of plaster were missing around where wooden trim had framed the safe in the wall. The wooden trim sat on a shelf. A steel casing under the trim area connected the safe securely behind the studs in the wall and behind the plaster. Dillon had been right; to get this sucker out you'd need the right tools and lots of muscle.

Pauline gripped her purse tighter still. "Let's leave. We're supposed to be going to a funeral, not trying to create our own. Somebody could be hiding upstairs."

"Or in the rose garden." I dashed to the windows.

I didn't see anybody. The door was still secured from the inside. But I knew I couldn't leave the cookbooks still on the shelves behind now. We'd scared somebody away, perhaps, and they hadn't yet gotten to the books on the shelves that might contain the safe's combination. The visitor couldn't have been Jordy. He definitely wouldn't have left books lying about on the floor like this. He would have taken them all with him.

"We've got to get into this safe," I said. Two walls of books weren't cookbooks, I realized. Just the shelves on the back wall with the safe. Whoever was here hadn't had time to use the rolling ladder to get to the cookbooks near the top. "I need your help carrying these cookbooks to your car."

"We'll get dusty and sweaty before the funeral. And we're in heels."

We considered our sheath dresses, crisp and fresh, the royal blue and red colors bright and unsullied.

"You're right," I said. "As usual."

"And as usual you're ignoring me."

"BFFs. We need to hurry."

It was around nine thirty and the service started at ten. I grabbed a steak knife for protection, kicked off my flesh-toned pumps, and then went up the stairs. Luggage with wheels on it was in Lloyd's master bedroom closet, which somebody had also left in disarray. I thought about John Schultz wanting to get in the house, and wondered if he'd finally picked a lock. But so many others had access, too, it seemed. Erik and the professor, and maybe Mercy and Kelsey, maybe Piers because of his association with Erik, and of course Libby. Maybe Libby had been here to get a suit for Lloyd to wear in his casket and had left the closet this way in her rush and she had nothing to do with the mess downstairs. My intuition said I was close to figuring out who murdered Lloyd.

In the library, I climbed the ladder and tossed books down for Pauline to catch. It was just like playing basketball again. We stuffed two large rolling suitcases with cookbooks.

After grabbing rubber gloves and towels from the kitchen to protect us from the thorns, we picked a dozen roses in as many colors and shades, found a vase in the kitchen, locked up the house, then headed for the funeral.

St. Ann's Church had been built in the middle of a wildflower prairie a few miles between Fishers' Harbor and Egg Harbor. It sat amid woodland and apple and cherry orchards dotting rolling hills. In the springtime, this drive was a breathtaking sea of pink and white blossoms with a perfume in the air that made you smile no matter what your troubles were.

As Pauline drove, I was reminded of our farm. "Pauline, we have to find a way to get my grandparents back together."

"Sophie is a wise woman. She'll figure this out."

"Not this time. Gilpa's moving for real down to Brussels because of me and my big mouth. I'll have my parents mad at me, too, but worse, I might not see Gilpa at the shop early in the mornings. The morning with just the two of us is our special time." My heart was cracking like ice on Lake Michigan in winter.

"Maybe Sophie's church lady friends will know what to do. They'll be serving the church lunch afterward. We can ask for their help."

"Good idea. Never thought I'd say that about the church ladies."

My guilt and shame spun inside me like a tornado. The more I tried to help others, the deeper in trouble I got and the farther I pushed people away. What was wrong with me? Pauline had said that I didn't trust my own success. Who could blame me? My fudge success had apparently caused all the trouble to happen—perhaps even caused a murder. If I hadn't picked Lloyd to be a fudge judge, he might still be alive.

I shook off my own sorrows. "How's Laura? She couldn't come, you said."

"She's not feeling well again."

"The babies okay?"

"Ava, I think she's miserable mostly because her husband's not here."

I didn't have a cure for that. "Maybe we should go over there and help her with the refurbishing of that old room in the back of the bakery. Maybe we'll find secret cavities in her floors or walls filled with a million dollars. That'll cheer her up." Another idea struck me. "We need to check Lloyd's house for secret floorboards. Maybe that fancy inlaid floor in the dining rotunda is really a trapdoor to treasure!"

Pauline slowed down for a corner. "We're not going in that house again. No way."

"We have to find out what's in that safe."

"Just ask Libby for the combination. I can't believe I didn't think of that sooner. I'm starting to think like you—convoluted."

"I'm creative. I don't think she has that combination, Pauline. Lloyd didn't want her gambling his valuables away. In fact, I'm surprised Alex Faust got a key from her that worked. I would've thought Lloyd had changed all his locks."

"Maybe Lloyd's lawyer gave her permission to have a key to get in to get clothes for the funeral."

"Likely. But let's not spook Libby today and tell her what we just saw. She's going to be especially fragile today."

"How did she feel about you and Sam getting shot at after you asked her for the keys to the lighthouse?"

"We didn't tell her about being shot. On the way home, I doused our lights yards away from her house, then slipped the keys under her mat. She needed her sleep for today."

"But what if that was Kelsey shooting at you? Libby needs to know that woman is certifiably crazy. Lloyd would want us warning Libby. Maybe Kelsey was the one ransacking Lloyd's house. Everything was rather neat; maybe it was a woman burglar."

Of course my friend could be right on all counts. I'd had the same thought minutes ago in the house. Our prime suspects, in my opinion, were Erik and Kelsey. "Let's wait to talk to Libby later. A funeral isn't a nice place to tell a widow that the person who may have killed her husband might be living with her and wants to kill her, too. After she steals her blind."

When we arrived at St. Ann's, at least a hundred or more people milled about outside under the tent the funeral home had rented. There was a line leading up the sidewalk to the church. With my roses in hand as my excuse, I cut into the line and strutted inside.

I set the vase of roses down on a nearby table filled with pictures of Lloyd. Several easels had been set up to accommodate dozens of photos, from baby pictures to some taken last week by golfing buddies at Peninsula State Park. There was also a photo with my grandfather and other card-playing buddies in the basement of this church, taken maybe only weeks ago.

Lloyd was laid out in a peaceful pose in the open casket. He wore a three-piece navy suit. He should have been holding a golf ball or deck of cards in his hands. Instead, he held nothing. Not even one of his precious cookbooks. That saddened me. Details matter at one's funeral. *Get it right, folks.* Makeup had been applied on his neck, which confirmed there was some mark there. The mark was thin, unfortunately about the size of the small, slim twine ropes we sold in the shop. But twine was ubiquitous; heck, I now recalled seeing it in Lloyd's rose garden to help hold up the bountiful blooms.

My gaze connected with Jordy, standing maybe ten feet from me, talking to a very tall man I didn't know. Jordy was in full uniform, holding his hat in his big hands. He had a look that said he wanted to talk with me.

My phone buzzed in the pocket of my dress. I rushed away from the casket to the unused coatrack corner in the opposite direction of Jordy. Cathy Rivers was calling.

"What is it, Cathy?" I whispered.

"The Riverboat Cruise Corporation owns other companies that have to do with tourism, including a wine tour business."

"Wine tours?" The neurons in my body waved red flags before my eyes. "John Schultz's wine tours?"

"Yes."

"But you can't possibly believe he's the one putting in the offer to buy my fudge shop and the cabins on Duck Marsh Street. He doesn't seem the type." *He has hairy feet. He wears Hawaiian shirts all the time. He can't possibly be that rich.* "Is he some corporate spy?"

Cathy laughed. "I don't know. He might know something about RCC's offer to buy up the village harbor properties."

We hung up. Pauline obviously didn't know she was falling for a rodent, and one that she thought was about to propose to her. I imagined he'd already planned the proposal for the night of my fudge contest adult prom when we would all be in our fancy fairy-tale gowns. John would make sure it was captured on camera for his dratted food channel show he was trying to sell. I realized now that TV show story of his was merely a cover for him to be nosing around our properties. I wasn't about to let him bamboozle Pauline. I wanted to find a giant piece of sticky rat trap paper and watch John squirm while I grilled him.

But Cathy had said she wasn't sure; she'd said, "I don't know." I had to find John Schultz right now.

He wasn't in the church, so I glided outside. Pauline was talking with some fellow teachers. She said John was in the church basement, videotaping the church ladies making the lunch. I decided to wait instead of making a scene in front of women who created prayer chains and aprons for me.

"Why do you want John?" Pauline asked.

Hmm. I'd have to lie to my best friend. "I wanted to

make sure he was videotaping the food from the best perspective. Funeral food in our neck of the woods is much more than gelatin molds with mayonnaise on the side."

"I happen to like mayonnaise," Pauline said.

"So do I, but with Belgian fries, P.M., not with lime gelatin in the shape of a rooster."

Pauline's friends started a conversation about collectible gelatin molds or tins, so I excused myself to go find Jordy and ask him about the autopsy report.

In my rush, I almost fell over when my heels poked too far into the lawn. The gentleman who caught me from behind was the stranger Jordy had been talking with. He was probably six feet eight inches tall at least—a giant. And handsome as heck. He was my age or thereabouts, with elegant, wavy short-cropped, brown hair as neat in appearance as his dark three-piece suit.

"I'm so sorry," I said, looking up at a chiseled chin.

"I'm not," he said. "Are you okay? You didn't break a shoe, did you?"

With smooth grace and big hands, he helped me move from the soft lawn to a portion of concrete sidewalk. I was floating on his strong arms. My heels checked out okay. Indicating his attire, I said, "You must be one of the pallbearers."

"Yes. I'm Parker Balusek."

"How do you know Lloyd?"

"I'm his attorney."

"Really?" I smiled big-time at my luck.

Parker laughed. "You expected to meet some old codger in pinstripes reeking of expensive cigars and wearing diamond cuff links." My mouth barely came open before he added, "That's my boss. I'm new to the firm but have been working on Lloyd's business as of late."

My heart bounced around like a joyful bunny amid rows of carrots in my grandparents' garden. "Then you've been working with him on the plans with the, uh, Riverboat Cruise Corporation."

"Indeed. I specialize in real estate law and rights involving historic preservations and zoning. You may have heard of the efforts to preserve the church in Stangelville? I was raised there. Recently, I went over the historic preservation status documents for the church."

People came from across the country to see the St. Lawrence Catholic Church in Stangelville, a Czech-heritage community that was not too far south of us in Kewaunee County. The church was built inside with the detail of a European Czech cathedral.

Parker asked, "You know Professor Faust? He's been in touch with me about local history."

"Yes, he's got quite a cookbook, which includes pictures of some of Lloyd's older properties, like Oosterlings' Live Bait, Bobbers and Belgian Fudge and Beer. I'm Ava Oosterling, the fudge part of that. My grandfather was Lloyd's best friend and runs the bait shop. We're located right in the harbor on the docks."

"Then I suspect you see the professor a lot, too. He said he's recently become interested in shipwrecks. It's interesting that he's made a connection with John Schultz." A look of distaste crossed his face.

"Interesting? How so?"

Parker flipped his head about, looking at the crowd. "John's not here, is he?"

"In the church basement. What's wrong with John? He's been hanging around in Fishers' Harbor since May."

"That's when he was asked to, let's say, take a new position, one that kept him out of the office at RCC. It was that, or else."

"'Or else'?" I lowered my voice. "Was he about to be fired?"

"Let's say he doesn't present the corporate image that RCC likes, but John has enough seniority that he could cause them legal trouble if he were fired. A man in his fifties might sue for age discrimination."

This was starting to sound far more serious than mere

corporate spying. Could John have possibly sought revenge against his company by messing up their deal here in Fishers' Harbor? Could he have murdered Lloyd as revenge against his bosses? In May, I'd been suspicious of John killing the actress. Maybe my instincts were dead-on about John being deadly after all. Sam had brought up the possibility, too, and I trusted Sam's instincts above everybody's. But John was the man my friend Pauline liked, possibly loved. A wooziness came over me. I needed a piece of fudge to think this through, but all I had in my pockets were Goldfish crackers.

Parker reached out with a big hand to steady me. "It's hot out here, isn't it? Reminds me of the basketball camps I taught in the summers."

"Basketball? You played?"

"Yeah, for Marquette. Before I went to law school there, but I coached for them in a few of the summer camps while I finished law school."

"I have somebody I want you to meet."

It was a no-brainer foisting him off onto Pauline while I went in search of John. Pauline would love reminiscing about her basketball-playing college days with Parker. From a distance, they looked like a perfect couple. I was shocked with my matchmaking abilities. She had to forget about John Schultz.

I ducked into the church's side door that led to the basement but somehow missed John. The women gave me pause, though.

The church ladies were rushing about setting long tables with plastic tableware and coffee carafes. Each of them wore an apron. Of course. When you volunteered here to help at a wedding, funeral, First Communion celebration, or kermis, you wore an apron. These women looked *angelic* in their aprons and *beautiful* no matter what their build, wrinkles, or reputation. The realization dawning in me felt like a tiny window sliding open inside me with fresh air rushing in.

Back upstairs, the service was about to begin. Organ music had turned into a dirge to get us to our seats. I hurried up the stairs to the vestibule. I was about to go inside the nave when my eyes caught sight of a briefcase that looked familiar. It sat under the coatrack. I looked about. I was alone. The pallbearers were outside getting instructions from the funeral director. Within two seconds I'd tried the briefcase latch and it opened. Erik hadn't thought to lock it. I blanched at what I found inside—a small pad of ruled paper that kids used to practice their lettering. I was about to reach for the pad when the voices of the pallbearers grew louder. I clicked the briefcase closed, then scurried to join my grandmother Sophie, breathless from my discovery.

Grandma was in the front pew, on the other side of Libby, holding a box of tissues. Libby had the aisle seat. My parents were in the pew in back of us.

My grandfather was one of the six honorary pallbearers. He walked down the aisle beside the casket, along with two members of Lloyd's card club, plus the attorney Parker Balusek, Professor Faust, and then Erik Gustafson. I flinched. Seeing Erik's hand on Lloyd's coffin was maddening. I wanted to scream that he was a murderer.

I wondered who else was involved, who else had learned about the possible bribes Erik had taken from Piers Molinsky. Giving the church nave a perfect gawk, I didn't spot Piers or Kelsey. That, too, felt odd, because if Cody were right about guilty people showing up at a funeral, those two chefs weren't guilty of Lloyd's murder. I searched for John Schultz. He was at the back of the nave, still videotaping.

When the casket was settled into place, I scooted over, closer to Pauline on my right, expecting my grandfather to sit next to my grandmother. Instead, he walked around to the end of our pew and sat on the other side of Pauline—far away from my grandmother.

The emptiness in me continued through the luncheon, when my grandparents said nary a word to each other. I noticed that others left them alone, a sign that their war had gone public.

When I spotted Sheriff Tollefson finishing his second piece of German chocolate cake, I followed him outside the church.

"Jordy! Wait. I need a ride. We need to talk."

"I'm not a cab service," he said as he kept on walking into the blacktopped parking lot. He settled his brimmed hat on his head.

"You questioned my grandmother, and that action contributed to my grandparents having troubles. So you're going to help me get them back together."

"I'm not a marriage counselor." He lengthened his stride.

My left calf hurt like heck now, but I hiked faster to catch up. "Jordy, that's not funny. I bet you want to know what I've found out about murder suspects as much as I want to know about the autopsy report. Want to trade information?"

He stopped to wait for me at the parking lot, looking like he was suffering indigestion, but I knew better.

I persisted. "The autopsy report will be released to the public anyway, so tell me now, was Lloyd poisoned?"

His slim runner's frame went ramrod straight. "The M.E. found something, yes."

"I think Kelsey poisoned him. But I also think she's working with somebody else. Two people are responsible for Lloyd's death, not just one."

"Who?"

Too many people with prying ears were lingering near their cars and chatting. "Give me a ride and we'll talk."

"Get in."

Chapter 20

I got to sit in the front passenger seat of the sheriff's cruiser for the first time ever. I pointed out to Jordy he was treating me like an equal.

He growled back as we pulled onto the country road, "If you would stop being such a pain in the ass, somebody might ask you to be his date to the dance."

His tanned face deepened to the hue of ripe tart cherries.

I had to look out the window to recover. "I just don't know if we'd work, Jordy."

"I'm not asking for me."

"Oh?" To my surprise, disappointment popped into my head. "Who are you asking for?"

"I'm not asking. I'm just checking. To see if you're amenable to going with somebody who asked me if you'd gotten a date yet."

"Holy cow. Some grown man asked you to ask me if I was free yet? This sounds like high school. Who's this mystery man?"

"I can't tell. Ava Oosterling, are you free or not?"

"Did you stop at the Troubled Trout? Who's got the odds on me now?" When he hesitated I slapped the dash in disgust. "Jordy Tollefson, you put money down on me and somebody going to the prom on Saturday night, didn't you?"

"I might have. But the guy still asked me to ask you about it."

"There's some chubby fisherman I might say yes to. I don't even know his name, but I'm starting to think dating a stranger would be a lot better than old boyfriends." My heart lurched unexpectedly at the prospect. I thought of Sam and Dillon, my whole being feeling the tender and timeworn hold they had on me, like the northern white cedar trees—called the trees of life—whose roots had held fast the Niagara Escarpment cliffs on our Lake Michigan shores for maybe two thousand years.

Jordy growled again. "So, what do you have for info about the fudge smudge?"

"Is that what the murder of a fudge judge is called at your department now?"

"Yup."

We had to slow down for tourists turning onto roads that took them to a beach or local winery. I asked Jordy again about the autopsy.

He said, "The preliminary report is that Lloyd ingested deadly mushrooms."

"Any leads?" Kelsey came to mind, shoving aside what I'd just found out about Erik.

"No. It could've been an accident. Your grandparents are friends of his. Did he mention to them anything about going mushroom hunting or buying mushrooms from somebody?"

"No." My brain burned with a yearning to blame Kelsey, but I stuck to the facts. "The last time they were together with Lloyd was at the fish boil. He seemed fine. I saw him arguing with Kelsey King, though."

"Did you hear what the argument was about?" Jordy was braking for more tourists who had slowed ahead of us to stop at a massive garden and lawn ornament shop hemmed with a white picket fence.

"No. But I'm pretty sure Kelsey was making a play for him, and maybe he rebuffed her. Kelsey's been staying at

Libby's. She knows Lloyd through my fudge contest, and Pauline and I think Kelsey might be a gold digger who's befriending Libby to get at Lloyd's treasures, or now, to get her hands on Libby's inheritance from Lloyd."

"I didn't see the little blonde at the funeral."

"No. She wasn't."

"Did you notice anybody else there you'd consider a suspect?"

I felt so mixed up now. The missing cups and saucers came to mind. John Schultz and the professor had been in the house and both had interest in cups. But I couldn't betray Pauline and get John in trouble until I had proof that was solid about him. But then there was Erik Gustafson. I explained seeing him at the house with a briefcase, then finding the pad of paper in his briefcase at the church.

Jordy said, "It's just a pad of paper he could have bought anywhere."

"I don't think so. Erik is acting odd. He's nineteen and carrying a briefcase instead of a backpack. Nobody his age carries a stodgy briefcase. It's big enough that it could've hidden those cups inside it, too."

"So maybe the professor put him up to it."

"And risk his reputation and career at the university? I don't think so. Erik, however, is just starting his career and has nothing much. He needs money."

Jordy nodded. I could almost hear his brain working. We were at the outskirts of Fishers' Harbor now.

I asked, "Have you questioned all the renters in the cabins on Duck Marsh Street, in case somebody had some grudge against Lloyd?"

"Yes. None of them know Lloyd really. They're just vacationers, but I have all their names, and the names of those who left on Sunday, in case we need to question them again."

He'd just said "we," as if I were part of his team. "And you checked out the shop owners along Main Street who rented their space from Lloyd?"

I knew the answer to that one already. Jordy would have done his job and questioned them all. People like Travis Klubertanz and his wife who ran the market weren't murderers. Their worst offense might be that they had a kindergartener who was a klepto. And elderly Milton Hendrickson, who ran The Wise Owl Bookstore, had been friends with Lloyd and was a friend of my grandfather. The artists in the other spaces I'd checked out earlier through Pauline's association with them; their rent was based on their commissions from the sale of their artwork, and none of them had a beef with Lloyd.

Jordy said, "Everybody had kind things to say about Lloyd, except for Milton Hendrickson."

"The Wise Owl's owner."

"Yes, but his complaint was about a card game they had recently and he was mad because he wouldn't get a rematch with Lloyd. Milton's thinking of retiring."

"That's too bad. He's been there on Main Street since I was a kid. Whenever I visited my grandparents they'd send me over to his store with five dollars to buy a book."

After passing the auto body shop with my crumpled yellow truck still in one bay, it reminded me of Dillon and his dog. "Pauline and I saw Dillon's dog playing in the park with rope. It could've been the rope Kelsey used to tie up Lloyd."

The squad car lurched to the side of the road with tires squealing and spraying gravel. I hung on to the door handle. Jordy flicked on his red-and-blues, drove straight ahead into a flat grassy ditch to get around a line of cars in front of us, then took a sharp turn onto a route that skirted Fishers' Harbor. He was obviously headed for Peninsula State Park on the other side of town. "Why the hell didn't you tell me about this rope in the woods before?"

"It was just a piece of rope. Rope is everywhere."

Within ten minutes we were careening onto Shore Road. We scattered a couple of cars. Golfers stared at us as we sped by.

We drove to the trailhead that Pauline and I had used to chase after Kelsey.

Still in the car, Jordy said, "You're in your fancy duds. You stay here."

"Nothing doing."

After twenty minutes of fighting brambles off-trail and swatting at mosquitoes in the woods, while I tried not to ruin my sheath dress or get my heels stuck in moss underfoot, we found the rope in the small clearing. Jordy bagged it carefully.

He used a small pocket magnifying glass to take a look at it. "There are some spots. Could be blood. Or it could be bug juice and this is nothing but a piece of rope some camper with a tent left behind. We'll know later."

"I never saw blood on Lloyd's neck when I saw him Saturday morning."

"There was a raw burn on the back of his neck and a wrist. Apparent struggle."

Gooseflesh popped up on my bare arms. Lloyd had struggled to free himself.

As we turned to head back, the sun spotlighted white mushrooms around the clearing, which made me stop. "A fairy ring," I said, "and just what Kelsey might have found."

"What's a fairy ring?"

"Basic botany, Jordy."

"Don't start drawing me your pictures. I can see the mushrooms."

This fairy ring was maybe thirty feet in diameter, ringing the small clearing. The grass had been eaten down in spots by the deer, so the mushrooms' ecru-colored tops showed easily. I leaned down for a closer look at one.

"Chlorophyllum molybdites." The tops were shaped like satellite dishes about three inches in diameter, and underneath they had rows of what looked like paper files. "Fairy rings are formed when the spores from mushrooms spread out around them, and then the original plants die off. What's left is the outer ring."

"These are poisonous?"

"They'll make you violently ill. You might have a worse reaction if they're ingested with alcohol. Somebody who knows about wild plants could possibly use them to subdue a person, maybe try to get him to sign away his life, Jordy."

"Lloyd had alcohol in his bloodstream."

"What was the time of death?"

Jordy had knelt down to bag a mushroom. "The medical examiner says around one or so Saturday morning."

"Kelsey had to have been at Libby's that night. Lloyd gave Libby a ride home after the fish boil. Maybe he stayed late and Kelsey stirred up something nice as an apology for their skirmish earlier, a dish to soak up their drinks. His dish got mushrooms slipped into it. Did you ask Libby about the night before we found him dead?"

Jordy stood up with the bagged specimen, giving me a tired expression that said he had more work to do because of me. "Yes, I did. But I never asked her about food. I can ask her later today, after the burial and after she's had a chance to collect herself."

"You're a nice person, Jordy, when you want to be. I almost want you to ask me to the prom."

He grunted in reply as we began our walk back.

"Did you find anything useful with the piece of my Cinderella Fudge I picked up in the parlor of the lighthouse?"

He grunted again. "We picked up the edge of a fingerprint. The DNA analysis will take a while."

The idea that my fudge could be a key to solving the case tickled me. I had a toothy smile that nobody but the squirrels and mosquitoes could witness.

After we emerged from the woods, Jordy and I peered about the environs of the lighthouse. Behind it, we walked to the rock wall. A regatta of sailboats was floating by on Lake Michigan.

He said, "It wouldn't take much for an accomplice to help the murderer get away. Any small boat would do. You said somebody else might have been in on this."

I told him about Professor Faust witnessing Piers trying to pay off Erik Gustafson, another of the fudge judges, but more important, Erik was someone involved in the secrets surrounding Lloyd's real estate deal.

Jordy asked, "You really think Erik murdered Lloyd?"

"He has a lot to gain if the village controls the real estate. He'd be a nineteen-year-old millionaire of sorts. It's not really his real estate, but as village president he would feel powerful."

"Erik would also have too much to lose, though, if he murdered Lloyd. He loves Door County, too. What about John Schultz?"

His mention of John surprised me. "Why consider him, Jordy?"

"The guy is everywhere. And he's irritating as hell. It's only a hunch."

I couldn't hold back anymore. "John chose Kelsey as a contestant and asked her to come here. He knew her. Maybe they're buddies in crime."

"Sounds like I need to have a longer talk with Libby and Kelsey about everything. And then John."

"I've been thinking about John, too, as a suspect, but John may have only put the two of them together so he could get access to Lloyd and his house. John didn't murder anybody. But he might have the stolen box in his possession. He loves treasures and drama." Then a huge revelation popped into my head. "What if John ran me off the road? He may have videotaped my accident for his TV show. Kelsey may have told him to tail me."

Jordy looked confused.

I explained, "I suspect Kelsey's been watching my every move. She always seems to be one step ahead of me, and out here in the woods, and I think at Lloyd's house because she can get the key from Libby."

Oops.

Jordy's gaze hardened. "When were you at his house?"

I confessed to my house visits but didn't tell him about

the cookbooks in Pauline's car. I didn't want to get her in trouble, on top of my turning in her boyfriend. I remembered the gun cabinet then, and told him about a rifle being missing, and then maybe one being returned when the professor and Erik had visited. "You questioned Dillon about the gun found in the back of his truck, but he said Lloyd had shown him his hunting rifles previously and that's why his prints were on that one. So who put that weapon in his truck? Who do you think is trying to frame Dillon?"

"A frame-up?" Jordy blinked hard; then his face softened. Maybe he was considering my supposition. "Libby verified that rifle was Lloyd's. Dillon Rivers said he didn't know how it got there. It also showed fingerprints belonging to Lloyd, Libby, and the professor."

"But not Erik? The professor?"

"He said he'd started to pick it up, then thought better of it. Libby corroborated that. He said he'd never touched it before then."

"So how did it get in the truck and why? And do you think it was used to shoot at me and Sam?"

"We're testing for that."

Was Erik wily enough to wear gloves when handling those rifles? Probably. The professor was certainly smart enough to wear gloves if he were the guilty person, but his fingerprints were on everything, showing he had nothing to hide. The thought of Erik's possible involvement in the murder kept flashing in my head. "Maybe all the rifles in Lloyd's gun cabinet should be given a second look. And that safe needs to be opened, Jordy. It could hold valuable information."

Jordy said, "Stay out of the house. I've hired somebody to come and open the safe."

"When will that be?"

"Friday. Why?"

This was Tuesday. My life couldn't wait until Friday, but Jordy wouldn't appreciate me trying to boss him around. "It doesn't matter. All we need to do is talk with John and

Kelsey and Erik, with maybe some verification from Libby about loose ends, and this will be over."

Jordy said he'd have a chat with Erik at the bar later. He suggested I call Kelsey to have her meet us. I did. To my surprise, she and Piers were at my fudge shop, which I found frightening since I'd ordered them to stay away. In the car, I told the sheriff, "Step on it."

When Sheriff Tollefson and I arrived at the fudge shop close to one o'clock, Cody was running a fudge-making show that was delighting the tourists. Kelsey and Piers were stirring new batches of fudge in the copper kettles—and both of the confectioners had on frilly aprons. Piers's stout frame was pretty funny in a lacy pink pinafore apron. He wore a matching toque on his head. They looked innocent—by design?

Cody's girlfriend, Bethany, stood between the dueling chefs in a powder blue apron, helping three of Pauline's kindergarten Butterfly girls stir fudge ingredients. All three girls had their hands on one four-foot wooden ladle. The girls, too, wore aprons, which had obviously been pinned in the straps to help them fit their tiny statures. They could barely reach over the lip of the kettle. The ladle looked like a giant oar and they were rowing in a chocolate lake. Little Verona Klubertanz was standing in front of her three friends and the copper kettle reciting the fairy tale "Rapunzel."

The story of "Rapunzel" is a pretty grim Grimm's fairy tale. An evil enchantress steals a girl child and locks her in a tower, and when she's a teenager a prince tries to help the captured girl escape. But the evil enchantress blinds him with thorns. I was a little shocked that little Verona knew the gruesome story by heart, but I had to remind myself that kids liked being scared and the story had a happy ending I couldn't recall. Right now I had other things on my mind, like solving a murder committed by the very woman standing there next to Pauline's kindergarten students in my shop.

As far as I was concerned, Kelsey was the evil enchantress who had done away with a prince—Lloyd Mueller. Instead of using thorns, she'd poisoned him with mushrooms.

Jordy managed to catch Kelsey's attention.

She flounced outside with us in the yellow apron I'd worn once. It almost matched her long blond hair. We sat a few yards from the shop on the picnic table, with Kelsey facing us and the sun. Boaters coming and going and the hubbub of the harbor continued behind her.

Jordy said, "Have you been in the woods lately, Miss King?"

Kelsey flipped her long tresses back off her shoulders. "You know darn well I've been in the woods. Looking for ingredients to cook in my fudge. But I promised not to pick anything illegal."

I said, "Mushrooms are legal."

She contorted her face. "Why would I pick mushrooms?"

"Kelsey, cut the crap. You've been following me. Pauline and I saw you running in the woods. You ran from Lloyd Mueller's house this morning, I bet. You shot at me and Sam at the lighthouse last night after dark."

"No, I didn't."

Jordy asked, "Can you prove that?"

She had to think too long. "I didn't do those things. Honest."

I said, "You were singing on the lighthouse the other morning. Mercy Fogg saw you. The singing was just a ruse to cover up something. You were at the lighthouse making sure you'd cleaned up any evidence left behind. Did you search the grounds, too, for any box of rifle ammunition you might have left behind? How about a piece of fudge not finished because you suddenly got interrupted for some reason in your plot to murder Lloyd?"

She paled. Was she guilty or just good at looking like a confused fish caught in a net, which I would have to throw back in the water?

She said, "I was singing because I like to sing. It's fun to sing on top of a tower like that, and inside, too. Libby gave me a key to get in to practice. Honest, I didn't shoot at you. I hate guns." She licked her lips, blinking several times.

Either she was a good actress or her distress was real. I sided with actress for now.

She said, "I can prove I wasn't in the woods doing anything wrong or shooting at you."

"How?"

"Somebody set up a trail camera in the park around the lighthouse sometime. I saw cameras when I was out looking for dirt to cook with." She added, looking at Jordy, "I'm not taking dirt anymore. The trail cameras will prove I was only singing." She described two locations for cameras, both in the woods near the lighthouse.

Jordy let Kelsey go back to making fudge.

He said, "I've never heard of cameras there. I'll call the DNR and lighthouse society to see if those cameras are something new they just put up. They always let us know where those are and when they install them. Probably in my paperwork waiting for me on my desk."

"We could find our killer this afternoon, Jordy."

"We?"

I shrugged at him.

Trail cameras use infrared night vision and tell you what time the photos are snapped. A lot of rural residents here used them to see what kind of critters walked by the house at night. It was entertainment.

Jordy and I got up from the picnic table as a seagull swooped in to beg. I tossed one of Lucky Harbor's crackers into the lake for the bird. It flapped away to get the treat just as Lucky Harbor came from nowhere to launch into the water to gulp at the cracker. The seagull screeched in disgust at his loss. Lucky Harbor hauled himself ashore in the reeds past my grandfather's dead boat, then came over to shake, spraying my fancy dress and dousing Jordy's uniform.

Jordy said good-bye and then sauntered back to the squad car.

Lucky Harbor wagged his tail while he panted at me, looking up at me with his doggy smile.

I was about to call Dillon about his dog when Pauline pulled into the parking lot and then came running.

"Why haven't you been answering your phone? Laura's in the hospital."

"She's having the twins?"

"I don't know. Maybe worse. She fainted. I found her on the floor of the Luscious Ladle and called an ambulance."

Chapter 21

Oosterlings' Live Bait, Bobbers & Belgian Fudge & Beer was in good hands with Cody and Bethany, so I changed clothes and hopped into the passenger side of Pauline's small sedan to head to the hospital to see Laura Rousseau. Lucky Harbor wanted to go with us, but cookbooks already took up the backseat.

As we drove through Main Street, Lucky Harbor followed us, catching up with Dillon, who was working with Al. Melancholy struck me. Dillon's reason for being here would be over soon. Then what for us? The memory of the kiss in the rose garden lingered, as did the fun ride in his mother's car, his apologies, his changed ways.

Because of the heavy traffic, Pauline took side streets to skirt around town. We were out in the countryside, passing the turnoff to St. Ann's, when she said, "I bet you thought you were clever, leaving me stranded at the church with Parker Balusek."

"Didn't you talk basketball?"

"I'm not going to date Parker. My kindergarteners won't like it."

"It's great alliteration. P and P, Parker and Pauline."

"They'll giggle over it being pee and pee."

"Well, John Schultz is worse. That's Pauline Mertens

Schultz. PMS. The junior high kids will scrawl that on your dusty car windows."

"I'll be able to handle that. If he proposes to me."

"If? Is there trouble in paradise?"

Her arms went stiff against the steering wheel. "He's obsessed with diving suddenly, especially now that Professor Faust is excited about it, too."

"The professor wants to write something other than cookbooks so he can please his faculty buddies."

"It pleases John, evidently, more than I do. Now he's planning two TV food and travel shows. You saw him at the funeral. He didn't even sit by me. He was too busy with his camera. Why would he want to videotape a casket rolling through a church?"

Because he murdered the man? No. But maybe he inadvertently helped the murderer. My heart beat faster. "I've got something to tell you about John."

She flashed me a hopeful look. "Did he buy me a ring? He asked you for my size?"

Oh dear. Her question made me remember that we had to find that box with the ring in it. I didn't care what was inside it anymore, though. I had a hunch that whoever had it was the murderer. But I had to lie for now. "I missed him in the church basement, but the church ladies said he had a certain look in his eyes. They were tittering."

"Tittering?" Her voice went up an octave. "Maybe they teased him about having a reception for our wedding in that church basement."

Pauline was a lost cause. A sick feeling came over me. I popped a couple of Goldfish crackers to settle my stomach and keep my mouth shut.

At the hospital, a couple of nurses called me by my first name. I'd obviously been here too many times lately.

We found Laura flat on her back in a bed with her legs elevated. Monitors blipped next to her. She was awake. Her short blond bob had fanned out in angelic fashion on the small pillow.

"How ya doin'?" I asked, rubbing her arm in greeting as I sat down in a chair on the near side of her bed.

"Bored," she said. "The babies seem to be settling down."

Pauline took the other side of the bed. "That's good. I found you on the floor in that room you're fixing up. Do you remember anything?"

Laura winced, rubbing her mounded belly. "Not much. I went to see how Piers was doing. He was carrying some kind of a box, but I was behind him."

"A box?" I shot up from the chair. "What'd it look like?"

"I didn't see it clearly, but I swear he fumbled with the lid to toss a ring in it."

"A ring! It's our box. What type of ring?"

"Green? It looked big, like costume jewelry. He said he had to take it back. He left. Then I felt dizzy. That's the last I remember."

I sat back down, collapsing into the memory of Lloyd's words about Piers perhaps bribing Erik. The possible conspiracy involving several people in murder and money swirled in my head. "But you and the twins are okay, thank goodness."

"I just have to lie perfectly still for a day or two. And I've already gone through all the magazines."

"How about we look through cookbooks?"

Pauline and I retrieved the suitcases from her car. After wheeling them into Laura's room, we each took a stack. Our goal was to find numbers to the safe or anything else of that ilk. With three of us thumbing through the old volumes, you'd think the process would be fast. But we kept pausing on recipes. Pauline had lots of sticky notes in her big purse, so we marked pages to come back to later. Pauline volunteered to make the raisin butterscotch pie; Laura had dibs on experimenting with strawberry soda-pop cake that she thought would make great muffins; and I marked two recipes for combining possibly into a new fudge recipe for kids—marbled brownies that could be made with cream cheese from my parents' farm, and another odd recipe for date bars made with candy orange slices. Pauline's kindergarteners could cut up the orange slices for me with their snub-nosed scissors.

It was lunchtime, so I went down to the hospital's cafeteria and brought back garden salads to munch on while we turned pages.

Our salads were almost gone when Laura announced, "Handwritten numbers!"

Pauline looked. "But those are for the length of fish."

Indeed. The cookbook had photos. There was Hans Mueller again, with Bram Oosterling and Clement Van Damme. Somebody—probably Lloyd—had handwritten the fish types right next to each fish and the fish's length in inches.

But then I recognized our folly. "There's no way that trout is only thirteen inches long."

We squealed with success. The numbers had to be the combination to the safe.

Pauline and I told Laura we'd be back when she could be released. We left most of the cookbooks for Laura to go through to pass the time, but Pauline and I took the books with the recipes in them we liked so we could copy those.

When we arrived at my cabin, a shiny yellow Chevy truck was parked out front—just like the one I'd crunched in the accident.

Pauline asked, "Did they fix it that fast?"

"They couldn't have," I said. We got out and went over to it. "Here's a note." It was under a windshield wiper. "*Found this on sale online. Owner in Green Bay. Your auto body shop bought it as a loaner. Keep it until you find a new vehicle. Dillon.*"

Pauline said, "Way to go, A.M. This is nice of him."

"No." I was boiling mad. "He's doing it to me again."

"What?"

"He's being nice. Notice he didn't actually buy this and

give it to me. He knows I would never stand for that. He knows he can't buy me like he once did."

"So now you're mad because he's changed, and he didn't buy you a car? All he did, Ava, was look around for you online to find a truck that matched yours. You loved your yellow truck."

"That's just it. He's being really careful to do everything the way I would want it done."

Pauline squinted her dark eyes down at me. "He wants you. What do you want?"

I wanted the peace found on this little street with its canopy of maple trees. But there was no peace—I also saw my grandparents' home across the way. My first duty was to get them back together. Their hearts were far more important than mine. A plan hatched in my brain.

Pauline asked, "So, what are you going to do, A.M.?"

"Drive the yellow truck, P.M. Because I think it'll help get Gilpa and Grandma Sophie back together. That and the aprons."

"Aprons?"

"Yes. I have a plan to get my grandparents back together. And you can help. Is there some kind of field trip or two you can plan for the Butterflies that would require Cody and Bethany to chaperone and be away from the shop for at least a day, even two days?"

"Of course. There are tons of educational things to do in Door County for kids. I can send them on the ferry to Washington Island to the nature center at the schoolhouse there, and to the ostrich farm, and—"

"Great. Line up all those things, please. Thanks." I squished Pauline in a hug.

She grunted. "Are you going to tell me what plan you have up your sleeveless blouse?"

"You'll see."

She left for home. I went inside to my cabin to drop off the cookbooks on the kitchen counter, where I discovered a note sticking out of the toaster.

An icy gale seemed to whip through the kitchen.

Orange letters were sideways in the toaster. I gingerly picked the note out by one corner, then set it on the counter.

Who will be the next fudge judge to die because of you?

I swallowed hard. The judges were Erik, Libby, the professor, and Dotty. My grandmother was pretty close to two of those people. The realization that Dotty and Libby were in danger felt as if Grandma Sophie had been threatened, too. The shock of it sent tremors through me.

Jordy told me not to touch a thing. Maria Vasquez was across the county in Baileys Harbor and she'd be there within the half hour.

Too agitated to just stand around, I called Dillon. I didn't tell him about the note. I thanked him for the truck, but my voice was cracking. I needed him to help me get my grandparents back together. But I was having second thoughts about my plan now.

"Anything wrong, Miss Fudge?" Dillon asked.

I suggested I'd buy him a beer at the Troubled Trout so we could talk. Since it was going on four o'clock already, he offered to meet for dinner at seven instead. I accepted.

A knock at my screen door revealed Grandma Sophie standing there with a pie in her hands. "Hello, Ava honey! I have a pie for you to take to Sam."

Seeing Sam tonight was decidedly not in my plans. And I didn't want my grandmother seeing the note that threatened Libby and Dotty.

"How nice, Grandma." I let her in, the smell of a strawberry pie thawing my nerves a little. "Let's put the pie over here on one of the boxes." I led her into the living room area. "Maybe you should save this pie and invite Sam over again to your house, Grandma."

"He's got that bad shoulder now. He'd be so appreciative of you bringing it over to him."

Grandma's matchmaking was transparent. She wanted

me carried over the threshold of the house Sam had bought for us eight years ago, with the key given to me as a shower gift. I'd never stepped across that threshold.

My cabin was redolent now with aroma of fresh strawberry pie. I plastered on a fake smile. "I'm not sure this will make it to Sam's. I've got some ice cream. Want me to bring it over to your house and we'll eat this? With Grandpa?"

Grandma Sophie tossed her cloud of white hair back. "Honey, I don't need that old goat. Why don't you come stay with me?"

"You and Grandpa need to patch things up. I've got my mouse to keep me company."

"Bah. And where's your pet mouse?" She headed into the kitchen before I could stop her. "Bah and booyah!" she shrieked. "Orange crayon again. Neat, legible writing. We have to warn Libby, honey."

"Why Libby? And you're not upset about Dotty maybe being threatened?"

"Dotty's got guardian angels watching her. Libby seems to be having bad luck lately. She told me that Kelsey asked her to be a fudge judge. I think there's more to all this than fudge."

I escorted my grandma to the sofa in front of the fireplace. "More what?"

"Somebody wants to do away with the Muellers so that he or she can take over their estate. Is there some long-lost relative we don't know about living in our midst?"

I hadn't thought hard enough about that angle. Was there some illegitimate son or daughter? I went to the screen door to watch for Deputy Vasquez. "Lloyd was pretty sure he had no relatives left here." I recalled the cookbooks my friends and I had just pawed through this afternoon. "Grandma, one of the cookbooks of Lloyd's has old photos of Bram Oosterling. Some old cousin, right?"

"An older cousin of your grandpa's. Bram was an only child like your grandpa. Bram's branch of the family is back in Belgium."

"He was with a Clément Van Damme and Hans Mueller."

"Clément? Let me see that book." She rose from the couch.

"Pauline has it. It had a recipe for raisin butterscotch pie she wants to try. Who's Clément?"

We went onto my front porch to sit in the rocking chairs to wait for Maria. A mother duck and her ducklings were nibbling their way through the grass in my lawn on their way to the marsh.

Grandma said, "Clément Van Damme is one of my relatives, related somehow to Henrik, that shirttail relative who runs that brewery near Madison in Flanders. Some kind of fiftieth-cousin-twice-removed thing."

"And Hans Mueller is Lloyd's grandfather."

"That's right. Hans and Ruth. They would have emigrated from Germany about the same time as the Oosterlings and Van Dammes who came over from Belgium to work as laborers and farmers in the 1850s." Grandma's sniffle startled me.

"What's wrong, Grandma?"

"Your grandpa says he's staying at the farm to help with the haying. Says the village can have the shop. He's giving up."

I swallowed hard. This was my fault. And it was playing right into the hands of the murderer. Her talk of our ancestry gave me a clue to Lloyd's murder, but I didn't want to involve Grandma Sophie. I got up from my rocker to give her one of our famous Belgian hugs that never stopped. "Grandma, I won't give up." I decided to put my secret matchmaking plan in motion. "I could use your help tomorrow because Cody and Bethany are on a field trip with Pauline's Butterflies. Will you come over to help sell fudge while I take over Grandpa's bait shop?"

"Of course, dear. You don't need to fail just because Gil is being an old poop. I'll bring a batch of cinnamon rolls hot from the oven for the fishermen."

"Don't get too carried away in your kitchen tonight. I want people to buy fudge."

Maria pulled up in her county squad car. Grandma and

I spent the next half hour watching her lift fingerprints off the doorjambs, counters, and toaster. She even lifted prints in my bathroom. She said criminals were like anybody else; they used the john before they left a crime scene just because the toilet was handy. As soon as Maria left, Grandma and I disinfected everything.

At around six o'clock, I put on my nicest black jeans, a red nautical blouse with rolled-up sleeves, and black leather sandals and gathered my hair into a ponytail with a red ribbon.

I checked in at my fudge shop. Kelsey had left, but Piers was helping Cody wrap fudge for a customer. I bit my lip to hold back from asking about the box and ring. Piers was explaining the finer points of the candy, including not refrigerating it. "You keep that there fudge at room temperature," he said in his booming voice. "You can freeze it if you must, but seal those suckers tightly to keep the fudge from soaking up the aroma of the salmon you just caught in our lake and shoved into your freezer before rushing off to take in the stage play over at the park."

He said "our" lake. This new Piers vexed me, but I wondered if helping a woman pregnant with twins had softened him somehow. Or was this "good ol' boy" act only a cover? What had he done with that box and ring? I'd ask him later.

I headed to the Troubled Trout early in order to question Erik. I found a seat at the far end of the bar, my hands shaking a little at the prospect of Erik being a possible murderer, or at the least a thief. Erik did a double take, but I asked for an expensive wine to mollify him, then asked to see the betting cards. The square with the biggest dough on it for dancing with me was for a Spuds Schlimgen.

"Who's Spuds?"

Erik set a glass of Door County's finest cherry-and-moscato wine blend in front of me. "Spuds Schlimgen? Mows golf courses. Last I heard he was taking care of Alpine, Stonehedge, and Peninsula."

"A friend of Lloyd's?"

"Golfing buddy, yeah. They've been in here for drinks together."

I figured if this Spuds guy asked me, I'd say yes. But I had to keep to my plan of action to get my grandparents back together. After shoving my credit card over to Erik, I said, "Put a hundred on Dillon Rivers for me, okay? That buys several squares, right?"

His eyes went wide. "You and Dillon?"

"A woman can hope." My insides were whirling. The fat lie had serious ramifications. "We're having dinner here tonight."

I'd worn red on purpose. Men noticed red. They also thought it was romantic—Valentine's Day stuff. Erik would likely be telling everybody at the bar later tonight he'd seen Dillon and me canoodling. By ten o'clock the whole town would know. By tomorrow the church ladies would have their social media networks sizzling with the news. I wanted all of it to happen. It was my plan.

But before Dillon got here, I needed to ask Erik important questions.

"Erik, what's really going on with the harbor? Any news?"

His body stiffened as he poured a beer from a tap for another customer. When done, he came back to me. "Lloyd's lawyer has to go over everything, and they can't get into Lloyd's safe until Friday."

"What's in the safe? The will?"

"That, I'm sure, and I guess they're looking for personal papers directing the actions of the trust. Parker told me a trust relies on the notes kept by the owner of the trust."

"So nothing can move forward until all the papers are gathered up, including those in the safe."

"Yeah."

I also thought about the missing box. Did Piers have it in his possession yet?

"Erik, Alex Faust said he saw you being given money by Piers Molinsky a week ago. True?"

Erik grinned instantly, naturally. Not a cover-up. "True. Piers is from Chicago. He actually thought that we need our palms greased here to get things done. He heard about the publicity over Lloyd selling his real estate and Piers wanted to be considered highly in the bidding for space in the new development for a muffin shop."

"Competition for my fudge shop?"

"I guess so."

That rat. I'd been cutting my own throat by giving him Cinderella Pink Fudge to experiment with. But then I thought about Lloyd's throat, and his gruesome ending. "Erik, did you have anything to do with Lloyd's death?"

"What the hell? No!"

Customers turned heads our way. We waited for them to resume their chatter. As I turned back to Erik, I happened to spy the jar of crayons behind him.

"Those crayons behind your bar—the threats to me and my fudge judges have all come in orange crayon, neatly written. Did you write any of those notes?"

"Are you crazy?" He seemed genuinely shocked.

"Have you noticed anybody odd taking the crayons with them instead of returning them to the jar?"

"You mean like somebody maybe taking them to write those nasty threats? You know, anybody can get crayons everywhere."

I had to laugh at myself. I really wished solving the mystery of the notes was as easy as matching a mere crayon. "I guess I'll have to give up on the crayon angle, won't I?"

"Yup. Besides, the only person out-and-out stealing my crayons is Verona Klubertanz. She hangs on to everything when she comes in with Travis for our mac and cheese. She even stole some crayons off the table over there yesterday when Libby was waiting for a food-to-go order for the professor." He nodded toward a nearby booth.

That made me perk up. "What were they up to?"

"She said Professor Faust had a book signing arranged for another lighthouse, and she was helping him since she was going to stay away from the Eagle Bluff Lighthouse for a while out of respect for Lloyd. Funny thing was, I gave her a bunch of my crayons because she said the lighthouse had a coloring contest and the docent called Libby to bring some along."

"Why is that funny?"

Erik shrugged. "Just seems like a coincidence you ask about crayons, and Libby asked for my crayons, too. Everybody wants these old stubby crayons of mine all of a sudden."

I wasn't tracking on the crayons anymore. Maybe Kelsey had pilfered them from Libby in the past, or maybe not. Putting that behind me, I asked a more important question. "Why were you and the professor at the house when we were there in the garden? What's the real reason, Erik?"

He shrugged again but this time turned as red as cherry wine. "He knows a lot of stuff. He's a professor, Ava. I'm nineteen. I've never been to college. I asked him to help me."

Then I swallowed hard and coughed up the big question. "You had a pad of paper in your briefcase. I saw it at the funeral. Same type of paper was used for the notes around the rocks."

The corner of his mouth twitched ever so slightly while he went to pour a drink for a customer. When he came back, he said, "When we were at Mr. Mueller's house, the professor and I collected a lot of things off the desk, papers that belonged to the village about the real estate stuff. I guess the pad of paper was on the desk."

This felt like a dead end, and Erik seemed innocent enough, yet his stories always had an aura about them that intrigued me. Was he a good liar? And if Erik was innocent, did that leave Kelsey King as the main suspect?

By the time Dillon got to the Troubled Trout, I wanted to leave instead and get back to fudge making. That would help me sort this out. I also needed to talk to Libby. To warn her about Kelsey. Grandma had been right. Libby had to be the fudge judge referred to in the note. But I was also chickening out about asking Dillon for a favor this evening. I realized what I was about to ask him was all wrong.

Dillon and I sat in a booth. With my heartbeat rushing. I was staring across the table at a handsome man who could take my breath away in a rose garden. I told him so.

Dillon took my hands in his on top of the table. Sparks skipped up my arms. I think other people saw the sparks, because they paused as they passed our booth. I must have turned as red as my blouse.

My cowboy's eyes were undressing me. I, in turn, imagined myself in a bad screenplay I might have written, the one where I was ripping the shirt off Dillon's broad shoulders, with the buttons arcing in the air like the sparks between us.

The meal of lake trout with a medley of fresh vegetables was probably nice, but we barely ate; food wasn't what would satiate us.

Once we'd pushed our food around our plates enough, Dillon said, "I have my mother's hot car. How about we have Erik put this in a picnic basket for us? Enjoy an evening drive with the top down? The car's top, that is, but if you want—"

"Dillon!"

"You match the paint job."

Amused and trying to ratchet my breathing down to a manageable level, I said, "Now, that's a line to endear a man to a woman's heart. And that reminds me, I need to call your mother."

"What about?"

"I need a U.S. senator's help with something. She said she knows a few."

"Indeed she does. What's this about?"

"Can't tell you. It's part of a surprise I'm planning for the fudge prom on Saturday night."

"So I have to wait?"

"Yes. And spend lots of money bidding on fudge and pies for charity."

"Can I take you as my date?"

My insides flip-flopped in utter turmoil. "Maybe. Clearly, though, Spuds Schlimgen thinks more highly of me."

"Spuds? That old duffer? He hangs out with Al Kvalheim. What about us young guys? Give me a shot."

His dark eyes softened. The honesty found in them made me want to slide under the table. I didn't deserve this guy as a friend. "Dillon, I have to confess something."

"This sounds bad."

"It is. Earlier today a sudden plan came to me that would get my grandparents back together. The plan involved you and me pretending we were dating again, and in that way my grandfather would get all concerned and come back to live with Grandma across the street to keep an eye on me."

My mouth went dry. I grabbed for the last of my water in the glass sitting and sweating near the candle on our table.

Dillon stared at me for what seemed like an hour. He sat there still as stone.

I was starting to sweat. "I'm sorry. It was a bad plan. I don't know why I thought you'd go along with such a thing. It'd be using you, and you're too nice for that. You've changed. It was mean of me to hatch such a stupid plan, considering what we used to mean to each other. Please forgive me, Dillon."

I exhaled a huge breath. But I still couldn't breathe; I waited for him to say something.

He finally thumped his fingers on the table; then he broke into a wide smile. "It's not a bad plan. I just asked you to give me a shot. It's real. I asked you first. So, do you want to date me or not?"

"For real?" Not only was sweat pouring down my back, but my heart was doing some kind of circus trapeze trick inside my chest and wouldn't stop.

"Yeah. Let's start over. You've changed a lot, too, in eight years. You're a really interesting person, and there are eight years of life we've both lived that have shifted our souls a little. We're practically new people."

"But our dating would still be a scandal."

Dillon laughed heartily enough that heads turned. He leaned toward me with a glint in his eyes. "Isn't that exactly what you wanted?"

"Yes, but— "

"I loved you once enough to marry you, and I love you enough now to help you get your dear grandparents back together. I don't see much wrong with your plan at all. In fact, it's not a bad plan. It's a very good plan all around."

He grabbed his water glass and raised it in a toast.

I felt as if he'd put a cushiony safety net under me, but my heart was still flipping about on that trapeze. I smiled again, thinking about the hundred dollars I'd just put down on his name behind the bar. Now it seemed like kismet to have done so.

Wiggling to get out of the booth, I said, "Let's take a ride in that car of your mother's. After I run an errand. Meet me back at my cabin?"

"I could drive you. What's the errand?"

I wished I could lie, but my conscience wouldn't let me. "I have to drop off a pie at Sam's place." My nerves were jangling louder than my shop's cowbell in my head. "My grandmother thinks that will make Sam fall in love with me again."

"I hate to give you bad news, but the guy *has* fallen back in love with you."

The cowbell in my head just rang louder in alarm. "And you?"

He had an arm around my shoulders, his hand rubbing my arm as if to warm me as we walked out into the crisp evening air. "Totally in love."

I gave him a big kiss in front of everybody in the parking lot of the Troubled Trout.

Dillon let me drive the red Corvette back to my place. He left to go check on Lucky Harbor while I drove in the yellow pickup truck with the strawberry pie to Sam's house.

Sam smiled when he saw me. I wished he were smiling for the pie, but I knew better. And I felt bad about what I had to tell him.

"Hi, Sam." I was standing awkwardly on his porch, which was flanked by lovely red rosebushes. A porch swing was just begging for company, but all I wanted to do was flee. But Sam invited me in, and I accepted. I owed him that much.

He took the pie to his kitchen. I stood in the living room.

The inside of the small home was stunning in unexpected ways. I'd thought I'd see quaint quilts and lots of homespun, traditional decor in earth tones, but instead the interior was sleek in white, with a white couch. The paintings on the walls were by the best photographers and landscape painters of Door County. Red roses in a vase sat atop a glass table in front of a stone fireplace that cradled crackling flames.

When I told him I was back together with Dillon, he merely nodded, as if he didn't believe me. "I see," he said.

"I'm sorry, Sam. I didn't expect this, either."

He chuckled in a stiff way that made me feel worse for coming here.

I said, "The place is beautiful." It was the wrong thing to say. My jaw began to tremble. I wanted to cry. Sam had created this nest for the two of us.

It seemed then that the moment stretched on forever.

Sam finally nodded. "Thank you for bringing the pie and for telling me about you and Dillon. I'll always be your friend. I'm always here if you need me."

I rushed forward to give him a quick kiss on his cheek, then thought better of it. I touched his good arm instead, giving it a squeeze. I nodded to his other arm and shoulder. "How are you doing?"

"One day at a time, but I should be healed within a couple of weeks if you need a partner to climb lighthouse towers with again."

When I got home, I called Dillon. Back in his mother's sports car, with Dillon beside me in the passenger's seat holding another pie, I asked, "How the heck did you and Sam get along on that boat ride to the shipwreck with John?"

"We did it for Cody. He invited us both."

"Have you ever wondered why?"

"To go fishing."

Men could be so dense. "Cody was matchmaking, comparing the two of you on my behalf. I'm sure of it. I hope he doesn't mind that it's not Sam I'm dating. He likes Sam a lot."

"So do I. Sam's a good guy. So is Cody. We'll work it out. I doubt you'll witness a duel on the harbor docks."

Dillon's humor made me laugh. It always had. I hoped that dating him this time around meant I'd get to learn more about all the other sides to Dillon, and find them as wonderful.

I pointed the Corvette out of town.

"Where are we going, Ava?" Dillon asked.

"Libby Mueller's. She needs another pie. It's a good excuse to find out how Kelsey King poisoned Lloyd at Libby's on Friday night. When we're there, look around for lined paper, stolen cups, rifles, crayons, and mushrooms."

Chapter 22

I parked the red Corvette next to Libby's old gray Honda. It was around eight in the evening and still light out. Dillon, holding the strawberry pie, nodded to the small house and beater car. "Let's hope she gets a good chunk of money from Lloyd."

"I'm sure he did right by her."

"You ever think she might have had something to do with his death?"

"Many times, Dillon. But the two of them had always gotten along, and there's no need for Libby to murder Lloyd; she knew she was likely going to get an inheritance from him. Libby and Lloyd remained good friends all the way to the end."

"You're sure? What if Libby was secretly angry about Lloyd hiding her things in that box? Or what if Libby thought Mercy was paying too much attention to Lloyd's matters?"

"The problem is that Libby's easily swayed by people like Mercy and Kelsey. All we need to do is prove Kelsey poisoned Lloyd."

"But what about that box? Piers Molinsky has it. Did you report that yet?"

"I can't report it. I didn't see it with him and Laura fainted, so I'm sure the sheriff won't find her reliable."

"Do you think Kelsey knows about the box? Maybe she and Piers uncovered it together at your shop."

"Conjecture of course. But it could be that Kelsey is using Mercy's vile letters to keep Mercy shut up and out of the way while Kelsey ingratiates herself with Libby."

Libby came to the door. She swooned over the fresh strawberry pie.

"Thank you! Please come in. We'll have a piece right now with coffee."

"You're sure you're not too tired?"

"It doesn't matter. I could use the company. After today, it feels like a morgue in here, no pun intended."

Libby's demeanor about the funeral encouraged me to be forthright. "Dillon and I just came from dinner at the Troubled Trout. That's the last place I saw Lloyd, on Friday night at the fish boil. He was happy that night. You and Lloyd were together."

"Luckily, yes. I have that nice memory." She waved at us to take seats around her small dining table between the kitchen and living room. She grabbed cups from the cupboard. I craned my neck automatically, looking for Lloyd's antique cups, but couldn't see around the cupboard door very far. "What a lovely night that was," Libby said. "The good memories gave me strength to get through today."

I let my gaze travel about for paper, crayons, cups, the wooden box, but only saw a small tablet and pen on the kitchen counter near a telephone. I wouldn't be able to riffle through drawers, so I settled into my agenda to figure out how Lloyd was poisoned. "Somebody mentioned that you had several friends stop by here later on Friday night. That was nice, too."

Libby poured the coffee. "It was quite a houseful. Kelsey and Piers were here for a short while. Lloyd had invited them. Alex was here. Erik Gustafson stopped by briefly after he got off work. Mercy was here, but my dear friend had a few too many, so Erik drove her home while the rest stayed. And of course John Schultz was here."

"John?" Pauline must not have known about that or she would have mentioned it.

"He was videotaping everything."

"Everything? Were my guest chefs cooking?"

"I was mostly. Alex was telling us about his cookbook's recipes and how the Native Americans had settled Door County eleven thousand years ago, which Kelsey loved because she said they'd be eating chemical-free plants back then."

"Not necessarily true. Chemicals and gases come up from the earth all the time, but go on."

"She was mixing up something from her forest foraging in a fry pan, I recall. I didn't eat. I'd eaten enough at the fish boil."

Bingo! "But Lloyd ate some?"

"Oh yes. Alex served it up with a great flourish."

"Everybody ate what Kelsey fixed?"

"I didn't really notice. It was a mishmash of people in this tiny space."

"John videotaped the dinner?" I had to be sure.

"Indeed. He liked the atmosphere. He said something about calling his show 'The Friendship Foodie.'"

"Hmm. Libby, you must have heard by now about the autopsy."

Dillon kept quiet, drinking his coffee.

Libby eased down in a chair across from me. "I don't know how he could have been poisoned. We were all right here, eating everything."

"Libby, Kelsey may have poisoned him. When you weren't looking, she slipped something in his food. Then she followed him after he left because she knew he'd be woozy."

"Kelsey? That sweet girl?"

I reached across the table to take her hand in mine. Her bones were thin. Although she had dyed her hair to look younger, her face wore plenty of wrinkles. "I'm sorry. Kelsey's been using you to get access to Lloyd's things. But I think we have a way of catching her red-handed. John was videotaping. All it's going to take now is for the sheriff to get his hands on that video. He might be able to see Kelsey doing a sleight-of-hand trick to put poisonous mushrooms in the skillet. The sheriff is also checking on possible video or still-action cameras that somebody may have set up at the park by the lighthouse. Perhaps John set them up. He may have inadvertently captured Kelsey doing harm to Lloyd that night."

Libby gasped. "Kelsey?" She slapped a hand over her mouth as she choked back a cry. I comforted her as best I could in the horrible reality we were in, and then Dillon and I excused ourselves.

When we got back on the road, with me driving again, which settled my nerves a little, Dillon said, "Good work back there, Deputy Oosterling."

"Poor Libby."

"You're right. She's the type of person who gets taken in by people."

"Lloyd told me that Libby needed him watching out for her. People here are kindhearted, Dillon. It leaves some of them easy prey to charlatans."

"All that's left to do is to call the sheriff. Then we can get back to what's really important."

His lascivious smile made my breathing pause. The feeling was so warm and good that I resented having to think about a murder. I squeezed the steering wheel, wishing I could fall into Dillon's arms instead. The murder had to have been accomplished by more than just Kelsey, yet Kelsey was so bullheaded and prideful I also couldn't imagine her asking anybody to help her or share the riches she'd get from her plot to soak Libby.

As I drove us back in the red Corvette to my cabin, with the crisp night air whipping my ponytail in the wind and clearing my muddled head a little, my instincts and womanly intuition told me I was a fool about everything and everyone. This blaming Kelsey was all too easy, and frankly, anything that came easily in my life hadn't been worth spit.

Did that apply to Dillon? Was I already falling too fast for him all over again? When Dillon kissed me good night on my front porch, the answer didn't matter. He took me in his arms the way a good man should. His lips were hungry, eager, encouraging. I was floating in his arms, an ethereal experience in a heady mist of romantic ardor. I imagined us going inside, stripping off our clothes, tumbling in each other's arms on the couch before we landed on the rug, where we'd make love in front of my fireplace.

I kicked at my door to open it, trying for some Hollywood movie star move while Dillon kept peppering sweet kisses down my neck, but he stopped.

We both stood back to catch a breath. He looked disheveled. I think my hands somehow were everywhere in his hair. I patted my hair and found my ponytail gone, my hair loose about my shoulders. A gray mist felt cool and damp against my hot face as I looked into his eyes.

"Do you want to come in?" I said.

"Better not," he said. "I want to do this right this time."

"Oh." This time. Not like eight years ago. When we'd been a tad too hasty and eloped. But darn him, I ached inside. I remembered . . . all that other stuff that he was mighty good at, and I wanted it. A wanton woman, I know.

Dillon saved me from my thoughts with a big, goofy grin. He reached out with a finger to tip my head up and then kissed me sweetly, lingering just enough to make my knees wobble. He said, "I'm already liking this plan to get your grandparents back together."

"Dillon, it's more than a plan. I really do have feelings for you."

"I know. I have feelings for you. The feelings are real. But I want to go slow. You deserve that. You deserve a different me this time around. I'll keep saying it if I have to." He cocked his head, indicating across the street. "I saw the light go on over there. Your grandmother's watching. One more kiss to help the cause?"

We chuckled together and kissed again, this time hugging a long time before we parted. His warmth and kindness seeped into me. I hoped that I was giving something back to him in this deal. It felt raw and new to me, as if Dillon wasn't Dillon and I wasn't me. Could we really start over? Was it this simple? Was it too easy?

He roared off in the Corvette, probably waking up the entire neighborhood. I saw my grandma let her curtain drop back in place. I smiled.

On Wednesday morning Grandma Sophie was at the shop by seven. I'd been there since five a.m. making fudge and helping fishermen, and savoring my time with Dillon last night. It was amazing how the taste of a wonderful kiss could linger on and on even better than fudge.

Grandma's face lit up at my apron. I wore a lilac-checked, lace-trimmed apron over a white blouse and denim shorts. My heavy shoes didn't match, but safety was more important than looks when I was hefting my copper kettles. For Grandma I chose the frilly pink, satin-trimmed full-bib apron and helped her into it. With her white hair, she looked like a tall helping of cotton candy. Very sweet. Just as I wanted her to appear.

While Grandma was busy with our first fudge customers, I slipped to the back with my phone and called my mother.

"Hey, Mom, how's Grandpa?"

"Out in the barn helping with the milking. And he plans to stay forever, he says. He's done with the city life."

"I see." Our tiny village of two hundred wasn't exactly a big city, but Grandpa was in a stubborn state. "Mom, I wanted to tell you something before you heard it off the church lady grapevine. Dillon and I are back together."

Her scream on the other end of the phone almost broke my eardrum. I held the phone away from me while she jabbered incoherently. I caught a few words, including, "Are you freakin' crazy?" and "You're not too old to take over my knee!" And the big kahuna warning was invoked, too: "Wait until your father hears about this!"

I knew getting back together with Dillon would take all my courage. I sent up a tiny prayer that Mom and Dad would forgive me later for this. They certainly didn't want Gilpa back on the farm trying to take charge, I was sure.

Lucky Harbor showed up outside the shop's door at around nine, wagging his tail and panting at me through the glass. I wasn't going to let him in, but Pauline showed up with Bethany and the Butterflies and everybody tumbled inside.

Pauline said, "We're here to buy fudge to take with us to Sister Bay. We're going to visit the goats on the roof of Al Johnson's Swedish Restaurant, then take fudge to a nursing home."

"Sounds good," I said. I ached to launch into the news about Dillon and me, but I didn't want to spoil any surprise for my grandmother. I was expecting Grandpa to be flying through the door within the half hour.

Grandma Sophie was already twirling in place for the little girls, who were giggling and calling her a princess.

A fisherman walked in right then and said, "A princess fer sure! Both of youse look like princesses."

The fisherman's pals came in next, all of them engaging me and Grandma in conversation immediately. Grandma flirted right back! She led them over to Grandpa's side of the shop, helping them with their purchases. I was getting a little scared now that she didn't care if Grandpa came back soon!

Pauline raised an eyebrow, looking down at me in silent questioning.

I leaned over with a whisper. "This is perfect."

"How can you be happy when your grandparents are breaking up?"

"Patience. You'll see. Now tell me, how's Laura? I was just about to call her."

"She's not feeling well again. Can't keep food down."

Verona butted in between us. "I puke when I eat too much cake, but I don't puke up fudge."

I said, "That's a compliment to me, I think. Thanks, Verona."

"Who's Laura?"

I knelt down to Verona's level. "Laura Rousseau. She runs the Luscious Ladle in Sister Bay."

"Oh. I remember her. We made bread there with Miss Mertens."

"That's the place."

"Miss Rousseau is having two babies, she said."

"Yeah. That's why she's a little sick today. I'm worried about her."

Verona wiped her dark hair back off her forehead. "She'll be okay, just like Rapunzel."

"What about Rapunzel?"

"She didn't feel good for a long time because she was locked in a tower, but she had hair longer than mine and she let a prince climb up it. Then she was happy, but then an evil person poked her prince's eyes out." Verona looked at me with wide eyes.

I said, "That's awful. And sad."

"But it's not sad. The prince wandered around for a while, but then he found Rapunzel had jumped from the lighthouse tower and run away and had two babies, too, just like Laura. Rapunzel was so happy to see the prince that she cried and her tears fell into his eyes and he could see again and they lived happily ever after. Does Laura have a prince?"

Who knew where the army had sent Laura's husband? "Oh yes. She has a prince." *He just isn't here, sadly.*

"Then Laura will live happily ever after. Her babies will come out of her belly and they'll be in pink dresses just like the dolls in your store and eat Cinderella Pink Fudge, just like Rapunzel did," Verona said, skipping away to rejoin her friends at the tea table in the corner.

I got up from my crouch, mesmerized by Verona, and thinking.

Pauline said, "Just like that. Problems are solved with

your fudge. Can I try the new batch you made? I can smell the raspberry flavor from here. My mouth is watering."

"Fudge for breakfast?"

"Why not?"

"I confess I eat it for breakfast all the time. My new batch doesn't have a name yet."

"It has to be Rapunzel Raspberry Rapture Fudge. Verona would love that."

"Verona loves a lot of things too much." I was keeping my eyes on her in the aisles with the dolls and purses. Lucky Harbor was with her, his nose sniffing everything she touched. He kept licking her hands, which seemed to prevent any shoplifting.

I led Pauline over to the new raspberry fudge covered on the white marble slab. "Time to taste-test before Saturday's contest. I'll make another batch, once I get feedback from your Butterflies. How are the wagon floats coming?"

"They're darling puffs of crepe paper streamers and glitter, all designed to look like Cinderella Pink Fudge."

"Great. The last I looked at the sign-up list, we had thirty-five locals bringing fudge to the contest and dance on Saturday. This could be big. John's camera will be busy."

I gave Pauline a tiny bite of the Rapunzel Raspberry Rapture Fudge. With the piece in her mouth, her body turned to jelly before my eyes. She shimmied in place. She settled into a nirvana grin. Her eyes went dreamy. Afraid she might faint, I pulled up the stool from next to the window so she could sit down. Orgasmic gasps came from her mouth after she'd finished swallowing.

"You like it?" I asked.

"A.M., it's fantabulous."

"That's not a word."

"I teach kindergarten. We make up words all the time. It's epicurean excellence, extremely edible, with enjoyable excitement, exuding the essence of exuberant effervescence."

"This is E week?"

"Exactly. We're now on vowels."

By now Lucky Harbor's nose was sniffing the edge of the table, along with the fingertips of six little girls named for cities. I gave each of the girls a piece of the fudge and tossed Goldfish crackers into Lucky Harbor's mouth.

They scooted outdoors to get in the van Cody had borrowed to take the girls on their field trip to Washington Island.

Pauline and I cut up the rest of the new fudge, moving it from the window to the kitchen. We wrapped it fast and put it inside boxes that I taped shut. I had to keep this flavor a secret from Piers and Kelsey.

In the kitchen, I shared in one big breath with Pauline the news about Dillon and me and what we'd found out at Libby's last night.

"Wait a minute," she said. "You and Dillon . . . ?"

Her eyes weren't sparkling like I needed them to do. "It feels right. For now." I cringed after adding the last words.

"For now. See? Already you're not sure this is a good thing. Dillon ruined your life. You're barely recovered. Your shop is in danger of disappearing in this mess with Lloyd's murder. . . ."

I deserved this scolding after how I'd reacted to her dating John Schultz. I forced the conversation back to the fact that John could possibly help us solve the murder case.

Pauline said, "I doubt the sheriff will find actual videotape. That's not done much anymore. John would know where it is, though, online or in a chip or flash drive."

"Let's call him."

"Right now he's following Alex Faust around to some book signings."

"Oh, that's right. Libby mentioned something about that happening. She's helping with those, too. Thank goodness she has something to keep her mind off the murder investigation."

"They make a nice couple. Like me and John."

"Yes," I said, reassuring her, "like you and John."

"Then after the book signings, John mentioned he was diving again at some shipwreck site, with the professor along with them."

"So John hasn't shared his passwords with you, P.M.?" I meant it the way it sounded—John didn't completely trust Pauline as lovers should do if an engagement was imminent.

"No, A.M."

Her scowl almost made me feel guilty. But not quite. I handed her some wax paper to wrap more fudge. "Pauline, have you ever thought about how the future might be with him? You have a steady job and he'll always be following his bliss-of-the-moment, not sharing it with you."

"But that's what I like about him. I can live vicariously through him. Like you do through Dillon."

"You're insinuating that I'm the dull one and I like him just because he's adventurous?"

"It's the other way around now. He's got the steady construction job, and you're chasing murderers around."

I stopped wrapping. "Really? Our roles have switched?"

"Yes, Ava. You've become impulsive, as if you're trying to prove something to everybody."

"But I am."

My phone buzzed in my pocket above my breast in the pinafore apron. I jumped.

It was Sheriff Tollefson. "The DNR doesn't have any cameras in the park."

"But Kelsey said she saw them there."

"She could have lied. Not the first time I've been lied to in my career."

I told him about John videotaping the party and maybe leaving cameras out at the park after videotaping out there earlier. Jordy said he'd look into that angle, but he insisted he'd looked everywhere. But this would take a while because he'd also need a warrant to go looking in somebody's personal online files or cameras.

After I got off the phone, I punched in Kelsey's number.

She sounded groggy, but I persisted. "Wake up, Kelsey. It's after ten in the morning. You lied about the cameras."

"No, I didn't. I swear. I can show you where they are."

"Fine. I'll pick you up in ten minutes."

"I can't do that. I agreed to work and sing at Legs and Toes at lunch and again at dinner."

"Fine. After dinner. What time are you off?"

"After nine it slows down."

"It'll be dark!"

"What's the big whoop? I know where the cameras are. Bring a flashlight."

I didn't have time to get upset with slippery Kelsey because of a commotion out front in the shop. Pauline and I raced out. Grandpa was there, shooing fishermen out of his shop!

"Just git! Git out!" He was flapping his hands at several men crowding through the front door. The cowbell was clanging several times as the door got jostled.

"Gilpa," I said after the customers had cleared out, "what's going on?" I smothered a smile.

A certain pungent odor was in the air. He'd rushed here straight from the barn, as I suspected he would. He was wearing bib overalls that had a few specks of cow manure on the legs. A long-sleeved, blue chambray shirt underneath that he'd rolled up to the elbows wasn't much cleaner. My face ached from holding back my triumphant smile.

He turned to me with fire in his eyes. "Those darn men weren't showing your grandmother proper respect. I caught one of them winking at her when I walked in."

Out of the corner of my eye I could tell that Grandma was not amused and was about ready to walk out. She was bustling about, pretending to be busy, but her every action was performed with stiff precision.

"Oh, Gilpa, it's the apron. Doesn't Grandma look cute in that pink apron?"

"I suppose so."

"You suppose? You know so."

I dragged him over to Grandma. "Why don't you two talk this out?" I turned to go.

"You come back here, little A.M.," Grandpa said. He pierced me with his steady, dark eyes. A hand combed through his silver hair. "I'm here about you. What's this I hear about you and Dillon getting back together? That is not going to happen, you hear? Your father was ready to fall over with a heart attack this morning. Me, too. You cut that man out of your life—"

"Gilpa, it's just that with you changing your life so suddenly, I felt I could change, too."

"I didn't change. The rest of you changed. And not for the better."

"That's because we need you in order to be better." The only way to deal with Gilpa was to outtalk him. "You wanted to apologize to Grandma about hiding the box, didn't you?"

"What?"

Grandma said, "You do, Gil?"

Gilpa rubbed a hand around his whiskered face. "This is about that dastardly Dillon. Ava honey, let's you and me have a talk out on the docks in private."

I grabbed Pauline's hand and began running for the back hallway. "Can't do that, Grandpa. The sheriff called and Pauline and I have to go do something for him right now."

We were out the door with the fudge from the kitchen and racing across my lawn before I said, "I think my plan just worked."

I was ahead of Pauline, rounding the corner of my porch.

She said, "But you're dating Dillon. You still have to face your grandparents and parents with this big change. Your grandpa sounded mighty mad."

"All the better for now." I raced through my front door. "Let them discuss together how to save me. It'll get them back together. They'll have to talk about dating and love and pretty soon they'll be in each other's arms."

"You're a genius, A.M."

"Thank you, P.M."

I set my armful of fudge on my counter first. "I win."

We were puffing from our race. Pauline said, "Can't run in these shoes." She had on ballerina flats.

Tossing my apron aside, I said, "Come on."

"Where are we going?"

"To Lloyd's. I told Grandpa I had to do something for the sheriff, and I never lie to Gilpa."

Pauline had a good laugh about that, but as we got in the new yellow Chevy truck that Dillon had found for me, she said, "Dillon's not going to quit on you this time, you know. You're in trouble with this fudge contest and prom dance of yours. It's going to be like an engagement party for you two. The whole town's going to show up for that E word."

Anxiety scratched through me like a jagged fingernail. "I'm not going with Dillon. I've already asked somebody."

"Who?"

"I can't tell, Pauline. I'm sorry. I really can't tell in case this new guy turns me down at the last minute. He's kind of a big shot."

Pauline was never happy when I kept secrets from her, but she quickly shifted with me to the task at hand: cracking Lloyd's safe.

Minutes later we parked on the road on the other side of the wooded lot, then walked through the woods to Lloyd's home. We were inside his house, in the sunroom and library, dialing the safe's second number we'd found in the historic cookbook, when the unmistakable creak of the front door echoed through the house.

Footfalls slapped our way before we had a chance to hide.

Chapter 23

Mercy Fogg barreled into the sunroom, then screamed when she saw Pauline and me standing next to the table. She was carrying a crowbar.

Pauline took off one of her ballerina flats and flung it hard at Mercy's head.

Mercy ducked. "Stop! Miss Mertens, are you crazy?"

Picking up a lamp from the table to use as a weapon, I said, "Why are you here, Mercy?"

"Probably the same reason you are. I saw your zippy yellow banana parked over on the road and suspected you were over here. So I came to help." She hefted the crowbar.

"Help? With what?"

"With breaking into the safe. I've been hoping you'd get into that thing, but it's been taking forever."

I put the lamp down, though I kept my eyes on her crowbar. "You've been watching us? Waiting for us to break in?"

"Yeah. I didn't want to break into it myself. Libby's my friend. She wouldn't like that."

Pauline asked, "How close of a friend?"

Mercy tossed Pauline's shoe back to her. "It's not what you think, Missy Mertens."

"Maybe," I ventured, "you and Lloyd had something going on."

She laughed. "Lloyd wasn't mean enough for me."

Mercy let those words hang in the air while she switched the crowbar from hand to hand in a menacing way. She wore a sleeveless blouse that showed off the bulging muscles developed by her truck driving and manual labor around our village and county. Pauline let a whine slip from her throat, while I licked my dry lips.

"Mercy, you may be mean, but Libby is your friend. You must be just as bothered by Lloyd's murder as we are."

"He's just one more rich guy out of the way, if you ask me."

"That's a little cold," I said, though I recalled my grandmother had wished him dead herself.

Mercy leaned the crowbar against a bookshelf, then hustled around me to look out at the rose garden as if she'd seen ghosts. "Lloyd had his secrets. Like this garden. I've wondered how many women saw this view."

"Lloyd? Women? You're talking about Kelsey and him?"

Mercy scoffed. "A man doesn't live for ten years after his divorce like a monk. They hit it off the minute you introduced them last Monday. Isn't that when the chefs came to town?"

I gulped. I'd been hoping my suspicions about Lloyd and Kelsey weren't true.

"Sunday, actually. They came to the shop on Monday."

Mercy stalked the view of the rainbow-hued rose garden. "He was always behind on his taxes. It was no surprise to me that your fudge shop ended up in the hands of the village."

"We don't know that for sure yet. That's why we're here, hoping to find the trust papers. We don't know who he named in his trust. Even his attorney, Parker Balusek, doesn't know."

"Parker. Young, cute, and saves churches. Your type?"

"Pauline's type."

"Not my type." Pauline had her shoe back on. She dropped her butt into the chair where she'd sat on Friday.

Mercy said, "Alex mentioned that Parker had become interested in Namur's little historic Catholic church, the one the Belgian Club has saved."

"Yeah," I said, getting nervous. "St. Mary of the Snows Church. My grandparents have been active in saving the historic buildings around Namur and Brussels."

"Isn't that where you were supposed to have a wedding eight years ago?"

"What's your point, Mercy?"

"Lloyd tried to buy that property after you left town. Alex Faust knew all about it because he was doing some research on the church for a book, but when you eloped with Dillon the publicity surrounding the property interrupted the sale. Alex backed off and turned to writing his cookbooks instead. His faculty had frowned on the sleazy nature of Alex's writing about you jilting a guy at the altar and heading for Vegas with Mr. Hunk."

"When did you learn this about Professor Faust?"

"Friday at Libby's impromptu party."

"So Lloyd was overextended eight years ago, even before my grandfather seemed to get behind on his taxes." This matched what Cathy Rivers had said about the state of the economy a decade ago.

"The debts are why Lloyd and Libby divorced. Lloyd was constantly in need of money to pay bills, and Libby was constantly worried."

"Sorry, Mercy, but Lloyd told me you and Libby gambled every cent he didn't nail down."

"We gambled, yes, but Lloyd liked to golf more than worry about investments. Have you priced a set of golf clubs lately? Memberships to country clubs?"

If Lloyd had his problems with money, what did that mean? He was still rich until his death. He owned Duck Marsh Street, several buildings on Main Street, and the fudge shop. Mercy wasn't panicking; she wanted to see what was in the safe as much as I did. But I didn't trust her.

At a stalemate, we agreed to leave instead of risking the

wrath of the sheriff. Each of us knew we'd tattle on the other if one of us dared break into the safe.

As Pauline and I drove back to my place, she asked, "So, what do we do now?"

"We hope the cameras show us what we need to know. That's all we've got. When will John be back from his diving expedition this afternoon?"

"Late, I'm sure. He has to wait for Alex to finish his book signings before they go out on the lake."

"So we'll pick up Kelsey, find those cameras, then meet up with John to see what he captured at Friday night's dinner. And we watch for Mercy tailing us."

"Ava, you think Mercy's the killer? Not Kelsey?"

"Mercy seems plenty mad at Lloyd for all his missteps in life, right up until the end with Kelsey, but there's no proof Mercy's connected. I don't think she did it. She'd love it if I got her arrested and made a fool of myself. She'd sue me for defamation of character."

Pauline laughed. "But who's left as our suspects, Poirot?"

"Who wants to get rich the easy way, Hastings?"

She stopped laughing.

The mosquitoes in the park were thick, as if somebody had dumped pepper in the air. We'd worn long sleeves and pants and sprayed ourselves, though, so pushing through the underbrush was tolerable. Except for the limbs we didn't always see that hit our face or the downed wood underfoot.

It was after nine o'clock. Pale light seeped through the trees from the lighthouse beam directed into Lake Michigan. We were coming out of the woods and approaching the lilac bushes that flanked the lighthouse grounds.

Kelsey led the way, complaining the whole time. "I'm too hot."

"Show us the darn cameras and we'll get out of here," I growled at her. "I thought you knew where they were."

Pauline said, "Come on, Kelsey, think. I'm tired of lugging this computer around." Pauline had my laptop in her big purse. Once we found the trail camera, I wanted to plug in the flash drive from it to see the pictures that would prove who the murderers were.

I poked at Kelsey. "Move it. Pauline needs to get back to her boyfriend."

Pauline said, "Actually, John called and said they were going to be in after dark. He and Alex were staying out until the very last minute at the shipwreck site."

The three of us hadn't quite taken another step when a light blinked on in the lighthouse in the historic living quarters on the second floor.

Kelsey said, "Libby. She likes to come over to tidy up when nobody's here."

We stayed behind the lilac bushes near the old outhouse. Sure enough, it wasn't long before we saw Libby come outside with what looked like a dustpan to shake it into the grass.

"Did she come over here the night Lloyd died? Before or after the party?"

"I remember hearing the door open and close at her house, but I was mostly asleep. I'd had too much to drink."

"But first you'd made Lloyd sick and maybe he took a walk to try and get some fresh air."

"That's not true." She swatted at a mosquito. "I'm getting out of here."

She started to push past the lilacs, but I caught her by the elbow. "You're not going anywhere. You poisoned Lloyd with the mushrooms or some plant from this park, didn't you? You know we'll see you doing it when we look at John's video."

"I didn't do anything except drink too much. And feel sorry for Libby."

"Who helped you? Piers? Mercy Fogg?"

Pauline intervened with a hand barely visible between us. "Wait a minute. Didn't Kelsey just say that she was drunk? A drunk can't tug a body up the stairs of a lighthouse."

Kelsey said, "Exactly."

"Sorry," I said to Kelsey. "I just had to be sure. I don't want to believe who I think did it."

Kelsey asked, "Who?"

"Who was left at the party late that night? Libby."

Kelsey went wide-eyed in the dark. "I think you're right."

Then she ran through a gap in the lilac bushes and leaped onto the rock wall behind the lighthouse. I thought she was running away, but then she stopped and reached up to a tree branch. She hurried back with the camera.

"Here," she said. "This is the second camera. Sorry I can't remember where we put the other one."

Pauline scrambled to get my laptop out of her purse. Junk overflowed onto the grass. "You really think Libby murdered Lloyd?"

"There are motives that I haven't wanted to admit to—money and avenging ten years of her living in her simple little house and him keeping her valuable ring from her. However, I don't think she acted alone."

We put in the flash drive. All it showed on Friday night was Libby outside the lighthouse in the dark, cleaning. The time on the frames said it was three in the morning, though.

Pauline, Kelsey, and I looked at one another with a sad realization. Libby had likely indeed killed Lloyd. Nobody would come out here then just to clean.

Appearing sickly in the meager light of the laptop, Pauline said, "Maybe Libby didn't know he was lying dead behind the tower?"

"No," I said. "She was here tidying up to destroy evidence of her being here with Lloyd—and his killer. Which she's doing right now. She knows we're onto her. Come on."

I marched fast, with my laptop in my arms, to the lighthouse, with Pauline in tow. I expected Kelsey to run away, but that didn't matter to me now. Kelsey wasn't the accomplice. Was it Erik? I was still waffling slightly on him and two others.

Pauline kept repeating, "Don't go in there, Ava."

I flung open the door with gusto to surprise Libby. To my

shock, she stood in the gift shop with the missing chest in her arms. "How did you get that, Libby? Wait. Let me answer that. You drove me off the road."

"I don't know what you're talking about," she said. "Kelsey used my car all the time."

I said, "You'd like us to blame Kelsey. You used me, Libby. I invited those chefs for my fudge contest, and you saw that you had a few patsies for your crime, didn't you?"

Kelsey came up behind me. "My rental broke down. I drove her car sometimes."

Libby said, "She borrowed my car all the time. She's nuts. She killed my husband."

I wanted to believe Libby, but there she stood, hugging the chest in her arms. I was trembling as I asked, "Who really helped you kill your ex-husband?"

She shifted her arms around the chest. Her left hand appeared. The huge emerald ring sparkled in the light.

That confirmed for me what had been going on. It confirmed for me who her accomplice was. It wasn't Erik. "That's your engagement ring, Libby. Why are you wearing that now? Ready to start a new life?"

"I wanted to put it on. To remember Lloyd."

"Liar."

"I feel alone."

"How alone? Who helped you murder Lloyd? Say it! Say his name!"

Kelsey, Pauline, and I stood blocking her passage to the door to the outside.

Libby's gaze held on Pauline a bit too long.

I turned and screamed at Pauline, "Call John!"

"John? Why?"

I couldn't even speak at first because of my shock.

Pauline found her phone and called. "There's no answer. What's wrong? Why am I calling John?"

"Because . . . because he's out in a boat after dark with a murderer! Alex Faust is behind all of this!"

Chapter 24

We tumbled outside, leaving Libby behind, with me on my cell phone calling nine-one-one. Then something hard hit me alongside the head. The phone and I went flying into the dark abyss.

I was seeing stars but not the kind in the night sky.

Kelsey said, "Stop!" to somebody, and then the echo of something like a board hitting a skull smacked the night air.

After another hit I heard only Pauline groaning from a short distance away.

When a rifle barrel appeared an inch above my face, I squinted upward from the ground and saw the silhouette of Professor Alex Faust, his body backlit by the lighthouse beam above us. He stood next to his briefcase resting at his feet. How had he gotten here so fast? I thought I knew.

He said, "You just had to snoop, didn't you, Miss Oosterling?"

"Despite your warnings? In your neat, perfect handwriting on paper pilfered from Pauline's purse at my shop sometime when you were there with your books?"

"Paper is paper. I didn't steal her paper."

"But you did. I saw a pad of paper like the kind she uses with her students in Erik's briefcase, where you put it. Erik said you had scooped all kinds of papers belonging to Lloyd in your briefcase. You were stealing things there, like rifles for doing your murderous deeds, and then you placed one in Dillon's truck to get rid of it, hoping you could implicate him."

I scrambled fast near his feet and grabbed the briefcase. It popped open under my hands, but not before Faust snatched for it. I slapped his face, got the notebook, flipped fast through the pages. Disney stickers fell out. In the back, there were several notes made in Pauline's handwriting, simple notes about what to buy at the store for her classroom. I looked up from the ground. "This is Pauline's. You stole it. You're guilty as hell."

The way he grinned down at me in the dark made me shudder. His pearly whites looked ready to eat me alive.

"It's a busy little fudge shop," he said in almost a purr. "Easy to sneak around in when you're wrapping fudge in your fancy pink paper and Miss Mertens is fussing with sticky children."

I lay back on the dewy grass, my head smarting from being hit with the rifle. The light beam signaling out to the ships prompted me to ask, "Where's John?"

"He's out on a dive, the last I heard."

Pauline whimpered.

My head was throbbing, but I lurched up to my elbows. "You bastard. You left him out there on his dive. He's out there alone in the water, in the dark."

"And soon he'll have company. We're going to take a boat ride. Libby, sweetie, get the rope."

Libby scuttled to the shed, rattling her keys in the lock. She came back and handed them to Alex. "They don't work."

He tossed her his set of keys.

Sitting up fully, I scoffed. "You made new sets of keys for everything. New locks and keys for Lloyd's house, too. New locks and keys to his gun cabinet, I bet. You just waltzed right into his house, and his life. You loved his library; you went through Lloyd's books, and stacked them neatly even when you were searching for hidden money or the combination to his safe. That was a huge clue that seeded my suspicions about you, Professor. You were planning on moving in after you married Libby. You used her."

"I love her."

"Funny joke, Professor. What's going to happen when your university buddies find out about this?"

"They won't."

"If you get away with this, they'll admire you, won't they? You hope. After you marry the rich Libby Mueller and end up owning half of Fishers' Harbor, you'll show those tenured creeps you're more than a mere cookbook author. Am I close?"

I could see Libby's shadow backing away. Maybe if I kept talking to Alex, distracting him, she would decide to side with saving our lives and call for help.

I fixed my attention on Alex standing over me. "You never got over the sting of them forcing you to publish or perish. And now you're so close to fortune, if not fame, but my family and I have been trying too hard to solve the murder. That messes with your plans. You could see that my love of my fudge shop and grandfather was going to be a problem for you. But this will all work out, won't it? Kelsey will drown in Lake Michigan with me and Pauline, and you'll set up rumors that Kelsey murdered Lloyd by poisoning him to cover up their affair. All a lie because Kelsey's just an innocent pawn of yours in this, too. You'll say Kelsey and I struggled on the boat. You'll posit that, at least, or maybe you'll say it's a murder-suicide. Kelsey is creative, but you likely loved it that she was fighting with Piers Molinsky in my shop for all the world to see. You're an opportunist, a real Tom Ripley, aren't you? Just like the guy in the Matt Damon movie *The Talented Mr. Ripley*. Your plan was set."

"A thesis worthy of a Ph.D., Miss Oosterling."

"Maybe a nice thank-you to us all would be appropriate in the acknowledgments page of your next book? For dying to get out of your way? You realize of course that nobody knows yet exactly what Libby gets in the trust or will. Maybe Lloyd left her—I mean, you—nothing."

"Shut up. You Oosterlings need to go back to the Old Country. I'm sure Lloyd took care of his lovely ex-wife just fine."

Unfortunately, Libby had come back with several lengths of rope. Which wasn't "fine."

Alex said, "Tie their hands and feet."

"Libby," I said, "you're better than this."

Ignoring me, she tied up Pauline, who was out cold on the grass, barely visible in the dark a few yards from me. I was sitting up and scoping things out, though I was dizzy. I felt sicker when I saw Libby put a rope around Pauline's neck and snug it down tight.

"Don't, Libby!" I yelled.

Alex whipped me alongside the head again with the rifle barrel. I went down hard on the ground.

"Shut your trap," he said. "Or you'll get worse from me right now."

He wasn't going to shoot, because that might bring campers over to see what was going on. He'd just beat me to death on the spot.

"What happens next?" I dragged myself up to my hands and knees, determined not to get tied up.

He nodded toward Lake Michigan. "Somewhere out there, the boat will get a hole in it and go under, while Libby and I will take the rescue skiff and motor back, a harrowing experience for us to tell in the national press. Kelsey became uncontrollable."

The beam above us shed enough light for me to make out a sizable boat at anchor within wading or swimming distance of the shore. It had to be the boat John and Alex had used to go diving. The skiff was likely just below the steep hill. Alex had arrived while we were inside the lighthouse with Libby.

"So you plan to drag three of us over the rock wall and into that boat? That's a lot of hard work, Alex."

"Libby and I managed to get Lloyd up the tower stairs by using a winch off the boat. We can surely roll you three down this embankment, then use fishing gear to haul our catch into the boat. You're not much bigger than a giant muskie or coho salmon."

This was sounding way too easy for him. I was sweating, praying, losing my mind and my hope.

Libby finished trussing Kelsey. I was next.

As Libby reached for my ankles, I kicked her in the face, rolled over fast, then crawled like hell. She uttered a loud "Oof."

I was scrambling to my feet when Lloyd's rifle stock socked me in the ribs. The breath whooshed out of me. I collapsed on my hands and knees. My body dumped over onto the ground, stiff with the shock of emptied lungs.

Something stomped on my belly then. With big paws. Lucky Harbor.

His tromping worked like a bellows, pushing my diaphragm back into action.

With a gasp, I got up as Lucky Harbor leaped up on Professor Faust, making the man lose his footing. I grabbed the rifle as the professor went backward onto the ground with Lucky Harbor licking him in the face.

I held the rifle on the professor. "You must have been eating fudge on the boat. Just like you were all enjoying my fudge in the lighthouse parlor the night of the murder."

He gave me a guilty-as-charged look of surprise as Lucky Harbor kept on licking his mouth. The professor tried to get up repeatedly but couldn't. I didn't even need to hold a weapon on him.

Libby made a run for it, but a blur of legs whirling like a helicopter's propeller took her down in a heap. Kelsey.

A moment later Kelsey emerged close to me in the darkness, taking the last of the ropes off her wrists. "We learned in self-defense class how to get out of ropes. But I'm not sure Libby's heart was in it, either."

"Thanks. Sorry I was wrong about you at first. How's Pauline?"

"Out cold. Not good."

"She's going to be really mad at me when this is over, especially if we don't find John."

I called nine-one-one again to ask for Coast Guard help to find John. The dispatcher said the sheriff was already on his way; they'd done a location search on my cell phone call minutes ago that went unanswered.

Exhausted, I sat in the grass with the rifle. Lucky Harbor came over to me, boinking his nose into my shoulder. I tossed him my entire pocket's worth of Goldfish crackers.

A couple of hours later, Pauline and I waited at my cabin for word on John's rescue. It didn't come as the hours ticked past midnight.

Pauline now had a bruise on the left side of her face to match the eggplant hue on her right side. She was lying on my couch sniffling, swearing, sighing.

My bruises were going to look pretty fancy, too, by morning. I started a fire in the fireplace to ward off the chill and dampness coming in off the lake. Lucky Harbor lay on the rug next to the couch, watching my every move. I thought back now to the rose garden and the dog's extra attention to the professor's shoes. They had probably smelled like the park area and some essence of Lloyd. Lucky Harbor knew all along who the killer was, just as I had suspected.

Dillon and Jordy had arrived at the park almost simultaneously that night. Libby and Alex were hauled off to jail. Dillon had wanted to take me home to the condo where he was staying, but I refused. When he heard me relate my story to Jordy about what Lucky Harbor had done, Dillon said that it'd be good to keep the dog for the night, reminding me that dogs had a way of reassuring people. Whatever the feeling was that I had for Dillon grew a little bit that night. For a man to let you borrow his dog is a big deal. Maybe that's even real love. I went over to sit on the floor next to the couch to pet the handsome, chocolate-fudge-colored American water spaniel.

The next thing I knew, my phone buzzed in my pocket.

I'd fallen asleep next to Lucky Harbor on the floor. His head rested across my legs, as if to make sure I didn't go anywhere without him.

It was Jordy. He said, "I'm sorry. But there's still no sign of John."

When I got off my cell phone I looked at the time. It was five in the morning. The windows were rectangles of gray morning light.

Pauline was stirring on the couch.

I dreaded telling her the news.

Grandpa and Grandma knocked on the door about a half hour later. They'd just heard about last night's goings-on. They hugged me and Pauline long and hard with lots of "I love yous" and "Thank God you're safe." Pauline was crying.

Grandpa said, "No tears, A.M. and P.M. Move it, move it. Get on the boat."

"You don't have a boat, Gilpa." He'd lost his mind.

"We're taking Moose Lindstrom's boat. I already called."

Now I knew he'd lost his mind—in a good way.

Grandma winked at me. "You gals get going with Gil. We have to find John. I'll take care of the shop."

We trundled off fast across the backyard, down the docks, past several slips, and to the very end of the harbor, where Moose's *Super Catch I* swayed in the light ripples of the water. Moose was already aboard firing up the engines in a big rumble.

The four of us were out onto Lake Michigan within seconds. The eastern sky was pink. Shadows were still deep.

Since the Coast Guard was searching currents from the shipwreck site where John had last been allegedly, according to the professor, we took a different tack.

Grandpa said, "John's a stumpy guy, but smart enough. Maybe he caught hold of some debris that helped him float."

Pauline wasn't cheered.

But then I thought, My grandpa is always right. Even snatching a foam cooler from a boat can save you in the water.

"Grandpa, if he floated, where might he go in these currents?"

"Let's see, after about ten hours?" My grandpa looked toward the sunrise. It was now past seven in the morning. "Toward Death's Door."

Pauline began bawling at those words.

Death's Door was the area between the northern tip of Door County and Plum Island, where many ships over the centuries had sunk because of treacherous channels. It wasn't likely that a man could float all the way to Death's Door from where Alex Faust had abandoned John, but the current was headed in that direction.

Another hour later, we spotted an unusual-looking buoy off Ellison Bay. Pauline screamed, "It's him! It's John!"

She leaped up and down, calling his name again and again, waving madly.

The way her face lit up in the morning sun—well, it was like the sun was inside Pauline and the brilliance of the moment evaporated all her bruises. This kind of pure happiness healed anything. Magic was in her heart. The magic was true love.

I got tears in my eyes. I'd been such a fool. John Schultz was the perfect man for my best friend. If he made her *that* happy . . .

Gilpa gave us a three-way hug. "A.M. and P.M., we did it!"

John's wet suit helped save him, the Coast Guard said. He was able to ward off hypothermia, and luckily the top layer of the water was fairly warm in July. John said he had grabbed hold of the paddle that Alex Faust had tried to clobber him with and used that to help stay afloat until he got lucky enough to come upon some floating fishing net buoys before he smashed up against the tall buoy marking some shoals. The professor had shot at him several times in the dark, missing every time. John was lucky to be alive.

His video camera was still aboard the boat Alex Faust had commandeered after leaving John out in Lake Michigan. But the professor likely didn't realize John was smart enough to upload his materials to the Internet regularly at a Web site used for storing video. Professor Faust was not going to be pleased to find that the video did indeed show him putting poisonous mushrooms in the pan just before dishing it out to Lloyd on Friday night. John hadn't realized what was happening; to some people mushrooms are just mushrooms. John tried to blame himself for not saving Lloyd Mueller.

Later, after the rescue and back on land, I confessed to Jordy that I thought my mention of the video camera to Libby might have exacerbated the situation for all of us. Libby likely called Alex Faust and told him he had to get that camera from John and kill him in order to save their plan to marry and take over Lloyd's estate. Libby was old school with electronics, so she also didn't realize John saved it all online.

All in all, the whole situation was sad. My grandfather's best friend was gone.

It took us all morning to finish making statements. Jordy was talking in private with me around noon behind the fudge shop. A stiff breeze was blowing off the lake. Clouds were bunching up for a storm. The fudge shop and docks out front were crowded with half the town plus all the area tourists, it seemed. The press from Green Bay had shown up. I'd also gotten an e-mail from Jeremy Stone, the Madison newspaper reporter who'd been something of my nemesis in May; he was on his way.

It was blessedly quiet behind my shop next to the burning bush. I was wearing a pink-flowered pinafore apron with lace that stood up high enough on my shoulders to brush my cheek.

Jordy had on his full tan-and-brown uniform and brimmed hat, ready for the cameras out front. He tucked a notepad back into his pocket with his pen. "You got lucky, Ava. This could've turned out another way."

"Lucky? See this bruise on my face? My leg? The stitches in my head? My ribs hurt, too. You should deputize me and give me combat pay and time off."

He managed a quirky, crooked smile. I was getting respect because I'd been right about a hunch or two. He'd told me they'd found a crayon in Faust's coat pocket, presumably Pauline's missing one. Jordy said murderers often kept incriminating evidence because of their egos. Faust thought he was clever, using something as simple as a crayon to threaten me. The partial fingerprint on the fudge matched Libby's prints, but the bite mark fit Faust. It gave me the creeps to think of Libby feeding Faust a bite of my fudge before they hauled Lloyd up the lighthouse staircase.

Jordy said, "Well, I'm done here. You take care."

He didn't move, though.

I didn't want him to move. Some bond had formed between us through all this trouble. I didn't have a name for it, though. It wasn't quite friendship. We were somehow respectful of each other in a new way.

I said, "So, what'd you find in the box? Did Libby say who stole it?"

"Alex Faust took it after running you off the road. Amazingly, he lost the darn thing and Piers found it and returned it to the lighthouse, thinking he'd find Libby there."

"Piers? When? How?"

"Alex had stopped by the Luscious Ladle to pick up some muffins to take to a book signing. He was in a hurry. Evidently, Alex pulled the box out of his trunk, thinking he'd put it inside the car, but then he left without it. Piers found it in the parking lot."

I laughed. "So, what'd you find in it?"

"Just Mercy's nasty letters."

That disappointed me. But then I brightened with an

idea. "I know the combination to Lloyd's safe. Want to go look at it now instead of waiting for Friday?" I flicked my ponytail tantalizingly at him.

"Did you go back into that house after I told you to stay out of trouble?"

"Of course." I fished about in the pocket of the pink-flowered pinafore apron. I showed him the key to Lloyd's house. "I'm legal, remember?"

"Faust probably changed the locks. That key won't work."

"I can find a way in on my own."

"You shouldn't be going in there without an escort."

"I'm staring at my escort."

"You sure have a way with words."

"And diagrams. Want me to start drawing diagrams of how I can get into Lloyd's house without a key, Jordy?"

"No way. Come on."

But when we got to Lloyd's house, Parker Balusek was there that day locking up. With new keys. He'd had the locks changed today. He carried a thick satchel.

"You opened the safe?" I asked eagerly.

Parker patted his leather satchel. "My firm will be going over the papers right away. We'll let you know what we find out about the town's property."

"Parker, what about the offer on the property? Has the offer been withdrawn?"

"Yes."

"Who was it that was going to buy the harbor property and Duck Marsh Street?"

"It was the Riverboat Cruise Corporation. I got a phone call not an hour ago that said they'd withdrawn their offer. It seems that John Schultz demanded they withdraw or he'd sue them for age discrimination. The guy might still have grounds to sue them, because he was let go for presumably not a good enough reason, as John puts it, but at least he sent a chill down their backs that helped you and others in Fishers' Harbor."

Since Parker and I had had the conversation only yesterday about John's shaky employment status with RCC, we both burst out laughing. It's amazing how life works. John, the man I'd detested and suspected of skullduggery, ended up being the guy to save Fishers' Harbor. For now, anyway. Who knew what the future would bring from those papers tucked inside Parker's briefcase?

Thunder threatened us if we stayed much longer, but I had to ask, "But do you think the village owns the property? And my shop?"

"It could. I suspect the village is owed back taxes."

"There's an emerald ring Libby is wearing. You might ask her to sell that to help make things right."

Parker shook his head. "Sorry. Personal property. Can't take somebody's ring to pay off taxes. We'll look at other angles first." He started for his car in the turnaround by the fountain, then said, "You're very cute in that apron."

My face went scalding hot. I'd forgotten I still had the thing on.

Jordy stepped between us, clearly muscling in. "She hasn't decided yet who will be her date for the prom on Saturday night."

Oh dear. The church ladies hadn't spread the gossip around yet. My grandmother wasn't about to tell them Dillon and I were getting back together. I needed to make a fast escape. "Gee, I've got to run. I've got one more recipe to dream up before Saturday afternoon. Jordy, we're down one judge. Do you want to be a fudge judge? One without a deadly grudge against me?"

He laughed.

Then the sky opened up in a deluge. We ran for his squad car.

Chapter 25

The rains came off and on the remainder of the week, as if cleansing us all of the murder. The soggy forecast made me worry about Saturday's fudge festival in Fishers' Harbor. But Saturday dawned misty and then the sun burned through by ten for the parade.

Sam appeared from out of the crowd on the sidewalk to stand next to me. His arm was still in a sling. The way he looked at me, with a bit of a scowl, made my heart come into my throat and my palms sweat.

"You're some gal," he said, looking me over. "Does your dress match those bruises?"

"Sam, be nice. I'm not going to the dance with Dillon."

"What're you up to now?"

"A surprise for a friend. Can we still be friends, Sam?"

A glint came into his blue eyes. "Always. I figure it's only a matter of time before Rivers slips up again. I've always had your back and I won't quit now."

"Thanks, Sam. For accepting my choice. You're a good guy."

Pauline's Butterfly summer class of girls paraded down Main Street with their red wagons decorated in Cinderella Pink Fudge fairy finery. The girls wore wings on their backs, crowns on their heads, and pretty dresses in various pastels. Each wagon carried a box that was decorated to look like a piece of fudge. Each piece had wings on top, mimicking the marzipan wings Cody and I often shaped by hand to go on pieces of the Cinderella Pink Fudge.

Several other shops and artists filled out the parade with floats, tricked-out bicycles, costumed pets, and more. Clowns tossed candy for children to grab. My grandmother and grandfather rode by together in the Peninsula Belgian American Club's car. It was decorated with a BOOYAH IS BEAUTIFUL sign and advertisements for autumn kermises. They had a big pot of booyah cooking outdoors now near the docks for consumption later at the adult prom dance.

Dillon waved at me from across Main Street. He held on to Lucky Harbor, who wore a doggy clown costume of his own, with a funny hat on his head and balloons tied to his leash that Dillon was giving away randomly to kids on the sidewalk.

I gave him a wave back, then excused myself with Sam. "See you later, Sam. The bar under the tent opens at five, music at seven. I'll make my entrance at eight. That's when I'll have a big surprise. Please be there. You'll like it."

I ran off fast, letting him fret.

By one o'clock, Kelsey, Piers, and I were standing on the dais outside my shop on the docks, each with two plates of new fudge in front of us. The crowd had already voted on their ten favorite fudge batches made by local residents. Those were being sold off piece by piece for charities. But now it was time for the celebrity round. I wore the green-checkered pinafore apron with matching green-checkered toque on my head. I even had on lipstick. Kelsey rolled her eyes at me, but I was in this to win it. I wanted to look like Audrey Hepburn. Kelsey and Piers wore their plain white chef's aprons.

The first round was created for fun flavors.

Jordy, Erik, Dotty, and Mercy eagerly dipped into their taste-testing. I had invited Mercy Fogg to be one of the judges so I could curry her favor, in case she won the next election for village president. Pauline told me I was shameful and insane, and that Mercy would be the death of me yet. "Mercy is as wacky as Kelsey."

Kelsey's fun flavor was called Sunshine Sparkles. It was her dandelion-infused fudge. She'd filled her fudge with wild plant and flower seeds, too, in her effort to make the fudge fiber rich. She had poked a dandelion on top of each piece, too, which the judges were expected to eat. To me, the fudge looked like dark suet cakes for woodpeckers and chickadees. Kelsey was not destined to become a fudge confectioner. But I had become thankful for her karate kick ability; she had a future as an exercise instructor.

Piers had made Blueberry Boppity-Boo Fudge. He'd used white chocolate, which meant the fudge was blue from the berries in it. The kids in the crowd loved it and clapped loudly. Even some of the Butterflies broke ranks from me and clapped for Piers.

My fun flavor? I stuck with my Rapunzel Raspberry Rapture, part of my Fairy Tale Fudge line. I served the bites of fudge with a big dollop of whipped cream on the side from our farm. Then I drizzled fresh raspberry wine sauce made at a local Door County vineyard over the top of that cloud of white and the fudge. The topper was a big, newly ripened raspberry from the Klubertanz Farm. I sprinkled pink luster dust here and there to make it sparkle in the sunlight.

Mercy ate her entire plateful. Then she ate the leftovers on the other judging plates. Dotty wasn't even done savoring it when Mercy snatched the plate from her. The rapture on Mercy's face, though, was priceless; I'd named my new fudge treat appropriately, thanks to Pauline's nudge.

The judging had to wait for Mercy to finish eating.

Pauline said into the microphone, "Folks, it's lavish, luscious, lovely, lip-smacking luxuriance."

The first round ended in a tie between Piers and me; we each got a nine. No ten! Piers was from Chicago, and Mercy loved Chicago people, so despite my Rapunzel Raspberry Rapture giving her an excellent epicurean episode, I think she voted against me.

Kelsey managed to receive a composite score of three. She did not worry me.

The four judges cleaned their palates with a drink of fresh, cold milk provided by my parents from their Holsteins.

In the second and final round, where we were supposed to impress the judges the most, Piers presented something he called Lambeau Field Fudge. Lambeau Field is the home of the Green Bay Packers football team. The fun fact about that is that Curly Lambeau started his Green Bay Packer team during the same season that Hercule Poirot debuted in Agatha Christie's novels—in 1920. My heart sank because Piers was playing hardball. For a Chicago Bears fan to step up on the dais with a Green Bay Packer fudge theme is a signal that the world has finally come to an end. Bears and Packers are arch rivals. The crowd knew this. The people clapped and hooted.

Piers's second fudge was also colorful—two-toned, to look like the Packer green and gold colors. He'd layered mint green fudge with lemon-flavored fudge, a bold combination for taste buds. Piers borrowed my technique of decorating fudge and had applied little chocolate paste footballs on top. He put a bobblehead doll of Aaron Rodgers, the quarterback, on the plate to the side of the fudge. Piers was a formidable foe. An icky feeling of defeat swept over me.

Kelsey was next. She presented what she called Velveeta Va-voom Nettle Nibble Fudge.

My panic deepened, because anything made with Velveeta cheese had a chance of winning for the novelty alone, despite the nettles. That gooey cheese was also incredibly cheap as an ingredient. A favorite salad at Pauline's school was one made with pasta, peas, bacon, and cubes of Velveeta tossed with some mayonnaise. I attempted a protest. "That's not real fudge! It's made with a block of Velveeta melted down with powdered sugar and cocoa dumped in, all squished with your hands. Kids make that all the time."

Kelsey flipped her long blond hair in a pert way. She was dazzling in a purple-and-pink shorts outfit, with her purple-glitter shoes. “There were no rules on how to make our fudge. My Va-voom variety is healthy. You get protein and calcium, plus the greens I added.”

“That could be green mold or moss or marijuana you collected at the park.”

The crowd gasped. I'd gone too far. “Just kidding about that last thing. Sorry.”

My nemesis wiggled her shoulders in protest and looked poised for a karate kick to my face. But she smiled, relaxing. “Cooked nettles are quite edible.”

I looked at the judges, all of whom were tasting her gelatinous fudge. Of course Mercy was going for a second piece immediately.

Then Dotty said, “This isn't bad at all.”

“Dotty!” You'd think one of my grandmother's friends would take my side.

Pauline stepped to the microphone. “Let's move along to our final entry in Round Two. What is your flavor, Ava?”

I felt like a dope. While Piers and Kelsey had gone for something very entertaining for Round Two, I'd put together something that now seemed too sappy. And maybe it would be perceived as taking advantage of a dead man.

I stepped to the microphone. “My flavor is, well . . . It's called ‘Lloyd's Rose Garden Fudge.’ It's made with rose petals.”

The crowd went quiet. I was horrified. Everybody stared up at me on the dais. My mistake was in the nuances of differences in regional taste bud habits. In California, whole restaurants were devoted to eating with flowers. I'd been using flowers in my cooking for the TV series crew for years. In Wisconsin, flower petal salads or petals sprinkled on ice cream was still a novelty. With a glance toward my father in the crowd I could tell he, too, wondered if I'd gone loco. Flower petals were something that cows and goats ate.

Pauline came to my rescue at the microphone. "Tell us about the recipe."

"It's a special fudge to honor Lloyd Mueller. He was my grandpa's best friend, but just as important, he was a friend to all of us. He let a lot of people skip paying him rent when times were tough. I wouldn't even be here in my shop if he hadn't let my family keep the bait shop running during lean years."

I looked to my grandmother in the crowd. She nodded. I didn't look at my grandpa because I knew I might choke up.

Dillon was in the crowd, too, smiling, nodding for me to go on.

Continuing on, I told the crowd, "Lloyd had a beautiful rose garden. Red roses, as you know, are a symbol of love. He also had yellow roses, and they're a symbol of friendship. I picked petals from all of Lloyd's roses and made a rose petal fudge in his honor so that he could be with the fudge contest in spirit. Rose varieties in Wisconsin are hardy and endure. When I made this fudge, I thought about how wonderful it is that friendships like my grandpa's and Lloyd's could endure over a long time. I hope you like my new flavor of fudge, which has the fragrance of friendship."

Pauline winked at me for my alliteration; her gesture made me glow inside. I set about feeding the judges a piece of "Rose Garden Fudge." The confection was white, with dried rose petals folded within the sugar treat like nature's own confetti. I had crystallized some of the petals and sprinkled those around on the plate, including atop a large dollop of whipped cream.

My grandpa hopped up on the dais to hug me prematurely before the judges were done tasting.

The crowd burst into applause. Those who had been sitting in the chairs stood up. The four judges took a second bite of the fudge. Mercy had paused to dip a rose petal into the whipped cream. She placed it on her tongue. I could tell she was rolling the flavor sensation around in her mouth. Her eyes crossed. I feared she hated it.

Mercy's lips wiggled about some more. "I didn't know perfume was edible. . . ." She peered about at all the people waiting for her vote. She was loving this attention, something I knew she sorely missed since being deposed as our village board president. Then she crowed, "This is delicious!"

Kelsey snatched a piece to nibble. Her entire body transformed with an ambrosial expression on her face. "I should have thought of this. There are organic roses all over Door County. You beat me fair and square."

Coming from the woman who had been my mortal enemy last week, that was a high compliment.

The judges handed in their scores to Pauline.

The crowd at the harbor went silent. Only the motors of boats on the lake and the wind snapping the tent could be heard.

Pauline finally took the microphone. "In last place with a four-point-five total score . . . is Kelsey King with dandelions and nettles in Velveeta cheese."

The crowd clapped politely. I felt sorry for her now. There really was a recipe for Velveeta cheese fudge that I'd found in one of Lloyd's books I'd left lying around my shop. Kelsey had obviously tried the recipe in her desperation.

But I was sweating, and back to worrying. Piers the Packer man looked smug, despite my rose petal triumph.

"Out of ten points, Piers has received a nine-point-seven!"

The crowd whistled and cheered, chanting, "Piers, Piers! Go, Packers!"

A nine-point-seven? Could I possibly beat him? I'd received a nine in the first round. Who would win? Packers or mere petals?

The crowd quieted. Pauline had taken position at the microphone. "And the winner is . . . Ava Oosterling!"

The Butterflies squealed right below me in the crowd. John was trotting his heft through the crowd to get all kinds of video. My parents and grandparents joined me on the dais for a big hug.

My grandpa whispered in my ear, "Honey, that was lovely. Lloyd would be proud of you. I'm proud of you. Thank you."

My whole family along with Pauline bounced up and down and all around me with boisterous hoots in what we call a "jump around." Pauline told me that the sympathy for Lloyd won out; I'd received a perfect score in the last round and the combined scores in the contest showed that I'd won over Piers by three-tenths of a point. Roses beat Packers!

I spent the rest of the afternoon selling fudge and pies. Jeremy Stone showed up and gave me a thumbs-up for my inventive and tasty fudge flavors. He wanted to take photos of me later in Lloyd's rose garden and at the lighthouse for an exclusive story that he promised would be front-page news. How could I resist! I still dreamed of getting my fudge into Hollywood's Emmy and Oscar swag bags.

Before I knew it, it was evening and time to change into my dress.

Pauline and Laura came to my cabin, insisting on helping me get ready. They wore beautiful gowns that shook my self-confidence; Pauline was stunning in a strapless ball gown in her new favorite color of tangerine, and Laura wore a powder blue, shimmery thing with lace sleeves that tented well over her big belly. When I emerged from my bedroom, my BFFs went stone silent.

I almost turned back inside and shut the bedroom door. "Is that a good silence or should I change back into a pair of shorts and a T-shirt?"

Laura was tearing up, though she did that a lot lately. She had made my dress from old-fashioned satin and netting that Lois and Dotty had found while cleaning out a house for an elderly couple who were moving to a nursing home. The color was pale pink rose, a tender and delicate color so unlike me that I held my arms and hands away from myself so that I wouldn't mar the beauty of the fabric. It was tea length, grazing my calves, with an empire waist and cap sleeves. The old-fashioned netting overlay went from my empire waist to the end of the skirt. Dotty and Lois had even found one of those stiff petticoats that held the skirt out just so.

Pauline said, "You don't look like you. And that's a good thing."

"Gee, thanks, P.M."

"Hush, A.M." She rushed to me. "This calls for your hair to be up."

While she fussed with my hair, Laura said, "You look like Cinderella."

Titus took that moment to scoot from the kitchen to look up at me before passing us on his way to the underworld of the couch.

Pauline nodded. "Yup, Cinderella. Titus is getting ready to turn into a horse to pull your carriage to the ball at the castle."

I countered, "I think he's off the hook because the old fairy tale calls for rats to turn into the horses. Mice helped sew the dress in the Disney movie."

Laura settled onto the arm of the couch. "Rats, mice—they don't matter when you have us."

"And I thank you both," I said, with the glow of friendship burning bright inside me again. My taste buds and nose recalled the perfume of my winning Rose Garden Fudge.

Pauline said to me, "So, if it's not Dillon, who's the mystery date that this dress is perfect for?"

"You'll see soon enough when we make our entrance. Now help Laura over to the harbor and no peeking toward my cabin. I'll be there as soon as my date arrives."

"Jeez but you're bossy, which you know I totally ignore. Do one last thing for me before we leave," Pauline said, dragging me back into my bedroom and in front of a mirror, where I got a good look at myself. "What do you think?"

The kindnesses happening to me were overwhelming, like spotting a rainbow the very first time in your life. Pauline had made the most beautiful loose bun on top of my head with wavelets of my summery auburn hair cascading down to my neck. "I really do look like Cinderella. Pauline, thank you."

"Ah, shucks, it's nothing. Now you're taller than me for at least one night."

Once Pauline and Laura scooted out of the cabin, I grew nervous from my excitement over what I'd planned next.

It was around eight o'clock when my date and I were ready to leave my cabin to make our grand entrance at the harbor. I called John on his cell phone. "You ready to get this on camera?"

"You got it, Ava."

I smiled at my secret date; then we walked across my lawn to the back door of the fudge shop, went through the dim hallway, then through the shop with the lights off so nobody could really see us through the windows, and then with great aplomb, I opened the door. The cowbell clanged. I took a deep breath.

We stepped outside.

The crowd muttered, then quieted, not knowing how to react. Who was I with?

I stood there with a man in full uniform. Army uniform.

A cry went up in the crowd. It was Laura's voice. I stepped aside to let the man beside me—Sergeant Brecht Rousseau, her husband—rush to meet his pregnant wife. They hadn't seen each other for several months.

None of us had dry eyes after that. The school band played "God Bless America."

Dillon rushed to me. "So he was your date? How did you . . . ?" Then he cocked his head. "My mother."

"Yup. She knew a senator on the right committee who could get him a special leave. He had to come from halfway around the world, but it happened. They moved up his leave or something so it was all legal. Thanks to your mother and her reputation for giving generously to some political campaigns."

"She's my date. But I'll ditch her for you. Want to take a fast ride in her car?"

Dillon was being his old cowboy self, ready to put me on a horse and ride away into the sunset. My heart said, "Do it." But Pauline was right, and Dillon was right. It was time to take things slowly, to appreciate each moment of life, to savor things just as I loved to savor a sublime piece of fudge. I could feel that I was different today; something was changing inside me. For the better, I hoped. From a secret pocket in my dress, I took out the betting card I'd saved from the Troubled Trout. "Not so fast, Dillon. Looks like our sewer guy won after all. Excuse me while I find Al Kvalheim."

Another voice in the crowd stopped me. "I'll be wounded more if you don't give me the first dance." It was Sam. He had his arm still in a sling, but his eyes glistened with meaning. He had my back. He probably always would. He looked handsome beyond compare in a crisp white shirt rolled up to his elbows that showed off his summer tan.

Before I could hunt down Al for the dance I owed him, bearded, stout Spuds Schlimgen stepped forward. "Hey, this little apron honey gal was supposed to be my date."

Parker Balusek's tall, slender frame eased through the crowd to join the lineup. "Step aside, men. I believe she's waiting for me."

I said, "I am?"

"You are," said Parker, bowing in a suave way, to the amusement of tourists holding on to beers, wine, plates of pie, and fudge. One person threw rose petals from his plate of Rose Garden Fudge onto the dock at our feet.

Dillon had his arms crossed, chuckling now from his stance in the crowd, enjoying my discomfort.

Before I could bolt, Al's chubby figure showed up next to Parker, though I barely recognized our water and sewer guy. Al was wearing a crisp striped dress shirt, tie, and dress pants. He was clean! He shook a friendly fist in the air. "I won her fair and square, guys."

"Hold on, or I might have to put you all under arrest," another familiar voice said. Jordy Tollefson emerged, off-duty and wearing casual pants and a blue, long-sleeved shirt that showed off his body's V shape from his broad shoulders to his trim waist. "I believe you owe me this dance . . . Miss Ava Mathilde Oosterling."

My mouth went dry. When my middle name got invoked, I knew emotions ran deep. What exactly was running deep in Jordy?

This Cinderella at the ball took a step back. Six men of various shapes and all with big grins on their mugs were staring at me. Me! More in the crowd had begun to enjoy our show. Quick side bets were being made. I glanced at John and Pauline, and sure enough, John had his camera rolling. I stood there with my hands and arms akimbo like a still-life doll from my shop, frozen in my confusion.

Verona Klubertanz raced full bore at me but stopped just short of touching my dress with hands filled with fudge. "You're not Ava! You're Cinderella!" She pointed to the six men. "And those are the six rats who go poof and turn into horses."

The crowd laughed, which broke the tension. My breath came back.

"Thank you, Verona."

But how was I going to get out of this gracefully? Who was I going to choose for the first dance? And why had they all stepped forward like this? Why had Dillon backed off? Then he hoisted a big pickle jar I hadn't noticed because of the crowd. It was filled with money.

He yelled out, "Who wants a dance with Ava Oosterling? All the money goes to new playground equipment for the kids."

So that's why Dillon wasn't first in line for a dance with me. But he'd left me adrift in a sea of eager smiles from the other guys. My heart was thumping louder than Lucky Harbor scratching himself with a hind leg bumping against one of my shop's cabinets. Old Al was so cute. And Parker, well, there was a tall drink, as the saying goes; and he and I could talk basketball all night and keep us both happy. But maybe Spuds deserved to have the first dance for the way he recognized my "apron sexiness" in my shop. Then there was Jordy, arresting my heart in a new, though benign way that was befuddling.

A tap on my shoulder startled me. I turned around. It was my grandfather.

"Hey there, A.M. honey. Give your Gilpa the first dance?"

He'd saved me. As he always had. With glee in my heart, we danced to the spirited "Beer Barrel Polka." My pink netted skirt dipped this way and that like an inverted cup as Gilpa and I stomped about the Fishers' Harbor dock with arms pumping up and down.

Al got the next dance; then everybody began dancing with everybody else's partners—the children, and grandmothers and grandfathers, Pauline and John, Grandpa Gil and Grandma Sophie, my parents, Pete and Florine, and the tourists. I danced with every man on the docks, it seemed, earning a lot of money for the playground. Finally, I fell into the arms of Dillon. I saved my last dance for him.

I thought I heard my grandpa growl and my mother gasp, but my heart was soaring above it all and my head said Gilpa would still love me no matter what, just as he always had. Pauline gave me a wink as she and John passed by during a swirling, stomping polka with a loud tuba's *oompah, oompah*.

Lucky Harbor handled the commotion by leaping into the water repeatedly, then coming to shake all over me, begging for "fudge." Luckily for Lucky Harbor, Laura had sewn in the secret pockets just for the dog; I tossed him Goldfish crackers throughout the night.

Best of all, Laura and Brecht got to slow-dance into each other's heart. It made me smile to think that my fudge played a role in their reunion.

Coming home to Door County and Fishers' Harbor, and trying for this fresh start of my own with a goofy fudge shop was working out after all—even if I had "six rats" in my own love life to deal with in my future.

Chapter 26

The next morning was Sunday, gloriously, thankfully so. Tourists always slept in; my fudge shop could wait for me to wake up. I was beat and achy and itchy but for all good reasons. I'd gotten to bed by midnight, which was reasonable. However, Laura had called me at three a.m. to say her twins had been born. She thanked me profusely for bringing her husband home just in time. She'd given birth to a boy and a girl. She'd used Pauline's name and my name to create their middle names. The boy was Spencer Paul Rousseau, and the girl was Clara Ava Rousseau.

At seven o'clock—late by my usual standards—I hiked through the dewy grass to Oosterlings' Live Bait, Bobbers & Belgian Fudge & Beer to help my grandpa. Fishers' Harbor was so quiet that at first I only heard a lone, yappy dog bark as it was let outside at the end of my street. Robins seemed subdued for once. A misty fog patted my cheeks as it threatened to turn into rain.

My grandfather wasn't in the shop. I heard whistling, though. A few of Lloyd's small church cookbooks sat next to the coffeepot, so I grabbed them along with a cup of chocolate-laced coffee, then followed the pleasant morning trill of my grandfather's out the front door and down the first pier to his docked and dead boat. Gilpa was inside, tossing things in a bucket. Bolts, rags—everything was flying. Lucky Harbor was with him; the dog smiled up at me, his tail thumping on the floor of the boat and his dark eyes watching my hands in case they dove into a pocket to toss him a treat. I came on deck.

"What's going on, Gilpa?"

"Gotta clean up the boat. Looky here what I found." He held up a fishing net filled with pink purses, pink dolls, pink wrapping paper, and even crayons—all from the shop. Grandpa winked toward the dog. "He seems to think my boat is his storage unit for the stuff he steals from your shop. Most of these were behind a life preserver."

Boy, was I glad I'd never confronted little Verona Klubertanz! "So Dillon's dog is a thief."

"Matches Dillon's personality. He stole you once. He doing that again?"

I set my coffee on the small table in the center of the boat, then plopped down with the cookbooks on the gunwale. "Just because we danced last night doesn't mean I'm marrying him." Yet.

"Did you kiss him?"

"Last night? Yup."

"Before last night?"

"Yup."

"I don't like it."

"I know that, Gilpa. Maybe that's why I kissed him." I winked at him.

Gilpa gave me a look, then stabbed at his silver hair with his oily fingers. "Bah. You're nothing but a stubborn Belgian."

"It's inherited."

"Bah and booyah on you."

"Don't be so hard on Dillon. He helped me get you and Grandma back together, he found me a truck, and he and his mother helped me with information to solve Lloyd's murder. Not to mention he let me borrow his dog now and then."

Gilpa went back to gathering items from the boat.

I was looking again at the photos in the cookbook focusing on the history of the fishermen, including those who were my loose relatives who'd come here in the 1800s. What did the wives do while men went onto Lake Michigan for weeks at a time to fish in the 1800s or even before those days when the Woodland and Onesta Indians lived here in AD 1000? Those men had to have ventured far out into the treacherous waters for food in skimpy vessels. I had a feeling that Pauline would have to put up with John, too, leaving for days and weeks to follow his creative ideas and adventuresome spirit. I said as much to Gilpa.

"Pauline has a good head on those tall shoulders. Whatever she decides will be the right thing. I'm sure she'll be at the fudge shop to tell us one way or the other about John's intentions by the time the sun burns off the fog. My A.M. and P.M. are never apart for long."

He started whistling again. But within seconds he stopped with a big grin on his face. He was bursting to tell me something.

"What is it, Gilpa?"

"Parker Balusek sent me an e-mail early this morning. I called him back."

The cookbooks shook in my nervous hands. "And what'd he say about all the property woes we have?"

"Lloyd's trust gave his property to Cody Fjelstad."

I almost lost my seat and fell backward into the water. "Our Cody? Ranger?"

"That's the one." Grandpa waved a hand about the harbor, over to Duck Marsh Street, and then toward the backs of the buildings that lined Main Street. "Cody gets all of this when he's twenty-five. At least, that's what Parker says is in the estate papers, which should stand up in court now that the sale to a buyer hasn't gone through."

"But what about now? What about our shop?"

"It's free and clear. To you and me. The trust has instructions to sell Lloyd's house and use that to pay off the taxes and the lien on this property on one condition."

My heart plummeted into my stomach. "What's that?"

"Lloyd left notes in the trust. He wants us to buy the Blue Heron Inn. He wants it preserved."

"Us? We have no money to buy it. Lloyd didn't even own it."

"Ava honey, Lloyd was hoping we'd take a risk and get out of our old tired ways. We'll have to borrow money or make money somehow. Work twice as hard. Change is a good thing."

"You talkin' about me or you?"

He chuckled as he tossed more old tools into a plastic pail. "Parker said that if you and I own the bait shop free and clear, we might be able to borrow against it for enough money for a down payment on the Blue Heron Inn. I can't afford it alone, but with you winning the fudge contest with raspberries and Lloyd's roses, you're going to sell more fudge and become busier and need that big kitchen. Maybe together we can make enough money to meet the payments on that old bed-and-breakfast."

The breath had been knocked from my lungs. "And buy a boat?"

"No." He didn't even pause while tossing bolts into the bucket. "Money won't stretch that far. For now, I'm willing to go in with Moose and rent his boat so that I can help you buy that inn up on the hill. I'm donating this boat to a place Cody told me about that helps boys get rehabilitated and learn worthwhile skills."

"But this is your boat that you've had forever. Since I was a little girl."

"Ava honey, you're more important than any old boat. And you were right what you said the other day. It's time to let go of this piece of junk. Let's get the Blue Heron Inn up and running again, then think about a boat later. What matters is that our little shop will stay the way it is. At least for now."

A lump grew in my throat. My heart swelled with all the love pouring into it from my grandfather's sacrifices. "Grandpa, all of the changes will be hard."

"Nothing worth a spit in life is easy, honey. Now, I was figuring we'd better start planning that Belgian kermis thing for next July."

"It's a Founders' Day, remember? For everybody and not just Belgians. I want it to be for all of Fishers' Harbor and all of Door County, for all the immigrants and their descendents who have preserved the quaintness and good soul of this place. Maybe we could do a little kermis here, though, come this fall sometime. That booyah last night was pretty tasty; I wouldn't mind if Grandma and her church ladies made that again, along with all those pies."

"Smart girl. But is it okay if I invite somebody from Belgium to come over sometime soon, now that we have a whole big inn up on the bluff with rooms to fill and rent out?"

The way he looked at me told me something more was going on. He had a secret. I said, "You invited somebody already, didn't you? Who?"

"It'll be a surprise. A special delivery of sorts for you straight from Belgium." He nodded at the books in my lap. "A clue is in there."

"In this book?" I had it open to the picture of Bram Oosterling and Clément Van Damme with their big fish. "One of our relatives?"

"Well, yes and no. And it has to do with that darn cup John Schultz brought up from an old shipwreck."

A sudden flash of the imagery of the fancy script "AVD" on the cup came to me. "There was another Ava Van Damme? Did she lose her dinnerware service during a storm on Lake Michigan?" I didn't recall any tales about our ancestors dying on the lake like so many others, but now I wondered. Fortunately, the cups stolen from Lloyd's house had been found in Professor Faust's car and had been returned. I wondered about the tales behind that collection, too.

Gilpa grabbed his coffee off the table for a slurp. "Not an 'Ava.' Lloyd's lawyer says that among the safe's papers were notes about Lloyd's ancestor being helped by a Belgian by the name of Arnaud Van Damme. That would've been way back on your grandmother's side of things. I asked Sophie about the name and she didn't know it. But Parker called up one of his church history guys, and the guy seems to think Arnaud married some royal family princess by the name of Amandine."

A feeling akin to winning the lottery washed over me. Bubbles started effervescing in my veins. "So maybe what John has found is valuable? It belongs to a royal family? And we're related?" I stared hard at the young men of years gone by in the cookbook on my lap. They didn't look like royalty. "This person coming from Belgium might know more about the men in this picture? And a cup?"

"I hope so," Gilpa said, grinning behind his coffee cup. "In the meantime, Parker's going to talk with John about going back to the shipwreck site to explore even more. A full table service could be worth a fortune, Parker says." His grin turned into a wicked smile. "By the way, Parker said he'd be over later to work on the real estate offer for the inn with you. I suggested he make it noon and bring a picnic basket along and take you to one of our lovely beaches or lighthouse parks for lunch."

"You didn't!" But I could tell he was lying. "Stubborn buffalo Belgian." He'd got me. But then I got an idea and said, "Gilpa, a picnic sounds wonderful." A picnic with Dillon and Lucky Harbor on a secluded beach for lunch. "Could you handle the fudge shop this afternoon?"

"Sure. Seems I owe you. Now that I don't have a boat to preoccupy me, I've got time on my hands."

"Well, then, that gives me more time to experiment with new fudge recipes. If I'm going to be tested by people who enjoy fine chocolate candies daily in our motherland, I've got to roll up my sleeves and work on my art."

"Who knows! Your fudge might end up in the royal palace in Belgium. Maybe you and Sophie's friends can also make more aprons as gifts for our guests to take home with them? Those are a hit with both the ladies and the men." He winked.

"Leave it to Grandma's church lady friends to find the secret to a man's heart. It's not food; it's aprons!"

He grew somber then as he sat down on the stool next to the bolted table in the middle of the open cabin. "I'm going to miss this old bucket, but we're gonna be too busy to be sad about it, Ava honey." Then mischief came dancing back into his dark eyes. "Parker's a nice guy. You could do worse, you know."

He meant Dillon. Then he was laughing and ruffling the dog's fur. "I guess we all deserve a second chance. Even that Dillon fellow."

Gilpa's silver hair fluttered in the breeze coming off the harbor. My grandfather was happy in a new, wonderful way, despite saying good-bye to his boat. Perhaps I'd helped liberate him somehow, and he was happy to start a new journey in his life, one where he'd set sail for adventures on Lake Michigan as our ancestors did when they came to Door County from Europe. Grandpa looked young again.

Lucky Harbor poked his nose into my lap.

I got up, set the cookbooks a safe distance away on the table, then reached in my pocket for Goldfish crackers. I tossed them in the harbor.

The big splash from the dog jumping in drenched Gilpa and me. It was a baptism, I sensed. My life was ready to begin a new chapter. I was stronger. I needed to be, what with all the mysteries ahead of me to solve. What would become of my grandpa and me in the months and years to come? Would Dillon and I make it together finally? Could I run the Blue Heron Inn on my own? Who were Grandpa's visitors he'd invited? What if our family really was connected to some princess and royalty?

There was so much to think about all at once that I knew just what I had to do first in order to sort it all out—make fudge!

Recipes

Rapunzel Raspberry Rapture Fudge

PREPARATION: 10 MINUTES
COOKING TIME: 20 MINUTES

This is an easy recipe you can make on your stove top or in the microwave.

Before you cook: Prepare an 8-by-8-inch pan by either greasing it with butter on the bottom and sides or lining it with wax paper so that the wax paper comes over the edges. Spray the paper lightly with nonstick vegetable cooking spray.

14-ounce package semisweet chocolate chips
1 cup milk chocolate chips
14-ounce can sweetened condensed milk
2 tablespoons butter
4 teaspoons raspberry flavoring
¾ cup raspberry jam
Whipped cream (for garnish)
Fresh raspberries (for garnish)

Melt the chocolate chips in the microwave with the sweetened condensed milk and butter on medium heat for 3 or 4 minutes. Stir, and return it to the microwave as needed until it's melted and smooth. (Stove-top method: Put chips, milk, and butter in a medium-sized saucepan on medium heat. Stir constantly until it's melted and glassy.)

Add the raspberry flavoring. Stir thoroughly.

Pour half the mixture into the prepared pan. Using a spatula, spread a light layer of raspberry jam across the fudge, being careful to keep the jam away from the edges. Pour the remaining fudge on top, completely covering the jam. Let it cool and sit for a day.

To serve Ava's way, as a dessert: Cut fudge into 1-inch squares or any size you wish. (If you used wax paper in your pan, grab the edges of the paper to lift the entire pan of fudge out onto a cutting board. Remove the wax paper before cutting the fudge.) Serve on dessert plates with a dollop of whipped cream on the side and with several fresh raspberries atop the whipped cream and on the dish. Enjoy bites of fudge, cream, and raspberries in any order.

Rose Garden Fudge

Rose petals are lovely, edible additions to confections and desserts. Use organic (chemical free), fresh rose petals in your favorite colors for this recipe. You can find edible flowers in specialty shops or produce sections of grocery stores, and if not, you might do what I did—ask your neighbor for a couple of blooms.

Before you cook: Prepare an 8-by-8-inch pan by either greasing it with butter on the bottom and sides or lining it with wax paper so that the wax paper comes over the edges. Spray the paper lightly with nonstick vegetable cooking spray.

*2 cups semisweet chocolate chips**\
1 cup milk chocolate chips\
1 14-ounce can sweetened condensed milk\
1 tablespoon unsalted butter\
1/8 teaspoon salt\
1 teaspoon vanilla extract\
*2 tablespoons rose water**\
1 medium rose blossom in full bloom (about 2 inches across)\
*Optional: crystallized rose petals for garnish***

Prepare the rose petals that you want to go into the fudge. Pluck them from the blossom, then cut each into small edible pieces (half-inch diameter or smaller).

Put chips, milk, butter, and salt in a medium-sized saucepan on medium heat. Stir constantly until it's melted and glassy. This will take about 20 minutes.

Add the vanilla extract and rose water. Stir thoroughly. Pour it into a prepared pan. Sprinkle the fudge with rose petals. Work them into the top of the fudge with a greased spatula.

**Using white chips:* This is lovely when made with white chocolate and I prefer that variety because the roses show up so well against the white fudge—however, the rose flavor can be overpowering. When using white chocolate, reduce the rose water to 1 tablespoon.

***To crystallize rose petals:* Use whole petals plucked fresh from the blossom. Mix powdered egg whites or powdered meringue according to directions on the package. Dip rose petals in the prepared mixture; let the excess drip off each petal. Set these on waxed paper and sprinkle both sides with extra-fine sugar, such as bartender's sugar. Let them dry. Drying will take about two days, depending on the humidity in the air.

Belgian Booyah

I met Ron Anderson when he was making booyah at the second annual Pilsen, Wisconsin, kermis in August 2013. Bob and I were on our way to nearby Door County and had stopped by the kermis on a whim after seeing a notice for the fall harvest celebration posted in the nearby Stangelville church, where we'd stopped to gawk at the famous and historic European-style, ornate building. The sign on the bulletin board said "Booyah, burgers, and ring bologna." And anybody was welcome. How could we resist?

Two miles down the road we came upon a rural, barnlike ballroom filled with about two hundred people enjoying good food, Belgian pies, and polka music. Ron was out back stirring the booyah in a huge stainless steel pot over an open flame. The thick red stew smelled heavenly. When I asked about his recipe, he handed me one that was already laminated. So many people enjoyed his booyah that he'd begun giving it away as fast as nuns give away prayer cards to kids. With his permission, I'm offering Ron's recipe here for your own community's kermis. My adaptation of the savory stew follows, created to feed just 8 to 12 people.

Ron Anderson's Booyah

YIELD: 22 GALLONS
SERVINGS: 100+

40 pounds chicken, cut in half
6 pounds beef roast
8 bunches celery
8 cans green beans
2 large heads cabbage
10 pounds carrots

20 pounds potatoes
10 pounds onions
3 jars V-8 juice
3 16-ounce cans peas
3 16-ounce cans corn
6 16-ounce cans mixed vegetables
1 gallon diced tomatoes

Spices
3 tablespoons pepper
1 cup salt
3 tablespoons Accent salt
8 ounces Lawry's seasoning salt
1 jar chicken base

Take along
Bowls and spoons
Pails
Kettle, barrel, basket, hooks, paddle, and dipper
2 x 4
Knives, soup ladle, cutting boards
Roaster

Water to top of basket. Cook the chicken and beef 3½ to 4 hours. Bone the chicken and beef, then refrigerate. Turn down heat to a simmer. Add V-8 juice, tomatoes, cabbage, onions, and spices. Heat this for ½ hour. Do not boil it hard. Gradually add celery, carrots, green beans, mixed vegetables, peas, corn, and potatoes. When the potatoes are done add chicken and beef. Heat this for about 15 minutes. Turn off the heat. This stays hot for about 4 hours.

Christine DeSmet's Booyah

SERVINGS: 8–12

Use a stock pot that holds at least 5 quarts.

2 cups shredded chicken (adjust amount in pot to taste)
1 pound beef roast (optional/booyah is often chicken meat only)
½ teaspoon salt
½ teaspoon Lawry's seasoned salt
½ teaspoon pepper
2 medium onions, chopped
1 bay leaf
1 cup chopped carrots
1 cup chopped celery
1 cup canned green beans
1 cup canned mixed vegetables
1 cup canned corn
1 cup canned peas
2 chicken bouillon cubes
1 14.5-ounce can diced tomatoes
4 ounces V-8 juice (low sodium)
6 medium-sized red potatoes, chopped or quartered
Additional tomato juice (as desired for thinning the stew)

Simmer cut-up chicken in enough water to cover it; cook this until it's tender and falling off the bones. Remove the chicken pieces from the pot to a bowl. Save the water in the pot. Strip the meat from bones and set aside. Put the beef in the chicken-flavored water and simmer it for 30 minutes.

Add the 2 cups of shredded chicken back into the pot with all of the other ingredients. Add more water and tomato juice as needed if it looks too thick. Add more chicken if you decided not to use beef in this recipe. Simmer it for 90 minutes to 2 hours—until the beef is tender and can be broken apart. Do not boil it.

Serve this with crusty bread, cheeses, Belgian mustards, and a Belgian beer (made with Door County cherries or wheat!).

Acknowledgments

Many thanks to my readers who enjoy Ava Oosterling and her grandpa Gil, as well as Belgian chocolate, fudge, and the occasional tasty beer infused with Door County ingredients. What more do we need to be happy, right?

Many thanks to my taste testers at University of Wisconsin-Madison Continuing Studies, who weighed in with votes and comments on Rose Garden Fudge. They included Judy Brickbauer, Christina Finet, Vanika Mock, Ellen Morin, Laurie Scheer, Kathryn Sweet, Anne Voxman.

Thank you to my neighbor Ken Belmore for the lovely red roses to use in my recipes.

Much appreciation goes to Ed Felhofer, docent at the Eagle Bluff Lighthouse in Door County, who gave me the "mystery author murder tour"; lighthouse manager Patti Podgers; and writer and student of mine Cheryl Hanson, who gave me detailed notes about the lighthouse.

Whenever I have a question about the Belgians in Door County, Wisconsin, I go straight to wonderful Belgians Al and Theresa Alexander, who work with organizations like the Peninsula Belgian American Club and the Namur (Wisconsin) Belgian Heritage Foundation. Don't miss the September kermis in Namur!

My research took me to Kilwins confectionary store in Madison, Wisconsin, where manager Curtis Diller gave me tons of time and expertise—and great fudge.

Booyah recipe? Ron Anderson in Kewaunee County gave me a scrumptious one.

A big thanks to an important team: Danielle Perez, executive editor, New American Library/Penguin Group, for her continued support of this mystery series and for her creative suggestions; Neal Armstrong, for wonderful book covers; and John Talbot, of the Talbot Fortune Agency.

Thank you to my fellow Wisconsin Sisters in Crime author members who answer my many questions, especially Deb Baker (aka Hannah Reed), Kathleen Ernst, and Peggy Williams (aka MJ Williams).

Thank you for the great support from Joanne Berg, owner, Mystery to Me Bookstore in Madison, Wisconsin, and to the lovely stores in Door County and beyond who featured my book in their front windows and on special shelves.

Finally, thanks to my family for their support, especially the greatest guy a confectioner author could have—Bob Boetzer—who's sweeter than fudge!

Don't miss the next
Fudge Shop Mystery by Christine DeSmet,

FIVE-ALARM FUDGE

Available from Obsidian in 2015!

The royals were coming in two weeks to our tourist haven of Door County, Wisconsin—a thumb of land in Lake Michigan called the "Cape Cod of the Midwest."

The momentous event had panicked me, Ava Oosterling. It's why I was in an unused, stuffy church attic with my best friends, Pauline Mertens and Laura Rousseau. We were looking for a divinity fudge recipe while vowing not to find a dead body.

Divinity fudge is a white meringue-style confection and an American invention, though this type of fluffy nougat candy can be traced to ancient Turkish Europe and back thousands of years BC, when Egyptians combined marshmallow root with honey. Local lore said that a Catholic nun may have served school children divinity fudge. She allegedly left the handwritten recipe inside the church that Pauline, Laura, and I were cleaning.

Finding and making this divine recipe would help improve my reputation. Immensely. Since returning to Fishers' Harbor last spring, I had unintentionally combined my Belgian fudge making with helping our local sheriff solve two murders. I was determined to stay out of trouble and focus on fudge.

Nature was cooperating. Three hours ago I had been in my fudge shop, and everybody had been talking about how we'd be at our colorful best for Prince Arnaud Van Damme from Belgium and his mother, Princess Amandine. Today was the second Saturday in September. Door County's famous maple trees overhanging the ribbons of two-lane country roads bore leaves tipped in scarlet. The leaf-peeper tourists clogged our streets and roadside markets on the weekends to snap up pumpkins, apples, grapes, and everything made from our county's famous cherries.

I'd increased fudge production at Oosterlings' Live Bait, Bobbers & Belgian Fudge & Beer. I'd also opened a small roadside market in the southern half of the county near my parents' farm with the hope of catching more tourists coming to see the prince. My six copper kettles were constantly filled with fresh cream from my parents' Holsteins, the world's best chocolate from Belgium, and sugar. Favorite fudge flavors flying off my shelves included maple, butterscotch, double-Belgian chocolate with walnuts, and pumpkin. But I couldn't wait to serve the prince and princess my Fairy Tale line of fudges—cherry-vanilla Cinderella Pink Fudge and Rapunzel Raspberry Rapture Fudge.

This brouhaha over a prince could be blamed on my grandpa. Finding a divinity fudge recipe from the 1800s for the prince was Grandpa Gil's idea. So was asking the royals to travel here to tour our famous St. Mary of the Snows Church in Namur, Wisconsin. The tour would occur during our fall harvest festival, called a kermis. Last summer, Pauline's boyfriend, John Schultz, had found an antique cup during a Lake Michigan diving expedition. The initials on the cup were "AVD," which Grandpa thought might belong to Grandma Sophie's ancestor Amandine Van Damme. Grandpa searched Grandma's ancestry and found, lo and behold, that a few of her shirttail relatives were part of the current noble class in Namur, Belgium!

Our Namur—pronounced *Nah-meur*—is a wide spot in the road, a collection of a half dozen buildings amid farm fields about forty miles south of my fudge shop. It's within a stone's throw of my parents' farm, near the neighboring village of Brussels. Some of our towns were named for places in Belgium because the southern half of Door County was settled by Belgian immigrants in the 1850s, including my ancestors.

We were all shocked that Grandpa had called up the royals on his cell phone as if they were mere contacts. He'd reached some assistant, of course, but it had turned out Prince Arnaud was eager to bring more tourists to *his* city of Namur. The prince had accepted Grandpa's proposal to visit to our shock. But the prince saw this as a tourism mission, which could benefit both Namurs.

Jubilation here over this development was tempered by my reputation. The fishermen and tourists coming in to buy fudge kept saying that "Things happen in threes." One smiley-faced man asked, "Do ya think that prince is gonna take a powder? Ava, you stay away from him, ya hear?"

"Taking a powder" meant he'd die in yet another murder involving me and my fudge.

"I'm not superstitious," I insisted. "I'm scientifically minded."

Fudge making is about the exactness of heat and the precise crystallization stages of sugar. Depending on what type of fudge you were making, that sugar had to bubble and get to the "soft-ball" stage temperature of two hundred thirty-eight degrees. Divinity fudge—what the prince had said he wanted to try—needed two hundred sixty degrees.

Truth be told, even my scientific side was on tenterhooks. Divinity fudge is notoriously hard to make; you can't have a speck of humidity, or the egg white meringue will flop. And Door County is a peninsula surrounded by water and humid breezes. In addition, every time a climacteric event had been planned lately in my life, a body showed up, with my relatives wringing their hands over my involvement.

Ironically, this time my parents and grandparents wanted me involved.

Why? Because Prince Arnaud Van Damme was thirty-six (only four years older than me) and a bachelor who was going to inherit a castle.

My relatives aren't hot about my current boyfriend, Dillon Rivers. They have their reasons. My mother still slips at times and calls Dillon "that bigamist." A part of me can't blame them for trying to distract me with a handsome prince.

Oddly enough, my grandma wasn't enthused about her royal relatives traveling to Wisconsin. Ever since Grandpa contacted them a month ago, she'd been acting aloof about the visit, as if she didn't want to own up to being related to them.

"Grandma, how come you never told me about them before?" I asked her last week while she was making one of her famous cherry pies. We were in her cabin on Duck Marsh Street in Fishers' Harbor. I live across the street.

"I guess I forgot. They're so far back in my family tree, they're barely a twig."

A twig? She forgot royalty?! My scientific mind said something was amiss.

I asked her, "Are you mad at Grandpa for inviting them? Did he make up the story about the divinity fudge?" I had assumed he had all along. My search today in the church was merely to please him.

She'd heaved a big sigh as she pulled a fresh, steaming cherry pie from the oven. "He didn't make up that story about the Virgin Mary."

My overzealous, matchmaking grandfather, Gil Oosterling, told the royals the divinity fudge had allegedly been enjoyed by the Blessed Virgin Mother after she'd appeared in front of Sister Adele Brice in 1859 in the nearby woods.

The Blessed Mother?

Yes. That Mother.

Here? In Wisconsin?

Yes. It's true. A bishop even sanctioned it as the only such sighting in the entire United States. In December 2010, the *New York Times* did a big article on it.

Grandpa says that Adele—from the Belgian province of Brabant, where Prince Arnaud is from, too—hid the original, handwritten divinity fudge recipe within the bricks of St. Mary of the Snows church to protect it from the fire dangers presented by wood structures and stoves in the 1800s. Grandpa had told the prince I would make Sister Adele's divinity fudge recipe for dessert at the kermis, with the meal being served in the beautiful little church. Not only that, but Grandpa had said we'd present the original recipe document to the royals. Grandpa had learned the prince wanted to build a museum in Namur that would highlight the history and culture of our sister cities. Housing a priceless recipe in the museum would be like the famous Shroud being kept in the church in Turin, Italy. Thousands of people would visit Belgium each year. Grandpa said the recipe would come back to us on a two-year cycle or some such thing, and thus, thousands might visit Door County, too.

The prince had suggested the divinity fudge I made could be part of a fund-raiser for the church, which is now used as the Belgian Heritage Center. Princess Amandine was enthralled, too. She called divinity fudge "heavenly candy, white and pure as the robes worn by the nun and Blessed Virgin Mary."

Princess Amandine had told Grandpa that divinity fudge was a rare treat. She'd eaten it only once, and that was when she had been a little girl. I'd attempted to make it once and given up because all I'd made was goo. Supposedly there was something special about Sister Adele's recipe that made it foolproof. I was intrigued about this, but Grandpa was obsessed. There was mention that Grandpa and I might receive some special governmental medal of honor for this divinity fudge recipe.

This royal visit had gotten out of hand quickly.

But the church lacked a steeple. It had crumbled long ago. Selling tickets to see a prince and eat fudge would give a proper home to the three white crosses perched precariously on the peaked roof.

Pauline, Laura, and I had volunteered to be on the church-cleaning committee, a handy excuse to spy in every nook. We had just finished going through the beastly hot, stuffy attic bedroom above the kitchen. The bedroom was about eight by ten feet. One small window in the slanted roof let in light. The room had been used by a traveling priest back in the 1860s before a rectory was built. After finding no divinity fudge recipe, we'd hurried down the narrow stairs into the kitchen, panting.

Pauline glugged from her water bottle. She was red-faced and sweating, her long black braid frizzed from heat and humidity. "I'm done. This is stupid, you know."

"We have to look in the basement still," I insisted. My long auburn ponytail had gone limp, sagging onto the back of my hot neck.

Laura ran a hand up her sweaty forehead and through her blond bangs and bob. "We need a break before the basement. I like your grandfather, but this isn't my idea of a fun way to spend a Saturday morning. Besides, I've got to go home and bake bread all afternoon."

Laura ran the Luscious Ladle bakery. She supplied fresh-baked goods to our five-star restaurants. I sold her mouth-watering cinnamon rolls with gooey icing dripping off them at Ava's Autumn Harvest on Highway 57.

I waved a hand in the air, giving in, but only a little. "Take a break. I need to check on Grandma anyway, out in the graveyard. I'll be back in ten minutes. Then we head for the basement."

Pauline said, "All we'll find will be mummified mice and musty dust motes. At least I hope that's all we find. Things happen in threes, you know."

I hurried out without responding, though inside my head a voice reminded me that Pauline was always right.

* * *

Grandma Sophie was only a few yards east of the front doors, tidying what always appears to visitors to be an odd graveyard. In a boxy space under the lone giant maple tree, about thirty headstones sat in rows within *six inches* of one another. A joke around here says the people were buried standing up. What really happened was that in 1970, the priest had moved the headstones from the graveyard located where the lawn is now at the back of the church. Nobody had been buried there for at least a hundred years, by that time. The ground had been resettling, and the stones were sinking or toppling. To save the lichen-etched stones from disappearing altogether, they were moved. Because the collection sits in front of a blacktopped parking lot next to the church, people mistakenly believe the priest paved over the old church graveyard. But it's a myth that cars park atop Belgians at rest.

On her knees, squeezed in between the headstones, Grandma was fussing over the placement of potted yellow and orange mums.

Grandma's wavy white hair buffeted about her shoulders in the breeze.

"That looks really nice, Grandma. You look nice, too." She wore a red long-sleeved T-shirt, black denim jeans, and sturdy walking shoes.

"Thank you, Ava, honey. Did you find the recipe?"

"No. Are you sure Grandpa didn't make that up? Has he had the three of us looking for a nonexistent recipe?" Grandpa liked a good joke, so I was still suspicious.

Grandma Sophie grunted as she shoved at the ground to get up off her knees. I rushed to help. Last spring she'd broken a leg. She still experienced pain.

Once we stood together before the headstones, with my arm secured around her waist, she said, "My grandparents used to talk about that fudge recipe. My great-grandparents were there at the time of Sister Adele. They knew her personally. So I believe it's true, honey."

Her great-grandparents Amelie and Thomas Van Damme were buried behind the church. Their headstone sat in front of us—gray and weathered, a couple inches thick, a foot wide and three feet high, with a chipped, arched edge.

I said, "Maybe what they were really remembering was the Communion wafers. They're white, just like divinity fudge. Maybe Sister Adele made sweet wafers, and thus people just said they were sweet as fudge. They both melt on the tongue, after all."

"No, Ava, my grandparents were pious. They would not have joked about that. They weren't eating fudge for Communion."

A giggle escaped me, despite my trying to be serious for Grandma. "Maybe church enrollments would rise if they served fudge. It would be a whole new market for me."

"Honey, please be respectful. Your grandpa believes there's a recipe hidden here somewhere. People have looked for it off and on for generations now. It's time we find the darn thing and send it home with those people."

Those people. Her disdain for her relatives silenced me. A little research had told me that the prince and princess were active in charities to help the poor. They had assured Grandpa the recipe would travel back to our community to help with fund-raisers to benefit Door County. The royals appeared to be good people. What wasn't she willing to share with me? Grandma stood as still as the statues before us, her physical being as sturdy as her conviction. I said, "I'll do my best to find that recipe, I promise."

Grandma pushed a pouf of white hair off her face. "Your grandfather will be over the moon."

"The moon, wafers, divinity fudge, your hair—all white. Your hair is as divine as divinity fudge, Grandma."

That got her to smile, finally. Then she shook her head. "This graveyard is so embarrassing. Your grandfather should never have invited them."

"But the prince and princess are related to the people laid to rest here. They'll want to pay their respects. They're interested in the early settlers from Belgium and the generations carrying on here now."

Many of the other names in front of us were familiar because the families still lived in the area. I recognized Coppens; a high school classmate of mine, Jonas Coppens, owned a small farm up the road from my new market. He was spreading mulch around right now several yards across the lawn at a historic schoolhouse. I growled because I recognized a woman with him, Fontana Dahlgren.

"Fontana is supposed to be helping us dust and polish the inside of the church."

"That floozy? Don't count on it." Grandma shuddered next to me, my body absorbing her tiny earthquake. "I suppose she'll be flirting up a storm with the prince. Maybe that's good; at least we won't have to entertain him and his mother."

"Grandma? What's wrong? You haven't liked this idea of them coming since the moment Grandpa broke the news. But Grandpa and my father—your own son—and my mother would love to marry me off to the prince. Not you?"

The fine wrinkles around her mouth quirked with a grimace. "The prince and princess are barely related to us. They're all about fuss and appearances. There's a reason some of us sawed ourselves off from the branches of the family tree and departed for America. This visit is going to end up in a disaster."

She began limping away from me, toward the historic schoolhouse. She'd meet up with her church-lady friends who were on cleaning detail, too.

My heart held a dull ache, and my stomach felt as if it were a dryer with a bunch of old bolts tumbling in it. I vowed to figure out what was upsetting Grandma about this visit and fix it for her. Certainly a little fuss wasn't the issue, because Grandma loved our kermises and making her famous pies. Could it be *me* she was embarrassed about? Or our entire family? We were plain people, just farmers, fishermen, and fudge makers. I thought that was good enough.

But Grandma was confounding me, something I confessed to Pauline and Laura when I got back inside the church a minute later.

My girlfriends and I were standing near the bottom of old wooden stairs leading into the dim, dusty cement church basement. This room was about ten by twelve feet. It was empty, save for a row of plumbing pipes lined up in the middle of the floor. A meager bulb lit the area, turning shadows into muddy brown in the corners of the floor and the joists overhead. Cobwebs hung down; they stirred from our sudden appearance.

Pauline stood directly behind me on the wooden stairs. "I tell my kids all the time not to go into strange places." She was a kindergarten teacher in Fishers' Harbor. "This is the dumbest thing you've ever gotten me into. No recipe is hidden down here. I think your grandmother's upset because your grandfather has gone lulu."

"It feels like more than that, Pauline. She mentioned something about the royals being about fuss and appearances. Do you think I embarrass her?"

"Heck, I'm embarrassed by you all the time. Including now. You bought into your grandfather's fudge story, hook, line, and sinker. He's a fisherman, and he knows how to reel you in with a tall fish tale. Or fudge tale."

Laura, bringing up the rear of our human train on the stairs, said, "Can't we just say we looked and not do it?" She sneezed.

I told them, "I can't lie to my grandfather about looking for the recipe. I owe him a lot."

Last spring, Grandpa Gil had resuscitated my life. I'd spent eight years in Los Angeles in a grunt job for a TV show. Then Grandma Sophie broke her leg in April. Grandpa asked me to return while my show was on spring hiatus. He had the idea of moving his minnow tank over in his bait shop to let me turn half of his building into a fudge operation. He'd also moved the singular apostrophe in his sign to make it the plural Oosterlings' Live Bait, Bobbers & Belgian Fudge & Beer. That kind of love couldn't be ignored. I quit my show and stayed.

With Grandpa's kindness resonating in my soul, I stepped onto the cement basement floor. As I walked over to the pipes to inspect them, I held on to my ponytail while moving to the right to keep away from a cobweb trailing from the joists.

Laura wasn't so lucky. "Ick. They're all over in my hair."

She'd somehow missed copying my stealthy move. Her blond bob looked like it was snared in a hairnet. As a baker, she was used to wearing hairnets, so maybe she'd cope with this better than Pauline. She was six feet tall—taller than me by two inches—and too dressed up for cleaning a church and poking around for recipe scripture. She wore her favorite designer sleeveless tangerine top and shorts. Laura and I had on denim shorts. I was in a faded pink T-shirt, while Laura wore a threadbare blue-and-white-striped short-sleeved blouse.

Pauline shook her black braid to rid it of a cobweb that had broken loose from its mother ship overhead. "I've seen enough."

"There's a doorway over there," I said, pointing toward a passageway, intentionally ignoring Pauline's whimpering.

I was enjoying the exploring. Although I'd grown up nearby, I'd never been in the basement or the attic of the church because their doors were located in the kitchen. The kitchen used to be the sacristy, where priests and altar boys would get ready for Mass.

I also hadn't been inside this church since I'd jilted my fiancé here the night of our wedding rehearsal eight years ago. That was the same night I'd eloped with another man—Dillon Rivers, whom I divorced a month after that, then didn't see for eight years, and now was dating again. Memories—bad, embarrassing ones—had been hitting me like darts from the moment I'd promised to look for the recipe in this church. At first, I couldn't force myself to come back here. My stomach had rolled for days, as if it wanted to purge my mistakes. That would take a long time. But I knew if I were going to fully embrace living in Door County again, I had to do a mea culpa and face what I'd done. Pauline and Laura were gems to volunteer for the kermis cleaning committee with me. Entering the church this morning had caused my breathing to stop for a moment, but the search for the fudge recipe had helped take my mind off past romantic disasters.

The next room in the basement was empty. Another small space, it smelled of chalky dust and time standing still. It spooked me. A brick chimney stood in the far corner. A rusty lid covered a hole in the brick where a furnace pipe used to fit.

I said, "Check the sills at the tops of the walls and the joists. I'll check the chimney. I can almost sense that Sister Adele was here."

Laura said, "Do you honestly think Sister Adele came down here? With a recipe?"

"Sure," I said. "She may have had to toss wood in the furnace now and then. Maybe she spent a whole bunch of time down here. This space would've been cozy with the furnace blazing. She probably had a rocking chair in a corner at one time. She could have built a secret cubby behind a brick for her valuables."

Pauline scoffed. "What valuables? She was a nun. Don't they vow a life of poverty?"

Laura answered for me. "She had a rosary. I'm sure she thought that was valuable."

"And she had the recipe," I reminded them.

Pauline said, "Have you ever thought your grandfather made up this story to keep you busy looking, and thus keep you from spending too much time with Dillon?"

"I've thought of that, but both Grandpa and Grandma are sincere about this fudge story."

"I still don't get why nobody found it before now."

"Pauline, it took a gazillion years for people to find and authenticate the Shroud of Turin."

"So now you're comparing this divinity fudge recipe to the Shroud?"

"Yes. If the Blessed Virgin Mary ate this divinity fudge, then the recipe is just as priceless."

My fingers scrabbled across the rough, dust-laden edges of the brick and cracked mortar, checking for a hiding place. A pebble of mortar popped onto the concrete floor.

Pauline backed away a step. "Watch it. I can't get these clothes dirty."

My BFF had worn her favorite outfit today because she'd be meeting up with her boyfriend, John, a tour guide, at the potluck picnic lunch for the church cleanup committee. John was on a bus somewhere in the county with thirty leaf-peeper vacationers from Chicago. The lunch would be held at my new market.

I popped off the metal covering over the chimney hole. Rust and soot flakes spewed out. They fell to the floor near my feet, sullying my running shoes. There was no recipe. I reached down for a handful of rust, wiped it on my pink T-shirt, then bombed the front of Pauline's shorts.

Pauline gasped, brushing at her shorts and legs. "What are you doing?"

"Proving to Grandpa that we were trusty fudge archaeologists doing our best to unearth ancient, sweet divinity hieroglyphics."

"When Lent comes around next spring, I'm giving you up instead of booze this time. And forget your Christmas present this year."

With a smile, I pushed the thin metal covering back in place. "Must I remind you that it was Grandpa who rescued John last summer when John got left behind on his diving expedition by that creep? And John was the one who found the ceramic cup that Grandpa thinks belongs to Grandma's ancestors at the bottom of Lake Michigan. That's why Grandpa called up the royals in the first place. The initials on the cup are 'AVD,' which might be the other Amandine Van Damme way back in Grandma's lineage.

John finding the cup led to the idea of bringing the current Princess Amandine here for the kermis, and that sparked Grandpa's memory about the story of Sister Adele and this church and the divinity fudge. So you're the cause of this search for a recipe, not me. I'm actually the one getting filthy in order to help you and John."

Laura was giggling.

Pauline pulled madly on her long braid to vent her frustration. "You always manage to turn things upside down and around so that you're never at fault."

"And you love me for it. What're you getting me for Christmas?" I peered up at her in a wide-eyed dare.

Pauline took a deep breath, looking down her nose at me in a double dare.

A dead black-and-red box-elder bug was stuck in her hair above one ear, which I didn't mention. Instead, I reached up with my thumb and smudged the tip of her nose.

She smudged me back.

Laura said, "Hey, what about me?"

We burst out laughing. Pauline and I wiped our hands on Laura's blue-and-white-striped blouse and gave her cheeks a sooty pat.

"Perfect," I said. "Grandpa will believe we did our best, and we can put his silly story to rest."

Laura took a selfie photo of us with her cell phone. "It's almost noon. I have to get back to start the bread and relieve my babysitter."

Laura was the mother of twins born in July. Little Clara Ava had my first name as her middle name, and Spencer Paul got his middle name from a shortened "Pauline."

I said, "Nobody's leaving yet. We still have the choir loft to inspect."

"Your grandpa will never know if we skip that," Laura said.

Pauline huffed, "But Ava won't lie to him. Cripes, let's go get it done."

"Thanks, Pauline," I said. "Just ten more minutes, Laura,

and then you'll be free to go home to Clara Ava and Spencer Paul."

We headed up the stairs to the kitchen, then went into the nave. We marched up the center aisle through shafts of colors striping the pews from the stained glass windows.

Laura said, "Wasn't a Fontana Dahlgren on the list for helping us clean the church? We could leave the loft for her to clean. By the way, who is she?"

Pauline and I shared a mutual snort. Laura was our new friend, whom we'd met last spring when she opened her bakery, so she didn't know Fontana.

"Fontana's outside bothering Jonas Coppens. My grandmother calls her a floozy," I said. "Fontana is mad at me, and that's why she's not in here helping."

Fontana, divorced from Daniel Dahlgren, ran Fontana's Fresh Fare, another roadside market a few miles south of mine on Highway 57. She sold her own homemade soaps, perfumes, lotions, and makeup, along with a few pumpkins to lure the tourists. My market, which focused on pairing fudge flavors with local wines, and fresh organic vegetables, fruits, and dairy, sat on land owned by Daniel and his new wife, Kjersta. Fontana had already stopped by my market to suggest that it was unfair competition for me to be located so close to hers, despite our goods being so different. I suspected the real reason Fontana was upset was that I'd made friends with the new wife of her ex.

Pauline added, "I heard she didn't qualify for the choir that will sing for the prince at the kermis. Maybe she's pouting and refuses to step inside the church now."

"It's more likely she took a look at our names on the cleaning crew and discovered no men to flirt with, so she said the heck with it."

"Jonas is a hottie," Pauline said, spritzing lemon oil on a long pew that stretched across the back wall.

Laura set to work dusting the front railing of the loft while I tackled the antique pipe organ.

I filled Laura in on Jonas. We'd grown up with him. He'd

lost his parents in a car accident when he was in his twenties. He now ran the family farm northeast of our farm and across Highway C, which intersected with the village of Brussels. He'd never married, but I'd heard plenty of times from my parents that he'd be quite the catch.

Pauline said, "Fontana is merely practicing on Jonas. The prince is her target. I'm surprised she's not at one of the spas getting a pedicure so her feet look good in glass slippers."

Poking about for hidden doors and drawers in the organ, I moaned that we hadn't even found odd scraps of old newspapers I could take to Grandpa. He and I loved treasure hunting in old books and anything with the printed word.

Laura, who was wiping at the organ's pipes halfheartedly, said, "At least we didn't find a body in the church."

"Yet," Pauline said, coming to stand next to me at the organ.

I gave her a punch in the upper arm, then raised my right hand. "I swear that no bodies will be found in this church now or during the prince's visit. Grandpa won't have to add 'and Bodies' at the end of our shop sign, though the alliteration should be appreciated by you, Pauline." She loved word games for her students. "Besides, I've changed."

Their loud guffaws echoed back from the altar at the opposite end of the church. Two tall angel statues with candles on their heads stood sentry at the steps up to the altar. I imagined they were laughing, too.

Laura pulled a piece of cobweb from her hair. "Does your family believe you've changed into somebody who doesn't always get in trouble?"

Pauline said, "Not if they're hot to marry her off to a prince and have her move over to Belgium. Sounds like a way to get rid of her. We should chip in for plane fare."

With smugness, I said, "I won't invite either of you over to my castle, at this rate. Pauline, a dead box-elder bug in your hair just dropped off to the floor."

She bent down with a paper towel to pick up the bug. "Aha! It's the dead body we knew we'd find."

"And that's the last one," I reassured them. "I have no time for crime anymore."

With Dillon's help, I was refurbishing the Blue Heron Inn in Fishers' Harbor, which my grandfather and I had recently acquired with a big, frightening mortgage loan. It sat on the steep hill overlooking our bait-and-fudge shop on the docks. With the inn, my new roadside market, my fudge shop, the prince's impending visit, and keeping a semblance of a romance alive, I was doing my best to stay out of trouble.

I stopped inspecting the organ for secret doors, then plopped my butt on the bench, giving in to frustration. "I was really starting to like the idea that the recipe might exist."

"What about the bench you're sitting on?" Laura asked.

With gleeful, silly hope, I launched myself up, opened the bench lid, then screamed as I jumped back, letting the lid drop with a loud clap.

Pauline came closer. "What—?"

I pointed at the bench. "A bloody knife."

We three huddled around the closed bench, staring at the lid. I said, "Open it, Pauline."

"No way. Maybe it's just your imagination."

We gave Laura an imploring look. She shook her head. "I faint at the sight of blood."

I lifted the lid. Slowly.

We stared down at a hunting knife—about seven inches long and smudged with red on its blade and white bone handle.

Laura choked out, "Maybe that's cherry juice."

I said, "I work with cherries in my Cinderella Pink Fudge. That's not cherry juice."

The smeary knife lay across sheets of music. Dried blood droplets mimicked musical notes on the five-lined staff of "Ave Maria."

I leaned in closer.

"Don't touch it," Pauline said.

"I'll call the sheriff." I had my phone out already.

She snatched it from me. "You're not getting involved. You know you have bad luck. We're walking away from this and letting somebody else find it."

Laura had paled. "That's a good idea. I need to get back to my babies."

Pauline shut the lid of the bench with a bang.

A sudden corresponding loud *thud* from below made us jump. We stared wide-eyed into one another's eyes. My heart was racing.

Voices—chattering—drifted up to the loft. The noise had been a door likely slamming against the wall after being caught by the breeze.

We scrambled to look over the railing. It was John's tour.

I whispered, "Crap. They're not supposed to be here. This is cleaning day."

Pauline plastered on a smile, then waved at John below. She whispered back to me, "I don't want John involved in whatever your bloody knife means. The last time he tried helping you, he almost ended up dead."

"It's not *my* knife."

"You found it. And I know how you are. Criminally curious." She looked down her nose at me with her sternest teacherlike demeanor. "I'll make sure they don't come up here. Forget the knife. Promise me."

But she hurried down the stairs to the nave before I could actually promise.